FEB 2009

D0065582

Corner Shop

By the same author

Bitter Sweets

Corner Shop

ROOPA FAROOKI

ST. MARTIN'S PRESS   NEW YORK

This is a work of fiction. All of the characters, organizations, and events portrayed in this novel are either products of the author's imagination or are used fictitiously.

www.stmartins.com

Library of Congress Cataloging-in-Publication Data

Farooki, Roopa.
    Corner shop / Roopa Farooki. — 1st U.S. ed.
        p. cm.
    ISBN-13: 978-0-312-37556-0
    ISBN-10: 0-312-37556-5
    1. Bangladeshis—England—Fiction. 2. Bangladeshis—Social life and customs—Fiction. 3. Intergenerational relations—Fiction. 4. Interpersonal relations—Fiction. 5. Domestic fiction. I. Title.
    PR6106.A765C67 2009
    823'.92—dc22

                                                                2008038354

First published in Great Britain by Pan Books, an imprint of Pan Macmillan Ltd

First U.S. Edition: February 2009

10 9 8 7 6 5 4 3 2 1

For the dreamers and players who inspired this book:
my husband, my two sons;
and for my father, in memory

We are the dreamers of dreams . . .
We are the movers and shakers,
Of the world for ever, it seems.

Arthur O'Shaughnessy

In this world there are only two tragedies.
One is not getting what one wants,
and the other is getting it.

Oscar Wilde

PART ONE

Dreamers

The Fabulous Destiny of
Luhith 'Lucky' Khalil

THIS IS LUCKY'S MOMENT, and the moment is everything. It's not the anticipation, it's not the memory,
it's now. It's his silent prayer, joining the prayer of the
legions staring at their TVs with hands gripped around
their pint glasses and covering their open mouths. It's the
unnamed force that has made each obsessed individual
wear that white shirt, or hang that red-crossed sheet from
their window. It's every murmur, and whisper, and song,
and shout and cheer that's been swept into the ether,
captured on the radio waves and carried on the wind and
clouds, gathering in the swirling atmosphere above the
stadium; a tornado of hope funnelled down towards him,
the last man on the field, where a single movement of his
foot can realize or destroy every English dream. He is one
man, making a sacrifice for millions. The moment is everything – take it, Lucky, it's yours.

He runs and strikes, his left foot connecting, the ball
shooting like a bullet towards the goal, and then there is
nothing but the moment. Sweeter than the dread pregnancy of anticipation, more potent than the complacency of

has-been memory. Maybe later there will be press conferences and parades, or documentaries and disappointment; maybe later he will be written into the history books or struck from them with shame. But now there is only the perfect stillness as he stands spread-eagled at the centre of the spinning world.

There is only the moment, and you. And you have done well, my son.

Lucky awakes with a start, dripping with sweat, panting, almost sobbing. Lucky has a destiny – worse than a destiny, he has a dream. It wakes him at night, so terrifying is this dream. It torments him, because it tastes real; he tastes the blood on his bitten lip as he stands at a white dot on a foreign field that will be forever England, and stares into the faceless enemy whom he knows looks just like him. It torments him, because when he wakes he weeps with disappointment that it is just a dream. This dream belongs to him only – he has mentioned it to no one, it's so outlandish that he doesn't dare to share it. This dream is so bizarre, so miraculous and out of reach of the most overvaulting ambition, that he may as well dream about becoming God. He dreams that one day, he will score for England. He dreams that one day, his lucky left foot will win the World Cup for England.

Lucky wipes his damp forehead, and kicks off his duvet. He quietly opens his window and looks out onto the moonlit crescent, silent and empty in the early hours of the morning. It's been raining, and he sees his blurry reflection in a puddle on the street, the water gathering in a dent in the pavement that his officious dad makes frequent complaints to the local council about. He imagines his reflection leaping up and running away, like Peter Pan's shadow, and that he might have to chase down the street to find it. He wishes he could run away down the street himself; to kick a ball, and just keep following it as it rolls. He is not yet fifteen years old, but he feels trapped by the weight of his destiny, of his dream. Even his posters commiserate: Princess Leia in shining white with a chunky weapon slung defiantly over her shoulder, and Darth Vader in glossy black wielding a light sabre, twin guardians on his wall. Both of them seem to be saying with a mixture of pride and sorrow, 'It is your destiny, Lucky,' as though it is something he will never escape. He watches his watery reflection splinter and disappear with the early drops of rain; turning to go back to bed, he stops short as he sees two figures in his doorway, their outlines thrown into relief with the light behind them, a braided brunette draped in pale folds of cloth, and a dark demon in shadowy robes, his face an inscrutable mask. He looks at the posters to check that the figures are still there and haven't leapt out of their paper into his room. He blinks at the couple in the doorway, and then gets back into bed.

'You should bloody well knock,' he mutters crossly to his parents, before turning his face into his pillow, dismissing them. His father, a swarthy Bengali with a gleaming cap of neatly cut hair, well built verging on stout, yawns and adjusts the belt on his charcoal Marks & Spencer dressing-gown.

'Told you it was nothing, Delphine,' he says, shrugging

his shoulders at his son's rudeness, for once too tired to tick him off about it. 'I've got a Very Important Meeting this morning, I'm going back to bed.'

Delphine sits on the edge of her son's bed, the creamy pleated silk of her dressing-gown falling demurely to her ankles, her braids tumbling girlishly over her shoulders. Her own mother used to braid her hair at night, and it is a habit that she persists in, although sometimes she looks at herself before she goes to bed, looks at her braids and her naked, unfamiliar face, and feels faintly ridiculous. She smooths down Lucky's hair, reminded of the downy perfection of his rounded head when he was a baby. 'Was it a bad dream?' she asks. Just the slightest hint of her native French accent remains, and adds an extraordinary charm to her voice that most people cannot place. He says nothing, and she feels for a moment bereft, nostalgic for the time when she could comfort away the worst *cauchemar* with just a gentle touch of her hand and a brush of her lips on his forehead, like magic. I should let go, she thinks to herself – not for the first time, and not only in this circumstance. As though letting go was so easy. She shuts the window against the increasingly persistent patter of the rain, then leaves the room.

In the morning, by the time Delphine has released her hair from her braids, letting it fall in loosely structured waves down her back like a forties' movie star, Lucky has already demolished his cereal and toast and is heading out of the door. He leaves the kitchen as she walks in, says 'Bye, Ma!' abruptly, kisses her out of habit rather than affection, and runs down the stairs to the street, a ball under his arm. As she puts the coffee on, she can see him place the ball carefully in the wet dent on the pavement, kick it down the smart tree-lined crescent, and run after it. Jinan joins her in the kitchen, already showered, suited and booted for his Very Important Meeting, his brown face so well scrubbed that it is practically glowing, his hair looking impossibly smooth. 'Has Luhith left already?' he asks.

'Mm-hmm,' assents Delphine non-committally, busying herself with the coffee to avoid the inevitable discussion about 'the boy' that Jinan seemed so fond of having in the mornings.

'Why has he left so early?' persists Jinan.

'Practice?' hazards Delphine. She knows that it's not practice, as practice is on Mondays, Wednesdays and of course, on Saturdays.

'It bloody well better not be. How much more practice does the boy need? It's not exactly rocket science, is it? Kick the ball, ball goes in the goal, most goals wins,' says Jinan, warming up to his usual theme. 'It's not like he's training for a black belt in karate or something. Something *useful*.'

Delphine sighs, and wonders whether to leave the kitchen so that the discussion might be terminated before he gets to 'When I was his age . . .' She coughs to distract Jinan. 'So, where's your meeting this morning? Are they picking you up?'

'Berkeley Square. No, I'm driving,' he replies efficiently, refusing to be diverted. 'The problem with Luhith is that he doesn't know what he wants to do. When I was his age, I knew exactly what I wanted to do . . .'

'Yes, I remember,' says Delphine shortly, and Jinan stops in embarrassment. His wife is fully six years older than him, and when he was a fourteen-year-old schoolboy, she had been a twenty-year-old woman, an unattainable goddess who belonged to the world of the grown-ups. She had seen him play *Hamlet* in his school production, for God's sake. Sometimes Delphine made him feel that he was no older than Lucky, for all that he was now a moderately successful lawyer with a six-figure salary and Very Important Meetings.

'Well, I'd better go,' he says, downing his coffee. 'I'll get breakfast at the meeting, they always provide those little Danish twisty things at the Berkeley Square office.'

'Nice,' nods Delphine.

'Yes, they are, rather,' says Jinan, recovered back to being the man of the household, rather than just another little boy. 'Have a nice day, darling.' He puts his arm around her and kisses her on the back of her head, on the loosely structured waves. 'You look lovely today, darling. Really minimal.' It is then that Delphine realizes that she is still in her white pyjamas and still wearing her alien, naked face.

Lucky follows the ball down the crescent where he lives, past the smart Knightsbridge apartments with roof terraces and shared gardens (with crisp signs stating 'No Ball Games' in ornate curly script), past sweeping stuccoed streets and the snappy little boutiques, and finally hops on the tube at South Kensington. He gets off at Hammersmith and follows his ball on a long journey way past the Odeon, down the back streets to the slightly shabby road near the council estates where his grandfather lives, in a proper terraced house, an on-the-ground house with a garden in the back for a kick-about. The house was divided long ago, so that the upstairs is a flat and the downstairs is a corner shop. It is long past eight a.m., but the shop still isn't open. Lucky presses the buzzer to the flat, but there is no reply. He presses it again, more insistently. 'Dada?' he calls up to his grandfather, and throws his ball with expert precision so it bounces against the frame of the bedroom window, deliberately avoiding the glass in case it breaks like it did once before – not that his grandfather had been bothered. He had got his insurance company to replace it, blaming local yobs; he had grinned conspiratorially at Lucky while he made the call, whispering across the mouthpiece that it was barely a lie, anyway. 'Dada!' Lucky shouts again.

Portia, his grandfather's paper girl, comes out of the neighbouring greasy spoon cafe; elfin and crop-haired, she is the most efficient part of his grandfather's shambolic enterprise, and sometimes even illegally minds the shop for him on weekends when he is otherwise engaged at the races or the bookies. Lucky catches his ball and asks her casually, 'Have you seen my grandad?' He has a massive crush on Portia, who is almost a year older than him and possesses the specific and uncomplicated beauty that is occasionally produced by parents of mixed race, but he thinks he has managed to hide his adolescent yearnings with some success.

Portia shrugs her shoulders and lights a fag, offering her packet to Lucky. When he shakes his head, she replaces the packet in her school blazer. 'I think the old git's hung-over, or something. I've been waiting for him for over half an hour. I won't have time to deliver the papers now.' She shouts up towards the window, 'Oi, Zaki, move your idle butt and let us in!' There is no twitch of the curtain at the window, nothing. She and Lucky just stand there, joined by unwilling affection and admiration for the man who is ignoring them, who cares so little about what people think of him that he doesn't even bother to open his window, much less his shop, unless he feels like it. Zaki needs nothing from anyone, but despite this, everyone adores him and would do anything for him; he is sort of Lucky's hero.

'Why do you call him "Dada"?' asks Portia eventually. 'Is that his nickname or something?'

'It just means "Grandad" in Bengali,' replies Lucky. 'I've always called him it.' Portia absorbs this information without comment, and as he feels uncomfortable with the silence, he finds himself adding awkwardly, 'I guess it could be a bit confusing to some people, it sounds a bit too much like "Dad", doesn't it?' The silence returns, with even less promise than before.

'I'd better get off to school, then,' Portia says finally. She pauses, giving Lucky the chance to offer to walk with her; her school isn't so far from his. When he doesn't, she smiles – a small smile to herself, correctly interpreting his offhandedness as shyness rather than rudeness, and strolls off, flinging her long scarf over her shoulder. Lucky sits down on the pavement with his back to the wall, and imagines his grandfather sleeping soundly in his bed with an empty bottle of Jack Daniel's and winning ticket from the bookies on his bedside table, maybe with another beautiful woman by his side. He absorbs the scene through the bricks of Zaki's on-the-ground house, and imagines his grandfather opening his eyes and saying to him, for once seriously instead of irreverently, 'It's your destiny, Lucky. You can forget all the crap they teach you at school, as long as you remember this. You're not destined to be one of them, to be a something-nothing. You're going to be something special. And you're going to do well, my son.'

Lucky gets up and does a few more experimental throws towards the window, and after shouting 'Dada!' and then 'Zaki!' and finally 'Dada-Zaki', eventually gives up and heads off towards school, following his ball expertly down the pavement and across the green.

Zaki groans and turns over when the banging on his window-frame finally ceases; shielding his eyes from the intrusive light, he reaches over to the other side of the bed ... where there is no one. Ayesha, his occasional girlfriend, must have left in the night. Zaki is in his early fifties, and still handsome even with his greying hair, his utterly unfettered life having taken no toll on him. He has never had to address a meeting dry-mouthed with apprehension, he has never had to stand sardine-packed into a steaming, stinking tube in rush hour, he has never had to wear a grey suit, or bite his tongue when faced with an obnoxious client or superior. His heart has never pounded with the fear of missing a deadline, although it has occasionally pounded with the elation of his horse coming in over the final fence, or the ball bouncing around the roulette wheel and dropping with a chunky clink into his number. Zaki mutters out loud, 'Persistent little bugger . . .' before falling back asleep; he says it with something like pride.

Burnt Toast and Other Small Tragedies

DELPHINE SITS AT HER dressing-table and looks with disappointment at her bare face, at the first signs of wrinkles that she has so far managed to keep at bay with outrageously expensive creams that cost her more per month than her gym membership. Well, at least she used the creams, which is more than could be said for her gym. She doesn't like her face without make-up, it doesn't look like her, but as though some gawky maiden aunt has taken her seat and pushed her into the background. The only time she ever felt beautiful with a scrubbed face was when Lucky was tiny, and used to press his chubby little wristless paws into her cheeks with wonder, gently tugging at her nose and eyebrows, memorizing the landscape of her face as though it was an enchanted kingdom to be lost in. She massages the cream carefully into her skin, all the way down to her throat, and begins to paint her face back on, bringing her eyes out by defining them with liner, and making her lips at once soft and precise with lip-pencil. She pulls on her designer tracksuit, determined to go to the gym; whoever said that French women didn't get fat hadn't seen her paternal grandmother, a ruddy-cheeked country-woman from Les Landes who had got so small and stout in old age that she had become practically square. Perhaps Parisians didn't get fat, but she knew that her corn-fed Landaise genes were just waiting in the wings to make their big appearance, which was why she had to pummel them occasionally back into submission with workouts and weights.

Her hair clipped back, her face familiar again, Delphine makes herself some toast and orange juice. The toast burns while she is trying to hack off shards of the ice-cold butter that she forgot to take out of the fridge to soften. She scrapes the toast, attempts to eat it, then throws most of it away. The smell lingers in the kitchen, throughout the apartment, but she tells herself she doesn't mind – it's only burnt toast. She puts on her ballet pumps, satisfied that she is ready to face the world, or at the very least the two streets she needs to walk down until she gets to her gym. Then she remembers, just as she is ready to head out, that it is the cleaner's day to do the washing, and that she hasn't yet stripped the beds. She doesn't like the cleaner to strip the beds, it seems too personal for a stranger to see where her body has pressed into the mattress, where her husband and son stretch and sigh and snore, the little marks and creases, and yes, sometimes stains, of intimacy. She efficiently strips her bed of the beige, taupe and cream bed linen (beige, taupe and cream! When did everything in her house, in her life, suddenly become beige, taupe and cream? So absurdly neutral, so . . . Really minimal, darling). She piles it all in the laundry basket, and goes to Lucky's room to do the same. Remembering his grumpy remarks the night before, she feels slightly guilty for opening his door without knocking, even though he isn't there. Privacy is so important to teenagers, she remembers; it's how their secret worlds are created.

She goes into the room, and begins to take off the pillowcases, printed with photographic images of grass, like sleeping in a field. Looking about her, she finds it funny that Jinan says he doesn't know what goes on in Lucky's head; Lucky may not wear his heart on his sleeve, but he pastes it up all over his bedroom walls. One wall is dedicated to *Star Wars*, with enormous poster images of Leia and Darth Vader displayed like religious icons, and smaller pictures of that fluffy, bear-like creature (Chew-something? Chewy?) and Yoda and spaceships and other paraphernalia. There's no Luke Skywalker, she notices; it's as though the main character isn't needed – in his world, Lucky himself is the hero. The next wall is all football: heroes and villains, strikers and keepers, an enormous photograph of the boys of '66 wielding the cup, and some action shots of his own local team. Funny that for someone who loves football as much as Lucky, he doesn't support a specific premiership team; he celebrates every game without prejudice, cheers every good goal or spectacular save. The final two walls are covered in touristy sites and scenes of Bangladesh and France; it seems rather wistful, as though anywhere might be better than here. It wasn't as though she or Jinan ever spoke nostalgically about either place; Jinan had been brought up in England, and could barely string a sentence together in Bangla, and when she was a girl she couldn't wait to get out of Les Landes. On the shelves she sees framed photos of Lucky's friends and team-mates, arms draped over shoulders in easy, unspoken affection, and one of him with his grandad, Zaki, but none of her and Jinan. And what else did I expect? she thinks, whipping off the duvet cover with a sudden, irritated violence. Did I think that I could manage my own son's feelings, just as I've pretended to manage my own? I made do, I settled for someone, and I was stupid enough to think that no one would notice, not even me. Her eyes begin to well up and she shuts them tight for a moment, then carries on.

Delphine finishes putting everything in the linen basket just in time, as she hears the cleaner's key turn in the lock, then the doorbell rings as a warning as Kasia realizes that someone is still in the flat. 'Good morning, Mrs Khalil,' trills Kasia, letting herself in after a polite pause. Delphine has told her hundreds of times to call her by her first name, but for some reason Kasia prefers not to. She had been a nursery teacher in her native Poland, and was intending to retrain in London; she wasn't the best cleaner, but she was punctual and cheerful, qualities that Delphine admired as she no longer had them herself.

'Hi, Kasia, I'm just heading out,' says Delphine, snatching her sunglasses from the stand in the hallway to cover her eyes. She has wound herself up so much that a single kind word from someone, anyone, even the punctual cleaner, might have her blubbering in a quivering heap in her hallway.

'Is everything all right, Mrs Khalil?' asks Kasia with concern, wondering what has happened to irritate her normally civil client, whose face is unusually pale and tense.

Delphine pauses for a moment at the doorway, absurdly

touched by a relative stranger's kindness. She is tempted, for a small trembling instant, to cry and confide, but masters herself quickly. Cross with herself for her silly weakness, she snaps, 'For God's sake, Kasia, why can't you just call me Delphine?' as she grabs a jacket and walks out of the door.

Delphine doesn't go to the gym. She follows her son's path, along the crescent and the snappy little boutiques where they know her by name, and takes the tube to Hammersmith.

Zaki, who has finally got up, has bribed the girl who works in Orla's Cafe to deliver the papers, and is sitting in the cafe himself with a cup of coffee as thick as tar and equally thick slices of toast. He sees Delphine hesitating on the edge of the green, and finally walking purposefully towards his shop.

He gets up, and waves from the cafe doorway. 'All right, Della, what are you doing here?'

'I might ask you the same question,' says Delphine pertly, feeling more cheerful already. 'I thought you were meant to work next door?'

'I'm diversifying,' explains Zaki with mock seriousness, going back to his moulded plastic seat at the cafe window. 'I thought I might start doing breakfast too. This is just research.' He gestures expansively towards his coffee and toast.

'The research looks delicious,' says Delphine, noticing that his toast was enviably golden and perfect.

'You can get your own, you know I don't share food.' He shouts to the plump, bleached-blonde owner who is left minding the cafe on her own. 'Orla, another round of toast for Della here, and get her a coffee.'

'Decaf latte, please,' corrects Delphine, and seeing both Zaki and Orla look at each other and snigger, suggests, 'Or a regular cappuccino?' As Orla raises her plucked eyebrows and shakes her head in mirth, Delphine concedes with a sigh, 'OK, just coffee, then.'

'You're not in Kansas now, Dorothy,' says Zaki. 'Honestly, Della, asking for a decaf latte in Orla's place, it's practically bad manners. You'll be asking for Parma ham, Parmesan and rocket on the toast next.'

'Why can't you just call me Delphine?' she retorts, for the second time that day, although with much less annoyance, accepting the cup of gritty filter coffee from Orla with a smile.

'You know why, Della. It sounds too much like "dolphin" – it makes me think that you might start making high-pitched squeaking noises and jumping for fish—'

'That joke's not got any funnier,' interrupts Delphine. 'Why don't you ever act your age?'

'Jinan acts my age for me, so I'm free to act my shoe size,' Zaki replies cheerfully. 'Anyway, you didn't answer my question. What's the girl doing so far out of Knightsbridge . . . again?'

'I was just in the neighbourhood,' says Delphine lightly, stirring her coffee. Zaki looks at her with frank disbelief, so she embellishes extravagantly, 'Lucky's school asked if Jinan or I wanted to join the board of governors, so I said I'd pop in.'

'Why do you even bother lying to me, Della?' asks Zaki, almost kindly. 'There's no cold day in hell that would have you turn up at Lucky's school dressed like that. You look like you rolled about in your walk-in wardrobe and wandered out with whatever stuck . . .'

Delphine looks down at herself, her designer tracksuit and ballet pumps absurdly topped with a smart tailored jacket with military brass buttons that she had taken unthinkingly from the hall cupboard, her aviator sunglasses sitting on top of her head. 'I just felt like talking, I suppose.'

'Oh, bloody hell, Della, I don't want to talk about *that*. Go complain to your girlfriends about your husband, not me. It's not on, you know, it's downright . . .' Zaki hesitates, trying to find a snippet of vocabulary that Delphine will accept '. . . *gauche* to whine to your father-in-law about your husband.'

'Whereas it's perfectly acceptable to whine to an old boyfriend,' says Delphine, looking straight at him. She drops her metal spoon on the yellow Formica-topped table with a tinny clink.

Orla, fascinated by the exchange that she pretends she's not listening to, has almost forgotten about Delphine's toast. She brings it over, burnt, thickly buttered and unapologetic. 'You can blame Zaki for the toast; he nicked my girl to deliver his blessed papers, so I'm having to be everywhere at once.'

Delphine stares at the toast that she was so looking forward to, more burnt and even less appealing than the toast she had made that morning, and despite herself, her lower lip starts to quiver. She suddenly feels small, exposed and unable to cope with the slightest mishap. 'Oh, for

God's sake, have some of mine then,' says Zaki, swapping their plates brusquely and sprinkling sugar on her burnt slices.

'Why do you put sugar on them?' asks Delphine conversationally, her way of thanking Zaki for not letting her break down in public.

'It reminds me of the parathas that Jinan's mum used to make us for breakfast,' replies Zaki. 'Nadya wasn't a great cook, and they were usually quite burnt too, but we just covered them in sugar and then they tasted fine.' He pauses, and asks, 'Why did you really come here, Della?'

'I guess you make me feel better,' she answers honestly, surprised by his persistence with this question.

'Well, you make me feel worse,' he says abruptly, thinking of his sorry, stupid son; so successful in meaningless ways, such a spectacular failure at the things that mattered, and he didn't even know it.

Delphine says nothing, and sips her gunky coffee, trying not to make a face. She knows that Zaki is right, that it's not appropriate to lean on him so much. But his suggestion of her speaking to her girlfriends about it is laughable; the girls all think that she has a perfect life. She's the one that got away, the one that skipped out of the rat race, the one who has the perfect (younger!) husband, wealthy and adoring, the one who has the perfect, talented offspring, the one who has nothing to do but look down from the balcony of her streamlined Starck-interiored nest in Knightsbridge and float airily through the swish cafes and smart shops until it's time to whip up the perfect risotto for her family, then perhaps meet the girls for a cocktail at Zuma, or attend a lecture at the Royal Geographical Society or wine-tasting at the Institut Français. She knows that she is envied, and sometimes she feels that this envy is all she has. That and her private little meetings with Zaki, who despite everything that has happened between them, always does make her feel better.

Zaki sighs, and seeing the genuine pathos in Delphine's fine-featured face, feels his brusque mask melting away. 'Would you like to come next door, Della? I'll let you work your way through the gossip mags. Or even the glossy mags. Take your pick, as long as you put them back on the shelf.' He downs his coffee and adds magnanimously, 'If you like, I could even attempt to make you a latte with that shiny contraption that you and Jinan got me last Christmas . . .'

Delphine smiles, and nods gratefully. 'It's a Krups, we've got the same one. I'll show you how to use it, if you like.'

Zaki goes to settle up with Orla, and looks back at Delphine waiting for him at their table. He thinks with some regret that his late-morning visit to the bookies will have to be abandoned.

The Teenage Washerwoman
of the Bangshi River

WHEN ZAKI FIRST saw Nadya she was sixteen years
old, washing clothes with her family by the Bangshi
River, the muddy water transformed on her skin into daz-
zling dewy pearls that rolled down her arms towards the
tips of her slender fingers. She was laughing with the children, who were trying to help her soak and beat the
clothes, amused rather than annoyed by their clumsiness.
While she worked, she sang little songs to entertain them,
occasionally stopping to kiss the youngest infant, until the
tottering little girl squirmed and giggled with mock protest, '*Na, Apa, na!* Too much!' Zaki was only eighteen
himself, and stood transfixed by the sight of her cold,
clean arms, her carved profile cast into relief by the thick
hair pulled back and wound into an untidy bun, the milk
chocolate skin that melted from the back of her neck into
the rough cotton sari blouse; it was as though he had
wandered into a dream. The tableau was so fresh and pure
in its innocence and glowing colour that it was almost
unreal; he was half expecting cartoon doves and helpful
bluebirds to land on the girl's shoulders and wring her

clothes with a cheerful twittering before laying them on the flat rocks to dry.

'Zakaria!' his father shouted behind him, from their car. 'Zakaria, hurry up! How long do you need to take a bloody leak?'

Mortified, Zaki shouted back, 'I'm just washing my hands, Baba,' and looked contritely at the girl for the crude way in which she'd been alerted to his presence. However, she simply looked back over her shoulder and smiled and nodded at the young stranger, showing no sign of embarrassment. She nudged the children to nod politely, too.

'*Asalaam alaikum*,' he said respectfully, as he walked swiftly to the river to dip his hands in the cool water. It was clearer close up than he had originally thought; the muddy colour was just the reflection of the earthy bed.

The washerwoman nudged the children again, who chorused '*Walaikum asalaam*' indifferently, before carrying on with their washing game.

'*Apnar naam ki?*' he asked the girl, but she just smiled and shook her head. It wasn't done to talk to strange young men. Especially a strange young man with such an appealing expression, even with his Baba as an unwilling roadside chaperone. Zaki's father shouted at him again, and he turned to go, unwilling to leave with so little ceremony, without giving the magical moment its due, without giving the girl some small token to remember him by. He had nothing to leave her apart from his name, which he gave to her carefully, hoping she would remember their brief encounter, '*Amar naam Zaki. Zaki Khalil.*'

He went back to his father's car and saw her turn around and watch him as he was driven off. He hadn't noticed before that she was quite pregnant, the demure sweep of her cotton sari almost concealing the bulge. His father had paid no attention to the group by the riverside as he had been complaining to the driver about the heat. 'Ouf, Zakaria, what took you so long?'

'What was the hurry, Baba?' asked Zaki. 'There was the most beautiful girl by the river.'

'Mr Mujib is waiting for us in Dhamrai, and he said he'd get us a good deal. I'm not telling him we're late because my intellectual son has suddenly got an eye for village damsels,' said Zaki's father irritably. He looked critically at Zaki, who was wearing flared trousers that were too fitted at the waist, and some sort of paisley polyester shirt that he must have bought while at university overseas. His hair definitely needed a cut, he looked like a goddamned harami Beatle. 'You have no head for business, son, but by God you're going to learn.'

Ignoring him, Zaki leaned towards the driver. 'You're from around here, aren't you, Abdur? Do you know that girl's name?'

The old driver looked disapprovingly at Zaki. 'She's married. And she's about to have her first child . . .' His silence was eloquent, and he refused to say anything further.

Zaki's father finished the sentence for him, '. . . and so what business is it of yours to know her name?'

Despite them both, Zaki found out later that her name was Nadya, meaning 'moist with dew' – an appropriate name for a girl who took in washing.

As a young man, Zaki had a dream. He had won a place to university overseas, but not to Oxford or Cambridge or even an Ivy League college in the States; he had won a place to the Sorbonne in Paris. He dreamed of being a Left Bank intellectual, like Sartre, and he was searching for his own Simone de Beauvoir, his soul mate; someone with whom he would live an unfettered life, free from petty concerns and practicalities. He had just spent his first year at college, and his father, furious at how little his son seemed to be learning, had insisted that he spend his vacation mastering the family trade. Mr Khalil ran the Khalil Emporium in Dhaka, selling saris, shawls and traditional village brassware. He had dragged Zaki unwillingly on this buying trip to Mr Mujib's factory. Zaki didn't scorn his father's profession, but neither did he admire it; it was just the way his father was, as though someone had marked 'Shopkeeper' on his wristband when he was a newborn baby, and it was a label he had kept.

Zaki's label, if he had one at all, was 'Dreamer'. Hopelessly romantic, he believed that he had fallen in love at first sight with a village beauty, who had already been sold off in marriage and fallen pregnant at a tender age, probably to some local lout who beat her for breakfast. Zaki believed that if anyone could save her, it would be him. Of course, it was just a dream, and no one was more surprised than Zaki, driving himself on another buying trip to Dhamrai, to find out that his father's chauffeur had lied. The young washerwoman wasn't married after all, but widowed, as her husband had fallen into the river and drowned. The less kind gossips pointed out that the husband was drunk when he fell in, and that his family, having no one to blame, decided to blame Nadya for not giving him proper attention. Nadya had returned to her family home, to the consternation of her parents, who had wasted a good dowry on their now pregnant and therefore unmarriageable daughter; they were hoping that her child might be a boy, in which case they might persuade her husband's family to take her back. Zaki took in the news from the villagers with interest, and then asked for directions to Nadya's parents' house; he had a business proposition for them.

Zaki began to take an unprecedented interest in his father's emporium, and particularly in the goods produced by the Dhamrai factory. Mr Khalil was pleased by Zaki's change of heart, but couldn't help being suspicious when he saw that some of the stock was arriving damp. Zaki explained with wide-eyed, convincing innocence that some of the more highly discounted shawls were emerging rather grubby from the factory, and so he was getting a local washerwoman to clean them for him, at a much lower rate than they would have had to pay in Dhaka. Mr Khalil unwillingly congratulated his son on his initiative.

Towards the end of the summer, Zaki was spending the last of many long afternoons he had passed by the Bangshi riverside, while Nadya and her younger brothers and sisters cleaned the shawls that he had purposely muddied on the journey from Dhamrai. Nadya, now heavily pregnant, was no longer required to be reserved around him, and accepted his presence cheerfully; she was chatting to him about her baby and future plans. 'I hope it's a girl,' she said decisively, 'as then I'll stay at home, and can bring her up with this rabble.' She straightened her back with a grimace, rubbing the heel of her hand over the lower part of her spine before squatting back at the water's edge to continue her work. 'If it's a boy, they'll want me to go back to my in-laws, and I'll end up being an unpaid maid for them. If I'm to be a maid, I'd rather go to Dhaka with the baby and be one there.'

'Have you ever thought of going further than Dhaka?' asked Zaki, sitting with his feet dangling in the water.

'Like where? Chittagong, maybe? I'd like to go to the seaside,' said Nadya.

'No, further than Chittagong,' said Zaki.

'Further than Chittagong?' frowned Nadya. 'What, you mean Calcutta?'

'Further even than Calcutta. Go on, guess where I'm thinking of!'

'You are a silly boy. And this is a silly game,' said Nadya, turning her attention back to her washing.

'I know that I'm a silly boy. But humour me. If you guess right, I'll give Padma a present,' said Zaki winningly.

Nadya looked at her littlest sister, tottering with her brothers, who were showing her how to peel a mango. She smiled affectionately as Padma dripped the juice from the mangled mango skin into her mouth. 'OK, I'll play,' she said. 'How about Delhi?' Zaki shook his head. 'Bombay?' He shook his head again, but splashed the edge of her sari with his foot. '*Arré!* Stop that, I'm thinking.' She paused, and hesitated just briefly before splashing him back cheekily, accidentally on purpose, as she dipped a shawl in the water. 'Karachi!' she said firmly.

'Wrong,' announced Zaki, splashing her even more as a punishment.

'Stop that, you little . . .' Nadya just managed to stop herself muttering an expletive. 'See, you'll have me swearing in front of the children with your silly games. What a waste of your poor father's money if this is what they teach you to do at that big university.'

'What big university?' asked Zaki innocently.

Nadya looked at him impatiently, as he was clearly acting dense on purpose. 'Allah give me patience with you. Your big university in Paris, of course . . .'

Zaki leapt up. 'That's it! That's it! You won the prize!' He ran to pull her up by her hands, but she pushed him away so that he almost fell comically into the water.

'Paris? Why would I think about going to Paris?' said Nadya with suspicion. 'And where's my present for Padma?'

'It's right here,' said Zaki. Suddenly nervous, he pulled a little square package out of his pocket and opening it, showed Nadya a beautiful ring set with a pearl and tiny diamond.

Nadya looked at him with dawning comprehension. '*Na, Zaki, na!* Too much!' she said in shock. She added in a hushed whisper, 'It's too much for a little girl like Padma.'

Zaki was dry mouthed, and said quickly, 'I didn't really get it for Padma. I thought it would look beautiful on her eldest sister. I thought she might honour me by accepting me as a father to her baby. I thought she might come to Paris with me, as my wife.'

Nadya said nothing for a moment, and turned away from him. When she looked back her eyes were filled with tears, as she reached out and closed the box that was in his hand. 'Put it away, silly boy,' she said, her voice very precise and firm. Zaki thought he might cry himself with the humiliation of being rejected by the girl he adored, but then she added, 'Now go and ask my parents, and for God's sake do it properly this time, without any silly jokes. And offer my mother the ring as a present . . .' She shook her head ruefully, wiping away her tears with the end of her sari before giving Zaki a playful and affectionate push. 'Go on,' she said, 'I don't know what they teach you in college, but it's certainly not how to propose.'

Zaki looked at her in stunned silence, and dashed off. He then ran back to Nadya, held her by the tops of her cold, clean arms to kiss her suddenly and warmly on her perfectly formed lips, then raced towards the village. 'Stop washing those clothes immediately,' he called back over his shoulder. 'As your future husband I command you to never wash anything ever again.' He ran into the village with great boyish bounds. 'She said yes!' he told the stunned villagers, 'She said yes!'

The Unexpected Helpfulness of Hiccups

L UCKY LEAVES HIS SCHOOL shortly after four o'clock and, strolling across the river, finds himself back at his grandfather's corner shop. The shop is open this time, and he walks in to find Portia installed behind the counter, eating a chip butty and reading *Hello!*

'Hello?' he says, wondering if she'll get the joke.

'Very bloody funny, I don't bloody think,' she retorts, recrossing her legs under the flip-top door of the counter. 'Someone's already been through this one – the quiz has been done.'

'Where's the boss man?' asks Lucky, opening the fridge door to get himself a Coke so that he has somewhere other to look than at her wonderful legs – not too thin, and certainly not too big, with a perfect curved shape to the calf.

'He naffed off to the bookies the moment I walked in the door, and I only popped in to get my wages. I'll report the daft bugger one day, leaving a minor in charge of this place, it's not on. And that's a pound please.' She puts down her chip butty, and stands up officiously.

'Family doesn't pay,' lies Lucky, as he doesn't have much cash on him.

'You're not my bloody family,' says Portia. Looking at Lucky, she tosses back her trailing school scarf and mutters, 'Oh, forget it. Like I care if your grandad goes out of business.' Lucky looks at her in surprise as he realizes, from that off-handed and bad-tempered remark, that she does care, she in fact cares very much. Her righteousness discomfits him; he is embarrassed by the tacit implication that perhaps she cares more for his grandfather than he does. He guiltily empties his blazer pockets into his hands, and counts out an untidy shrapnel of coppers and silver, which are nestling among the bits of gum wrappers and fluff, until he reaches a pound. He hands the money over self-consciously, without saying a word.

'Ta,' says Portia indifferently, popping it into the till, which makes an old-fashioned 'ker-ching' noise. For some reason, this noise delights Portia, and he sees her suppressing a giggle. 'Private joke,' she explains, as Lucky takes his usual seat on the other side of the counter. She companionably passes him the *Hello!*, while she moves on to the back page of the *Independent* to do the sudoku and the quick crossword. She's a bright girl, Lucky thinks to himself, watching her chew the end of her biro thoughtfully. She understands numbers and words, she can tease out hidden meanings and sequences where all I can see is a chequerboard jumble. He feels humbled by her all over again. He flips open the *Hello!*, looking at the quiz she mentioned, and recognizes his mother's handwriting. His mum must have popped over this week; probably watching some arty French movie at the Riverside Studios; there was very little else that would draw his perfectly polished mother to this unfashionable backwater. Looking at Portia's profile, the chewed biro and her elfin hair dissolving into down at her neck, he searches for something to say.

'That's my mum who's done the quiz, although she's not normally a quiz sort of person,' he says, much more calmly and casually than he actually feels.

Portia looks back over the quiz with interest. 'So she's mostly 'B's. A shopaholic who would rather a night out with the girls than a steamy night in with a hot date.'

'Yuk,' says Lucky, making a face. 'Don't talk about my mother and hot dates, that's just . . . gross.'

Portia smirks knowingly. 'Boys are all the same. They all think that their mothers are virgins. Of course your mum dated before she met your dad.' Portia pauses, and adds slyly, 'She even dated Zaki, didn't she?'

'How do you know that?' Lucky asks, annoyed. Of course he can already guess how she knows as Zaki shares this story freely, professing to find it hugely funny that he was the one who first found his future daughter-in-law and unwittingly introduced her to his son. By contrast, it was a source of acute embarrassment to Lucky's dad that his wife once went out with his father; the sort of thing that happens in soap operas and sitcoms and has no place in real life. Especially not a life as precisely ordered and organized as Jinan's. The first time Lucky's parents met, Delphine had been Zaki's date at Jinan's school play. The next time they met, years later, had been at some meeting at Delphine's company offices where she had completely failed to recognize him. The funny thing, thinks Lucky, is that in some ways Delphine and Zaki were probably seen as a more normal couple than Delphine and Jinan. After all, Zaki was only a dozen years older than her, which wasn't so odd. It was more unusual for his dad to be half a dozen years younger than his mum; young enough for her to have babysat him. Lucky has the impression that his father's relative youth embarrasses his mother much more than her long-ago liaison with her future father-in-law; perhaps that's why his father is making himself so old before his time.

Portia has ignored his question, and gone back to her sudoku. Without looking up, she continues as though he hadn't spoken, 'Now, girls are a lot less gooey when it comes to their mums. We see them for who they are.'

'Your mum's German, isn't she?' says Lucky, wondering if he can manipulate this into some sort of accusation, to get his own back for her remark about his mum and Zaki. He starts to hum 'Two world wars and one world cup, doo-dah, doo-dah,' but then decides against it. Looking at the top of Portia's head as she bends over the paper, her long, thick lashes fanning against her cheeks, he wonders if she would be more or less beautiful if she had longer hair. Less, he decides. Lots of beautiful girls had long hair, but there was something about Portia that made her unlike anyone in the world. And the cropped hair hid nothing from sight; there was something so very vulnerable about her exposed ears with the tiny silver hoops in them.

'She's a bloody slapper,' retorts Portia fiercely. She speaks without warning after what seemed a long pause, as though the words had been bubbling up slowly inside, and then simply had to be spat out. The sudden unfiltered anger in her tone causes Lucky to stop and stare at her. Perhaps his look might even be interpreted as reproach, as though his teenage goddess has revealed her feet of clay, showing him that she can be vindictive and unkind, but Portia returns his gaze unrepentantly, lifting her chin a little higher in the air.

Zaki saunters in and sees the kids locked in a staring battle; perhaps it was some kind of juvenile mating ritual. 'Are you two in love or something?' he asks, and is amused to see Lucky almost blush.

Portia's fierceness evaporates with his arrival. 'Ker-ching?' she asks mysteriously.

'Ker-ching,' Zaki confirms, just as mysteriously.

'I thought you looked pleased with yourself,' she grins finally with delight. 'So, have you won me my wages?'

He nods and hands her a couple of crisp notes with a flourish. 'My last nag came in. Thank your mum for me, Lucky; if she hadn't rolled up this morning, I'd have lost everything on a bad tip in the first race.' Zaki looks at his watch. 'Too early for a beer. I'll make us Irish cappuccinos to celebrate; I learned how to do the foamy milk thing this morning.' He grabs the *Independent* from Portia, and strolls towards the stairs. 'Bugger, I was going to do the sudoku . . .' he complains to her as he passes.

'Don't make mine Irish,' she calls after him, 'I'll get in trouble.'

'Make mine a double, Grandad,' Lucky calls impulsively, seeking obviously to impress. He looks at Portia, and shrugs his shoulders with a sheepish grin. 'I'm always in trouble anyway,' he explains.

Hours later, once they have finally been thrown out by Zaki, Lucky and Portia are sitting by the river in Hammersmith on the benches thoughtfully supplied by one of the pubs. Portia had been unwilling to go home for some reason, and Lucky had found himself walking along with her, simply by having forgotten to say goodbye and walk in the opposite direction. It was far easier to be pulled along by her sheer magnetism. He wasn't the only one drawn to her; she got wolf-whistles even with her cropped hair, and even in her school uniform. Maybe because of it. Portia, however, was unimpressed by any such attention. 'Fuck off, perverts,' she had snapped to the perpetrators, muttering, 'I hate bloody dirty old men.' She had pulled Lucky by the arm to walk closer to her, as though he would protect her. She was different from the other schoolgirls Lucky knew, who complained that the 'boys' their own age were too young for them, and sought out the older lads instead; they were of an age when an extra two or three years appeared to lend limitless sophistication. Portia's light touch on his arm gave Lucky goose-bumps through his blazer, and he had taken to his appointed role with gusto, glaring at any others who dared to eye up Portia, as though he was a burly bodyguard, not a sporty schoolboy who was just a bit tall for his age.

On the grey river-bank, Lucky looks at Portia's profile in the increasingly poor light, as she blows smoke artistically into the breeze, and the traffic twinkles along the bridge. It is late, and they would both have been expected home some time ago. He is sure that his parents would have called Zaki by now. He wants to say something serious to Portia, something more than asking what she plans to do for the weekend, or whether she's seen some well-reviewed movie – the usual dull things that he asked her when Zaki wasn't with them. 'Portia, why do you . . .' he starts to say, but the solemnity of the moment is ruined by an irritating little popping noise that stops him in his tracks, accompanied by a flutter in his abdomen, the sound so featherlight at first that it takes him a moment to realize that it is coming from him. He only has the bloody hiccups; and now he can't stop, and they're getting louder and more noticeable.

Portia bursts into peals of giggles, a rare, musical sound that he can't appreciate through the fog of his humiliation. 'You utter lightweight – one double Irish cappuccino and you're hiccuping like the neighbourhood drunk,' she says affectionately.

Lucky suddenly feels hopeful rather than foolish, and tries to say between hiccups, 'I just wanted to know, why do you . . .' Another hiccup interrupts him, and Portia bursts out laughing again. 'Oh bloody hell, I'm off home,' he mutters, and pushes himself up from the bench.

'No, stay a minute,' says Portia, pulling him back down. 'Please,' she adds appealingly. 'I'm sorry for laughing. What did you want to say?' Patting his hand, she adds, 'Hold your breath for a minute; it helps sometimes, I think.'

Lucky holds his breath, but is sure it's the warmth of Portia's hand on his that calms his hiccups away. He feels suddenly grateful for the hiccups; without them, she wouldn't be touching him so gently, and looking at him so intently. 'I wasn't going to say anything, really. I was just going to ask, why do you not like your mum?'

'Who said I don't like my mum?' asks Portia, frowning

❧ 35 ❦

so adorably that Lucky wants to touch the slight furrow that appears on her otherwise smooth forehead. 'I love the silly cow. I just said that she's a slapper. Ever since she and my dad split up, she's come home with one random guy after another. And the last one looks like he's staying – he's always at home, and he's a real sleaze . . . I can hear them sometimes when they . . . you know . . . it's just gross. I guess she's trying to prove something to my dad, that she doesn't need him, something like that.'

'Yuk,' says Lucky sympathetically, thinking how horrific it must be to hear a parent doing . . . stuff. Parents shouldn't have sex lives, or love lives, or anything like that – they should behave themselves and do what's expected of them, normal things like slouching on the sofa in front of the TV, complaining about interest rates or the neighbours, or arguing in DIY shops about walnut flooring. At least, that's what his parents did; he feels a flash of gratitude for their thoughtful lack of demonstrativeness. 'Why don't you stay with your dad?' he suggests helpfully. Portia's dad is an actuary (Lucky has only a vague idea of what an actuary is, and assumes it's some complicated form of accountant), he is half Jamaican and half Scottish, and according to Zaki, utterly humourless and dryer than sandpaper.

Portia shrugs. 'I guess I think that it would be letting her down, proving to my dad that she's a bad mother. She's got low enough self-esteem as it is. I think she needs me.' Lucky nods with recognition; he feels needed by his mother too, although not in quite such an obvious way. His mother's needs are more insidious, and harder to express.

'It's hard, to be needed, I think,' he says, but then

considering this, adds, 'But maybe it's better than not being needed?'

Portia gives him a small, slight smile and, shivering slightly, walks over to the river, and looks down into the murky, inky depths. 'Did you hear that they pulled somebody out last week, just over by the bridge?' Somebody, some unknown body, had decided that they'd had quite enough of being needed, or not being needed, and had decided to stop being at all, just to become part of the river instead. To get caught up in the current, and swept away along the dark, hidden secrets of the rocky bed; to bump along the bricks of the bank, and to look up finally at the stars, and the twinkling lights of the traffic on the bridge. What would they have chosen for their final journey? she wonders. Would it have been an impulsive leap, something to be done in an instant or never done at all, or would it have been planned, considered? Would they have taken off their shoes, or left them on just to feel them get washed away? Would they have filled their pockets with stones, or expected that the heaviness of their heart, that the weight of their expectation, would be enough to enable them to sink into the current's embrace. She feels a sudden, dangerous empathy for this somebody, even envy for their decisiveness, and their success. If she fell into the river, would she care enough to fight it and float?

Lucky isn't sure if he's meant to say anything in response; there is a dark side to Portia, he realizes, something you wouldn't expect from someone with such a fresh, open beauty. He can see it in the way that she is considering the bridge; in the vengeful, injured tone she used when she insulted her own mother. It intrigues him, rather than puts him off. He finds everything about Portia interesting. 'Poor sod,' he says eventually, 'they must have been desperate. There must be nicer ways than that to end it all.' Portia turns to look at Lucky, and he wonders if he's said something stupid. 'I don't mean that it's ever nice to end it,' he feels the need to clarify, 'only that it's such a cold and wet way to go.' He realizes belatedly that he now seems even stupider; whatever drives someone to suicide is probably significant enough for them not to be much bothered about the cold and the wet. It's now dark as well as late, and Portia's needy, randy mum is probably worried about her, but Portia is just standing by the river and lighting another cigarette. 'Are you all right?' he asks. 'It's just that I think we ought to start heading back – your mum's probably wondering where you are.'

Portia smiles at Lucky, who can be so serious and quiet, and touchingly schoolboy awkward. Despite his height, he is just a little boy who plays with balls. He is uncomplicated in his unblinkered admiration of her, in his blunt and ineffective way of disguising it. 'How am I ever meant to know that you like me, if you never tell me?' she asks him simply. She stands close to him, kisses him firmly on the lips, and turns to walk away. But Lucky instinctively pulls her back to him, and before he has time to think about what he is doing, unthinkingly returns her chaste kiss in kind. His mouth is warm and dry, and for a moment, for a small, miraculous moment, Portia feels safe. She feels she might have found her reason to stay afloat.

They walk back to the tube station together, Lucky both unsure and elated about this new intimacy. Portia is holding his arm again, even though it is now dark and there are no further wolf-whistles to be protected from. This, thinks Lucky, is what heaven must be like, to have a beautiful girl holding him by the arm. Perhaps people even think that she is his girlfriend; the thought makes his back straighten with pride. Perhaps she *is* now his girlfriend, perhaps their kiss has sealed the deal; the wonder of this thought makes him start hiccuping again.

Portia tries not to giggle at the renewed attack, and waits until they reach the station before asking, 'So, what are you up to this weekend?'

'Pract—' Lucky starts to say, but is interrupted by Portia, who confirms his response with the answer to her own question.

'Practice. Of course.' She sighs. 'Well, good luck with it.'

'But I'll see you on Monday morning before school, at Zaki's?' asks Lucky, not even trying to be cool.

'Monday,' affirms Portia, as though exacting a promise. She doesn't try to kiss him goodbye or give him the opportunity to kiss her, but walks down the stairs towards her train, glancing just briefly over her shoulder at the tall schoolboy leaning against the wall.

'Monday,' repeats Lucky to himself, for once feeling that he is living up to his name. It's practically a date.

Lucky Khalil Against the Cosmic Forces of Darkness

LUCKY IS SOMEONE different when he's with his team. He's no longer reserved, and quietly confused – he is quietly confident, as he is doing what he does best, and what he likes best. And he is revered, as he is their star player. He plays in midfield, but his height makes him dangerous in set pieces. Club scouts have been aware of him since he was twelve, and although no one has offered yet, it'll have to happen soon. It has to. Lucky knows this because he has a dream, and just as he can't let his dream down, his dream won't let him down. The next match has my name on it, he tells himself anxiously; the next match is against a team from outside London, and their thirteen-year-old striker has attracted a lot of interest, and often drew influential scouts to his matches. Lucky knows that he has to acquit himself well in the next match.

His father lectured him over breakfast for not calling when he stayed out late the night before, and said that he wouldn't be allowed out until his homework was done. His mother ignored his father's lecture and drove him to the training ground, handing him his freshly laundered kit in a

Harvey Nichols bag. He now races into the changing rooms, still warm all over with the happy afterglow of his evening out with Portia, and with the unexpected, wholly miraculous finale. He considers sharing this news with the lads – his comrades, his compadres – and thinks it through as he pulls on his kit. The story changes with each iteration in his head, gaining or losing detail, but it always finishes the same way: ' . . . and then she kissed me.' No, he decides, that delicious moment was for him, and him only. Out loud, it wouldn't be something perfect and delicate, it would be twisted into something crude and base. Just a dry snog by the river. He is still thinking about this when one of the defenders thwacks him with a towel. 'Jesus, Lucky, you smell like a tart!'

'It's called being clean, Minger,' he says to Ming Bruce. Ming lived up to his moniker by being famously casual about personal hygiene; he always left and arrived for practice in his kit, looking for all the world as though he never bothered to take it off in between. Jackie, their hardest-working forward, grabs Lucky in a friendly headlock, and rubs the top of his slightly spiky hair enthusiastically.

'Aaw, you so purdy.' He grins. 'Minger's right. Even your hair smells sweet.'

'Oi! Geroff, you raving fag,' says Lucky good-naturedly, succeeding in shaking Jackie off him. He doesn't mind being ribbed for being clean, but in truth he's a bit embarrassed about his hair today. His own shampoo ran out, and he was forced to use one of his mum's flowery concoctions. 'You nervous about next week?' he asks the lads.

'What, you mean the match with Swindon?' replies Jackie. 'Nah, there's no shame in being shown up by a

striker like Felix Conway. Phenomenon Felix, they're calling him. He's in another league.'

'Well, you're not the one who has to bloody mark him,'
mutters Ming. 'I remember playing him last year. Flipping
knackering it was . . . Embarrassing too, the number of
goals he got. He'd only just turned twelve.'

'Yeah, poor Dunc,' says Lucky, referring to their hap-
less goalie. 'He was well upset. Didn't turn up for weeks.'
Lucky remembered seeing Duncan crying on the pitch
before the game was even over, and crying some more
afterwards. And Duncan wasn't even that serious about
football, not like the rest of them; he wanted to be a marine
biologist, or something similarly tweedy and specific. Dunc
had been heartbroken all the same; he was a big bloke, but
none of the squad mocked him or took the piss or told him
to stop being a girl. That's the thing about football, thinks
Lucky, there's a nobility in grieving for your loss, and when
you get to the hard end of it, everyone understands. Well,
everyone apart from people like his dad, a clueless spectator
who'd been nagged into turning up that day by Lucky's
mum. Jinan had assumed that the outrageous defeat was
representative of how Lucky's team normally did, and
thought it hilarious that the biggest boy on the pitch was
crying. Lucky himself had been a bit less understanding
afterwards; since as the second tallest in the squad, he'd
been forced to play in goal during the couple of weeks that
Duncan was licking his wounds. Shuddering at the memory, Lucky looks around. 'Where is Dunc, anyway?' Jackie
and Ming glance around the changing room at the rest of
the lads, and shrug. Lucky is prevented from further inves-
tigation as his coach, Harding, calls him up.

'I need to talk to you, Lucky,' Harding says a bit grimly. The tone doesn't suit his avuncular, rather cuddly exterior. 'I've got some news.'

'You're joking,' says Lucky, appalled by what Harding has just told him. Then, looking at Harding's overly solemn face, the lips uncharacteristically thin, decides that his coach is laying it on too thick to be serious, and relaxes. 'You really are joking,' he laughs. 'Good one, sir, you almost had me there for a minute.'

Harding sighs; the kid's wide-eyed optimism isn't making this easy. 'I'm not joking. Duncan can't play for the next week, and I need you to practise in goal. In fact, to play in goal.'

Lucky decides to play along, still not believing this news the slightest little bit. The lads and Harding were setting him up, that was all. Nice of Harding to be so sporting, and to make such a serious job of it; he was a good sort, really. 'So, what's wrong with Dunc?' Lucky queries lightly.

Harding shrugs his shoulders, much like the lads had done in the changing room. 'You tell me. His dad told me that he's ill, but he didn't give any details.' He rubs his forehead with the back of his hand, and it is the weariness in this slight gesture that finally begins to worry Lucky.

'You're really not joking, are you?' he asks, unable to keep the panic from colouring his voice. Harding shakes his head, and Lucky explodes with rage. 'Fucking bastard! The fucking bastard! He's too piss-scared to play against Conway, so he's letting us all down.' He kicks the edge of the stand violently, and then punches it for good measure. Ouch, fucking ouch. His hands aren't used to hard knocks, and he nurses his bruised knuckles, leaning against the stand.

'We don't know that now, Lucky,' says Harding remonstratively, 'he might really be ill.'

'If he's not, he's bloody going to be,' mutters Lucky unrepentantly. The dire consequences of Duncan's cowardice finally sink in, and Lucky feels his stomach churn. 'Hold up, sir. I can't play in goal this week. Any other week I would, you know I would. But it's the Swindon Town FC match next week, and I need to be playing in my proper position . . .' He doesn't need to say any more. Harding must realize that there'll be scouts looking at Felix Conway, but who might look Lucky's way instead. If he's not playing midfield, they won't be looking at him at all.

'I know, son, but football's about the team. First and foremost, it's about the team. You're the only boy in the squad with the height to cover the goal. And if you're not in goal, we'll be laughed out of the match . . .' Lucky is looking miserable and mutinous, and scowls in response. Harding is a kind coach, rather than a good one, and hates confrontation. But forced into this corner, he finally has the courage to say something he knows he should have said some time ago. 'The thing is, Lucky, that maybe you should see this as an opportunity . . .'

Lucky gapes at him – the old man has clearly gone barking mad. What opportunity could there possibly be in missing out on the biggest break of the season, the match which had his name on it, where the scouts would be watching? 'Are you taking the bleeding mick, sir?' he says sarcastically – a sign of genuine distress, as Lucky is almost never rude to his coach.

'No, really Lucky, I mean it. It gives you a chance to show what you can do in another position, and I've always felt that you weren't really playing to your full . . . potential in midfield.' Lucky is stunned by this assessment, and opens his mouth to protest, but the coach carries on. 'I mean, you're good, there's no doubt about it. You're easily the best player we have. But Lucky, there are hundreds upon hundreds of young lads about as good as you in midfield, and they're not all going to make it.'

'No, you don't understand . . .' Lucky begins, not at all sure how he's going to finish this sentence. How can he explain to the coach that he will make it, that he must? How can he explain that he knows he'll make it, because he has a dream, an actual dream that wakes him weeping from his sleep?

'Lucky, I do understand. You know you're a good player, and you're entitled to think you've got a chance. And I'm agreeing with you – you do have a chance. But not in midfield. Do you remember last year, when you played in goal for Duncan? Those two matches were the only clean sheets we kept; you even saved a penalty – a difficult one. And that was with hardly any training in goal. You could be a champion goalie. You're tall, you're fast on your feet, you're good with your hands, and I've seen how well you read the field when you do the throw-ins or corners. And if you're on the receiving end, when you jump for the ball, no one can get close to you.' Having said his piece, Harding feels a bit easier, and gesturing towards the battered stand, adds good-humouredly, 'And no one can say you're afraid of hard knocks or hard shots.'

Lucky kicks the stand again disconsolately. 'It doesn't look like I have much choice, do I?' he says miserably.

'You're still worrying about not getting seen next week?' says Harding. 'Let me tell you, if you manage to deny Conway, you'll get seen all right.' Lucky says nothing; all his righteous anger against Duncan has evaporated, leaving him with the bitter, familiar taste of disappointment, now tainted by doubt in his coach's judgement. He knows he's not meant to be a goalkeeper, because then his last four years in midfield have been wasted; he knows he's not meant to play in goal, because his dream says that he will score for England, and everyone knows – even a complete football div like his dad would know – that you don't score from goal.

'How was it, darling?' says Delphine. Lucky has said nothing since she picked him up, and she's now on the Fulham Road, driving down the final stretch towards the apartment.

'They've put me in goal, for the next week at least,' says Lucky flatly.

Delphine tuts in sympathy; from what she knows about football, being in goal is Not A Good Thing. 'That's a shame, darling. You get to run about a lot less, don't you?'

Lucky looks at her scornfully. 'Mum, it's not about running about. I don't give a damn about running about; I can run about in the bloody park if I just want to run about . . .'

'Language, darling,' chides Delphine. 'So that's not so bad, then. It's just for a week.'

'Mum!' protests Lucky with the specific type of right-eous indignation that only the young can muster. 'No way is it "not so bad"! It's very, very bad. In fact, it's bloody awful. It's the big game next week, remember?'

'That's right, darling. I'm looking forward to it. I was thinking that your dad should make more of an effort to come to your big matches – I'll make sure that he skips his golf and comes too, this time.'

'Oh no you won't,' says Lucky, thinking of the last time his dad turned up. 'I'm not having Dad seeing me in goal, embarrassing myself against a wonderkid striker. He'll just piss himself.' And then he'll wonder what the hell it is I've been doing for the last four years, and refuse to pay my subs, Lucky adds silently. So far, his dad has failed to show any support or understanding towards Lucky's football-ing aspirations, but at least he hasn't seriously tried to stop him, not yet.

Delphine considers arguing against this evaluation of Jinan, and then decides not to; teenagers have a built-in bullshit detector, and she privately agrees with Lucky that Jinan is probably best kept away from the stands. The only thing worse than a competitive and furiously keen parent spectator (of which there were plenty at this sort of event) is an indifferent and bored parent spectator. She changes the subject as they approach the Michelin Building. 'Look, darling, there's Bibendum. I was thinking of taking your dad there for our anniversary. What do you think?' Lucky looks at the stained-glass figure of the chubby Michelin man on the side of the building, bursting out of his white, bloated tyres, and stifles a laugh. 'Yeah, I think it would suit him fine.' Delphine sees what Lucky means, and disloyally permits a puff of laughter to escape before she controls herself. Poor Jinan has started to gain weight recently, getting middle-aged spread before he is even middle-aged – too much work stress and too many of those Danish twisty things at working breakfasts. She stops at the lights, and as Lucky stoops to fiddle with his trainers, she unthinkingly runs her hand over the back and top of his hair, as one might stroke a kitten.

'Mu-umm!' says Lucky again, with a different kind of indignation. Delphine realizes what she's doing, stops mid-stroke and quickly pulls back her hand with embarrassment.

'Sorry,' she mumbles, 'I thought you were . . .' Someone beeps her from behind; she finally notices that the lights have changed, and moves off. Lucky looks at her searchingly for a moment, then starts fiddling with his trainer again; but this time he doesn't stoop, and pulls his knee up towards his chest instead. Delphine bites her lip self-consciously, looking fixedly ahead. She had thought he was someone else, or not quite someone else, but an earlier self – his younger infant self, with downy strokable hair on the back of his soft, warm head. She had thought that he was still her little boy. She is so discomfited that she almost can't look at him as she locks the car, and says practically nothing as they head up towards their third-floor flat, with its balcony and roof terrace.

Lucky sits back on his bed, and looks accusingly at Leia and Darth Vader. Well, what now? he asks them sullenly. You two are a fat lot of help. Turning his back on them, he pulls out his *Star Wars* DVD box set, and selects his favourite scene: the seminal fight between Luke and Darth Vader, the ultimate battle of good versus evil. He pushes a chair against his door (there is no lock to Lucky's bedroom – there was once, but Jinan had it removed after Lucky locked himself in after a telling-off to do with homework, chores, and probably football), and switches on his plastic replica light sabre, swishing it around in time to the battle sequence like he is still ten years old, whacking his Darth Vader poster indiscriminately. In his enthusiasm he knocks a ceramic photo frame off the shelf, and instinctively dives to save it, getting a hand to it before both he and the frame hit the floor. His shoulder is sore from where he's fallen on the walnut floorboards, but he opens his hand and sees the frame perfectly intact. It's the photo of him and Zaki, taken during Lucky's birthday picnic last year in the park. It's funny to see Zaki outside; his grandfather is an indoor sort of person. Whenever Lucky thinks of him, he's always in a room somewhere, in the close clutter of the corner shop, in the seedy, sullen interior of the bookies, or looking surprisingly at ease in a dinner jacket at the tables of a windowless casino. Once upon a time his grandfather must have been an outdoor sort of person, he must have run around the river banks and banyan trees, among the paddy fields and mango groves depicted in the lushly idealized posters of Bangladesh that Lucky has pasted on his wall. He must have sat outside the cafes of the Parisian Left Bank with Lucky's teenage grandmother, while she wore skinny black polo-necked jumpers against the cold, teamed with extravagant seventies' flares printed with brightly coloured swirls. It's funny, he thinks, replacing the picture, that Zaki doesn't need to be outdoors to be free; closeted in his corner shop, he's free in ways that Lucky can't imagine – unfettered by romantic attachments or ambition, unconcerned about the opinions of family, friends or strangers. Lucky doesn't know what made Zaki this way, but there's something glorious about his blithe indifference – something cruelly heroic – that Lucky admires, as he knows he could never emulate it.

Turning his attention back to *Star Wars*, Lucky is just in time to see Darth Vader lop off Luke's hand. You and me both, Luke, he thinks – cut down at the crucial turning-point where one good strike could win both of our battles and decide our fates. Luke has lost his right hand, and Lucky has lost his position. But at least Luke survives his defeat, and is given a new hand along with the chance to fight another day; it is his destiny, as the digitized voice of Darth Vader tells him, tells both of them. And I'll fight another day too, thinks Lucky. I'll get my place back, and I'll get my chance – I just need to survive this next match. Lucky knows that he won't survive if he puts on a show as bad as Duncan. He can't risk it. When he's next shining on midfield, or converting a set piece with panache, he doesn't want the scouts to frown and remember him as the lad who was so appalling in goal against Swindon because he didn't even try; lack of team spirit, they would whisper, lack of professionalism, a real prima donna . . . we don't need that sort, however fast he runs, however fancy his passes.

Lucky sighs, as he now knows what he needs to do. He turns off the DVD, and pulls out a video and a sheaf of papers from the Harvey Nichols bag that had held his kit. While the video is rewinding, he shuffles through the printed papers and gets a biro to make notes.

'Lucky?' bellows his dad suspiciously. 'Lucky? You'd better be doing your homework, young man. I mean it this time.' Jinan knocks sharply on the door and pushes it open without waiting for Lucky to invite him in, scraping the chair that was propped against the handle along the walnut floor. Looking across at Lucky, who appears to be innocently studying on his bed, with bits of typed A4 all over his covers, Jinan suddenly feels foolish. 'Sorry about that, Lucky,' he apologizes. 'Didn't mean to disturb you.' Chastened, he shuts the door softly.

Lucky gets up and puts the chair back in place. He plugs his headphones into the TV, and begins to watch the goalkeeping master-class video that Harding has given him, scribbling notes to himself in the accompanying printed worksheets. Somehow, in a week, he has to become more than competent at a goalkeeper's craft; at the goal kick, the javelin throw, the overarm throw, the take-off, and most importantly of all, the save. He looks at the photo of Zaki and himself that he effortlessly dived to catch, and rubbing his tender shoulder once more, tells himself firmly, 'I can do this. I'll put up a fight they won't forget. And I'm going to show them all.'

The Troublesome Definition of Home

IL ÉTAIT UNE FOIS, il y a bien longtemps, une jolie petite princesse. Once upon a time, a long time ago, there was a pretty little princess, who was only a princess deep down inside, in her heart. In fact, she was a farmer's daughter, and she lived in a picturesque, wooden-framed farmhouse in Les Landes, in an idyllic part of south-west France that wasn't the Dordogne, and wasn't the Pays Basque, but was somewhere in between, where maize fields glinted gold in the summer, and on clear winter days the tempting snowy peaks of the Pyrenees could be glimpsed. She went fishing with her father, and caught her first trout in the local waterways when she was six. She went cycling with her mother around the little *chemins* that bordered the fields and the pine forest, and collected wild black-berries for jam and creamy puddings, and mushrooms for *galettes* and stews. She walked a cracked clay path from her house to the village school, where she and a couple of dozen little children learned their sing-song lessons, and played in the dusty yard. Occasionally the family would go into town, an almost foreign place a whole twenty minutes

away, for the local rugby game, or the *feria* at the bullfight-
ing arena. Her life was a postcard, a chocolate-box fantasy,
a glossy coffee-table book on the rustic simplicity of rural
France; the type of life that foreigners envied, and wished
they might live themselves.

Delphine, who knew nothing of how she might be
envied, hated her home, and couldn't wait to get away. She
found the maize fields depressing, even aggressive, in their
ubiquity; it felt as though every patch of land around her
that wasn't forest was enlisted into their use. She felt worn
down by the inevitability of their May to October cycle,
when they turned from green sprouts to meaty spears to
withered brown husks, so that in winter, an almost indecent
litter of dead leaves was strewn over the soggy land, like
bodies over an abandoned battlefield. The Pyrenees, with
their promise of snowball fights and *bonhommes de neige*,
and all manner of delightful ways of sliding or slipping
downhill, were only ever visited once a year on their family
vacation; although less than two hours' distance, the moun-
tains were all the way in the next *département*, and so were
practically foreign. (An actual foreign holiday would have
been unheard of, absurd, and roundly disapproved of – and
besides, most foreigners didn't speak French.) Delphine
wanted more for herself than endless discussions about the
state of the neighbours' marriages, village gossip about who
had decided to grow what in their garden, and whose
weeds were less innocent than they might at first appear.
She didn't want to spend hours picking yet more black-
berries from their thorny little bushes or rooting in the
damp undergrowth for yet more muddy fungi which they
would then be forced to eat rather than let go to waste; in

fact, the abundance of these foodstuffs during her child-hood would lead to her having an almost pathological hatred of them later in life, which she only just about managed to hide when served a wild mushroom risotto at a dinner party. Most of all, she didn't want her restricted, incestuous circle of a couple of dozen classmates to be her companions for the rest of her life. She read books, news-papers and magazines voraciously, went to the local single-screen cinema religiously once a fortnight when they showed the latest movie, and caught a glimpse of a wider world than she could see from her pine-shuttered window. She shocked her pious Grande-Tante Christiane with her flighty opinions, and announced 'Small village, small minds,' whenever she was criticized.

Delphine's pretensions to a different, if not (she only realizes now) better life were greeted with bemusement by her family, who called her their 'little princess' since nothing, they felt, was good enough for her. They said this in an exasperated rather than an indulgent way. She studied assiduously, and paid a great deal of attention to her English classes; when the time came for her to go to university, her family magnanimously told her that they were prepared for her to go to Bordeaux, Pau or even (heavens above!) Toulouse. But Delphine had her sights set on somewhere further than two hours away from the familial home, and went to study in Paris, where she shared a squalid basement flat with two other girls. She sloughed off her provincial chrysalis with an imported loofah in the cracked and tinny shower in their bathroom, and emerged shining and flawless, a social butterfly of the metropolis. She discovered the joys of bars, nightclubs, soft drugs, anonymity, junk food, casual sex, and above all, choice! She had never been happier.

She was happier still when, on completing her degree, her determination (and to some extent, her polished beauty) got her a highly sought-after job in the marketing department of a corporate giant, in charge of a range of low-end toiletries. With her unusually proficient English, she was transferred to London, which in the cut-and-thrust eighties was the city of her dreams. Her letters home, which had always been perfunctory at best, dried up altogether, and were replaced by dutiful cards at Christmas and birthdays, accompanied by tasteful presents that she knew her parents would never appreciate from places like Fortnum's. She felt no need to fill the months of silence in between. Her mother called her one day, at outrageous expense, 'to check that she was still alive', as London was a dangerous city; she added that Grande-Tante Christiane was praying for her. 'How does she know that God speaks French?' Delphine responded caustically. The sharp intake of breath down the line told her that she had probably gone too far, but she no longer cared. She had taken too much trouble to escape home to have its small-town tentacles grip hold of her once more.

One early evening, Delphine and her boss were being wined and dined at Mirabelle in Mayfair by their newly appointed direct marketing agency. They were eating ridiculously early, as her boss had forgotten about the dinner and made theatre reservations, with curtain-up at 7.30 p.m. Theo Stonebridge was a personable type with a sales background and a natural air of authority that disguised the fact that he was all style over substance. Delphine noticed with amusement how the Account Director and Account Supervisor, both wearing shiny black suits with loud ties, hung on Theo's every word, and laughed at all his jokes about their pitch presentation, however inappropriate or misinformed. They didn't have a clue that Theo hadn't even bothered reading their painstakingly produced pitch document, but had asked Delphine, a rising star in the department, to write him a one-page summary, and a two-line recommendation. Over their starters, the agency were polite to Delphine, but otherwise ignored her as the decorative French totty who was clearly too junior to have anything to do with the decision-making process. When Theo excused himself for an urgent call, the Account Director and Supervisor looked for a moment bereft, but then shamelessly cosied up to Delphine, asking her conspiratorially, perhaps even a little flirtatiously, 'So, tell us, Delphine. What does he really think of us? Why do you think we got the job?' as though she was an ally in the enemy camp, as though her opinion really mattered. Delphine sighed; perhaps they expected her to giggle and simper something in kind, in her oh-so-cute Frenchie accent, 'Oh, it's because you had the best looking team . . .' or something of that nature. Isn't that what they'd think a little country girl would say?

'I wouldn't like to presume . . .' Delphine started to say guardedly, unthinkingly supporting her chin, but then she saw that the Account Director was now supporting his own chin too; he was deliberately mirroring her! The oldest trick in the client-relations book, and the one that Delphine found the most patronizing. It took a huge effort for her not to snatch her hand away, but to remove it gently and put it on her lap, where she rammed it between her knees to stop it shaking. She continued without a break in her voice, her expression remaining pleasant, ' . . . but I would say that we were most impressed by two specific elements: the creative work you presented, and the flexibility of creative resource in the team structure you proposed. We liked the fact that you recognized that the purpose of commissioning DM creative work is not to win industry awards for your agency, but to get us the most responses per pound spent. We also liked the fact that the creative resource you proposed could be adapted to suit our requirements over the year, so we could brief for additional ad hoc projects as and when the need may arise. I would say that those were the key points of difference between yourselves and the others invited to pitch.' She paused, noticing that the bland grins had been wiped off their faces, and that they were listening to her intently. She allowed herself a small but winning smile as she took a sip of water.

The Account Director cleared his throat. 'Thank you, Delphine, for such a frank and informative answer to a question that was asked, I'm sorry to admit, in a rather frivolous manner.'

Delphine acknowledged the apology with a slight tilt of her head, as Theo returned cheerfully from his call. 'So, what were you kids nattering about?' he asked genially, taking it as his right to assume that nothing serious was said while he was away from the table.

'The team here was just grilling me on why we took them on,' said Delphine airily.

Theo smiled benignly. 'Of course they know why. We'd had enough of style over substance; with you guys, we got substance over style.'

Delphine stifled a giggle that she quickly turned into a cough; one thing Theo lacked was any sense of irony. 'That's exactly what I said, Theo, although it took me much longer to say it. I wish I had your economy of phrase.' She beamed at him insincerely, displaying an ability to flatter with intent, to network, to . . . schmooze, even, that would propel her quickly to the dizzy heights in her career that hard work, talent and integrity would have no chance of achieving alone.

Delphine would ask herself later, when she was a Knightsbridge housewife who had the great gift of time to think, and, if you like, obsess about such things, what exactly she did feel when flattering the boss or the head of the important account, or when agreeing coquettishly to dance with senior management at office parties? In the beginning she felt nothing – she was just doing her job, and doing it spectacularly well, if her career trajectory was anything to go by. In that first year in London, she already had an important position in the marketing department, whereas other graduates who had been taken on at the same time as her were still photocopying and envelope stuffing in Paris. 'I remember you from your second interview,' a married member of the board had said to her during the summer party, dancing a little too closely with her. He had sleek good looks, a desk littered with pictures of his photogenic spouse and offspring, and an appalling reputation for sleeping with his secretaries. 'You were . . . incredible,' he whispered in her ear. Delphine had laughed huskily, with a confidence she did not feel, and a few minutes later used the end of the song as an excuse to slip away from him. Why hadn't she felt compromised, grubby? She only felt these things later, looking back on her successful career with the cleansing halo of motherhood placed firmly above her head. She would look at her little boy, so beautiful and rounded and perfect, a Botticelli angel, with the potential for grace that she would never have, and admit to him tacitly, as though he was her confessor: yes, it's true, Delphine Loustalot was a corporate slut. But now she's something better. She's your *maman*.

At the end of that dinner, one of the waiters approached Delphine when she was collecting her coat, and asked her in French, 'Miss Loustalot, do you mind me asking where you're from? I couldn't help noticing that you were French.'

'A little town in Les Landes,' said Delphine, 'not too far from Dax.'

'I knew it! I'm not so far from you – I'm from a village in the Béarn. Really, it's heaven on earth.' He looked expectantly at Delphine, but she said nothing, just smiled and nodded.

When it became obvious that some answer was required, she asked, 'So, do you miss it?'

This was exactly what he had wanted her to say, as he responded passionately, 'Miss it! I dream of going back home! And instead . . .' he swept an arm dismissively towards the glittering Mayfair dining room, where the crystal chandelier scattered shards of twinkling light over the customers, '. . . I am stuck in this hole!' He spat the last word with disgust. Delphine looked at him with frank bemusement, and making her excuses, went to join her dinner companions upstairs, who were waiting for cabs in a sudden downpour.

Home, she realized, was something difficult to translate into French. It didn't really exist as an absolute concept, in a pure, unsullied state, like love or liberty. In French, you always had to qualify home by saying whose home it was – *chez toi, chez elle, chez nous*, your home, her home, our home. But in a way, the definition was simple, even if the translation was not: Home was somewhere which you were either trying to get away from, or trying to get back to. That was all there was to it.

Theo sailed off in a cab towards the West End, and the agency team decided to get out their brollies and make a dash for Green Park tube. It seemed to her that the English always remembered to carry an umbrella, however glorious a morning it had been when they set out. This was a habit that Delphine had not yet taken up; preparing for rain seemed too much like tempting fate – giving the rain an excuse to fall. The rain began to lessen, so Delphine decided to walk to the bus-stop rather than take a cab; her salary wasn't huge, and she couldn't claim back a cab expense so early in the evening. She teetered up Curzon Street in her fashionably high heels, unreasonably embarrassed by the clip-clop sound she made on the empty, sodden street. She was approaching Park Lane when the heavens opened once more, the rain falling heavily enough to soak right through her shoes so she could barely walk; forced to protect her head with her briefcase, this time she didn't hesitate when she saw a black cab approach with a welcoming yellow light. 'Taxi!' she yelled, so loud it was as though her voice echoed down the street, and when the cab stopped, she bundled herself in, only to find a tall, dark stranger in a dinner jacket bundling himself in on the other side. 'Who are you?' she asked at the same time as the dark stranger; she realized then that he must have been responsible for the bizarre echo she had heard when she hailed the cab.

'Aren't you together, then?' asked the cabbie. 'I thought you were together,' he added unnecessarily. 'So who am I taking, because I can't park here, you know?'

'It's the lady's cab,' said Dinner Jacket gallantly. He was in his early thirties, with hair as jet black as his jacket, and skin the colour of creamy toffee. His impeccable exterior was let down only by his slightly tousled hair, and the few drops of rain on his lapels; otherwise he could have been straight out of *On Her Majesty's Secret Service*.

'Thanks, you're very kind,' Delphine answered, hoping she hadn't stared at him too obviously. He was terribly good-looking, a sort of exotic angel. He was foreign, coloured and showy, everything her parents hated. 'Putney, please,' she addressed the cab driver.

'Putney?' said Dinner Jacket. 'I need to go to Fulham, for something very, very urgent. It's on the way. Would you mind if I shared your cab? I won't make a peep, you won't even know I'm here. I'll be your invisible cab companion . . .' he grinned appealingly and made a zip motion across his mouth, and Delphine found herself laughing, for the first time that evening, with sincerity. Her uninvited guest took her laughter as assent, and asked the cabbie, 'Could you take us to the London Oratory, near Fulham

Broadway, if you don't mind?' He reclined comfortably in the cab, stretching out his long, lean legs as far as he could, and broke his promise to Delphine immediately by asking her, with another winning, infectious smile, 'You're French, aren't you? I can tell.' Delphine, not normally given to romantic notions, thought to herself that if this was a play or a movie, then she and Dinner Jacket would end up getting married, and she would tell her children that she and Papa met sheltering in a cab from the pouring rain.

By the time they reached Fulham, Dinner Jacket had managed to wheedle Delphine's entire life story from her, listening with such flattering attention that she felt warm all over and disarmed enough to tell him about her career plans. He didn't treat her like a silly girl with ridiculous ambition, even though he was a grown-up – an obviously successful grown-up. He was different from all the other men she'd met in London, who had either been callow boys her own age or lecherous management; she felt slightly starstruck by his looks, his evening dress, his perfect not-too-young-not-too-old age. As he went to get out of the cab, Delphine realized that she knew nothing about him apart from his first name, as he had encouraged her to talk, but had volunteered nothing himself. 'Well, Zaki. Goodbye, then,' she said bravely, sad that their brief encounter had ended so abruptly. They hadn't even got stuck in traffic; it was the first time she hadn't been stuck in traffic on the way home in rush hour, and typically it had to happen when she was in a cab with a fascinating man instead of when she was on the number fourteen bus with grocery bags around her ankles, dying to get back for a hot bath. He hadn't even asked for her number.

Zaki turned around as though he was going to close the cab door, but then asked, 'Delphine, you know what might be fun? Would you like to be my date for this thing? Only if you're not doing anything tonight.'

Delphine's heart leapt, but she played it cool. 'I'm not sure I'm dressed for it,' she said demurely, gesturing hopelessly towards her boxy navy suit, her damp heels.

'Oh God, don't worry about that. You look nearly perfect. You should see what the rest of the old crows wear to these things. I'm the one who'll stand out, they'll think I've come in fancy dress . . .' He pulled her out by the hand and tossed a note to the cabbie, telling him to keep the change. It was the first time Zaki had touched her, and she was surprised at how sensitive her hand felt, as though he had given her a slight electric shock. 'Your hands are cold,' said Zaki, thankfully unaware of her reaction to his touch, and, taking both of them brusquely in his warm palms, he rubbed them roughly, as though she was a child, as though it was something he'd had practice at doing. He didn't let go of her hand as they walked along the pavement towards the entrance.

Delphine had assumed that the London Oratory must be a restaurant of some sort, and judging by Zaki's choice of dress, that it was hosting a swish event. Like the sort of thing she read about in *Tatler*, or *Harper's*. As they walked in through the gates, she realized that in fact it was a school, of the old, established sort; she immediately revised her expectations – a charity function of some sort, a gala event, perhaps? The truth became apparent as Zaki guided her through a throng of middle-aged couples in perfectly ordinary dress, and they came to the trestle tables laden with plastic cups of cheap, warm wine and damp peanuts in paper bowls at the entrance to a large hall. There were posters for *Hamlet* hung up around them, and a spotty young boy in striped tie and blazer ducked out of the hall and started ringing a bell. 'Take your seats, please. Five minutes to curtain,' he bellowed with a surprisingly deep voice, before going back inside.

'Great, we made it,' said Zaki, oblivious to the interested looks his dinner jacket was getting from everyone else. 'Jinan would have had my guts for garters if I'd been late for this one, after the fiasco at Christmas.'

'But this is a school play,' stated Delphine, more for herself than anyone else, in a state of utter confusion. 'You've asked me on a date to a school play?'

'Not just any school play, this is my son's starring role!' said Zaki proudly. 'I was worried that he was going to be a complete geek, but then he goes and gets the lead in *Hamlet*! Fantastic, isn't it?'

'Your son!' yelped Delphine, pulling her hand away from his. 'How old is he? I mean, how old are you? And where's his mother?' She felt that she was on the wrong end of a very unfunny joke; somehow, she'd been tricked into going on a date with some old married man.

'He's fourteen, I'm thirty-two.' He watched Delphine do the maths, her brow adorably furrowed with a mixture of annoyance and confusion. He explained his situation cheerily, dismissing it with a few words, 'I know, I know, I was young and foolish and in love. I got married when I was still a kid.' He paused before answering her last question more solemnly: 'His mum died eleven years ago, in a car accident in Paris.'

'I'm sorry,' said Delphine awkwardly, not sure if she was consoling him for the accident or making her own excuses, 'but I'm really not sure about this. I think I'd better go.' She felt genuine regret at walking away from this handsome man; he was terribly appealing but there just seemed to be too much baggage for her to cope with – an impetuous marriage, a youthful tragedy, and to top it all, a teenage son. She smiled uncertainly and turned to leave, but Zaki reached for her hand and pulled her back gently towards him.

'Please stay. I'm sorry, I should have told you before where we were going, but I thought you'd say no, and I really, really wanted you to say yes.' Delphine paused, her resolve already weakening. Zaki went on, 'And if you don't like me after tonight, you never have to see me again. We can go and have a drink after the play, Jinan's staying over with friends this evening.'

'Look, Zaki, I really don't know—' Delphine began to murmur again, but not with much conviction.

Zaki interrupted her, 'And for what it's worth, you really are the most beautiful woman here, not that there's a heck of a lot of competition.' Delphine allowed a whisper of a laugh to escape, and seeing victory was almost upon him, Zaki dealt the final winning hand: 'But I think that you'd be the most beautiful woman almost anywhere.'

'OK, OK,' Delphine held up her hands in surrender. 'The play, and then a drink. Just one quick drink.' Zaki smiled and took her by the arm to take a seat. 'But just tell me one thing: why the dinner jacket? Do you make a habit of overdressing for school events?'

'Oh, God, no. I'm only dressed like this because I was

playing at a casino on Curzon Street. They've got some stupid dress code. I was doing really well, too. I had to force myself to leave, or I'd never have made it to Jinan's play.' Delphine sighed; some of the mystique was restored. The handsome stranger in a dinner jacket at a casino – he really was from *On Her Majesty's Secret Service*. Of course, all the mystique was to disappear over their drinks and their subsequent dates, when she would find out that apart from being something of a professional gambler, Zaki also inexpertly ran a distinctly unglamorous corner shop in a backstreet wasteland behind Hammersmith station. For Delphine's purposes, he couldn't be less ideal marriage material if he juggled in a travelling circus. She knew that they had no long-term future as she hadn't come all the way from her provincial village to settle for a shopkeeper. She had loftier ambitions; she wanted – in fact, she needed – someone she could boast about at dinner parties – a doctor or a lawyer, someone who mattered, someone important.

But despite her better judgement, Delphine continued to see Zaki throughout that summer, each time telling herself that the next time would be the last, and each time relenting when he called. It turned out to be one of those long, hot summers; a golden summer of the sort that only exist in memory. She accepted flamboyant gifts and the bunches of flowers left outside her door with dizzy delight; she drank far too much with him and giggled and misbehaved like a teenager. There was laughter and there was certainly lust, and treating the relationship with the frivolity of an affair, she ignored his baggage as much as she could; she only saw Zaki's son, an impossibly tidy-looking boy with his head in a book, on three occasions during all the months that they dated, and then just in passing. Delphine only came to her senses when the weather cooled and their passionate moments began to approach tenderness; she realized that she was in danger of getting far too fond of her inappropriate boyfriend. Even though Zaki was undeniably unsuitable, and certainly not important, he had something that drew her to him, more than his humour and his winning manner; in a funny way, she felt at home with him. And like home, he was something she was either trying to get away from, or trying to get back to.

A Reason to Like Mondays

LUCKY IS TO WAKE on Sunday in a state of high anticipation; somehow, he let the events of Saturday's practice distract him from the most significant thing that has
happened to him all year: a kiss from the girl he has secretly
adored for months. With the inconsistency and rubber-ball
resilience of youth, the proportions of the goalkeeping tragedy seem to have shrunk overnight; there is nothing he can
do about it, so he has decided to accept it and simply move
on. He spent the previous evening studying all the magical
things that spectators think a goalkeeper does effortlessly or
instinctively, like when to put his hands in an 'M' or a 'W',
and how to close an angle into goal. Over the coming week
he will put his study into practice, and he will work hard
and be uncomplaining, and at the end of the week, he will
play in goal in a match against Swindon Town Juniors with
Felix Conway as their star striker. And he will either do well
with all his best efforts, or he will do badly despite his best
efforts; whatever happens, he will have the support of his
team and coach for his courage in the face of adversity,
unlike Duncan, who will be ribbed and scorned mercilessly

for his cowardice when he finally returns to practice. Lucky will insist on going back to playing midfield, and life will go on. He will live to fight another day.

And so, as Lucky awakens to the faint ringing of bells from the grand local churches, to the dappled spring sunshine pouring in through his window filtered by the young leaves on the elderly trees lining their street, he finds that he can think of only one thing: Portia. In fact, he does not think of Portia as one thing, but as a kaleidoscope of different images: the vulnerability of her cropped hair and exposed ears, lined with three silver rings along the lobe. The swishing of a school scarf over her shoulder. A moment of anger in the corner shop, or melancholy by the river. The casual way in which she offers her cigarettes and accepts his arm. The sight of her slim figure disappearing down the grey and grubby stairs to the tube. 'Monday,' she said. She promised to see him on Monday morning; not to bump into him accidentally (accidentally on purpose, for Lucky's part) at the corner shop, as had happened before, but to meet him and, by implication, to spend time with him. They have a date, on Monday morning, before school. Lucky just wants this day to be over; he turns over sleepily in bed, hazily absorbing and writing off the beauty of this Sunday morning, the bells, the sunshine; if he simply stays in bed all day, and then all night, it will suddenly be Monday. Lucky can't wait until Monday.

Lucky is dreading Monday. He has been forced up by his mother and is sitting at the breakfast bar in the kitchen with her, morosely drinking orange juice and pulling his croissant to pieces. He has managed to convince himself, over the course of the morning, that he is deeply in love with Portia, but that Portia feels nothing for him; that she was being kind, even sisterly, in kissing him so tenderly but so dryly. And he has nothing to help persuade him otherwise; he is ridiculously young, he is gangly and gauche, he can never find anything to say that can interest her, and he doesn't even dress well. He hides in uniforms – his school uniform, his team kit, his jeans and T-shirts and fleeces, and right now, he is still wearing a bloody Obi-Wan Kenobi dressing-gown with a Jedi hood, like a first year. If she could see him, she'd just laugh, and then make it worse by trying to pretend she hadn't. He will make a fool of himself on Monday, he knows it, and the seeming inevitability of his fate makes him almost begin to dislike Portia, as though it is all her fault and who does she think she is anyway, little miss thang who thinks she's so shit-hot just because she's got nice legs and can solve a sudoku?

Delphine, unaware of the teenage turmoil boiling up inside her son, is sipping her usual home-made cappuccino and separating out the Sunday papers, handing the sports and kids sections over to Lucky, keeping the magazines and the arts events for herself, and putting the rest in a pile for Jinan. Her husband, having stuck his weekly 'to do' list on the fridge for Delphine to take care of, is inexpertly toiling over a hot stove, frying eggs and grilling beef sausages with tomatoes, complaining that the only tomatoes he can find are either tinned plum or organic cherry on the vine – some new-fangled experiment of Delphine's.

'I keep saying I need beef tomatoes for Sunday breakfast, darling. It's easy to remember: when you get the sausages, think beef sausages, beef tomatoes.'

'OK, darling,' murmurs Delphine disinterestedly, looking at the list he's written. For some reason she has to pick up his dry-cleaning on Tuesday this week, rather than Wednesday. Another Very Important Meeting, no doubt. So many of the jobs seem petty and unnecessary; she sometimes suspects that by making her busy at home, Jinan feels that he is busy at home himself. She turns her attention to the glossy newspaper supplements.

'You will remember, won't you?' persists Jinan, clumsily dripping the hot fat over the eggs to try and cook the tops of them before the bottoms burn. The harsh sizzling succeeds in getting Delphine's attention where Jinan's plaintive tone has failed.

'Try lowering the heat, darling, and put a lid on to cook them through,' she says. 'And please use the plastic spatula on non-stick, you'll scrape the pan again.'

'Sorry, I'll remember next time,' says Jinan, chastened, swapping the spatula and dropping the greasy metal one with a clatter on the otherwise sparkling granite worktop, where it creates a tiny pool of fat.

'Yes, well, you keep saying that,' mutters Delphine, not quite under her breath, looking reproachfully at the dirty spatula. Jinan, already hot and bothered by the stove, puffs up with the injustice of her remark.

'Well, you keep saying that you'll remember about the tomatoes!' he retorts.

'Remember what, darling?' says Delphine infuriatingly. Seeing Jinan turn redder than the hot stove alone could justify, she holds up her hands in surrender. 'I'm only joking, darling. Beef sausages, beef tomatoes. I promise I'll remember next week. Look, I'm adding it to your list.' She leans over and makes a big show of lifting the magnet attaching his list to the fridge, and scribbling a note on the paper.

Jinan nods and attempts to smile, but secretly feels a little bit compromised. As though he has somehow been . . . managed, in the way a nanny would manage a little boy's threatened temper tantrum. 'Does anyone else want some eggs or sausages while I'm here? Luhith?'

Lucky, reading the sports section without enthusiasm, shakes his head. 'Athletes shouldn't eat crap like that, Dad. Full of cholesterol. This croissant's bad enough already.' Jinan smirks at his son's presumptuous mention of 'athlete', as though that were really a fit description for someone who kicked a ball about a bit after school, but he is prevented from making a comment by a warning look from his wife. Lucky, warming to his theme, carries on, 'Neither should you – you'll have a heart attack before you're forty if you keep eating like that.' Delphine nods in agreement and for a moment, Jinan is absurdly touched by the implication that they both care. He suddenly feels prosperous and full of hope, with his elegant wife who looks after his every need, his teenage son who has the stature and sportiness that he so conspicuously lacks, and his lovely home with a sunlit view across the trees of the crescent. He slides his eggs, sausages, and cherry tomatoes onto a plate and takes it to the breakfast bar. He's forgotten to make his toast and decides to do without it rather than risk have everything else go cold. Besides, an Atkins breakfast won't do him any harm; he's noticed that he's getting a bit cuddly of late.

'We should go out and do something, seeing as it's such a gorgeous day. What do you reckon?' he says, tucking in enthusiastically. The eggs are slightly too brown on the bottom, but the sausages are delicious, and the grilled cherry tomatoes burst in his mouth with an explosion of sweetness. He is tempted to tell Delphine not to bother about the beef tomatoes next week and to get these again instead, but decides against it; it might seem a bit temperamental on his part. He is the solid, dependable one, after all. His family rely on him to be consistent, to make his decisions and stick to them.

'Sure,' says Delphine. 'It says here that there's a fantastic Anish Kapoor installation at the Serpentine gallery – it's listed as a must-see.' Jinan and Lucky, without looking at each other, sputter out a laugh in unison.

'Good one, Mum,' says Lucky. 'I needed cheering up.'

'Oh, suit yourselves, Philistines. I'll go by myself next week,' Delphine huffs.

'I was thinking about a stroll in the park, maybe a nice pub lunch somewhere?' Jinan suggests hopefully.

'Yeah, well, I'll pass,' mutters Lucky. His dad seemed not to realize any more that doing something wasn't the same as eating something; it seemed these days that his father was always eating, or planning to eat, or returning from eating. Was there a word for reverse bulimia, when you hoover rather than throw? Portia would know; she knew that kind of thing, because she could do crosswords and sudoku. 'Besides, I thought I might go shopping. I need to buy some bits, I'm growing out of everything.' This was a valid excuse. He already towered over his parents, who were both of medium height; in fact, Jinan was just an inch taller than Delphine, which meant that he was shorter than her when she wore heels.

'Fine, but I'd better come with you,' Delphine says. Lucky tries to argue, but Delphine is stern. 'I've told you lots of times, when you're sixteen you can buy your own clothes, but not before.' Then she adds, with incontrovertible logic, 'Besides, how do you think you're going to pay for it all?' so Lucky is forced to acquiesce. Jinan, suddenly abandoned by both spouse and child, realizes that he will need to have his walk and pub lunch on his own; he is too proud to argue his case, or point out that there is plenty of time to do the walk, have the lunch, and then go shopping. The flicker of happiness that he felt evaporates abruptly, and he now feels with certainty that neither his spouse nor his offspring cares very much after all. He wishes, for a bitter moment, that he could cause them the sort of pain that he is feeling now in his chest and deep in his insides; a feeling that he suspects is nothing to do with his newly voracious appetite, nothing to do with heartburn, but simply to do with his heart. He reaches for a croissant, wishing that either Delphine or Lucky will stop him, but neither of them does.

Lucky, meanwhile, is thinking only that he will have new clothes for Monday. But he is still dreading it.

'Nice top,' says Portia, looking over the side wall into Zaki's back garden, where Lucky has been practising dives in his freshly acquired gear to get rid of the tell-tale new look, kicking the ball against the wall and then saving it. 'Why aren't you in uniform?'

Lucky, unaware that he was being observed, is taken by surprise. This was not how he planned to see Portia on Monday morning. He had intended to be sitting casually in Zaki's shop, his cool clobber on show for when she walked in after her paper round, and be able to reach out towards Portia, to kiss her hello. Perhaps on the cheek, perhaps even on the lips. But instead she has returned early, and he is lying prostrate on the ground while she is on the other side of a wall, her lips nowhere within reach. Symbolic, he thinks grimly to himself.

'I was up at the crack of dawn, practising,' he says.

'I thought practice was tonight?' she asks, raising an eyebrow. She seems so casual as to be almost disinterested, and he feels foolish to have assigned such a weight of expectation to their meeting this morning.

'Normally it is, but this week's different. I've got to learn to be a cracking goalie in a week.' He explains the events of Saturday to her and gets quite overwrought by it all, although he is not sure if he is upset about Saturday or upset that their date has not proven to be a date at all, just a not-quite-accidental meeting.

She listens sympathetically and then says matter of factly, 'Well, what are we bloody waiting for, then?' and starts to ruck up her skirt. Lucky, still a bit upset, looks at her with horror, not having a clue what she is proposing.

Portia simply tucks her skirt into her knickers and adds, 'I'll help you. It's no good you trying to save if you're having to kick it yourself. Just tell me what you need me to do.'

Lucky is about to say that there would be little use in Portia helping him as his own strikes rebounding off the wall probably had more pace than anything she could kick or throw, but then he realizes that of course that isn't the point. The point is that Portia is showing she's in his corner, and he appreciates this gesture enormously. She climbs up the wall, manages to get one shapely leg over and calls out to Lucky, 'A little help here, please,' as the second one follows precariously. He goes and half catches her, half lifts her down, and as he deposits her, she is so close that she is standing on his own trainers. Portia stands on tiptoe, achingly near to Lucky, and brushes her lips very lightly against his, so gently and softly that it is almost not a kiss, but something even more intimate; a promise, a secret. Her lips feel wonderfully warm and slightly damp, as though she has just licked them, and Lucky feels his own lips melting at her touch – a liquid feeling that trickles all the way through to his fingertips, which are still lightly holding her waist, and right down to his toes, which still have the reassuring weight of Portia balanced on them. 'Is that better?' she asks.

Lucky nods. 'Yes it is,' he says. And suddenly, it all was.

Honeymoon in Paris

IT WAS AN ACCIDENT. That was all. Something as simple as an accident, on a busy street in Montmartre, where a cab swerved to avoid a bike and ploughed into a young woman crossing the street. She had been holding a little bag of croissants that she was bringing back for breakfast. She had been waving to her husband, who had been looking out for her from the tiny, outwardly ornate window of their shabby rented room on the second floor. Her smooth brown arms were bare in the spring sunshine and she was wearing extravagant flares in white and blue that swished around her ankles. And suddenly she was flying, almost gracefully; for an instant her body was perfectly parallel with the ground she soared above, her bare arms straight by her sides, and then she landed in a crumpled heap, the back of her head releasing a steady flow of bright red blood, her lips forming an 'O' of surprise.

Zaki ran down the stairs and forced his way through the gathering crowd. '*C'est ma femme!*' he shrieked, and when he reached Nadya, there was already a man authoritatively kneeling by her side. The man announced to Zaki that he was a doctor, and looked sorrowfully at him.

'*Je suis navré; je ne pouvais rien faire. Elle était déjà morte.*' Touching Zaki's shoulder, he added sympathetically, 'It was sudden, she would have felt no pain.'

Zaki ignored him and gathered Nadya in his arms, her blood spilling over him. She was so warm and soft, and he whispered to her, 'You're not dying. You're not dead yet. You're still here. I know you're still here.' He remained rocking her, whispering to her, until the ambulance arrived and she was taken to the hospital and formally pronounced dead on arrival. She was just twenty years old.

The last thing Zaki expected, in the dark and dizzy aftermath following the accident, was for his father to turn up in Paris. He had not left things well with his Baba, who had flown into a fury about the ill-advised elopement with a pregnant village girl and had insisted that Zaki annul the marriage or lose his funding for his college place at the Sorbonne. Realizing that his no-good-nothing son had no intention of annulling the marriage and that without money, Zakaria would have no choice but to stay in Dhaka and flaunt his stupid marriage with some local slut and her harami-bullshit-bastard, Mr Khalil reviewed his strategy. The scandal could ruin his business among the moneyed ladies of Dhaka, and he was nothing if not a businessman; he was, after all, one of the most successful shopkeepers in the new quarter. He would give Zakaria enough money to go back to Paris, on the condition that he stayed quietly there and never darkened his father's door again. The last words that Zaki's Baba had said to him when giving him his cheque and marching orders were, 'The next time I see you, Zakaria, it had better be my funeral, or yours.'

Zaki took up this offer cheerfully and, telling Nadya that college was greatly overrated, took up a casual job as a croupier in a casino that paid their modest rent and left them enough to live like students, in the unfettered and impractical way that Zaki had always dreamed of. They ate canned foie gras with bread and bananas in their room for supper, shopped for flamboyant clothes and knick-knacks at flea markets, and spent lazy afternoons in cafes and student digs with Zaki's liberal friends from the Sorbonne. Nadya liked the adventure of Paris, with its soaring, ornate architecture, and loved the serenity and order of the formal gardens and parks most of all. So when the baby was born, dark, fat-lipped, and furious, the teenagers were both so delighted with the cross little bundle they named him Jinan, a garden of paradise. Apart from writing his Baba a short note to inform him of the birth, and to include a happy photo of the three of them with the impertinent suggestion that it be displayed in the Dhaka dining room, for the next three years Zaki kept true to his word and made no further attempt to contact his father or to coerce further funds from him. He fully expected never to see him again.

And yet here his Baba was, at his door, looking fat and prosperous and saying, 'God, Zakaria, you look like seven kinds of shit.'

Making coffee on the little gas ring, Zaki asked his father, 'So, how did you know?'

Mr Khalil looked at his unshaven, hollow-eyed son; it was like he was in costume, with his patterned polyester shirt and grubby white flares. He seemed helpless as a child; all around him were the signs of collapsing domestic routine, piles of unfolded nappies and unwashed dishes. Mr Khalil felt a twinge of concern, of guilt even, that he suppressed sternly. This was all Zakaria's fault, after all. He deserved no sympathy. No one had forced him to drag the poor girl out of her village in the first place. 'Your address? You put it on the letter, simpleton,' he said condescendingly.

Zaki shook his head, too numb and weary to muster any indignation about the insult. 'No, I mean, about . . . my wife.' It still hurt too much to say Nadya's name. It still hurt too much to get up in the morning and to go to bed at night. It hurt too much to do anything, but he was forced to carry on for Jinan, whose impotent infant fury had subsided with his mother's death, replaced by an unnerving gravity and solemnity that terrified Zaki more than his tantrums ever had.

'I heard from the embassy. And don't flatter yourself that I came all the way from Dhaka just for you. I was in London taking care of some business with your Chacha Syed and Auntie Uma,' Mr Khalil said testily. 'So, you don't have tea?'

Zaki shook his head. 'No, not proper tea. But there's camomile somewhere, I think.' He looked around helplessly and started opening jars with a wild-eyed hopelessness until even Mr Khalil took pity on him.

'Coffee's fine, Zakaria. Coffee's fine,' he said hastily, before his son could make the room even more disorganized than it already was. 'So, where's the boy? Her boy, I mean,' he asked, peering round. With the state of the apartment, he wouldn't have been surprised if the child was asleep under a pile of laundry somewhere.

'You mean my son,' said Zaki, some of his old fire returning at the needling implication that Nadya's child was nothing to do with him. 'His name's Jinan. He's at the *maternelle* – nursery school. They thought it was best that he keep to his routines. I'll pick him up after lunch.'

'Isn't he a bit old for nappies?' asked Mr Khalil a bit meanly, looking pointedly at the piles around them.

'He's only three and half,' snapped Zaki. 'He's needed them again since the accident. For God's sake, the boy's lost his mother and you're criticizing him for not being potty-trained!'

'Ouf, Zakaria. Always so touchy. I was just making bloody conversation,' muttered Mr Khalil.

Zaki poured out the thick coffee into a cup for his father and thumped it in front of him on the brightly painted table. 'Why are you here, Baba? Are you here to gloat? You've done that now, so you can bugger off and leave me and my son alone.'

Mr Khalil took his coffee cup and drank it with obvious distaste. After a pause, in which Zaki looked mutinous and stared obviously at his wrist-watch, Mr Khalil added, 'So why do you think I'm here? I'm here to clean up the mess you've got yourself into.' He looked around at the untidiness of the apartment for emphasis.

'Well, thanks for the offer, but I can do my own

washing-up and laundry,' said Zaki, deliberately mis-understanding.

Mr Khalil had had enough of his arrogant son's moody nonchalance. 'For God's sake, Zakaria!' he exploded, popping one of his shirt buttons open in fury. 'Look at yourself! You can't take care of yourself, let alone an infant. This isn't Bangladesh, you can't expect the authorities out here to mind their own business. They'll take the child away and put him into care. And even if they don't, how are you going to bring him up here? You can't work *and* look after him.'

'Well, what do you suggest I do?' said Zaki in frustration.

'The most obvious thing is to give him back to his people, and get on with your life,' said Mr Khalil. 'Abdur knows his father's people, his *real* father's people,' he added for emphasis, talking over Zaki before he could object. 'He's their grandson, they'll be happy to have him. They're not so badly off, you know. The grandfather sells tickets at the local cinema, I believe. I could take him back and you could return to college. And do a proper subject this time, like business or accountancy, none of this philosophy bullshit.'

Zaki looked at his father in outrage. 'You must be joking! He's my son! I've brought him up, and now you want me to abandon him to some provincial strangers who chased away his mother and who haven't cared enough to enquire whether he's alive or dead? He's just lost his mother and now you want him to lose his father too? Get out of here, Baba. I mean it, get out. Before I do something I'll really regret.' Zaki stood up in anger and smashed his coffee cup violently on the floor, his grief-stricken lethargy evaporating. At that moment there was a knock on the door and a woman's voice trilled out, '*Coucou! Nous sommes là!*' Zaki went to the door and saw Flavie from the fourth floor standing there with Jinan. 'You forgot, Zaki?' she asked in French. 'It's Wednesday. Today is morning only at the *maternelle*. I saw this poor little angel waiting when I went to pick up my Véronique, and I thought I'd bring him home for you.'

'God, it's Wednesday!' said Zaki, slapping himself on the forehead in frustration. His father shot him a look that was both irritated and pitying; he didn't understand French, but he could see exactly what had happened. His son was so hopeless that he couldn't even pick up a child from infant school at the right time. Sometimes he thought that there was nothing of him in Zakaria at all; he was all his mother's son, and his mother had been hopeless too – a lovely, long-limbed dreamer with a sickly pale complexion and such an infuriatingly weak and wilful constitution that she had dropped dead of diabetes in her thirties, a simple disease of too-much-sweetness that she should have been able to manage. Mr Khalil didn't so much mourn her death as resent her for it; she had abandoned him with her equally weak and wilful teenager to manage. What a bothersome burden, thought Mr Khalil, to have to admit that his proud blood coursed through Zakaria's feeble, foolish veins; sometimes he thought that blood was not worth as much as people thought it was. Zaki was fortunately too harried to notice his father's disdain and was gabbling his thanks to Flavie with desperate gratitude. '*Flavie, je te remercie infiniment!* Thank you so, so much!' He had dropped to his knees and was giving Jinan an enormous hug, which the little boy simply accepted, displaying neither pleasure nor annoyance. 'I'm so sorry, Ji-Ji. Baba was silly to forget. Say thank you to Flavie.'

Jinan obediently thanked her and held up his cheek to her for a kiss goodbye. Then he walked solemnly over to the fat, dark stranger in the chair and wordlessly held up his cheek politely for a kiss as well. Mr Khalil looked astonished; he had never encountered the French tradition of kissing a child when you enter their home, and unsure what to do, pecked the soft little cheek warily. Seemingly satisfied that etiquette had been met, Jinan toddled sturdily over to the corner, walking carefully past the broken shards of the coffee cup with a slight sigh, and pulled out a wooden box of toys and oddments from under the table. He tipped out a few items and then neatly replaced them all apart from an oversized book with extravagant illustrations on its well-thumbed pages. He lay on his tummy and turned the pages, reading out a story to himself in a broken combination of French, English and Bangla. His sleek cap of dark hair was impossibly smooth and neat.

'This is him, this is Nadya's son?' asked Mr Khalil in amazement. He had been expecting to see a scruffy village brat with a streaming nose and a screaming mouth, or perhaps a milky-faced weakling. Not this well-mannered, studious little prodigy. Not this chunky-legged, strong-looking thing with skin as dark chocolate as his own. And the boy's toy box was the tidiest thing in the apartment. 'He can read at three?'

Zaki looked at Jinan proudly, the distraction of the past few moments having made him forget his firm intent to throw his father out. 'No,' he said with a rueful smile, 'of course he can't read, he hasn't even started school yet. His mamma used to read him that book; he knows each page by heart. He's remembering, not reading.'

'Mamma's gone,' Jinan said sadly, looking up at the mention of his mother. 'She went away up there,' he explained to the fat man in the chair, pointing to the sky through the window. He asked Zaki hopefully, 'Is it time for lunch?'

'I'm sorry, Ji-Ji, I haven't bought anything yet,' said Zaki wearily; yet another thing he had failed to get right that day. 'This is your daddy's daddy – he came over and surprised me. Let's go to the shop and get something.'

'No, let's go out for lunch,' said Mr Khalil, surprising himself even more than Zaki. 'I'll treat us.' He said conspiratorially to Jinan, 'Do you know what a daddy's daddy is called, in Bangla?'

Jinan nodded. 'Dada,' he said simply, taking Mr Khalil's hand with appealing trust. Mr Khalil was momentarily speechless at the small shock of affection that went through him with the little boy's touch. He wished that his real son was half the man that his fake grandson promised to be. Blood, he thought to himself, really wasn't everything.

It was over lunch that Mr Khalil came up with another suggestion for cleaning up Zaki's mess. His cousin Syed had been inexpertly running a corner shop with his wife in an unfashionable part of London. Mr Khalil now owned the shop, albeit with a mortgage, as a result of having covered all of his cousin's debts; he had been in London to look at selling the corner shop, but now had a better idea: his son could take it over. Working for himself, Zaki could run the shop and look after Jinan at the same time; he could just close it when he had to take Jinan to nursery or school. And on the condition that Zakaria stayed at the shop and paid his father a rent from his profits to cover the mortgage, Mr Khalil would eventually sign it over to him; it would be his and Jinan's inheritance.

'I'll need to think it over,' said Zaki quietly, watching Jinan being fussed over by the avuncular owner of the little brasserie. He was showing him the fish-tank in the corner, and how the tiny treasure chest popped open every few seconds with a jet of bubbles that caused the rubber scuba-man to wobble with excitement.

'Think all you want, Zakaria,' said Mr Khalil cheerfully, 'but you don't have much choice. You'll not get any other inheritance from me, you know. Not once I'm married again.' Registering the surprise in Zaki's face, he realized some explanation might be in order. 'Of course, you didn't know, did you? I'm to marry again. I've been a widower for eight years and I've had enough of having to organize the house as well as the business. I'm marrying Iqbal's daughter, she's a wonderful administrator.'

'Faiza? She's barely older than me,' said Zaki in astonishment. 'Aren't you a bit old to start a second family? You're not a rock musician or a film star, you know.'

'Tch! Graceless as always, Zakaria. No matter, I accept your warm congratulations and shall pass your kind compliments to my intended,' said Mr Khalil smoothly. 'And she is at least ten years your senior, so you shall address her respectfully as Apa.' He added a bit tetchily, 'Besides, I am not yet fifty. Charlie Chaplin was much older than me when he married Oona O'Neill. And she was just eighteen. But they had a long and happy marriage and several children.'

'Like I said, you're not a film star,' said Zaki, just as the waitress brought over the dessert. 'Ji-Ji, your ice-cream's on the table,' he called out. Jinan didn't need telling twice; he leapt up from the fish-tank and returned to his seat instantly, tucking into his ice-cream with such speed and enthusiasm that Zaki spoke up distractedly, 'Ever since . . . you know . . . he's been eating non-stop. He never used to eat like this before. I think he's eating for comfort.'

'Nonsense,' said Mr Khalil, looking at Jinan with approval and shovelling down his *crème brûlée* with equal relish. 'He has a healthy appetite, that's all. It's good that he eats. When you were his age you ate nothing, you were just skin and bone; it drove your poor mother to distraction.' At the last mouthful, he added, 'Think about my offer, Zakaria. And think fast. Your Apa Faiza might have other plans for the corner shop in London once we're married.'

Zaki did think it over, and realized that he really didn't have much choice. His funds were already at rock-bottom; Nadya's simple funeral had used the last of their savings and he had been forced to leave his job after the accident to look after Jinan. The only money he had earned lately had been from playing chess for money with some of the residents of his building and he suspected that they had lost out of pity. His student friends had helped a little, but they were as impoverished as he was. He couldn't deny that his father's proposal made sense; he was qualified for nothing, but his summer helping out at the Khalil Emporium meant that he knew he could more or less manage a shop. He realized that his teenage pretensions to independence had been just that, and at the age of twenty-two he was being taken over and managed, with the best of intent, by his father and by his own familial ties. He agreed to his father's proposal with one condition: that he would never reveal to Jinan, out of spite or malice, that Zaki was not really his father.

When Zaki and Jinan arrived at the little corner plot in the backstreets of Hammersmith on a grey summer's day, a chill wind from the river whistled up the road, rattling and scattering the rubbish strewn over the nearby council estate. In the upstairs flat, the ghostly scent of Auntie Uma's cooking still lingered in the brown swirling carpet, and the crowded shop below was littered with Chacha Syed's disorganized and out-of-date stock, all the sticky shelves packed high in teetering confusion. Zaki finally understood that the tag on his wrist at birth didn't say 'Dreamer' after all. He didn't have any dreams any more; his dreams of an unfettered life with his gentle soul mate had been whisked away by a simple accident on a busy street in Montmartre. But he still had a son, and now he had a means to provide for him. The tag on his wrist at birth said 'Shopkeeper', just as his father's had done; this was to be his straightforward and uncompelling fate, and Zaki now accepted that he was helpless to escape it.

Shopping Lists for the Perfect Marriage

LUCKY IS IN HIS ROOM late on Friday night; although he has told himself again and again that tomorrow's match is no big deal, he still feels too anxious about it to fall asleep. So instead he is pretending to be asleep; it seems a sensible thing to do, as he is in trouble, and his parents are arguing. He is not sure whether the trouble came before the argument and caused it, or whether the argument happened first and the getting in trouble bit just happened to come in along the way. From the muffled snatches of conversation he has managed to overhear when the voices have become heated enough to be raised, it seems his parents have found out that he hasn't been doing his homework all week. He suspects that his form master called them after dinner and sneaked on him; it wouldn't be the first time.

Lucky is not too concerned about being in trouble in this way as it happens fairly regularly and the punishment is usually straightforward. He will obviously have to make up the homework and will probably have a week without television, or something like that; in school terms, it's pretty much a white-collar crime – it's not like he's been caught cheating in tests, smoking in the loos or menacing the first years. Nor is Lucky too concerned about the argument; his parents are always arguing, but they thoughtfully tend to save their big arguments for when they think he can't hear. He finds this habit comforting rather than evasive; it is as though the one fundamental thing they do agree on is that they should never let Lucky witness their fights, or get involved. So however bad the argument was, whenever he sees them afterwards they are always civil to each other in front of him and present a united front, even if he can tell that they're so pissed off with each other that they'd rather not even look at each other, let alone stay in the same room, let alone serve up dinner and make small talk around the table. With naive vanity, he unconsciously assumes that he alone holds them together, and that they will not separate as long as he remains between them. It'll all have blown over in the morning, he thinks to himself, finally falling into a fitful, mercifully dreamless sleep.

In the tastefully decorated living room, after taking the unsociably late call from Lucky's form master, Jinan is furious. 'But it's your job, Delphine,' he fumes. 'You can't keep letting this happen. If it's not your job to look after these things, what is?'

'Oh, that's just great, Jinan. Every time something goes wrong with our child, just blame it on me. Of course it's my fault,' she mutters sarcastically. 'Makes it easy for you, doesn't it? God forbid that you ever take the least bit of responsibility for your son.'

'Responsibility?' exclaims Jinan. 'You're accusing me of not taking responsibility for my son? You tell me, Delphine, when have you ever actually let me take responsibility? When he was a baby you'd hardly even let me hold him without supervision, you just kept shooting instructions at me – support his head, support his head *properly*. You made me a nervous wreck!'

'Now you're just being ridiculous,' she says. 'What on earth has holding a baby's head got to do with getting an adolescent to do his homework?'

'It's to do with you undermining me,' mutters Jinan.

'But you constantly undermine me,' exclaims Delphine, outraged. 'Nothing's ever good enough for you. I'm constantly pandering to you and putting up with your bad temper and criticism. You treat me like I'm one of your bloody staff who's failed to meet expectations in her annual appraisal. At least at work I only got appraised once a year, with you it's like a constant drone of things I've done badly or not at all. I didn't pick up your dry-cleaning on the right day, I didn't get the right tomatoes, I didn't know that Lucky hadn't done his homework . . . do you ever stop to consider that perhaps I didn't deliberately set out to forget the dry-cleaning, just to piss you off? And if you must know, the reason I didn't buy the beef tomatoes last week was because I thought I'd get you the organic cherry ones on the vine for a treat. I thought you might like them. I was trying to do something nice, and all you can ever do is snipe at me and complain . . .' Delphine is managing to get herself quite wound up, and feels almost teary.

'Look, I don't care about the dry-cleaning, or the tomatoes – get any damned tomatoes you want,' says Jinan with the intention of being soothing, but despite himself it comes out sounding truculent. He wishes now that he had said how much he enjoyed the cherry tomatoes; to admit he liked them now would make it seem as though he was being deliberately bloody-minded in going on about the beef ones, and justify her belief that he looked for trivial reasons to criticize her. It amazes him that he can make enormous, nail-biting decisions at work with confidence and integrity, but in his home he can get tiny decisions so spectacularly wrong. A simple decision about whether to say that the cherry tomatoes tasted nice or not. 'But I do care about Luhith's homework. I mean, what do you have to do that's more important than looking after Luhith?' Unthinkingly, he adds, 'I mean, what else do you have to do?' He realizes instantly that the last sentence shouldn't have been said aloud, even though he didn't say it with malicious intent, and in fact meant it honestly.

'What else do I have to do? How dare you!' Delphine practically hisses in anger. 'And you have the gall to stand there and tell me that this is about *me* undermining *you*? Nothing is more important to me than Lucky, and if you were the least bit capable or bothered about looking after your son, I'd have been able to go back to work years ago.'

'Oh God, not this again,' says Jinan wearily. 'Didn't we talk about this two minutes ago? I've got one thing to say to you, or rather two things: support his head, support his head *properly*! Besides, it's not like you even wanted to go back to work. You just wanted to stay at home and mooch needily over the baby.'

'I wanted to stay at home and try to be a good mother. And that's what you wanted too, if you remember. And I am a good mother. Do you have any idea why Lucky hasn't handed in any homework this week? Because I can at least make an educated guess. He's incredibly stressed about tomorrow, and I know for a fact that he's been practising around the clock. He's barely been sleeping. What do you expect me to do? Go down to the ground, drag him back kicking and screaming and stand over him with a stick while he writes out some poxy history essay?'

'Yes!' says Jinan, surprising himself with his vehemence. 'Yes, if that's what it takes. I keep telling you that he's taking his football too seriously, and now it's affecting his schoolwork. He needs to start focusing on what's important. I mean, when I was his age—'

'I don't want to hear about when you were his age. It's not about you, Jinan,' interrupts Delphine quietly, with sudden, dangerous authority. 'And it doesn't matter that his football isn't important to you, what matters is that it's important to Lucky.' She gets up and walks not towards their room, but the spare bedroom. 'Tomorrow, I'm going to get up and drive Lucky to his match, and you're going to do the decent thing and wish him luck. And after the match I will sit down with him, and make sure that he does all the work he didn't do last week, and all the work he's meant to do for this week. And that's all there is to it.' She looks at him from the gloom of the hallway and twists back her hair with a tired gesture. 'We all make mistakes sometimes. There's no need for you to make us all so miserable about it, just because we don't live up to your expectations.'

Jinan, unwilling to leave the discussion so abruptly, follows her into the hallway, even though he knows he shouldn't. 'I'm fed up with this, Delphine. I'm fed up with being accused of being a bad person, a bad father. I'm always the guilty one, I'm always the cause of all our problems; I make one little comment, and you interpret it as criticism and jump down my throat. You're difficult too, you know; you're bloody hard work sometimes.'

Delphine stops at the door and turns around. 'I know I'm difficult. I'm sorry.' She knows that in this matter he is right, and she feels she must admit this, if only to be honest to herself. She is difficult because she is unhappy, she is unhappy because she is dissatisfied, and she has no one on whom she can project her dissatisfaction apart from her husband. She knows that Jinan can't win with her, as what he says gets taken down in evidence, and what he doesn't say gets interpreted as disinterest. She also knows that Jinan needs her; despite his big talk, he needs her to support him, to prop him up, to put up with bursts of bad temper or sullenness and even pander to harmless whims. It is entirely possible that she needs him in the same way, but the truth is that she is too tired in their relationship to try any more, as though it was the trying that was so . . . trying in the first place.

Her softly spoken apology has knocked the indignation out of Jinan like a physical punch to the guts. He feels compromised once more, he feels small and insignificant, as though the idealized mother he doesn't really remember has just told him off. It doesn't feel fair.

He says plaintively, 'You know, my friends think we have the perfect marriage.' He hates the sound of his voice; it seems to him like that of a little boy whining, when he'd intended to end their discussion with a rueful and ironic master stroke.

'Mine too,' says Delphine, offering a truce, unintention-ally taking the petty consolation of the last word from Jinan. 'See you in the morning,' she says, and as she sees Jinan's well-scrubbed face fall slightly in defeat, she is suddenly unhappy with herself for only managing to sound polite, rather than kind. She shuts the door to the spare room behind her, looks at the clean expanse of beige, taupe and cream bedlinen stretched coldly across the bed, and remembers a flamboyant voice from the past saying irreverently and illogically, but somehow with authority, 'Something is only perfect because it can't get any worse.'

The Scent of Whisky and Regret

LUCKY IS THRILLED to see Portia at the ground when he arrives for pre-match training. In his experience, most schoolgirls tend to be unrecognizable when not in uniform, but Portia just looks even more like herself, and simply stunning. It's not as though she's dressed particularly sexily; she's wearing faded denims and a jumper, but with her long, slim legs and her short, cropped hair, she looks a bit like a model on her day off.

'Isn't that the girl from Zaki's shop?' asks Delphine, pulling up and parking. 'Pretty, isn't she?'

'Yeah, that's Portia,' says Lucky casually. After the initial excitement of seeing her, he now feels a bit intimidated; he can see himself with Schoolgirl Portia, but why on earth would Model Portia be interested in him? He still can't quite believe that she has picked an oversized, not very clever adolescent like him. He sees his mother is going to get out of the car too and says, 'Mum, would you mind just coming back for the game? You don't need to watch me train.'

Delphine looks at Lucky, looks at Portia, and understands. 'Sure, darling.' She waits for his usual abrupt kiss goodbye, the kiss that she values even though it is from habit rather than affection, but he just bounds out of the car towards Portia and doesn't even turn around to wave her goodbye as she starts the car and moves off.

Lucky stands very close to Portia. 'I want to kiss you but I think my mum's looking,' he says shyly.

'It's OK, I'm not going anywhere,' she replies, sliding her hands up and down his upper arms reassuringly. 'How are you feeling – not too sore? Not too tired. Not too scared?'

'No, I'm feeling perfect, just perfect.' Looking over his shoulder to check that his mum's Audi is out of sight, he pulls Portia to him in a bear hug, and kisses her warmly. For once she doesn't smell of fags, and she tastes sweet, like the Cadbury's fruit and nut bar that is sticking out of her back pocket. 'You feel perfect, too,' he says, feeling the warmth of her along his torso, the softness where her slim waist nips in above her jeans.

'Don't say perfect,' says Portia, between their kisses. 'If something is perfect it can't get any worse.'

'That sounds like one of Zaki's lines,' laughs Lucky. 'OK, almost perfect, how's that?'

'Much better,' says Portia. 'You don't mind me coming so early, do you? I won't get in the way, I couldn't face staying at home for another minute watching creepy Malcolm slop all over my mother . . .' She shakes her head in disgust.

'No, I'm glad you came,' says Lucky, surprised by the question. Portia has that melancholic, almost angry look about her again; he wants to ask her about it, but is interrupted by the arrival of a couple of his team-mates, with bags slung over their shoulders. They wolf-whistle at Portia and make teasing kissing faces at Lucky as they wander into the ground. 'Bugger off,' he shouts to them, secretly pleased to have been seen with her. 'I guess I'd better go in. I'll see you after the match.'

'I don't need to wish you luck, do I?' says Portia. 'It's practically already your middle name.'

Luhith 'Lucky' Khalil grins at her. 'You're right!' he says, and kisses her gratefully on the cheek. He races in after his team-mates, anticipating a barrage of questions about the gorgeous girl he was with and not minding the prospect one little bit.

Delphine has to stop around the corner, as she feels an absurd urge to cry and her eyes are fiercely blurry. She has cried over Lucky many times before, although never in front of him; she cried when he burbled his first word-like sounds, a little song of ma-ma-ma-na-na-nyum-num, she cried when he took his first steps, cruising around their chunky coffee table, and she cried when she took him to school. Hold my hand if you're scared, she had told him, but instead she had been the one to reach out for his soft little palm as she was the one who had been scared, watching him disappear confidently through the gates. She had cried with each little watershed that took him away from her, that made him depend upon her less; each moment that took away his infant perfection and marked the passage of time as he grew into something real and imperfect. Now he was practically an adult, with a girl-friend, and concerns of his own that had nothing to do with her. She feels a surge of bitter resentment towards Lucky for no longer needing her; she feels used and even cheated. I haven't forgiven him for having grown up, she thinks candidly to herself, horrified by her selfishness. Delphine pulls herself together, blows her nose, and goes to a cafe to wait until the game. Ordering a latte and a slice of guiltily comforting fudge cake, she understands, with a flash of empathy, why Jinan gains weight so easily. She leaves the cake untouched and, taking the latte in its paper cup, gets back in her car to drive to Hammersmith. She wishes that her own weaknesses were as simply diagnosed as her husband's; she wishes she could find comfort in the same straightforward way.

Zaki is in the corner shop poring over the *Racing Post* and feeling vaguely guilty about Lucky, who has his big match that afternoon. Oh, for Chrissake, he thinks to himself, it's not as though you haven't got better things to do with your time than stand in the rain and watch a load of zitty adolescents chase a ball around. Besides, the kid doesn't need you to be there – don't flatter yourself. No one needs you, you're just an old joke – the comic relief, an embar-rassment to your prosperous and respectable family, to your nitpicking lawyer son and your nit of a father; the former ignores him from the other side of town, and the latter ignores him from the other side of the world. Oh well, he reflects, in eleven years I'll get my free bus pass and be officially too old to be called a black sheep any more, so everyone will just call me 'eccentric' instead. Bad old, mad old, just plain old old, eccentric Chacha Zaki. He takes a slurp of his coffee, made the old-fashioned way with instant as he couldn't muster the energy to fiddle around with the shiny Krups machine that morning, and makes a face. He never minded instant coffee before, or even the thick gunk that Orla produced next door, but after just a few days of decent espressos, now he can't stand it. The trouble with getting something good, he reflects, is that you get used to it, and then when you don't have it, you miss it more than you ever enjoyed having it in the first place. You feel the loss more than you take pleasure in the possession. 'Just like relationships,' he says. Christ, he's talking to himself now, he really is a mad old man. The bell tinkles on his door as a customer wanders in, and he keeps his eyes down from long habit. Looking at people only encouraged them to engage with you, or, God forbid, interrupt your morning by buying stuff, which would then need to be reordered and replaced.

'Good morning, Zaki,' says Delphine with unusual formality, walking up towards the counter and sipping through the lid of a paper cup.

'Hello, Della,' responds Zaki, not bothering to hide his surprise. 'Why aren't you at the match?'

Delphine sits on the stool opposite the counter and slides her handbag off her shoulder. 'Oh, Lucky asked me to push off during practice. I was cramping his style with his new girlfriend.'

'Makes a nice change,' says Zaki, 'to have you wandering in here complaining about your son instead of mine.' He looks at Delphine, who is dressed impeccably in casual chic, with immaculately clean jeans and a simple, expensive-looking pullover. 'You look different today,' he says. There's a brightness to her eyes, a pinkness to her cheeks, but he supposes that could just be clever cosmetics.

'I'm feeling different,' says Delphine. 'I came to tell you something. I'm not going to come in any more and complain about Jinan to you.'

'Well, thank Christ for that,' mutters Zaki dishonestly, since the truth is that he quite likes Delphine's visits, even though he makes a great show of grumbling about them. 'Let me guess – you had a searching heart-to-heart over a civilized bottle of Bollinger and agreed to a revised household rota, marriage guidance counselling on Saturdays somewhere conveniently near Jinan's golf course, and perhaps to get side-by-side massages together every other week so you could bond away from the pressures of the home?' He says this all rather meanly, even though he knows he should be happy for them. 'Isn't that how you middle-class types resolve your little episodes?'

'Not quite,' replies Delphine calmly. 'I've just had enough of complaining. We had another quarrel yesterday over nothing, and I've had enough of that too. I'm beginning to wonder whether it might be less stressful for us all if I just left him.'

'What?' Zaki spits his coffee over the *Racing Post* in

horror. 'Not funny, Della – you know I can't take practical jokes first thing in the morning. April Fool's Day was last week.'

'I'm not sure that I am joking,' says Delphine. 'I'm getting so tired of us, of our stupid little quarrels, of his bloody weekly lists, of being constantly picked at. I'm becoming miserable, depressed and, God, I'm becoming downright . . . boring. Christ, I'm sorry, I'm complaining again and I said I wouldn't . . .' She sighs and peels the lid off her coffee, licking the foam off the plastic top unthinkingly.

Zaki pulls a bottle of whisky out from under the counter. 'Fortunately it's just gone noon, so it's acceptable to drink,' he says, pouring it generously into his coffee and taking a deep slug. Allowing himself to indulge after mid-day was almost the only way he differentiated his weekends from his weekdays. 'Would you like some?'

'No, but thank you for offering,' replies Delphine politely.

'No, thank you for refusing,' says Zaki, tipping the rest of the bottle into his mug so that the whisky is only slightly flavoured by coffee, rather than the other way round. He downs a bit more, then asks, 'So, does Jinan have anything to say about all this, about how down you've been feeling?'

'I haven't talked to him about it,' she says.

'So why on earth are you telling me?' asks Zaki. Delphine raises her eyes to his; she has misty grey eyes, chameleon eyes that can flicker from being cautious and assessing to appealing and otherworldly. They had been the first thing he'd noticed about her, over twenty years ago when he first saw her, a drowned yuppie rat in a good suit dripping in a cab. 'Oh,' he says knowingly, 'I get it . . .'

'Don't flatter yourself, old man,' Delphine says brusquely, with just a touch of her old humour.

'I don't mean that!' says Zaki, pretending to be offended. 'I really do get it. You want me to tell you how much Jinan loves you, and that he'd be heartbroken without you. You want me to pick apart and overanalyse that oh-so-troubling puzzle of men and relationships with you. You want me to gossip and offer comfort and sympathy.' He drinks his whisky coffee a lot more cheerfully and finally guffaws, unable to hide his mirth. 'Della, you want me to be your bloody girlfriend!'

Delphine flushes because she suspects he might be right. 'Well, I'm glad that my miserable life provides you with some entertainment. You're meant to be my friend, you're one of the oldest friends I have here in London. Why can't you stop joking for once and give me a bit of goddamned friendly advice? And why shouldn't you give me comfort, and sympathy, and some reasons why I should stay with Jinan?'

'Firstly, I'm not your friend. You stopped being my friend when you married my son – then you became my relation. You can't be friends with your family, it's like enjoying something you're forced to do, or paid to do. It never happens, you just resent the imposition too much,' says Zaki. 'Secondly, Jinan's an annoying little bugger. He wasn't always that way, but since he hit double figures there's been no stopping him, so I can't give you any reasons to stay with him. If I'd been married to him, I'd have left him when I got *my* first stupid weekly "to do" list from him when he was eleven years old. Baba, wash my PE kit, iron my uniform, buy me orange juice so I don't get scurvy, make my dentist appointment, get me a junior dictionary . . . Anyhow, the bottom line, Beautiful, is that I'm stuck with him – you're not.'

Delphine looks at him, dumbfounded. 'So that's your advice? You think I should leave your son because he's annoying, and he writes "to do" lists?'

'Yup,' says Zaki cheerfully. 'That pretty much sums it up. And don't hang around too long to do it, you're no spring chicken any more, so you might get left on the second-time-around shelf. In ten years' time, you'll be too old for me, even . . .' The bell rings over the doorway and a couple of local kids walk into the shop. 'Bugger,' mutters Zaki, before continuing regardless, despite his audience, 'But don't worry about Jinan, he'll be fine. Rich lawyers don't have any trouble finding dates, even if they're old and ugly. And Jinan is only thirty-six, and he's by no means hideous, if you like the well-scrubbed, clean-shaven look. He'll be with a nice blonde twenty-something secretary before you can sneeze "trophy wife". There's probably one with her eye on him right now, thinking "poor thing, that skinny Knightsbridge housewife isn't taking proper care of him".'

'Oh, fuck off,' says Delphine good-humouredly. 'I know exactly what you're doing, telling me that he'll be in demand and I won't – you're trying to scare me into staying with him.'

'Is that what I was doing?' says Zaki in mock surprise. 'I'm cleverer than I thought. Is it working?'

'I think I'd miss you more than him,' says Delphine innocently, drinking her latte. 'You always make me feel better.'

The kids come to the counter with comics and chocolates, forcing Zaki to put down his paper and help them. As Delphine watches him joke with them, her grey eyes mist over as she remembers the summer they met and dated – the silly pranks he played on her annoying neighbours in Putney, the nights in the casinos and days at the races, the sheer irresponsibility of it all. By day she'd been a buttoned-up, ruthless, ladder-climbing executive; by night she'd been like a schoolgirl with her secret, unsuitable boyfriend. With the distance of time, she feels a slight yearning, a sorrow for the young girl she had forced to lead such different lives, as though it wasn't really her who had done and felt all those things, but someone else. A previous self. She possibly even feels a little bit of regret for the ambition that the girl had that would never allow her to have a serious relationship with a shopkeeper, however fond she was of him. It's silly to feel sorry for that girl, she thinks – didn't the snobby little princess get everything she wanted? A successful career and a successful lawyer husband that she could boast about at dinner parties, and later, a lovely son and a lovely home, as far away culturally from her village as she could manage? Although, she thought, perhaps getting everything you wanted is also something to feel sorry about, since where did that leave you to go? Nowhere, apart from backwards.

How funny, after all these years, that the unsuitable man that girl had rejected so blithely, after one long summer, was the one still sitting here and listening to her confidences and making her feel better. She remembers Zaki's flamboyance and head-turning looks, but she doesn't remember what it felt like to kiss him, to hold him close and then let him go. She represses a dangerous urge to remind herself of those forgotten things, then she pats his hand and satisfies herself by giving him a warm, daughterly kiss on his unshaven cheek. She does not allow the kiss to linger; if she stays too close to him, he may notice her scent of coffee and regret. 'Do you mind if I go upstairs and make myself another latte? This one's gone cold,' she says. 'And then we'll go to Lucky's match. He could do with your support; Jinan's playing golf today.'

Zaki looks after her as she disappears up the stairs. He tells himself that he is glad that he helped; it was the least he could do after she had taken over the burden of his son from him, and those 'to do' lists and other annoying habits that he had never been able to persuade Jinan to break. He has always told himself that it was his job to make her feel better.

'But you always make me feel worse,' he tells the empty air that she has left in her wake. Talking to himself again, like the bad old, mad old, old old eccentric man he is soon to become. He downs his drink and is unable to resist touching his cheek where her lips brushed him so warmly, where her breath misted on him. What did she smell, when she kissed him? What else was there to smell on him but whisky and regret?

Captain Khalil on the Field of Battle

A S THE TEAMS spill out on to the pitch, a light drizzle starts. Symbolic, thinks Lucky, resigned.

'Oi, Lucky, you know what they say about blokes with big hands,' says Ming, as they get into position. Lucky says nothing and waits for the punchline. 'Yeah, big gloves,' Ming guffaws, whacking Lucky's massive goalie gloves for effect. When Lucky doesn't join in, he adds, 'Come on, cheer up, mate! It's not a bloody execution.'

'We don't know that yet, do we?' replies Lucky. 'Just mark your man, mate, and leave out the jokes.' He looks across at his nemesis, Phenomenon Felix, Curler Conway, a striker who can bend a ball, who can fly across a pitch so fast with such perfect timing that he barely needs to touch the ball to keep it ahead of him. Lucky has seen his photos in local papers and on the Swindon team website, but is always taken aback by how tiny he is in person. A short white kid with a round potato face and freckles who looks a bit of a geek. Like Lucky, Conway is captaining his team, but he isn't indulging in his usual banter with his team-mates; he just seems unusually focused and collected.

However, Lucky has been observant enough to see him glancing surreptitiously at the stands, at two particular anonymous-looking people in expensive all-weather gear, because Lucky has been doing the same. There are two scouts there, one from a London club, the other one from Manchester. Perhaps this game will be the big one for Conway, where he'll finally seal the deal and get an offer. Or perhaps he'll get more than he bargained for.

'Bring it on, Conway,' Lucky mutters under his breath. 'Let's make a bit of club history.'

It is only ten minutes into the first half when Conway has his first clear shot on goal. He has had to run the length of the pitch and has been sneakily fouled by Ming, but still, as he goes down, manages to put the ball accurately in the direction of the net, although not with much pace. Lucky, able to judge exactly where the ball was going, saves it easily, and throws it back out to Ming immediately. 'That's it, Lucky,' shouts Harding encouragingly. Lucky shakes his head; that was barely a save, even Duncan would have managed that one, but he feels his confidence surge despite himself. The second shot on goal is a tougher one; it is a free kick, and knowing Conway's curling ability, Lucky makes sure to hang back on his line, however tempted he is to come out to punch the ball clean away. The ball flies a neat and unexpected curve to the top right corner of the goal, and there are premature cheers from the Swindon supporters, who think it's unsaveable. But Lucky, so intent on the smooth trajectory of the ball that he seems half hypnotized, just manages to get the tips of his fingers to it, and ease it over the bar.

Conway is getting agitated – it is almost unheard of for him not to have scored halfway though the first half. 'Get me some bloody service,' he is heard shouting to his team, his voice unexpectedly deep and fractious for such a small, mild-looking boy. The third chance on goal Conway makes almost single-handedly for himself, dribbling past all the defenders with such swift precision that the other players look like they are in slow motion. Lucky, who has the clearest view of the pitch, is almost lost in admiration; bloody hell, he thinks, it's Michael Owen against Argentina in the France 1998 World Cup. He realizes that the only way he can deny Conway is by showing that he wants the ball more than him, and that he's willing to do anything for it; the battle is going to be less about skill than about nerves. Lucky recklessly abandons the goal and running out, dives for the ball, risking Conway's boot in his face. He falls badly, but the ball is safe, curled in tight against him, and Conway tumbles over him. 'Fuck me,' Conway says in furious shock, looking at his opposite captain; the idiot Khalil kid could have wound up with a mouth full of broken teeth. As the whistle blows for half-time, Conway, who shook hands pleasantly enough at the start, gives Lucky the filthiest look. 'It's not fucking over yet, you Frog–Wog mongrel.' Lucky, testing his shoulder, is surprised, as he'd never heard of Conway having a temper; he is also flattered, since Conway knowing his French and Asian background means that he must have looked him up on Lucky's own team's website. He says nothing, but hauls himself off the ground and smiles as he goes to meet his coach on the sidelines. He's rattled Conway; if he can rattle him, he can beat him. He just has to want it more.

In the second half Lucky saves two more goal attempts, to the delight of the home crowd who are singing a combination of 'I should be so Lucky' with 'Can Khalil do it? Yes he can!' He's never heard them get so excited before. Lucky has played some great games in the past, but there is nothing that compares to this – it's like he can't put a foot or a hand wrong, and he and the ball home in together with almost magnetic attraction. But his luck runs out in the closing minutes, when Ming gets overexcited and tackles Conway aggressively in the area; Conway takes his chance and drops like a stone. The crowd hiss and shout at him to get up; Harding yells indignantly at the ref, but Lucky just prepares himself for the inevitable penalty. He watches Conway preparing to take the kick among the boos and catcalls, and suddenly he feels very calm. I know you, he thinks; I know where you'll move, I know which way you'll strike; I know, because you're just like me. Conway strikes the ball and everything suddenly slows down; there is no noise apart from the blood rushing through his head and pumping an insistent tattoo behind his ears. There is no anticipation and no memory, there is only the moment, an elongated moment as the ball sails into the air, and Lucky leaps to claim it. He jumps the right way, but can't quite manage to get his hands behind the ball and instead unthinkingly tries to head it. The ball is travelling at 60 mph, and glancing off the side of his glove, gets him between the eyes and rebounds off him with a soft thwack into the side of the net. Lucky collapses in the goal, and the whistle is blown.

Lucky wakes to find his team carrying him off the field in honour, to the shrieks and cheers of the home crowd. 'Did we do it? Did I save it?' he asks, and has to look at the scoreboard for the answer. 'But we lost?' he's asking Jackie and Ming and Harding in bemusement, wondering why they are celebrating.

'Bollocks we lost!' contradicts Jackie. 'We went the distance, and he only got that penalty because he fell like a girl. I'd say Conway's tarnished his golden reputation today, and you, mate, are my personal hero!' He pulls at Lucky's sore head and places a smacking kiss on the top of it.

'Put me down!' Lucky protests, not quite convinced about the merit of the celebration, scouring the crowd for Portia, his mum, and the two anonymous-looking blokes he'd clocked before. He is finally deposited on the side of the stand and is barely up on his feet when he is knocked down viciously from behind with a sharp kick to his kidneys. He turns over on the ground to see Conway leaping over him and starting to punch him, his face twisted with fury. 'You bastard! You bloody Paki bastard!'

Lucky pushes him off easily, and holds him flailing at arm's length. 'Not Paki. Frog–Wog, remember? What's the matter, Conway? You won, didn't you?'

Conway stops punching, and his fury gives way without

warning to hot, angry tears. His guttural sobbing hits Lucky harder than his punches. 'You don't get it, do you, Khalil? This was my big chance, and thanks to you, I blew it.'

Lucky feels a surge of sympathy. 'Mate, I do get it,' he says, and reaches out to pat Conway on the shoulder, but he is shrugged off.

'Just don't look at me,' says Conway bitterly, embarrassed by his tears, and he runs into the dressing rooms. He's just a kid, Lucky thinks; he's just a little kid after all the passion and the penalties are over. He wonders whether he should go after Conway, but then hears a familiar voice shouting his name and looks across the ground to see Zaki and Portia standing together, waving furiously. It has been such a magical afternoon, so full of unexpected occurrences, that Lucky does not question Zaki's unusual appearance at the field, even though his obstinately indoor grandfather had expressed no intention of being caught out of doors on a damp Saturday afternoon. Lucky runs over to them. 'Where's Mum?' he asks, putting his arm around Portia. 'Isn't she with you?'

Zaki smiles broadly, and makes a slight, silent gesture with his head a little to the left and behind. Lucky sees her talking with Harding and the two anonymous men in their expensive all-weather gear. Talking intently. 'Omigod,' whispers Lucky and tries to join them, but he is pulled back by Zaki.

'Let your mum handle this,' says Zaki. 'This is what she's good at. You didn't see her in the old days when she was a marketing director; the woman can negotiate for England.'

'I don't want her to negotiate, I want her to say yes!' protests Lucky. 'Or maybe yes please.'

'And that's exactly why you're staying right here,' insists Zaki, while Portia nods in agreement, squeezing Lucky's hand fiercely. After a few more moments that seem like forever, Delphine turns and waves to Lucky and she, Harding and the two men begin to walk towards him. Omigod, he thinks again, feeling the blood rush to his mildly concussed head and hearing nothing but that insistent tattoo behind his ears – This Is Where It Begins.

The Management of Boys and Men

D ELPHINE IS SUDDENLY alive again. In the course
of one morning and afternoon, the delicate balance of
her forlorn life has unexpectedly shifted, her discontent-
ment has evaporated, and now, as she makes her usual
complicated dinner for her nearest and dearest, she feels
both expectant and happy. She feels on the inside what she
usually projects for friends and former colleagues on the
outside.

There is a simple reason for this turning of the tide.
After years of choosing to be a housewife and a mother,
Delphine has found a job – or rather, the job has found
her. During ninety magical minutes, her talented son has
confounded all her expectations, and in creating a victory
from almost certain defeat, has managed to attract the
interest of those with the power to turn his hobby into a
vocation. Suddenly, in the moments after the game, he
needed her as he has never needed her before – he needed
her not as a comfort provider, a tear-wiper, homework
helper or chauffeur; he needed her as one adult might need
another, as a hard-nosed representative and negotiator. He

needed her as a manager, and she found that she still had what it took to step effortlessly into this new role. Delphine sees a future, for Lucky and for her; she sees herself being useful instead of miserably indulged, and her son being propelled to fame, fortune and happiness as a result of his God-given talent and her conscientious management. They will be a team again; he will be her boy again.

'No, absolutely not. I've never heard of anything so ridiculous,' says Jinan, spearing home-made goat's cheese ravioli with roast poussin. 'How's he expected to get his GCSEs if he's playing for some club on the other side of London?'

'It's not just another club, darling,' explains Delphine patiently, 'he's been given a chance with the youth academy of a premiership club. If they accept him permanently, it means that when Lucky's nineteen he could be playing in the premiership – or even sooner, if he's good enough. He'll be playing with the best in the country.' She pauses, waiting for this to sink in, and adds, 'It means that he'll be a professional footballer; it'll be his job.'

'Professional?' sputters Jinan. 'How can he be a professional anything? He's not even fifteen yet!'

'I don't think you understand what an incredible opportunity he's been given; it's the sort of thing most kids just dream of,' says Delphine. 'And besides, it's what he wants to do.'

'He's doing this to spite me,' mutters Jinan unreasonably. 'He'll plough all his exams, and when he's finished chasing his stupid ball around, he won't be qualified to do anything at university apart from Physical Education at some former poly . . .'

'Oh, for God's sake, don't be such a bloody snob,' says Delphine, finally getting annoyed. She watches Jinan shovel down her lovingly prepared celebratory meal with no more regard for the melting perfection of the poussin or the perfect bite of the ravioli than if it were a supermarket ready meal, and wishes she hadn't wasted so much time on it. He didn't even look like he was enjoying it; it was just more fuel for his latest grievance. Was he even chewing?

'I am a bloody snob. And so are you. Why is Lucky doing this to us? What does he think he is, some kind of working-class hero?' Jinan finishes the last of his ravioli and looks momentarily bereft before spotting the focaccia that Delphine has sprinkled with roasted rosemary; grabbing a hefty piece, he mops up his plate. 'I mean, I didn't drag myself up by my bootstraps, and get to where I am via Oxford and law school, just so Lucky could jump back three generations and go back to working the fields in his *lungi*.'

'It's hardly working the fields, it's playing on a field,' says Delphine, wondering if she would feel quite as supportive if Lucky really had decided to work the fields and become a maize farmer in an idyllic part of south-west France. 'You wouldn't be so disapproving if it was cricket, or tennis.'

'You're right, I wouldn't be. Football's an oaf's game – we may as well have brought up Lucky on some council estate in Peckham. Name me one footballer who's gone to public school or got a degree,' mutters Jinan.

'There's no time limit on getting a degree,' says Delphine soothingly. 'We'll make sure that Lucky gets his GCSEs while he's doing his apprenticeship, and we'll give him a year or so to see how he gets on with the football. He can even do his A levels while he's under contract. And if it doesn't work out, he can do a degree then.' She thinks of two things that will sweeten this proposition for Jinan, and stroking his hand, adds gently, 'Just think of it as a gap year. Haven't you always said that you regretted not taking one? And I've made chocolate soufflé for dessert.'

'Soufflé, you say?' says Jinan, perking up. He follows Delphine into the kitchen with the plates, almost puppy-like, and looks appreciatively at the soufflé puffing in the oven. 'Smells amazing,' he sighs. He watches reverently as Delphine carefully removes it and spoons out the stiff, sweet crust and melting chocolate insides onto his dessert plate. He asks as he tucks in, 'So, you seem happy with all of this? You don't think it's a bad idea?'

Delphine hears the compromise in his voice and hides a smile. Jinan always came round to her way of thinking in the end. Perhaps she was lucky to have married him – there couldn't be another millionaire solicitor in Knightsbridge as easy to manage as him. 'I think we should let him have his chance,' she says. 'It won't do him any harm, and he'd resent us otherwise.'

'I guess you have to do this sort of thing when you're young,' concedes Jinan, scraping the remains of his soufflé from his plate, then helping himself to some more. 'You're right, I always regretted not taking a gap year and doing the whole Grand Tour thing. Then I was in college, then law school, and then we got married and had Lucky, and it was just too late.'

Delphine nods in agreement. 'You only regret the things that you didn't do,' she says. She checks her watch – Lucky will be getting back soon from Zaki's; she'd let him go there with Portia on the condition that he got his homework done. She gets up to make their decaffeinated espressos, and thinks of Zaki's stubbly cheek, of the poignant mustiness of his freshly showered skin in two-day-old clothes, and the scent of coffee and regret.

Decisions on a Dance Floor

DELPHINE IS IN A CAB on the way to meet the girls.
She is home alone for a couple of days as Jinan is
away on business in New York and Lucky is on a training
weekend with his team. He's been with the team's youth
academy for well over a year now, and with Delphine's
support is doing rather well. She got his contract renewed
without drama, and she even made sure that he kept on
top of his GCSE coursework. She was managing Jinan
rather less well; the night before he left, they had a fight
about something insignificant that they blew into epic
proportions. Of course, there was nothing unusual in
that, and although Lucky wasn't there as their audience,
they had been back to themselves the next morning. They
had even made love before they got up; or, rather, Jinan had
started to make love to her and she hadn't minded at first,
then found herself enjoying it and responding with enthusiasm. It was a habit, making love before one of them went
on a trip; like a stamp of ownership or an inoculation.
Afterwards, they had made polite small-talk while Jinan
packed for his flight and looked for his transatlantic plug

adaptors. What had made the fallout of their perfectly commonplace fight so unusual, so unprecedented in its awfulness, was the way Jinan had tried to make up for it before he left. He had held her close and told her that he was worried that it was all his fault after all. 'I married a brilliant executive with a soaring career, and over the years, somehow, I've made you ordinary. I've made you into a housewife, cook, driver and babysitter. No wonder you're not happy.'

'I am happy,' she had lied, hurt by the bitter accuracy of his charges. 'I've got everything I ever wanted.' It was bad enough that she knew she was ordinary, but it was too much that others should suspect it, and should know just how little space she took up in the world. The girl who had so much ambition, who believed that she deserved so much, had effaced herself. By getting everything she had ever wanted, she had somehow made herself into someone who hardly mattered. It was an unexpected tragedy, fulfilling your dreams too early; as she had only recently realized, it left you nowhere to go.

'We'll talk about it when I get back,' Jinan had promised, either not listening to her protestations or not believing them. He had picked up the tips of her hair to kiss them, as though he was too embarrassed to kiss her properly on their own front doorstep. Then, like a child asking for approval, he had said, 'I love you, you know. I love you so much.' He didn't wait for a response, but dashed off; he was probably afraid, with justification, that Delphine might hesitate in saying those words back to him. He did not want to witness a moment of doubt, or hesitation; in this matter, all he wanted was the last word. His unexpected declaration was just another kind of inoculation, thought Delphine.

Delphine, alone in the apartment, had spent the day preparing for her evening out. She had drawn a long bath, done her hair and nails and waxed her legs. She had played her Abba Gold CD and cackled to her friends on the phone while organizing and reorganizing exactly when and where they were meeting. She felt young and optimistic again, something she couldn't feel while Jinan was around, taking up enough space in the world for both of them these days.

Wandering through the hallway with a towel on her head, she had stopped to inspect a framed photo of Jinan as a baby with his parents. Zaki and Nadya were still in their teens, with fine features and infectious smiles, looking adoringly at Jinan; he was an unlikely candidate for such unfiltered affection: a dark, bald and rather cross-looking infant, with fat lips and fat fists. Jinan, unsurprisingly, didn't like the photo, but she had found it and put it up as there were so few baby photos of him. She remembered Jinan at fourteen, the age Lucky was now; such a grave adolescent, so meticulously groomed. And then she had met him years later, a twenty-something like her, but still so grave, still so smooth-haired and well scrubbed, with full lips that seemed sensual rather than fat. In the enormous meeting room with Legal, Finance, R&D and most of Marketing, she had stared at him, and he had stared back at her obviously enough to make her colleagues whisper, while she desperately tried to remember where she knew him from. It wasn't until he'd given his surname that she had burst out, 'So that's how I know you!' and her colleagues had laughed and said that they had thought it was just love at first sight. He had made his interest in her obvious from the start, and his youth gave him a certain naive glow that made him rather attractive. He had been a good catch, a nice-looking and ambitious young lawyer; he was everything she was looking for. She enjoyed being with him and she enjoyed being without him even more, as then she could boast about him to her friends and colleagues. She had enjoyed the awed enthusiasm with which he made love to her, and the refreshing lack of baggage he brought with him; no previous wives or bittersweet failed romances, no disagreeable siblings or bossy mother-in-law. The only baggage was hers, but he seemed more than able to handle it all, even her brief relationship with his father.

And if she wasn't sure that she loved him as much as she felt she ought to, it really didn't matter when he adored her as much as he did; he had enough love for the two of them. She recalled the impetuous words that he had breathed to her in their most intimate moments, in the strolls though the parks, in the art galleries and wine bars, in the reception of her office as he waited patiently for her while her meetings overran. 'I love you. I love you so much,' he had said, this lost, motherless boy, as though he had waited his whole life to be able to say those words to someone, and now couldn't say them enough. So, having already achieved everything she had set out to do in her career, she had been ready to move on to the next challenge, the next adventure, and to become a wife and a mother, a lady of leisure. She would leave her colleagues in the rat race and be free of the rush hour on the tube, of the pin-striped high fiving in meeting rooms in front of a flip chart; she would be the one who got away. It was possible that she had settled for Jinan, back then. Was it any wonder that they were both so unsettled now?

Delphine realized, at the moment when Jinan kissed her hair tenderly and left her that morning with a renewed declaration of love, that she would have to leave him. She didn't know how or when, but she knew that she would. She felt a great weight lifted from her; a little like when she had handed in her notice at work. She would no longer have to feign enthusiasm or try so hard, she would simply, at some point, walk away. She found herself singing along cheerfully to 'Dancing Queen'. It might have been the glass of Chablis that she had poured herself, but she imagined that she caught a reproachful glance from Nadya through the polished glass of the silver photo frame. Who would love her dark, fat-lipped little baby now?

As the cab goes down Curzon Street, Delphine spots a familiar figure in a dinner jacket strolling nonchalantly along. 'Zaki!' she calls out unthinkingly, yanking down the window. The cab pulls up and Zaki stops in surprise.

He opens the cab door and seeing Delphine inside, looking youthful and fragrant, her grey eyes beautifully made up for her evening out, smiles ruefully as he says, 'I'm confused, have I just opened the door to the past?'

Delphine laughs, feeling slightly uncomfortable. 'It's not raining this time, and I'm not in shoulder-pads and power heels. What are you doing over here?'

Zaki nods towards a canopied entrance a little way down the street. 'I'm going to the club.'

'I thought it closed down last year?' says Delphine suspiciously, although Zaki has no reason to lie. A romantic, extravagantly ludicrous notion flits through her head, that every Friday night since they broke up twenty years ago, Zaki has been on Curzon Street, in a dinner jacket, waiting patiently for her to appear so that they might fight over and share a cab, and she has finally arrived. How ridiculous, she thinks to herself. She slightly resents Zaki for giving rise to this fleeting fancy, and resents him for ageing so well, for keeping his slim-hipped figure on an appalling diet of whisky and take-aways, for wearing a dinner jacket with such insouciant comfort and panache that he might have been wearing his Levi's. What right did he have to haunt Curzon Street in a dinner jacket on Friday nights?

Zaki shrugs. 'It reopened a while ago under new management – same building, same gaming tables, most of the same staff. The only things that have changed are the name and the logo on the napkins. Ayesha and I have been coming most weekends.'

'Is she with you tonight?' asks Delphine.

Zaki looks around hopefully before eventually admitting, 'Nope, doesn't look like it. What about you? Out with the girls?'

Delphine nods, wishing she were a bit less predictable. 'Just Katie and Veronica. We're meeting at Ninos around the corner. We'll be out quite late.' She hesitates, then adds, 'You could come and join us if you like, when you're done losing your money.'

Zaki shakes his head. 'Oh no, Della! You won't get me that way. I'm not going to be listening in to a night of husband-bashing over Chardonnay. I've already told you, I'm not your bloody girlfriend!' He leans in the cab to kiss her quickly on the cheek, and strolls off.

In the cosy, busy basement bar of Ninos, Katie and Veronica have already nabbed a table on the tiny, sunken terrace, and ordered chips and pink champagne. 'So, I guess we're not doing dinner?' says Delphine, as she slides in next to them. 'Mwah, mwah!' she air kisses them jokily. She is glad that she's dressed up, as they have both made an effort and look gorgeous – Katie all blonde and curved and dimpled, with pink sequins on her skirt, and Veronica in a sleek black halter neck, her lips very deep red against her dark satiny skin, her Afro-Caribbean hair defiantly unstraightened and styled into a flattering mop of twists.

'And mwah, mwah, to you. We thought about waiting for you before ordering, but thought sod that, because we knew you'd be late,' says Katie indulgently, pouring Delphine a glass.

'And you've got no excuse – you live the closest. I had to haul my skinny butt all the way from Wimbledon,' adds Veronica, stubbing out a cigarette to dip a chip in tomato sauce. 'God, why do we always come here? These chips taste awful, I think this time I'm really going to complain . . .'

'You complained last time, Ronnie,' Delphine points out, 'and he'll say just what he said last time. Don't have a stinking fag before you eat.'

'But I need my stinking fags. You know what happened last time I stopped smoking, Dee,' says Veronica. 'My skinny butt suddenly wasn't so skinny any more. My trainer had this really annoying cutesie-poo phrase for it . . .'

'Sweet peach to plump pear,' recalls Delphine. 'Trainers are great for euphemisms.'

'Yeah, when what they really want to say is lightweight to lardarse,' giggles Katie. 'Until Ronnie stopped smoking, the Great Wall of China was the only man-made structure you could see from space . . . Ouch!' she squeals in outrage as Veronica whacks her indignantly on her own none-too-slim, pink-sequinned behind.

'You went too far,' Veronica explains dangerously, then all three of them collapse laughing.

'You're freakishly obsessed with your perfect butt,' comments Delphine, once they have calmed down.

'We've all got to have something perfect to obsess about,' says Katie. 'Ronnie's got her perfect butt, you've got your perfect man, I've got . . . wait a minute, what *have* I got?'

'Hair,' chorus Delphine and Veronica in unison.

'That's it,' says Katie, flicking her smooth, naturally platinum locks back over her shoulders. 'Typical – the only thing I've got that's perfect, anyone can buy from chicks in Eastern Europe and get glued on at a salon.' She munches her chips appreciatively. 'Speaking of which, Dee, don't you love Ronnie's new hair?'

'I do love it,' says Delphine sincerely. 'It really frames your face. When did you get the extensions taken out?'

'A few weeks ago. I felt a bit too chavvy having someone else's hair on my head; it felt vaguely exploitative. And I decided that corn-rows were too eighties for a hip and happening adland girl. So my hairdresser suggested the funky twists.' She twirls one experimentally. 'I think it helps with the smoking, anyway, as I can fiddle with my hair instead of having a fag.'

'I think we should take your funky new hair out clubbing tonight,' suggests Katie. 'It's been ages since we've done that.'

'God, no, Derek will flip. He's probably pacing at home right now, grinding his teeth. You should have seen him when I put this top on,' says Veronica, turning to show the smooth expanse of bare brown back that the halter neck revealed. Delphine and Katie look at each other knowingly; neither of them approve of Veronica's current boyfriend. Like Veronica, he is a high-powered media type, but he is also some fifteen years older than her, not nearly as good-looking, and incredibly jealous as a result. It doesn't help that Veronica looks so fantastic for her age; twenty-somethings wolf-whistle her as she walks down the street. Delphine is sure she had had more wrinkles when she was a teenager than Veronica has at almost forty.

'Come on, Ronnie, for me,' begs Delphine appealingly. 'I haven't gone out clubbing for ages . . .' Delphine hadn't even thought about going clubbing earlier, but suddenly the idea is irresistible; in her twenties, she had gone every weekend. Perhaps dancing would shake out that lost girl from where she was hiding beneath the housewifely veneer and expensive, tasteful make-up.

'And there'll be plenty of time to stay at home, knit twinsets and fetch Dull Derek's slippers when you're in your dotage – say in four or five years' time . . .' adds Katie cheekily. She is still in her mid-thirties and annoyingly smug about it.

'Mee-oww! Katie Kitten has claws,' exclaims Veronica. 'Oh, fuck it, let's go! I'll text Derek, his teeth will be down to powder by the time I get home.'

'That's OK,' says Delphine. 'Guys his age keep a spare pair in the jar next to the bed.'

'You bitch!' Veronica howls with laughter. 'Oh God, I'll wet myself . . .' She is still laughing as the charming owner of Ninos appears with a tray bearing olives, freshly made bruschetta and thick home-made crisps.

'For my favourite ladies,' he says smoothly, before winking at Delphine and Katie confidentially. 'So, is this one still complaining about my chips?'

'No! Me? Never! How could you think such a thing!' exclaims Veronica, rubbing her flat tummy with exaggerated glee. 'They're . . . beyond description!' When he has gallantly kissed their hands and moved on, Veronica adds, 'That's why we keep coming back here, isn't it? The clever bugger gives us free food.'

'Those damned consumer loyalty courses,' says Katie, through a mouthful of bruschetta. 'They'll get you every time.'

Towards the end of the bottle, Veronica raises her glass. 'Girls, I have an announcement. In fact, I've got news. Quite big news.' Delphine and Katie grin expectantly and raise their glasses; they know that Veronica has been in the running for a promotion at work. 'Derek's asked me to marry him.'

'What?!' says Delphine in horror.

'Oh God, no!' says Katie at the same time, with equal horror.

Veronica looks at them wryly, takes a sip from her glass,

and says, 'Did you two rehearse that? I think the normal thing you say is congratulations, or am I just a bit out of touch?'

'Sorry, sweetheart,' says Katie, recovering herself quicker than Delphine. 'I just didn't think that you and he were that serious. I mean, I know we've barely met him, but he's so unlike you, he's just so . . . so . . .'

'Old?' says Veronica. 'Girls, you may not have noticed, but I'm no spring chicken either. We can't all get young lawyers like Dee here.'

'It's not just that,' argues Katie. 'He's so stuffy, and self-important . . .'

'Well, he is important! He's a bloody MD of an ad agency, he manages about four hundred people. And he's not stuffy with me, he's kind, and considerate, and thoughtful . . . I mean, for Valentine's Day . . .'

'You mean his PA is considerate and thoughtful,' interrupts Katie. 'You're not telling me that he sends his own flowers and books his own restaurants . . .'

Veronica rolls her eyes in annoyance. 'And nor can we all have arty stay-at-home hubbies like you, who've got all the time in the world to call Interflora when they're not painting in their shed. Do you two ever stop to think about how lucky you are? All I've got is my career, my house and an overpriced convertible that's depreciating by the minute. I want the stuff that you two have before it's too late – I want a husband, and kids, and maternity leave, and stretch marks and holidays in bloody awful family-friendly resorts too.' She looks at Delphine, who is watching the cross exchange with concern, and appeals to her: 'You've been quiet, Dee. You understand, don't you?'

'I do understand, sweetie. And if you love him, I'm happy for you,' Delphine says simply, reaching out sympathetically for Veronica's hand. 'But if you're settling for him, I'm not. But I'll still understand, I guess.'

There is a long pause, in which they are all silent, while Veronica downs her glass of champagne in one gulp, and lights another stinking fag. 'Oh, bollocks,' she says resignedly. 'I hate you two for being right.' She adds plaintively, 'I just don't have the energy to put myself through the dating scene again; if you're a single woman hitting forty you may as well have 666 tattooed on your forehead and horns and a forked tail. I mean, at least Derek's nice, and safe and cares for me; he may not be Mr Right, but at least he's Mr Right-Here-And-Now.'

She looks so down that Katie puts her arm around her and suggests half-seriously, with impeccable pink champagne logic, 'Maybe you could marry him just for a bit? Have a couple of rug-rats, then give him the old heave-ho. I mean, he's used to it. He's been divorced twice already, hasn't he?'

'Maybe you're right.' Veronica brightens up. 'I read somewhere that marriage these days is just about finding someone to breed with before your biological clock winds down. The finding someone to get old and die with can wait for ages . . .'

'I'd say with modern life expectancy, you've got another thirty years to do that. Loads of time,' agrees Delphine.

Hours later, in a club off Trafalgar Square, having danced until her feet are sore and drunkenly told Veronica and Delphine everything that she dislikes about Derek, Katie has moved on to complaining about her husband.

'I mean, I get back from the office, shattered and starving, and Tony's just sitting there watching telly, and he's so bloody proud that he managed to pick up the right toddler from nursery and defrost some mush for her tea that his tail is practically wagging. He's made the house into an utter tip in the course of the working day, and all that he's done is rinse his own coffee cup while he's working on his so-called exhibition. And if I want to eat anything for dinner that doesn't arrive in a cardboard box on the back of a motorbike, I have to start a night shift in the kitchen.'

'You should have married a wife, not an artist,' says Delphine, not without a little irony. She has kicked off her own high heels and is rubbing her toes; her delicate strappy sandals were not made for walking or dancing, or anything more strenuous than dangling from a bar stool or nestling in a cab.

'I might not have married him at all if he hadn't knocked me up,' says Katie meanly, eating the fruit out of her cocktail. 'Well, there was that, and the fact that he was vegetarian.'

'I can't believe I was considering taking marriage advice from you,' says Veronica in disbelief. 'What has Tony being a vegetarian got to do with you marrying him? You're an utter carnivore.'

'Simple, it meant that he was the only boyfriend I ever

had who didn't expect blow-jobs. We struck a deal – I wouldn't make him eat meat if he wouldn't make me!' Katie's raucous laugh is all at odds with her pink princess appearance, and Veronica and Delphine collapse in giggles. 'Anyway,' continues Katie, swigging the last of her champagne, 'the vegetarianism and the baby aside – both good things, don't get me wrong – my point is that Tony is really getting on my nerves, especially since we got married.' Her big blue eyes suddenly look philosophical through the haze of alcohol, and she muses, 'Maybe all blokes are rubbish once they become husbands. They just stop trying to impress you once they've got you. Apart from your Jinan, Dee.'

'Yeah, Jinan's just yummy,' agrees Veronica. 'He's like the Mary Poppins of blokes: practically perfect in every way. I could eat him for breakfast, lunch and tea.'

'Not if he gets to it first,' mutters Delphine, breaking her cardinal rule of never showing discontent in front of her friends.

'Hello, do I spy a bit of trouble in paradise?' asks Veronica. 'Has the perfect man finally slipped up?'

Delphine shrugs. 'He's getting fat, that's all. I think he's stressed at work, so he's comfort eating.'

'Perfect,' sighs Katie dreamily. 'He's getting stressed and fat at work so you don't have to. Why can't Tony do that for me?'

'It's not just that,' protests Delphine, feeling a sudden destructive urge to tear down the walls she has built up, guarding the untrue image of a perfect marriage. 'We've not been getting on; we bicker constantly about stupid things; there's so much bad will, it's exhausting. And he keeps giving me these really irritating "to do" lists about what to buy and when to collect the dry-cleaning . . .' She stops, as she can see a mixture of frank disbelief and even irritation in the eyes of her best friends, both of whom work ten- to twelve-hour days while she flits around cafes and does rather little by comparison. Much as she enjoys managing Lucky's affairs, since his contract has been negotiated it has hardly been a full-time job, and one that can be mainly done at home and with her feet up. She knows what they're thinking, they're thinking exactly what Jinan said the evening before Lucky's big match: they're thinking, what else does she have to do with her time?

'OK, Dee, if you're claiming to be a dissatisfied housewife, how about a little pop quiz to get to the nitty-gritty?' Veronica suggests. 'When did you last have sex? When did he last tell you he loved you? Has he ever forgotten a birthday or anniversary? Come on, answer truthfully, you know we won't judge Jinan.' Veronica is clearly indulging her, providing Delphine with valid, cast-iron excuses to moan about her husband, so she won't feel too left out. And Delphine feels utterly disappointed with the answers that she has to give.

'Honestly? You're going to read too much into this,' she sighs. 'This morning. This morning. And never.'

Veronica and Katie look at each other, and put their arms around Delphine. 'Aaw! Poor baby!' says Veronica, unable to keep a straight face. 'That thoughtless bastard. How dare he still make love to you, and worse, tell you he loves you after sixteen years of marriage? It's just bad manners! If he had any decency he'd work harder on being impotent, surly and forgetful.'

'If it was anyone else I wouldn't have believed it,' says Katie, before pleading, 'Please can I have your life? Or just your man? Please!'

Delphine laughs despite herself. At the same time, she realizes her friends won't let her be like them: dissatisfied and hard-done-by. They need her to be successful, in her marriage, in her independence from the rat race, as otherwise they have nothing to aspire to. If she can't enjoy her life of unthinking ease and an adoring, wealthy husband, what hope do they have?

A bottle of champagne arrives in an ostentatiously branded ice bucket, and they all cheer. 'Who ordered Veuve Clicquot?' asks Delphine, as the slim waitress, looking effortlessly and annoyingly chic in jeans and a strappy top, unwraps the foil. 'I thought we were doing cocktails now?'

'We were,' says Katie, confused. 'I thought you must have ordered it while I was dancing. Ronnie, was it you?'

'Oh, bloody hell,' says Veronica, 'three suits waving their glasses at us at eleven o'clock. They must have ordered it – shall we send it back?' At that moment, the waitress pops the cork ostentatiously, and starts pouring. 'OK, I guess not.'

Katie, however, starts waving excitedly at the three suits and beckons them over, ignoring Delphine and Veronica when they ask her what the hell she is doing. 'Oh, relax,' she tells them. 'The one in the middle is cute. Maybe we can get Ronnie an alternative breeding partner to Derek.'

Veronica looks properly at him. 'The Chinese one with

glasses? You're right, he's got great cheekbones, he looks a bit like Chow.' She sighs, remembering the most promising of her past boyfriends, whom she had broken up with because of his disapproving, culturally insular parents, who barely spoke English despite having lived in London for twenty years. 'Now, Chow and I would have had beautiful children.' She joins Katie in waving, and is soon indulging in flirtatious small-talk. One of the suits, a nice-looking man in his mid-thirties, asks Delphine to dance, and she accepts, as the noise and movement of the dance floor would avoid the unwelcome intimacy of conversation. But even as she dances, she feels an absurd urge to hold her anonymous partner's hand, as though he were her boyfriend, and she has to resist touching him, even though she feels nothing for him. She feels odd, disconnected, as though her body has nothing to do with what is going on inside her head and heart, and her mind is an independent entity that floats freely about her insides without actually touching her – a ghost in the machine. There is, she thinks, something not quite right with her; how can she make love to her husband in the morning, and enjoy making love to him, and yet at the same time be quite coldly aware inside herself that she no longer feels the same towards him? How could she hear the words, 'I love you, I love you so much,' repeated with such sincerity, and yet only conclude that she must leave him? The disconnection might be a sort of illness, she thinks, as though there might equally be a cure. But then she remembers the young girl from Les Landes, the little girl who knew exactly what she wanted from life and was not to be dissuaded from her course by falling for an inappropriate man, a widowed shopkeeper with a teenage son who didn't fit into her vision of bourgeois dinner parties. That girl had been quite happy to enjoy herself with her unsuitable suitor for a summer, knowing that she had no intention of letting it last, but only of letting go. She realizes that there is nothing of that girl left in her, nothing but a thimbleful of ash, and that she was simply impersonating her singing along to Abba in her towel that afternoon, dancing in this club in the early hours. All that is left that links her to that girl, to that previous self, is the disconnection that they share between head, heart and body.

As she gets back to their low-slung seats set away from the dance floor, Veronica is earnestly telling the sympathetic Chow look-alike, 'Maybe I shouldn't have asked him to choose between his family and me, but I don't think I should have had to ask in the first place. Besides, I couldn't go back to Chow, even though we're still friends and meet up occasionally, because that would be going back, and I never go back. You shouldn't, it's always a mistake. But he was lovely,' she adds nostalgically. 'So cute, and *years* younger than my fiancé.'

Delphine couldn't see Katie anywhere, and was astounded to finally spot her slow dancing with the other suit from the group on the dance floor, his face buried in her neck and his hands stroking her back. She nudges Veronica urgently, 'Ronnie, look at Katie! Shouldn't someone have told that guy that Katie's married?'

Veronica looks at Katie and groans. 'For Christ's sake, shouldn't someone tell Katie that Katie's married? She can never hold her drink.' She gets up to go and save Katie from herself.

Delphine hadn't realized that her dance partner had

followed her back from the dance floor; he is looking at her now with genuine admiration. She looks back warily, smiling only slightly; he is probably a couple of years younger than Jinan and has the same fresh-faced, just-washed appearance, despite being in an overheated club. 'Did anyone ever tell you that you're the spitting image of Audrey Hepburn in *Charade*?' he says. 'Although you're a better dancer than she was.'

'You seem a bit young to know Audrey Hepburn movies,' says Delphine politely.

'They're my mum's favourites, I sort of became a fan by proxy,' he says. He really is a nice young man; he probably loves his mother, and he thinks she looks like an elegant film star. She knows she should be touched by his niceness, and by his compliment, yet despite this, disconnected Delphine doesn't feel flattered, she just feels rather embarrassed.

'Then I guess your mum and I would have more in common than you and I do,' she says unthinkingly, only realizing as she says it quite how patronizing she sounds.

Giving the young man an apologetic smile, she gets up and goes over to where Veronica and Katie are now standing at the edge of the dance floor; she is thinking about what Veronica said about going back. Perhaps you shouldn't, perhaps it was a mistake. But sometimes it was the only way to go.

'I'm all in, girls. Do you mind if I head off? I'll grab a cab upstairs,' Delphine says, waving aside protests. She doesn't kiss them goodbye the way she kissed them hello, with a mwah mwah to the air. Instead she kisses them properly, on both cheeks, with warmth and affection, as though touching them is somehow anchoring her to the here and now. As her lips leave Veronica's skin, she whispers, 'Ronnie, I really think you should call Chow.' Then she goes and gets a cab to Curzon Street.

She gets out of the cab at the Mirabelle restaurant, and walks down the street in her fragile, inappropriate shoes. If it rains, it'll be a sign, she thinks, but the sky is clear and even starry. There is no figure in a dinner jacket standing on the street. She feels foolish; she set out searching for ghosts, for a drenched girl and a handsome man on opposite sides of a cold, smart street; now she stands with little hope where the girl once stood, abandoned in the early hours of an early summer morning. She sees the doorman standing under the canopy outside Zaki's club, and goes over to see if he can call her a cab. But before she can ask, a voice comes out of the shadows, 'Della? What are you doing here?'

She doesn't answer his question. 'I didn't think you'd still be here,' she says.

'I was waiting for a cab,' says Zaki. 'And you?'

'I was just waiting,' she replies. 'We can share one, if you like?' She walks over in her unsteady heels and he instinctively reaches out and takes her arm, supporting her.

'How long were you waiting?' he asks. She looks tired and lost and whimsically lovely.

'Too long. About twenty-odd years, I think . . .' she says, and tiptoes up to kiss him lightly on the lips, just as his cab arrives. He feels tired and lost himself now, as though this moment was inevitable; as though the very act of her leaving him late that summer all those years ago was the act that would necessitate her coming back. As inevitable as the turning of the hands of a clock. Once again he feels wholly unable to defend himself against his fate; the cab arrives and he helps her in, opening the door to a place where there was no regret, and no guilt, and no happily-ever-after or what-might-have-been. He opens the door to the past, and gets in himself.

Rolling over in the beige, taupe and cream linen of Delphine's tastefully decorated spare room, Zaki gets out of bed and sits on the edge, looking at Delphine's lovely fine-boned face, perfectly at rest. 'You always make me feel better,' she had murmured, before falling asleep.

He leans over and kisses her hair where it falls on the pillow, so as not to wake her; he remembers that she was always a light sleeper. He remembers a thousand tiny things that he had made himself forget: the slight mole on her inside arm that was almost a freckle; the gentle curve of her back; the way her hands half curl into fists, then relax and open out like flowers. 'You make me feel worse,' he whispers to her, his skin branded where she had touched him, an ache deep down after the excitement and violence of surrender. He feels some guilt, there is no doubt about that, and without resentment he is aware that he has been used; managed, even. But most of all he feels helpless, taken hostage by the slim figure under the sheets, sleeping with innocent ease. Damned by such a slight body. As he dresses and leaves he sees the photo of his younger confident self in the hallway, with trusting teenage Nadya and helpless, cross-looking baby Jinan. He's let all three of them down.

He wants to say, 'I'm sorry,' but he is afraid of succumbing to hypocrisy; he is not sure whether this would be an apology, an excuse or a plea for understanding. What he really wants to say is 'Forgive me. Forgive her,' but he does not know what would expiate, and so he does not dare to say it out loud.

Delphine Loustalot in a Room of Her Own

IN THE EARLY HOURS of the morning after the night before, Delphine dreams that she is living several lives at once. In one life she has remained in Les Landes, she is a supervisor at the Trésor Public, she has married Jean-François, the neighbouring farmer's son, and they have two corn-fed, golden-haired children, with snotty noses and streaming eyes each spring due to all the Aquitaine pollen released from the overabundant greenery, and muddy clothes from tramping with the dogs along the clay paths. She and Jean-François are outwardly content, but he drinks and does nothing about the house, and she has become a slattern in protest, leaving the dishes to pile up until he concedes to her request to buy a dishwasher. They draw together in lonely desperation at night, flesh colliding rather than meeting, and laugh with complicit cruelty at the stupid *anglais* couple who bought the ruin in the fields for an exorbitant sum from his father. *Ils sont tous fous, ces anglais!* Grande-Tante Christiane comes on Wednesdays to watch the children when they are off school, and always arrives with a martyred air, looking at the state of the house and overgrown garden with disapproving eyes. On her departure, she never fails to remind Delphine that she is praying for her, and Delphine, sitting alone in her bedroom while her husband drinks pastis downstairs with his hunting buddies, asks herself, what have I done to deserve this?

In another life, Delphine has stayed in Paris, and on completing her degree does not attempt to be charming or manipulative enough to succeed in her graduate interviews with the marketing departments of the multinationals. She decides not to compromise herself for the sake of success in some anonymous corporation, and continues her studies. She becomes an academic, sympathetically reading Virginia Woolf and Simone de Beauvoir. She abruptly dismisses Rimbaud as a spoilt, foolish boy, and Sartre as a spoilt, self-important man. The former's beauty does not move her any more than the latter's plainness. She takes lovers, in both glorious and humiliating circumstances, but does not come across a man interesting or individual enough to marry, and it never becomes a sufficient priority to look for one. She looks with undisguised pity, perhaps even malice, at gooey-eyed mothers cooing over their dumpy offspring in the Jardin du Luxembourg, at suited businessmen braying into their mobiles as they ascend from the metro. She knows better than them; she is intellectual and independent, and while she walks with a determined step to her lectures and the library during crisp Parisian mornings, she unconsciously quotes her admired Mrs Woolf: What a lark! What a plunge! She is Clarissa Dalloway without the vicarious suicide, she is Isabel Archer without the poorly chosen husband, she is Jane Eyre without the banal happy ending;

she is better than all of them, as she is destined to be simply Herself. Her mind is like a golden bowl to which a new nugget of knowledge is added each day like a trinket, and she records all of its vicissitudes and intensely laboured thoughts with earnest dedication in her journal, for fear that its richness may be lost to posterity. Unfettered by family or material possessions, unbothered by the troublesome need to love or be loved in return, the journal is her preoccupation, and her sole occupation, apart from the one that pays her rent. And so, every evening, she sits alone in her small studio apartment, irritated by the constant creaking of the ancient plumbing, trying to marshal her subtle grey feelings, jumbled with splashes of embittered colour, into a black and white coherence that can be captured on a page. One such evening, a single thought comes to her through the buzz of her unconscious rambling, and although she dismisses it, it returns more insistently until she is forced to acknowledge it; she has never, she realizes, felt passion. She notices that she is simply a penniless, friendless spinster alone in a room, and she asks herself, what have I done to deserve this?

In another, closer life, Delphine has gone to London, where she charms, manipulates and compromises until she has become wildly successful in her chosen career and becomes a marketing director for a multinational at a surprisingly young age. She meets a handsome, unsuitable man in a taxi and begins a passionate love affair. She leaves him, and eventually finds a more eligible candidate to be her partner in life and love, and she escapes the cage of the boardroom to become a pampered Knightsbridge socialite, a perfect wife and mother. She is beautiful and liberated, appreciated by her family, envied by her peers. She has an income and a room of her own; she is blessed, and she asks herself, with breathy appreciation, looking at her chic surroundings, how did I get so lucky, what did I do to deserve all this?

In her final life, Delphine still goes to London, becomes successful and meets a handsome, unsuitable man in a taxi. And she stays in the cab, looking only at him, looking only at her. But this life has only just begun.

Delphine examines herself critically in the bathroom mirror. She is naked after her shower and her skin looks clear and flawless, even in the unforgiving morning light. It is just a few hours since she slept with Zaki and she finds it hard to believe that this experience, this misdeed, has left her unmarked. There is no damned spot to wash from her hand, no scarlet letter burned on her breast; she has never looked better. It seems as though she has got away with it. This thought fills her with a sudden, unreasonable fear; she has no intention of getting away with it, of abandoning what-might-have-been once more. She dresses quickly, her face unmade up, her hair pulled back into a ponytail. She races out of the apartment, down the three flights of stairs, and almost falls over Zaki sitting on the bottom step above the ground floor landing, with his coffee in a paper cup.

'Hello Della,' he says. 'You're in a hurry. Don't let me keep you.' He sips his coffee calmly, with too much concentration, looking out to the street through the glass panelling next to the front door.

'You didn't go too far,' replies Delphine breathlessly. His nonchalance is disconcerting and she sits next to him warily.

'Yes, I did,' he contradicts her. 'I went home, got changed and I came back. Then I thought I shouldn't have come back, so I went away again. I got as far as the cafe on the corner, then decided to come back after all. But then I couldn't decide what to do, so I just stayed here, on the step. And then you arrived.' He says all of this without looking at Delphine, then adds, 'I've just ended it with Ayesha, by the way.'

'Oh,' says Delphine inadequately. She pauses, and asks, 'Why?' and then feels foolish, as she already knows why.

Zaki looks at her with frustration, as though she is choosing to be deliberately dense. He shrugs his shoulders and says lightly, 'Well, no matter. It was never going to last, anyway, with me and Ayesha. We knew we were going to break up; it was just a matter of when. Her husband's coming back this year.'

'I thought she was separated, and he'd moved outside London,' says Delphine.

'Well, yes, but not entirely through choice. He's in Ford Open Prison, doing white-collar porridge for tax fraud. According to Ayesha he's quite enjoyed the time off; he's learned how to cook, garden and even improved his golf handicap. They should charge for that kind of rest cure; charge the inmates, I mean, not the taxpayers. Given that not all inmates are taxpayers anyway, as Ayesha's old man can testify.' Having taken temporary refuge in being glib, Zaki finishes his coffee and looks a bit sadly at it. Delphine is reminded of the expression that Jinan adopts once he's finished his dinner; it's not often that she sees any familial resemblance between Zaki and Jinan and it seems poignant, and somewhat poorly timed, that she should notice something now. Zaki sees her watching him, and explains, 'I was going to make a decision about whether to come and see you when I'd finished my coffee. I've finished it now, but I still haven't made a decision.'

'But I'm here now, anyway,' Delphine points out.

'Oh, you are, aren't you? Thanks for that, Della. Helpful as always,' Zaki says. He reaches for Delphine's hand and squeezes it just slightly before pulling her up by it. 'Why don't you come with me for another coffee, if you're not going anywhere? Maybe I'll be able to decide by the second cup.' He rubs her hands briskly; they are always cold, even on a warm day. Cold hands, warm heart, he thinks, remembering with a sudden painful flash the tingle of her cool hands sliding up his back in the early hours of that morning, the muffled sound of her excited heartbeat through the damp skin of her chest. His gut clenches with a spasm of desire, and he drops her hands abruptly and turns away. He is embarrassed by how he feels; he shouldn't feel passion any more. He's not a movie star or a rock musician who might be expected to have romantic entanglements and start new marriages and families in his fifties. He is a shopkeeper and a dilettante gambler who has already lived more than half his life. He is a grandparent. He should expect to spend the next thirty-odd years in a state of ease, illness and eventual decline. He shouldn't be indulging in his illicit, suppressed feelings for his son's wife. What would the extended, estranged family think of their liaison? he wonders. The neighbours, the friends and acquaintances?

Disgusting, filthy, incestuous, they would sniff; such a sordid affair. He's old enough to be her father. 'But I'm not!' Zaki would object. 'There's barely twelve years between us. I'm hardly old enough to be Jinan's father, let alone hers!' And how could they do such a thing to poor Jinan, who was such a hard-working son and faithful husband, so faultless and practically perfect in every way? 'But I found her first!' Zaki would cry impotently, although there was no one in the sniffing moral brigade who would listen. 'I was with her first!'

Delphine pulls him back to sit beside her again. 'OK, I'll come for a coffee. But I need to tell you something.' She takes both his hands and tells him urgently, 'I made a mistake.'

Zaki feels the liquid in his gut turn to lead and tries not to sigh; well, that was it then. She'd made the decision for both of them. Last night had probably just been about comfort and escape; instead of providing a safe, sympathetic ear for her to vent her frustrations, he'd provided a safe, sympathetic body. She'd used him, that was all, and he could hardly complain, as he clearly hadn't minded. He should have known better, he thinks with bitter disappointment; what was he thinking, dumping Ayesha and racing back here to sit like a lovesick schoolboy on her steps? When was he going to grow up, and start acting his age instead of his shoe size? 'Of course you did, Della—' he says wearily; he doesn't want her to say any more.

'No, you don't understand,' she interrupts. 'I made a mistake twenty years ago when I left you – I made the wrong choice. It's all but over between me and Jinan; I'm going to leave him.'

'You've said that before,' says Zaki, not daring to feel hopeful so soon after feeling humiliated. 'You were thinking about it fourteen months ago, and you even said it sixteen years ago.' In the weeks leading up to Delphine's wedding, she had once confessed to Zaki that she didn't really love Jinan and that she intended to call it off. Then she went and married him anyway. Perhaps it was time for Delphine to face the truth. 'Maybe you're fonder of Jinan than you think.'

'I will leave him,' insists Delphine. 'I need to find the right time, that's all, because I don't want to hurt him.' Trembling slightly because of the tense way Zaki is looking at her, his face taut and stiff as though he doesn't quite believe her, she adds, 'Of course I'm fond of Jinan; we've raised Lucky together, and he loves me. But don't you think it's time for me to be with someone I love, for a change? I think we both know who the true love of my life should have been . . .'

Delphine doesn't say any more as Zaki pushes her back violently against the stairs and holds her there for a moment, looking intently at her unmade-up face, her damp, scraped back hair, before kissing her passionately and unreservedly in the tidy communal hallway where anyone could walk in from the street or down from the flats and see them. But Delphine doesn't care. Pinned between the roughly carpeted stairs and the hard wall of Zaki's chest, she feels pinned back to her real life, the one that she hasn't started living yet, the one with the unknown ending that might turn out to be happy ever after. She feels as though her body is conducting lightning to the ground, and holds on to him with painful tightness in case the world spins out of place, when Zaki pulls back and sees tears welling in her grey eyes. 'God, Della, I'm sorry – did I hurt you?' He slides his hands up behind her back and shoulders, rubbing them where they collided with the staircase.

She shakes her head. 'No, you couldn't. Hurt me, I mean. Ever.' Reassured, he pulls her by the hand and drags her out of the front door to the street. 'Are we going for that coffee?' she asks in confusion.

'Sod the coffee,' says Zaki, 'we're going home.' He hails a cab, gives his corner shop address, and they bundle into it so quickly that it is almost comic. 'I've always liked you in cabs – they suit you somehow,' he says, pulling her into his arms and kissing her again, less urgently, but with slow tenderness, her skin melting under her clothes like chocolate. Home, thinks Delphine happily between kisses, is where you're trying to get back to.

A Teenager's Fear of Intimacy

LUCKY IS WORRIED about losing Portia. While he is training with the youth academy and struggling with his GCSEs, she is already talking about the A levels she intends to do. If she decides to go to university, he'll never manage to keep her – she'll hang out in scruffy bars accompanied by sensitive boys with stripy college scarves and double-barrelled names, and have clever conversations about obscure things. Lucky can never think of anything clever to say and is, on occasion, amazed by his stupidity. Just the other day there was some word game on TV, where you had to guess a word from its alternative meaning, and he had been genuinely astonished by the fact that 'quiver' did not just mean to shake, but was also the word for the things that arrows are kept in. He was similarly surprised that 'pride' meant a group of lions, as well as the quality of being a bit smug. He had been watching the show with Portia, and had hidden his shock; he wondered how many other words he had been innocently using, unaware of their other meanings, as though the world had a secret code into which he had not been initiated.

As if it were not already enough that Portia was too clever for him, the rest of the world had begun to notice her adorable, unspoiled beauty, and a scout for a model agency had asked her to go in to see them. Portia had been flattered by the scout, an elegant woman in her thirties with immaculate accessories, in the way she had never been flattered by crude male attention. She agreed to visit the agency after she'd finished her GCSEs.

Lucky can think of just two ways of keeping Portia before she soars out of his grasp: to marry her, or failing that, at least sleep with her, as he has heard on good authority that girls are always attached to their first. As he is just sixteen, marriage is not really an option; besides, he has broached the subject with Portia and she thought that he was joking.

'No one marries at sixteen unless they're knocked up or forced into it by fundamentalist parents,' she said dismissively. Lucky's argument that his grandmother had been married at sixteen fell flat, as he was suddenly unsure whether she might have been knocked up or forced into it.

As for the subject of sex, Lucky has no idea how to approach this with her; he knows lots about the theory, but has had no practice (his private practice on himself notwithstanding). If he were to believe his friends, which he doesn't, he would be the only virgin both in his class and on his team. Portia has shown no sign that she is keen to move their relationship on to this stage; it is true that she kisses him passionately in parks and in public places, her hands roving promisingly until he quite literally throbs, and the other day she sighed with longing under the willow tree in Hyde Park, as though it was as painful to her as it was to him that they couldn't go further. But in the privacy of their bedrooms, when they are home alone and meant to be doing homework and revision, she only shows interest in doing ... well, homework and revision. And when he tries to kiss her or put his hand somewhere more interesting than his GSCE physics file, she distractedly returns the kiss, returns his hand and carries on working, while he retreats in abashed embarrassment.

Lucky is not sure what to make of this public demonstrativeness and private reserve; if he was the sort to sneak a peek at his mum's posh women's magazines and read all the gross articles about shagging and emotions, which he wasn't, he would diagnose this as Fear of Intimacy. The only way he can think of getting over Portia's possible Fear of Intimacy is to get carried away with her somewhere public enough for her to feel safe enough to begin, but private enough to continue. However, he has no idea where this somewhere publicly private might be, and if she were happy to get carried away, how could he produce condoms in a way that wouldn't look manipulative and cynical? She'd probably slap him and walk off if she thought he'd planned anything, and accuse him, unjustly, of being a sex-obsessed adolescent intent solely on getting into her pants, when of course he was anything but.

Inspiration comes to him one afternoon when he stops by at Zaki's. The bell on the corner shop door jingles as he walks in, but the shop is empty. Zaki has probably nipped off to the bookies, so while Lucky is waiting, he surreptitiously pulls out a glossy magazine from the shelf and scans it quickly. Disgusting, just as he thought. Porn for girls. He is leaning back against the counter reading an article about the Emotionally Unavailable Man, when he accidentally knocks over Zaki's coffee from the counter top. 'Fucking shit,' he yelps in agony and utter surprise, as the coffee is still scaldingly hot and runs down his arm. 'Ouch, fucking ouch!'

'Lucky?' shouts Zaki from upstairs. He runs down, looking distracted and out of sorts; his hair is messed up and his buttons aren't done up properly. 'What the hell are you doing here? Why aren't you at school?' he demands, before adding, 'And why were you reading *that*?'

'Double free period for revision, so I left early,' says Lucky, wincing. 'Look, this is agony, I've got to get some cold water on it.' He starts to go upstairs, but is yanked back suddenly with surprising force by Zaki.

'Not up there, son. Use the garden tap, it's closer. Run it for at least five minutes.' He pushes Lucky towards the garden.

'Why were you upstairs? Were you having a nap?' asks Lucky, running the tap over his arm. He might be dense, but he wasn't so dense not to realize that something had been going on.

'Yes, I was having a nap,' says Zaki, 'and I'm going to finish it, so put the closed sign on the door on your way out.'

'Then why did you make a fresh cup of coffee just before?' persists Lucky.

'To keep me awake, of course, but then I decided I was too tired to bother fighting it,' replies Zaki smoothly, without hesitation.

'Bullshit,' laughs Lucky. 'Come on, Dada, tell me. What dragged you upstairs at such short notice? Was it a race you'd forgotten about, or a girl?' Looking at Zaki's mismatched buttons, he answers his own question: 'It's a girl, isn't it?'

'It's a fucking French farce, is what it is,' mutters Zaki. 'Get yourself home before I tell your mother you're skipping school, or tell Portia that her big pansy of a boyfriend was caught reading *Marie Claire*.'

Lucky heads home happily enough, as he realizes that he has found the perfect public–private place, with ready access to condoms. It's so obvious, he can't believe he hasn't thought of it before. He and Portia are always at the corner shop – it wouldn't be that hard for them to come at a time when Zaki was skiving off, maybe meeting his new girlfriend. And they could get carried away in the public shop, but this time they'd have somewhere to go to take it further; they could just go upstairs. It could be impetuous, unplanned, and it would make Portia his forever. His mother isn't there when he gets home, so he guiltily pulls out the coffee-stained *Marie Claire* that he has stolen and stuffed into his bag; there is an article on 'The Other C Word: Commitment' that he thinks he had better mug up on.

The Vicious Cycle of Marital Harmony

DELPHINE AND JINAN are eating breakfast together on a Sunday morning; Lucky has left early, as he's attending a workshop on media training that his academy manager has sent him to. Jinan has made himself grilled sausages and vine-ripened baby plum tomatoes; he hasn't made himself any fried eggs, in fact he hasn't made any for a long while, so Delphine's worktop remains spotless. He has also made toast for both of them, crisped to golden perfection and buttered carefully right up to the edges. He has used real butter for Delphine, and low-fat spread with cholesterol-reducing qualities for himself.

'Wow, darling. Utterly perfect toast,' says Delphine appreciatively, sipping her second cappuccino.

'Not bad, is it?' says Jinan, shiny from his exertions at the grill and clearly pleased with the compliment. 'The trick is to set it for two minutes exactly. And these tomatoes are gorgeous, where did you find them?'

'That new food emporium on the corner, where the Indian restaurant used to be. They've got some farmers' market type stuff in there, I thought I might pop in after breakfast and pick up some cheese to try out with supper tonight,' Delphine says.

'I've been meaning to have a look in there – why don't I come with you?' suggests Jinan. There is a pause filled with comfortable silence, then Delphine looks at the fridge. Something is wrong. Something is missing.

'Darling, where's your list for this week? Haven't you had time to do it?'

Jinan suddenly looks very serious. 'Oh God, we mustn't forget my list!' He dashes out and returns almost instantly from his study, trying to suppress a smile and looking very mischievous. He sticks it on the fridge with exaggerated care, and Delphine can see just one line, in thick marker pen.

'"Keep Friday Free"?' she reads. 'With triple exclamation marks? That's your list for this week?' Her mind is racing; what was she meant to have done for Friday? Was that when Jinan's Aunt Padma from Bangladesh was planning to stop by and see them?

'Yep, the good ship Khalil is on course and steady as she goes, and there's absolutely nothing that needs doing. So that's all you have to do this week, darling. Keep Friday free,' replies Jinan. He is as carefree as a little boy.

From the undiluted happiness of his tone, Delphine finally realizes that this is not a complicated way in which he is trying to show her up, and asks pertly, responding in kind, 'And may I ask why?'

'You may not,' says Jinan, 'as that would be telling.'

Delphine sighs. 'Oh, honestly, Jinan. You know you can't keep a secret to save your life. Tell me now and save yourself the trauma of not knowing when you'll give it away.' She adds wheedlingly, 'And I know you want to tell, anyway.'

Jinan purses his lips, tries and fails to avoid breaking into a smile, then gives in: 'Oh, go on then. I'm taking Friday off and I'm whisking you away for the weekend to Paris. I've booked the George Cinq for Friday and Saturday night.'

'My God! How sweet! I've always wanted to stay at the George Cinq,' exclaims Delphine. 'When I was a student we used to have coffees there and pretend we were residents.'

'I know!' says Jinan, just a little bit smugly. 'I just wanted to thank you for the last few months. I know you've been trying so hard, and it feels that we're . . . back to where we should be.'

'But what about your Saturday golf, and what about Lucky?' asks Delphine, still smiling but suddenly feeling very uncomfortable.

'Oh, bugger golf. And Lucky's away next weekend with the team – I checked,' says Jinan, before leaning in towards Delphine. 'I just wanted to do something to show that I love you. I love you so much,' he puts his arms around her and kisses her gently on the back of her neck, between her night-time plaits that she hasn't yet taken out. His lips feel very soft, and Delphine knows with certainty that he will want to make love that evening. Uncomplicated lovemaking, tender rather than passionate, with responses that are practised and automatic, and that she will acquiesce and enjoy the feeling of physical closeness and lack of controversy in the arrangement. Their married lips, their acceptable and wholly unremarkable married love.

It was an odd fact, Delphine realized, that as soon as she had started an affair with her husband's father, her marriage had immediately begun to improve. Everything was inexplicably better between herself and the man she had determined to leave. Perhaps it wasn't quite so inexplicable, as she herself had been happier. Reunited with Zaki, she felt like a girl in love again, and she felt free; her gilded cage, the ties of her perfect marriage and perfect Knightsbridge home, could no longer bind her. She wasn't strained and discontented around Jinan any more, she was relaxed and even cheerful, as she knew that the next bitter argument would be their last; she didn't have to put up with it any more, she would just walk away.

Even though she was happier herself, and she had every intention of coming clean to Jinan at the right moment, she still felt a twinge of guilt about the affair, and genuine sorrow for the hurtful blow that she was soon to deal him. As a result, she found she was being much, much nicer to him. When he had come back from New York, she had welcomed him like a returning hero. She had made him wonderful meals without resentment; she had listened to his work stories without interrupting or displaying obvious signs of boredom; she had accepted his little insights on topics varying from property prices to her household management without censure; she had even stopped snapping at him about the many small things he did that irritated her.

Jinan, touchingly lacking in any sort of suspicion, had not questioned the sudden change in the household climate. But he had responded to her sunnier mood, to her kinder treatment and lack of criticism, by blossoming like a flower. He'd reined in his comfort eating, had become appreciative of every trivial thing she did, had stopped being even slightly argumentative and begun to behave with an almost puppy-like docility, seeking her approval in a boyish way that might have been funny if it wasn't so heartbreaking. He loved her, he loved her so much. What did he really mean, wondered Delphine, when he said those words, this motherless man who had never had anyone to say them to before? She thought perhaps he really meant to say, 'Please tell me that you love me, please tell me that I'm good.' She would have to be made of stone not to comfort him, not to give him the affection he craved. It was, she considered, a vicious cycle of perpetual marital harmony: the more she knew she would leave their marriage, the happier she became; the happier she became, the better their marriage became; the better their marriage became, the harder it was to leave.

'You're what?' says Zaki in shocked exasperation. It is the middle of the afternoon, and he is wearing a chunky white towelling robe stolen from a hotel and making coffee in the flat above the corner shop. Delphine is in the bath; she will pretend to Jinan and Lucky that she went swimming, but in fact she is washing off the scent of Zaki from her skin, although she does not admit this even to herself. She had walked in through the back garden gate and they had made love almost immediately; complicated and passionate love, illicit and controversial love, during which she did nothing nearly so dull as acquiesce. They had barely made it to the top of the staircase, and it was only the carpet burn and bruises from the hard edge of the stairs that had eventually got them into the bedroom.

'Going to Paris this weekend, with Jinan,' repeats Delphine. 'So I won't be able to come over on Friday.'

'But why Paris? Are you seeing family or something?' asks Zaki, walking over to the end of the kitchen, where he can see her through the open bathroom door.

'You know I don't have any family in Paris,' replies Delphine.

'So, this is . . . what, exactly? Some kind of . . .' he half sniggers, as though he is making an unfunny joke, as though he is trying not to believe what he is saying, '. . . *romantic* weekend?' When Delphine doesn't contradict him, but simply shrugs with a kind of sheepish embarrassment, Zaki mutters, 'Oh, bloody hell,' and storms out of sight.

When Delphine gets out of the bath, using her own towel that she packed for her fake swimming trip, she can't see Zaki anywhere in the flat and the latte that he has made for her is cooling on the kitchen counter. Picking it up, she sips it, dresses and goes downstairs to the shop, where she sees him moodily marking up the *Racing Post*.

'Still here, then?' he says darkly. 'You've had your fun, I'm surprised you hung around for the cuddle.'

'Don't be like that. It's not my fault he booked the trip,' says Delphine.

'Yes it is!' contradicts Zaki. 'You're encouraging him to think there's some hope. He shouldn't be booking surprise trips to Paris, he should be secretly consulting divorce lawyers and telling his friends what a bitch you are. You're meant to be leaving him, remember?'

'And I will,' says Delphine soothingly, feeling a guilty thrill for the jealousy that Zaki is showing. She puts her arms around Zaki from behind, and presses herself against his straight, broad back.

'Well, when then?' he snaps petulantly, not responding to her embrace.

'I'm waiting for the right time. It's difficult when he's trying so hard, and thinks that everything's going so well. I can't just say, "Well, that was another pleasant day, thank you for all the kind attention, and by the way, I'm leaving you." It would be too much of a shock for him, it would just come out of the blue. If we had a fight, if we were arguing, then I could tell him; he'd at least be a little bit prepared. I just don't want to hurt him more than I have to.'

'Well, I'm all for not hurting Jinan more than we have to,' says Zaki, not quite mollified, turning to face her. 'But I don't believe for an instant that he's as unprepared as you think. He's not stupid, you know. We've been together for a few months now, he must realize that something's not right between you two. And this Paris trip is just plain weird. If you can't tell him now, how are you going to tell him after a romantic trip to Paris?' He pauses. 'And how are you going to avoid, you know . . . doing . . . making . . . having . . .' he hesitates, and seeing no glimmer of comprehension on Delphine's solemn face, just says it: 'Sex! How are you going to get out of having sex on a romantic trip away?'

Delphine's eyes widen, and she bites her lower lip unconsciously, something she does when she is uncertain or confused. She hadn't realized that Zaki thought she wasn't making love to Jinan; she was still his wife, after all. She realizes that her vapid assumption was rather thoughtless, and simply convenient for her own purposes. 'Zaki, I didn't—' she starts to say.

'Fucking hell, Della. You're still sleeping with him, aren't you?' interrupts Zaki, in complete and utter horror. He backs away from her, and when she doesn't deny it, he looks at her as though she's the worst sort of slut alive. 'How could you?'

'I thought you knew,' she says in a small, tremulous voice, adding in a smaller voice still, 'We're married,' as though that might explain it. How could she explain her curious disease to Zaki, her disconnection between her head, heart and body? How could she explain that she can be in love with Zaki, that she might even believe herself to be passionately and madly in love, with all the youthful recklessness that she didn't allow herself in her twenties, but still not mind sitting up in bed and reading the papers with Jinan. That she doesn't mind Jinan making love to her, and even enjoys the feeling of his flesh next to hers, the softness around his middle, the tickle of the hairs on his arms. A tiny persistent voice was nagging at her: why should she have to explain? Shouldn't he, of all people, understand at least this much about her already?

Zaki sits back down, as though he's been punched in the stomach. He suddenly looks very tired and weary. 'Of course – you're married. How silly of me not to have noticed. I must be getting senile.' Mad old, bad old, old old Chacha Zaki. A stupid old man chasing a dream, when he knew that all his dreams were gone. A cab in Montmartre in Paris, and a cab on Curzon Street in London; all just part of the same big road accident colliding to determine his fate. 'Please go away, Della. Just go.'

'I don't want to go away like this,' she says, trying hard not to cry. 'I'm so sorry, Zaki. I just thought you knew. It doesn't change anything; you must know how I feel about you.'

'I thought I did,' says Zaki, 'but then I thought I knew how you felt about Jinan, and I got that wrong. You clearly don't dislike him enough to stop sleeping with him.' He adds bitterly, 'Tell me, what's it like? Do you shut your eyes and think of England? Or even France, for that matter?'

Delphine can see that he is truly upset, but she has no intention of letting him go over something so . . . so . . . trivial, really. If it had been the other way around, if he had been the married one, she would have fully expected him to sleep with his wife; what were a few more nights of perfunctory marital sex when compared with the promise of a lifetime of happily ever after? 'Do you honestly want to know?' she says. 'Because it wasn't my intention to mislead you, and I don't want to be anything but honest with you. So I'll tell you if you want to know.'

'So tell me,' says Zaki. He doesn't mean it to come out sounding like a challenge, but it does anyway.

'It's fine. It's good, even. That's all,' she says quietly.

Zaki shakes his head, wishing he hadn't asked. 'Is sex just a habit with you, Della? Is it something that just happens after brushing your teeth and before your shower, just another part of your routine? Doesn't it mean something?'

'It means something with you,' Delphine says sincerely; she feels that Zaki is the only one upon whom her head, her heart and her body have ever agreed. Didn't he know what she was prepared to give up for him?

Zaki looks at her; she is pale with concern. He finds it hard to equate this damp, well-scrubbed angel with some grubby *femme fatale* who would cold-bloodedly sleep with two men for her own amusement. 'Are you using me, Della?'

Delphine sighs. 'I don't know how you can even suggest that.'

Zaki breathes deeply; he was older, perhaps he could sometimes – admittedly very occasionally – be wiser. It didn't escape him that she hadn't actually answered his question. 'Maybe you don't mean to, but you are. Maybe you really are fonder of Jinan than you like to admit.'

Delphine crosses the distance separating them and puts her arms around him again; he doesn't shrink or shake her off, nor does he dare to lean into her. 'I'll stop sleeping with Jinan. I won't go to Paris. I'll leave Jinan soon, I promise. Please trust me.'

'I don't trust you,' says Zaki, but then he pulls her onto his lap, and kisses her passionately. 'But I do love you, so I don't have very much choice.' Delphine is unsure what to say to this strange, mixed-up confession, but she isn't able to argue with him, as his insistent embrace distracts her. So she sits there in the corner shop, in full view of the street, kissing him back, just glad that the episode appears to be over.

The Dark Side of Love

LUCKY HAS ALWAYS known that there is something dark about Portia; he feels it in her sudden bursts of anger and abortive passion, and in the fragile sweetness of her concern. He feels it bubbling under the surface of her perfect skin; he doesn't know how he should deal with it, and so he simply accepts it, and embraces it as part of who Portia is. He likes to think that since they have been together, she has become rather more cheerful than the tragic, melancholic, undeniably interesting teenager she was when they first met. Although a small part of him, disloyally, doesn't want his Portia to become too happy, as he suspects that what makes her so interesting to him is precisely that bad-tempered melancholy. And much as this quality attracts him, it also has the additional benefit of putting off others; how else could he explain how he has managed to be with Portia for so long, a girl who is lovely and clever, whereas he's a gangly goalie with a smattering of teenage acne and nothing but the far-off promise of perhaps, one day, becoming known to followers of the beautiful game as a premiership footballer in the least loved position on the pitch.

Lucky struggles to marshal these confusing thoughts as he walks with Portia towards the corner shop, wishing that he had Zaki's clarity of expression. He is slightly ashamed of his selfishness, of the fact that he would rather have Portia be unhappy with him, than happy without him. He is so distracted by this that he has almost forgotten his undeclared purpose for taking Portia to the corner shop in the first place; he has been hoping that with their exams finally over, results counted and received, with him playing full time for his team and Portia having signed on at the interested model agency, that they might finally get round to having some sex. He is almost certain that now he really is the only virgin in his team. Portia notices his distraction and squeezes his hand.

'What's up? Are you thinking about the England Under-18 selection?'

'You what?' says Lucky, surprised. 'No, I'm not thinking about it at all. If it happens, it happens.' He considers this, and adds, 'Although I reckon I've got a good chance; most of the young goalkeepers aren't that good, I don't think. They're all a bit mad, goalkeepers, really.'

'You're a goalkeeper, too, remember?' says Portia. She is looking very pretty today, in an outrageously pink summer skirt and a crumpled cotton vest. Lucky doesn't like her dressed like this, in a girly way; he prefers her long perfect legs safely hidden in her baggy jeans. Fortunately, lots of other pretty girls come out in summer, with long flicky hair and little dresses showing off uniform expanses of bare, brown skin, so at least she doesn't stand out too much.

'Yeah, I know. I still don't feel like one. Sometimes I

think that I might still get a chance to play midfield, even after all this time; course, it's never going to happen,' says Lucky.

With that fragile concern of hers, as though she was really testing her capacity for tenderness rather than comforting him, Portia says reassuringly, 'Goalkeeper's an important position. Maybe even the most important. Every other player is expendable, but you can't play without a keeper.'

'Yeah, well, goalkeeper isn't so much a position as a bloody predicament,' mutters Lucky, repeating something he heard Zaki say once. 'And a keeper can't win a game for you. They can just stop you from losing.'

'You'll be happier about being a keeper once you're famous,' says Portia confidently. Lucky sighs; it's touching how Portia and his mother are so convinced that he will be famous, in fact, it's as though he is almost famous already. Famous-in-waiting. He's been famous-in-waiting for over a year now, and his future is by no means assured; if the club doesn't think he's good enough, they could release him from his contract without ceremony at the next renewal date.

'Prince of Wales,' says Portia suddenly, as they get to Zaki's. The door to the corner shop is open.

'Oh, he's in,' says Lucky, unable to keep the disappointment from his voice, and realizing belatedly how suspicious that disappointment might seem. He hopes that Portia hasn't guessed his impure intentions for the visit. She looks at him curiously, and before she can question him, he asks, 'What was that about the Prince of Wales?'

'What you just said: not a position but a predicament. That's a line from a play – being Prince of Wales isn't so much a position as a predicament. Can't remember which play, though,' she says, walking into the shop and leaning against the counter top. 'Zaki would know.' She pulls out a packet and lights herself a foul-smelling fag, trying and failing to ignore the face that Lucky makes. 'What?' she says in irritation.

'I wish you wouldn't,' he says, annoyed that his poorly laid plan has failed.

'Why, because it's like snogging an ashtray?' she says, bridling sarcastically.

'No, because each one takes three minutes off your life, and I kind of like having you around. I'd like to have you around for as long as I possibly can,' says Lucky. The tension disappears from Portia's face, and she puts her arms around Lucky and pulls him to her, kissing him with her smoky mouth, the flimsy fabric of her skirt feeling like nothing at all against his legs. She sighs as his hands slide down towards her bottom, with all the promise that she has shown so many times before, when she is sure that they will not be able to finish what they start. She slips her hand inside the back of his jeans and pulls him closer to her, so that his crotch is pressing against her, beginning to bulge uncomfortably. 'Zaki might come down any minute,' says Lucky, pulling back. His Dada couldn't be too far, his day's deliveries were still untidily piled all over the floor in firmly sealed boxes.

'I know,' says Portia regretfully. She picks up the abandoned cigarette, and takes a long drag before it burns out.

'Zaki? You there?' she calls out. There is no answer, but Orla from the neighbouring cafe sticks her head around the shop doorway.

'Oh great, you're here. Would you close up for your grandda', Lucky? The fine-looking eejit's buggered off again and left me to collect all his deliveries. I'll be giving him an awful slagging when I see him.'

'Sure, Orla,' says Lucky. 'Has he gone off to the races?'

'He's all over the gaff, that one; he's not been here all weekend. Probably off with some floozy,' says Orla, casting a dark and significant look towards the two of them, still standing in dubiously close proximity, before pulling the door shut with a firm and disapproving bang, so that the bell over the door jingles in sharp alarm, and the lock clicks shut.

Lucky can't believe his luck, and lets out a short, embarrassed laugh. 'So, where were we?' he asks shyly, leaning back towards Portia, and sliding his hands precariously up her legs, as though he expects her to slap him away at any moment. Portia, however, surrenders to the embrace, and kisses him back with enthusiasm; when he lifts her up on the counter top, so she can kiss him without getting a sore neck, she even wraps her legs around him. And then, something happens, and she begins to terrify him with the ferocity of her response, her soft caresses turning to digging nails into his back, and her warm, swollen kisses to fierce, biting teeth. It is as though she is trying to obliterate any semblance of babyish affection from their embrace. Lucky feels inadequate and totally unprepared for the unprecedented violence in her touch; he supposes that this must be passion, but he isn't enjoying it very much. In fact, he is no longer enjoying it at all. Portia pulls at Lucky's jean buttons, and he wonders if she is intending to fuck him there and then; he can't describe this as making love. 'I guess we should go upstairs,' mutters Lucky, no longer wanting to.

'Too far,' says Portia breathlessly, swinging her legs around to the other side of the counter, then slipping off, pushing Lucky down on the vinyl flooring there. She straddles him and kisses him furiously, biting his lower lip until Lucky thinks it might even bleed. He is suddenly aware that he is just a little, inexperienced boy, when all is said and done, and that Portia, not even a year older than him, knows more about everything, even though they have been together since she was fifteen, and she is as virginal as he is. As she pulls off his shirt, he wishes that they were back in a park or somewhere where he could stop all this without seeming like an idiot or a coward. He has fantasized about making love to Portia many times, and it has never been on a grubby vinyl floor; it has been in a bedroom, somewhere he might fiddle with her bra unsuccessfully until she helps him to remove it, laughing indulgently at his ineptitude. He has imagined lowering himself on to her while she holds on to him and gasps. He hasn't expected this feeling of helplessness as he lies flat on his back, almost as though he is being violated. He could cry, that the longed-for moment of finally getting it together with Portia is scaring him so much. It's like Santa Claus turning out to be the bogey monster.

Without warning, Portia tears herself away from him and throws herself, sobbing, into the corner. 'I can't! I just can't! God, Lucky, I'm so sorry.' Overcome with relief at the sudden reprieve, Lucky goes to her, hastily doing his jeans back up.

'It's OK, Portia. It is, really. Don't cry.' He thinks about saying something to put the blame on him, something like 'Sorry I rushed you,' but it was so patently untrue that he just didn't think it would be comforting. 'I'm not sure I was ready either, don't worry.'

'I really wanted to, Lucky, honestly. I don't want you thinking I'm some kind of prick-tease . . .'

'I'd never think that,' says Lucky, putting his shirt back on before she can change her mind. 'Look, let's go next door to Orla's and get you a cup of tea or a hot chocolate or something.' He'd feel a lot safer in public, where nothing could get out of hand, where a kiss would have to be one of babyish affection.

'No, she'll see that I've been crying,' says Portia, and tears are still rolling down her cheeks, unhappiness marring her smooth, caramel skin with blotches of unsightly red around her eyes and nose. 'Let's go upstairs, I'll wash my face.' Lucky reluctantly follows her, and for want of something to do, goes into the kitchen and puts the kettle on. After going to the bathroom, where she pats cold water on her face and steals some of Zaki's girlfriend's expensive face-cream, Portia just slouches at the kitchen table and puts her head down in the pillow of her hands.

Lucky carefully makes the tea, and is extraordinarily touched by the sight of her, so forlorn and vulnerable. He kneels next to her and puts his arms around her, pressing his face against her back, feeling guilty at how affectionate he feels towards her when she is distressed. He even fancies her again; there is something magnificent about her misery, something that makes her untouchable and irresistible all at once. I'm a frickin' parasite, he thinks with some shame, feeding on my girlfriend's unhappiness, turned on by it even. I'm a frickin' freak.

'You're so sweet, Lucky,' says Portia, stroking his hand. 'You're a saint to put up with me.'

'I'm really not,' says Lucky honestly. 'Don't worry about it. When we do . . . you know . . . do it, it'll be when you're ready.'

'I am – I'm almost seventeen, for Christ's sake. I want to be able to have sex with my boyfriend. And every time we start to do anything, it's always me that's made us stop.' She pauses, and takes a sip of her tea. 'It's like I'm scared.'

'Fear of Intimacy,' agrees Lucky knowledgeably, getting up and kissing her on her bare shoulder. He takes the seat opposite her, his long legs forced to sprawl out to the side as they don't fit under the table.

'That's not what I'm scared of,' says Portia. She looks straight at Lucky and says bravely, 'I'm scared you'll find out.'

'Find out what?' asks Lucky, having no idea of what she might be talking about.

'That I'm not a virgin,' she says, and looks away.

'But . . .' Lucky starts to say, and realizes that he has no idea what he might say to this bizarre revelation. How can Portia not be a virgin? They've been together since she was fifteen. There was no one she could have cheated on him with, was there? 'Since we've been going out, you've not . . . ?' he asks, not judgementally, just asking for confirmation. Portia, still not looking at him, tightens her lips and shakes her head furiously. Lucky absorbs the information; she's not slept with anyone since they've been together, so she must have slept with someone before. But she was only fifteen when they started dating, and fourteen when they first met. Fourteen! Realization sinks in, and he begins to understand the cause for Portia's dark moodiness, for her intolerance towards her mother's affairs, for her anger towards the men who whistled at her in the street, for the brooding gaze she gave the suicide bridge the first night they walked down to the river together. The embrace just now that was so vicious it was as though she was purging herself of something. The words come up in his throat and they are so enormous in their implication that they fill his mouth, expanding like a sponge against his gums, tongue and teeth, so he can't formulate them, let alone get them out: Abuse. Rape. His poor, poor Portia.

'Does anyone know about it? Your dad, your mum?' he asks at last.

'It's not what you think,' Portia says quietly, hanging her head with shame at the gentle sympathy in his voice. 'It was one of my mother's boyfriends. I was angry with her for causing the divorce, I wanted to get my own back on her. So I slept with her boyfriend, just because I could.' Lucky looks at her in horror, and Portia pauses, and then nervously stammers on, 'But it wasn't abuse; I let him. I mean I let him come into my room. I even pretended to like it.'

Lucky absorbs this, then starts shaking his head in angry denial. 'But it *was* abuse!' he explodes. 'You were just fourteen and confused, and that dirty old bugger used you. He took advantage of you because he fancied shagging an underage schoolgirl. Where the hell was your mum while he was banging her daughter in her bedroom?'

'You don't understand,' says Portia, the tears welling up once more and beginning to run freely down her face. 'It was all my fault. I was just a stupid little slapper. Mum never had a clue.' Portia doesn't want to talk about this; she has never wanted to talk about it, and already regrets her rashness in sharing her grubby little secret with Lucky. She doesn't want to remember how she had felt afterwards; she had thought that she was so clever in using her mother's younger, brash boyfriend, then she realized that she was the one who had been used, just treated like a piece of willing meat. Her mother hadn't even noticed what had been going on; perhaps that was what had made her most angry. Her mother should have known, and should have stopped it happening. Although the sex hadn't been painful or unpleasant, Portia had felt dirty, inside and out, for months afterwards. She would just be walking down the street, on the way back from school or on the way to the corner shop, when she would be struck with a wave of nausea and feel polluted, as though raw sewage was running through her, and that people couldn't help but smell it seeping out with her sweat and breath and the moisture in her eyes. She hadn't started to feel clean again until she had started seeing Lucky; she had preyed on him, even, letting his own unambiguous innocence wash through her until she was herself again, a schoolgirl with a schoolboy boyfriend. She had never believed that she had been abused; she took responsibility for her actions, and for the brooding, unresolved guilt that came with them; she wishes now that she hadn't told Lucky, and that there was some other way that she could have told him how deeply she regretted having sex with someone she didn't love, and that her first time should have been with him.

'The thing is, I know it was my fault, because it wasn't horrible,' Portia feels she has to admit, conscious that she doesn't deserve Lucky's righteous rage or his compassion. 'He was gentle. That's why I didn't want to tell anyone about it, I didn't want anyone to know that I wanted it to happen, that I'd led him on. That's why I didn't want to be gentle with you, I wanted to . . . just get through it. I thought if I could do it once, I could wipe out what had happened before, and be there properly for you.'

'Oh, Portia,' says Lucky, appalled at how much he loves her at this moment, at how her being a victim could only make her more lovable to him. Because it is obvious to him that she is the victim, despite her brave protestations. Swelling with emotion, he pulls her roughly into his arms and holds her tight. He'd have sex with her on the spot if she wanted to, however scared he might be. 'I'll never let anyone hurt you again. I'll try to make it all better. I promise.' As he makes this outrageous pledge, he feels at that moment quite strong enough to live up to it. Portia looks up at him with her big tearful eyes and starts to kiss him again, at first gratefully, then tenderly, then hungrily, and he lets her lead him to Zaki's spare bedroom, where despite his fears he tries his very best to keep his promise, and help expel the memories from her flesh.

Checkmate in the Corner Shop

Z AKI IS IN HIS usual seat in the corner shop, pretending to be looking at the *Racing Post*, but really looking at the clock, waiting for Delphine to arrive. He is slightly bronzed from their little break in Cornwall, where they spent the entire time outdoors and in public, in an attempt to redress the balance of all the time in London that they have been forced to spend behind closed doors and away from prying eyes. Jinan will be back from his business trip tomorrow, then they will be back to hiding as usual. Zaki sighs, doodling little love hearts and squiggles in the margin of the paper, and looks up hopefully when the bell rings over his door. It is only Portia, dressed for the heat in a pale strappy vest and loose white trousers, looking undeniably lovely, like the model in the making that she is shortly to become. She is also looking undeniably guilty, and Zaki knows exactly why.

'Shouldn't you be wearing scarlet, Scarlett?' he says testily.

'Why, Mr Khalil, Ah'm sure I haven't the faintest, teensiest, tiniest notion to what y'all could possibly be referring,' replies Portia in an over-the-top approximation of a southern belle.

'Bollocks you don't. And next time you and Lucky need a shag-pad, I'll thank you to ask first. It's called breaking and entering—' he begins to complain.

'Ooh no, it's called something much more romantic than that,' interrupts Portia, with a giggle.

Zaki can't stop himself laughing with her. 'Shameless!' he says, his annoyance almost completely evaporated. 'Well, happy as I am for you and Lucky that you've finally cemented your deep emotional connection with a scrappy adolescent bonk, I still think you could have found more subtle ways to flaunt it to me.'

'How did you find out? We left the room very tidy,' asks Portia.

'That was a giveaway, for a start; that and the fact that the spare room sheets had been mysteriously replaced in my absence. Then there was the rubber Johnny floating cheerily in the loo.'

Portia blushes prettily, and has the grace to look embarrassed. 'Christ, I'm sorry about that. I told Lucky to flush the bloody thing twice.' She sits uninvited on the stool opposite the counter, and leans conspiratorially towards Zaki. 'That's sort of why I've popped by; there's something I need to ask you. A favour . . .'

Zaki hastily folds up the *Racing Post* so that she can't see his hearts-and-flowers doodles, and tucks it up under the counter. 'No way, sweetheart. You two are grown-ups now, and you can find your own place to make the two-backed beast. You both have perfectly good homes, with regularly absentee parents. And whatever happened to behind the bike sheds?'

Portia smiles, and shakes her head. 'Not that sort of favour. It's just that I found out something yesterday, something that might upset Lucky, and I need you to do something to make sure that it doesn't.'

'Oh, sure, anything,' says Zaki, not really listening as he is looking at the clock fixed on the wall behind him, above the cigarette packets. 'Is that all, Portia? I'm expecting someone. Not that I don't find juvenile sex lives fascinating . . .'

'Thanks, Zaki. It's a small favour for Lucky. Just make sure that you stop shagging his mum,' says Portia. She looks up at him defiantly, as though daring him to contradict her, and her smile has evaporated, transforming her normally generous mouth into a thin, hard line.

Zaki keeps completely calm and gives nothing away. 'What on earth makes you think that I'm sleeping with Lucky's mum?' he asks. 'Just out of interest.'

Portia sighs. 'I see you're not bothering to deny it. I found her face-cream in your bathroom yesterday, and then I realized that you both went away on the same weekend. And I've just had an illuminating little chat to Orla about how often your dutiful daughter-in-law's been coming round to help out with your . . . accounts, was it?'

Zaki is silent for just a moment, but then he recovers and beams indulgently. 'All completely circumstantial. I had no idea that you were such a fantasist, Portia. Just because you're starting to have sex doesn't mean that everyone else is at it too.'

'I mean it, Zaki,' says Portia seriously. 'Don't treat me like an idiot. Lucky'll be crushed if he finds out what you're doing. You're his hero, and he doesn't need to deal with all your shit just because you can't keep your trousers on. She's your daughter-in-law; it's just disgusting.'

'You don't know what you're talking about,' says Zaki brusquely. 'What I do in my personal life is nothing to do with Lucky, and it's certainly nothing to do with you. And I can promise you one thing: I'm not doing anything wrong.' He pauses before giving her his best avuncular smile. 'So bugger off home, why don't you, sweetheart? Like I said, I'm expecting someone.' He pats her hand dismissively.

Portia seems to accept Zaki's ambiguous reply philo-sophically enough, and says nothing in response. But then she snatches her hand away without warning, and sweeps everything violently off the counter, so that the coffee cup, whisky bottle, jumble of pens and papers and coins and keys crash to the floor with a musical crescendo. Zaki looks at her and is momentarily horrified by the pale fury twisting her face; she looks almost ugly. 'Well, no need to tidy up for me as well, your smiling face is thanks enough—' he begins to say dryly, but is interrupted by Portia, whose simmering anger explodes.

'Shut up with your fucking stupid jokes, Zaki! I've had enough of your jokes, you smug old hypocrite! You think you're so special, don't you? You think you're so daring and unconventional just because you barely work and you occasionally fuck other people's wives. Well, you're not so bloody daring – you're nothing. You're just a parasite, taking over other people's lives because you haven't got one of your own. You're just a pathetic, drunken, middle-aged shopkeeper, and this time you've gone too far.'

'Stop, I'm blushing,' says Zaki, trying and failing to find something in Portia's ferocious tirade that wasn't true. 'Well, not everyone's destined to be supermodels and football heros, Portia. I hope you'll remember us little people when you're being interviewed for *Hello!* from your mock Georgian stately home.'

Portia takes a deep breath and calms herself; she looks at the broken shards of crockery among the other junk on the floor, and pushes them delicately out of her way with her sandaled toe, before sliding off her stool. 'I mean it, Zaki,' she repeats dangerously. 'Stop shagging Lucky's mum. You have to think of someone else for a change apart from yourself – have you any idea how many people you'll hurt if the truth comes out? I've had to keep enough dirty little secrets in my time, and I'm not keeping yours. If you don't stop what you're doing, you won't be leaving me a lot of choice.'

Zaki's face falls with her final threat; it seems that Portia, for whom he has nothing but affection, utterly hates him. The innocent schoolgirl has grown into a judgemental woman overnight, and he is not sure whether he has been standing too near, or too far away, to notice. She has seamlessly joined the sniffing moral brigade of all the extended family, friends and acquaintances whom he knew would condemn him with their snide mutterings: disgusting, filthy, incestuous . . . such a sordid affair. And he knew that there was little use crying to Portia, 'But I found her first! I was with her first!' as she seemed no more prepared to listen than the rest of them. Instead he says simply, 'I've not done anything wrong,' but now his words sound both plaintive and hollow even to him.

'Yes, you have,' contradicts Portia firmly. 'Just make sure you do the right thing now.' She bites her lip indecisively, before adding, with a whisper of her old affection, 'I'm sorry about the mess.' Zaki isn't sure if she's just referring to the pile of broken junk she's left on the floor. She walks out of the door, and doesn't look back.

Zaki checks his mobile, and sees that Delphine has texted him briefly to say that she won't be able to come over, with the promise of an explanation later. Just as well, he thinks through his disappointment – he didn't want her bumping into Portia. He goes upstairs and checks the bathroom; there's Delphine's Crème de la Mer, just as Portia said. Something like a hundred quid a jar. He takes it and puts it away in the broom closet junk box, but it looks bizarrely out of place, so he decides to tuck it deep down in the airing cupboard instead. He is unable to resist loosening the tightly sealed lid, the jar as smooth and heavy as a stone, and breathing in the lush fragrance to remind himself of Delphine's naked, scented face after a bath, before she piles on all that make-up to dissolve away her lovable imperfections into a dewy blank mask. His heart leaps when he sees her car pull into his parking space in front of the shop; she must have been able to come after all. He runs downstairs, but instead of Delphine racing gladly through the shop into his arms, he sees Jinan cautiously locking and double-checking the car, wearing a maroon cardigan despite the heat. He comes through the shop entrance hesitantly, seeming alarmed by the cheerful jingle of the bells above the door. Zaki realizes that he has been staring at Jinan in guilty shock for several moments; his son almost never calls him, never arranges to see him outside of Christmas or family birthdays, and he can't even remember the last time that Jinan came to visit him at the corner shop. Zaki finally gathers himself to greet him: 'Hey, Ji-Ji. It's been a long time. I thought you were in New York.'

Jinan looks as scared as Zaki feels; his normally swarthy colouring has lost its robust ruddiness, as though the blood has drained from his cheeks, and he is sweating slightly below his hairline. He remains at the door, then takes just two steps forward. 'Hello, Baba. I need to talk to you,' he says simply. He looks at the crushed mess near the counter and walks up to it, stepping around the broken shards of crockery carefully, with a slight sigh. He looks like he's about to cry, and Zaki sees, in the runny mirrors of his brown eyes, his own hypocritical, middle-aged, shop-keeper's face; an innocent pool reflecting a stormy sky, unaware of all the trouble that is soon to be unleashed. Everything he has known about Jinan – the irritating schoolboy lists, the anal preparation for his Oxford entrance exams during which every *Economist* and *FT* was carefully annotated, his pompousness about his legal career, the smugness in his wise property investments, even his marriage to an attractive Frenchwoman – melts away, like flakes of December snow hitting the damp London pavements. Everything telescopes down to one moment, to tiny Jinan brought helplessly to the door of his Parisian flat by the upstairs neighbour, because in his own selfish grief Zaki had forgotten about him; the moment where he put his arms around the unresisting little boy, and said, 'I'm so sorry, Ji-Ji.' He wishes he could put his arms around big Ji-Ji now, around that horrible maroon cardigan, and say the words again; but he is too afraid that Jinan will know what he is apologizing for. Portia is right – he is not so daring after all.

Upstairs, while his dad is busying himself in the kitchen, Jinan looks around his old bedroom. The crack that ran up the wall and along part of the ceiling is still there, no longer or shorter than it was when he used to sit at his desk and stare at it while he did his homework. There were cracks all over the house, which Zaki had never bothered to fix in all the years they'd lived there, but Jinan had always found this one particularly oppressive. Once he'd moved into his own place, he was amazed at how straightforward a job it was to get rid of them – a squeeze of Polyfilla, a bit of sanding, and a touch of paint over the top. The curtains are still the same too, with hideous psychedelic swirls that he used to look at through shuddering half-lidded eyes as he woke. His college matriculation photo is hanging crookedly on the back of the door, on the hook where he used to put his dressing gown. He has to admit that he's not terribly photogenic; despite trying to smile, he actually looks slightly cross in the picture, his eyes screwed up because of the bright outdoor light, or more likely because he hadn't yet got used to wearing contact lenses. The chunky, dark chest of drawers is still there, with its inappropriately lavish mouldings, and the matching wardrobe with tarnished golden knobs. They were a present from Dada Khalil, his grandfather, and were expensive and tasteless; well, perhaps that was unfair – it was just a different kind of taste, that's all; from a different time. His grandfather had always preferred substantial, heavy-looking things, rather like he was himself; things that occupied their territory with an almost imperial sprawl, as though they were not satisfied with the space they had and hungered for more; things that asserted his fortune with their sheer physical presence.

The dusty bedroom window looked over the back garden, and there was the same weedy lawn, with ancient, gnarled old rose bushes bearing blousy, loose-petalled flowers that sprinkled dark red and peach confetti with the slightest breeze. And the camellia had spread out monstrously, both above and below ground, cracking the patio paving. He had loved the camellia in spring, with its abundance of waxy, pale-pink flowers, each one a thing of porcelain perfection. He had spent years plotting and planning to leave this corner shop dump, studying to get the grades that would lift him out of the mire that his mother's death had resigned both him and his father to, and yet, it felt now, that he hadn't gone very far at all. Perhaps that was why he never came back here; the truth was that he was ashamed of having grown up in this shop, and ashamed of his father's shopkeeper status. But all his dedicated study and hard work and professional success had got him just a few miles down the road, to a flat where the overpriced pots on his rooftop terrace and balcony had never managed to sustain such overripe roses or such an extravagant camellia.

Zaki comes in with a pot of tea and two cups already poured. 'Here you go, Ji-Ji. Two sugars.'

Jinan starts at his entrance. 'I don't take sugar any more, Baba. Sorry, I forgot to tell you.' But then he pauses, cocks his head to the side, and reaches for the proffered cup anyway. Zaki remembers this little mannerism from when Jinan was a child; it was one he used when he was debating whether or not to select a toy – it was as though you could quite literally see him think. 'In fact, I think I might go back to having it with sugar. I prefer it that way. Any biscuits?' he asks hopefully.

Zaki goes downstairs to the shop and brings up a mixed selection. He sets them on the table in the sitting room, and Jinan sinks down on the sofa and takes the biggest, most chocolatey one without hesitation. 'Why are you driving the Audi?' Zaki asks, watching him curiously as Jinan dunks the biscuit and swallows it in a couple of bites, then reaches immediately for another. Zaki doesn't bother saying that it is Delphine's car; he thinks with illogical superstition that if he can get through this conversation without saying her name, everything will somehow be all right.

'Mine's still at the airport. I had to get a cab back from there, as I'm not meant to drive long distances. I shouldn't really have driven here, even, but I couldn't get a cab, and I couldn't face the tube.'

'Why aren't you meant to drive?' asks Zaki, not sure if

this was old news and something he was already meant to know.

'I was ill in New York, that's why I'm back a day early. Tachycardia.'

'Oh, it's not that bad,' says Zaki carelessly. 'I wouldn't have chosen a maroon one, but it's certainly not tacky. Not enough to make you ill, anyway.' Seeing Jinan's blank face, he feels forced to explain, 'The cardigan, I mean. Tachycardia? It's a joke.' Jinan still looked blank. 'Oh, never mind,' says Zaki, wishing he could control his impulse to make flippant comments about everything. No wonder Jinan kept his distance from his mad old, bad old Baba.

Jinan nods and continues as though Zaki had made a much more appropriate response; the response he should have given instead of the one he actually did; in this habit Jinan has always been much like a politician. 'Yes, same thing that Blair had once. Heart murmurs. Gave everyone quite a scare, I can tell you. I didn't tell Delphine while I was in New York, I didn't want her to worry too much. So I waited until I got back.'

'But you're all right now?' Zaki asks, surprised by the concern he feels. Jinan nods, and Zaki says nothing further, waiting for him to explain why he has come to see him for the first time in months when he is ill and should be staying at home in bed. He studies his tea and his nails, and looks up expectantly when Jinan speaks again.

'It's Dada's birthday soon, you know. Do you want us to include your name on our card, and the present?'

'You send him a card *and* a present?' asks Zaki. He couldn't even remember exactly when his father's birthday was; he always called him about a week too late, and each time promised himself that he'd write the proper date down somewhere, then forgot it all over again.

'Yes, well, I don't send it. Delphine normally picks out something nice for him. As long as it has a conspicuous Harrods logo on it, and comes in a big box, he seems to like it. Handkerchiefs this year, I think it is. Decent-sized ones for serious nose blowing, none of that faffy putting in your breast pocket stuff.'

'He'll like those,' says Zaki. He is still waiting for Jinan to explain the reason for his visit when his son pipes up again, as though struggling to fill an embarrassing gap in the conversation.

'So, have you heard from anyone in Bangladesh recently?' Jinan asks, reaching for a third biscuit, which he munches with an appreciative nod towards his father. Zaki shakes his head, but says nothing, wondering what Jinan was at such pains to avoid talking about, and afraid that he already knew. Jinan fills the silence hurriedly. 'Yes, well, we had Auntie Padma over recently. She's travelling since her divorce – you remember her husband ran off with that singer from Calcutta?' Zaki nods with sympathy, as though he already knew that his wife's baby sister was divorced, when in fact he hadn't even heard; he wonders why Delphine hasn't told him. She and Jinan were much better at this keeping in touch business than he was. Jinan carries on, beginning to gabble slightly, 'Well, she seemed to take it very well, Auntie Padma. Seems silly that she's my auntie, she's barely two years older than me. Delphine is older than her, of course, so she doesn't call her Auntie. In fact, it's Padma that calls her "Apa". Apa Delphine, like she's her older sister. Like Mamma was. Sounds weird, doesn't it?'

'Yeah, I guess it does,' says Zaki, feeling he should interrupt just to let Jinan take a breath. He is reminded of Jinan's school plays, when he had those long soliloquies, and of how, when he was rehearsing, he sometimes forgot to breathe, just speaking quicker and quicker until he got to the end. 'But Padma's doing OK, you said?'

Jinan nods. 'Yes, she's always been very strong, and her kids are already in college, and she's got a good settlement, so she seems very cheerful about it all, considering. Good riddance to bad rubbish is what she said. Let him run off with a two-bit singer. Good riddance to bad rubbish . . .' Jinan's voice starts to crack, and the tears that have been threatening to spill out since his arrival finally roll down his round cheeks and pool around the sides of his nose, before dripping down to puddle on his philtrum and upper lip. Even my tears aren't photogenic, thinks Jinan; in the movies, when people cry, their tears fall in a nice straight line down their cheekbones. He smears them away from his mouth with the sleeve of his cardigan. 'Delphine's been planning to leave me,' he finally blurts out.

Zaki sits bolt upright in shock. He cannot effectively reconcile the guilt and the relief that this statement releases in him with the surprising, overwhelming urge to comfort his son, who suddenly seems so small and lost. He cannot think of an appropriate response, so he takes refuge in an inappropriate one. 'So, how about a drink and a game of chess, eh, Ji-Ji?' he says cheerfully. 'G and T for you, isn't it?' and all but flees the room.

'Didn't you hear me?' asks Jinan quietly, when Zaki

returns with the drinks on a tray and the chessboard under his arm.

'Of course I heard you,' says Zaki, trying to imitate some of the bullishness his own father used when faced with a topic he didn't want to discuss. 'But what's it to do with me?' He starts to set up the chessboard with the same swift fluidity with which a dealer might shuffle a deck of cards. He makes his first move, nudging his pawn forward, and sits back with his whisky.

'It's everything to do with you,' says Jinan unhappily. He pauses, not noticing that Zaki, despite his determinedly casual pose, is actually holding his breath. 'You're the only one I know who knows what it's like to be left by her. Apart from Jean-François in Les Landes, her first boyfriend, but he doesn't speak English.' He shrugs his shoulders, and leaning forward, sends out his own pawn.

Zaki lets out a surreptitious sigh, and carries on playing. 'What makes you think she's planning to leave you, anyway?'

Jinan bites his full lower lip. 'She's been seeing someone. She's not at home when I call, she says she's at the gym or over here, but she doesn't answer her mobile. She made up some flimsy excuse to cancel our trip to Paris. And she's different; she's stopped criticizing me, she's stopped correcting me, she's stopped arguing with me. At first I thought it was a good thing. And then I realized, it's like she just doesn't care any more. It's like she's given up on us.' He looks frankly at Zaki. 'Baba, is that what it was like with you?'

Zaki sips his drink thoughtfully, as though he is giving

this matter full consideration. 'It was a long time ago,' he says finally. 'It was amicable enough, as break-ups go. She was quite young, and I was quite immature. Still am, I suppose. Guess some things don't change.'

'But some things do,' says Jinan, making an uncharacteristically daring attack on the chessboard. 'She's been planning to leave me, but she won't be leaving me now. Not for a long while, anyway.'

'That's not like you,' says Zaki in surprise at the move – normally Jinan was more defensive in play than a seventies' Italian football team. Forced to send in his rook for cover, he asks casually, 'Why not?'

'At least, I think she won't leave me now,' says Jinan, clutching his gin and tonic and sipping it gingerly. 'When I went away to New York this weekend, I knew she'd be seeing him. But then I got sent home with a malfunctioning heart. She was seeing her bit on the side while my heart was breaking. Imagine how guilty she's feeling right now. She can't leave me this way, she'll want to make it up to me, to look after me. She was lovely to me when I came back, absolutely lovely . . .' He pauses, and says timidly, 'I know what you're thinking . . .'

'I doubt it,' says Zaki truthfully, now unsure whether Jinan was really ill or not.

'You're thinking that I'm being a coward. I should confront her; good riddance to bad rubbish and all that. Like Padma. Can't imagine her faking an illness to guilt-trip her adulterous husband back.'

'Faking?' repeats Zaki for confirmation. 'So you don't really have a case of tachycardia? Apart from that maroon monstrosity, I mean.' It had never occurred to him that Jinan would resort to such extreme tactics just to hold on to Delphine for a little bit longer.

Jinan carries on as though his father hasn't spoken: 'But I don't want to confront Delphine, and have all that unpleasantness between us. I don't want her to leave. I don't blame her for looking elsewhere; I guess I've not always been certain that I deserved her. But I thought that if I made myself successful enough, rich enough, and loved her enough, that I would deserve her, eventually.' Jinan keeps drinking slowly, looking intently at his fallen pieces rather than at his father's face. 'You see, I don't want anything to change with me and Delphine. What I want, most of all in the world, is for everything to stay exactly the same. Haven't you ever felt that way, Baba?'

Zaki looks at Jinan shrewdly; his son has never, ever spoken to him this way before. But then he has never, ever had the risk of his world falling apart. Except for the one time, when he was three, that it actually happened. 'Yes, of course I have. I felt that way with your Amma, in Paris. And then there was the accident, and everything changed.'

'Do you think that you and Mamma would have still been together, if she had lived?'

'I don't know,' says Zaki. 'Maybe she would have had enough of me after a while. But I couldn't imagine myself ever leaving her. She was so lovely and fresh and trusting; she went from her village to an unfriendly house in Dhaka to a cramped apartment in Paris, and nothing ever fazed her. As long as she had you and me, she was happy.'

'I wish I remembered her more,' Jinan says simply. 'I was so little when she died, I don't know if I was even able to tell her that I loved her.' He looks frankly at Zaki, expecting an answer. 'Was I?'

'You were a very eloquent toddler,' reassures Zaki. 'And your mother loved you, she loved you so much. She told you that all the time, and yes, you even knew how to say it back. Don't you remember?'

Jinan shakes his head, and biting his lip, tries to avoid his mouth twisting, his face crumpling, as his tears begin again. 'Was I . . . a good boy? Did she know I was good? Did she tell me that I was good?'

Zaki looks at him ruefully. 'You don't understand, Ji-Ji. Yes, you were good. But she didn't love you because of that. She'd have loved you if you'd been the meanest little brat in the world. She didn't have conditions. You didn't need to earn her love, or deserve it. She was your Amma, and that was enough.'

Jinan nods. 'Did you see Delphine with Lucky, when he was born? I didn't think she'd be a natural mother, I thought she'd be back at work in twelve weeks. But she adored him, it was like he was the whole world to her, even before he was cute, when he was just this ridiculous little purple screaming scrap. That's when I realized how much she could love. And I thought, if she could just love me a fraction as much, then she might, she might . . .' he hesitates, and says with embarrassment, as though the words might shrink in contact with the air, '. . . give me back what I lost when Amma died. Unconditional love. But you see, that's what I can give Delphine; that's what makes me worthy of her. She doesn't have to earn my love, or deserve it. I can give her what I need the most.'

Jinan curls himself into a ball on the sofa, hugging his

knees like a child, concentrating only on the chessboard. He sees Zaki looking curiously at him, and asks, 'Are you ashamed of me, Baba?'

'Why would you think that?' asks Zaki.

'Because I'm a weakling, and a liar. Because I'm nothing like you or Amma; I'm not a free spirit who could move unfazed between continents. The thought of moving out of corporate law, or moving to a bigger house in the Home Counties gives me a nervous rash. I always thought that you'd have preferred a different kind of son; someone creative and unconventional. Someone brave.'

Zaki looks at his son, who is still biting his lip. He has Nadya's mouth, he realizes; the plump lips that had looked so voluptuous and sensual on her look rather fat on her son. He feels ashamed that he has let Nadya down; her child is the only thing he has left of her, she entrusted him to Zaki. And he has been such a poor excuse for a father that Jinan feels like he is a disappointment, just as Zaki was a disappointment to Dada Khalil. He has been such a poor excuse for a father than he has somehow forgotten the lesson that Nadya taught him: that of unconditional love. 'I'm proud of you, Ji-Ji. I've always been proud of you, and I've never been as proud of you as I am at this moment. You are a wonderful father, and a wonderful husband, and Delphine is lucky to have you. No one else will ever give her what you can.'

Jinan looks up at him, uncurling in wonder. 'You mean that, Baba?'

Zaki nods, and puts his arm around him. 'You are so much like your mother. I trusted her like I've trusted no one on this earth. You are the best thing she could have left me,' and he finds that he means it when he says this. His poor, lost little boy. His motherless boy, just looking for someone to love, to love him so much, to tell him that he was good. 'The game's over,' he adds in a humbled voice.

'Have you won?' asks Jinan, looking in confusion at the board.

Zaki resists the urge to glance at him sharply; he is reminded again of Jinan's school plays, of the slightly overplayed wide-eyed innocence at the final reveal, of the sense that it was all acting after all, just an actor with a carefully prepared script in hand. Zaki doesn't want to follow this line of thought too far; it doesn't matter any more. It doesn't matter if he has been played to, all that matters is that the game is at an end. Zaki realizes without malice that Jinan is far more devious, and far cleverer than he has given him credit for. 'No, you have,' he says. 'Didn't you see? I'm in checkmate.'

It turns out that it was Zaki, rather than Delphine, who was fonder of Jinan than he thought.

Big Fish, Little Fish, Cardboard Box

FLOWERS, NECKLACE, DRESS, thought Delphine on the morning of her engagement party. Flowers, necklace, dress, in that order. I'll go and pick up the flowers from Columbia Road Flower Market, and put them in water for tonight. I'll go and buy that necklace from Hatton Garden, and I'll collect the dress from the dry-cleaner on the way back. That would keep her busy until it was time to take the cab to the venue: a party boat moored on the north bank of the Thames, not so far from Temple. The boat was Jinan's idea; his firm had recently had an office party there and it had apparently been a great knees-up, a real blast. These were good things, he hastened to reassure her when her brow furrowed adorably. Knees-up, a blast; she knew what these words were meant to mean, but there was something she disliked about them beyond the slightly distasteful innuendo that only a foreigner would register; it was the juxtaposition, she realized. One referred to elderly tea parties, the other to adolescent outings. It reminded her that Jinan was both too old and too young for her. In any case, she had smiled and let Jinan have his way, as he had already agreed to her ideal wedding – something small and perfect with lunch at the Ritz or the Savoy, with the minimum number of guests for her provincial parents to embarrass her in front of. Flowers, necklace, dress, she reminded herself firmly. She had things to do, and she didn't have time to think about anything else. She certainly didn't have time to think about who might be there at the party that evening; about ex-boyfriends or future father-in-laws who might be inconveniently bundled together in the same dinner jacket, whom she hadn't seen for some six years. Another person who was too old and too young for her. No, she had no time to think about that at all. She stepped out of her Victorian flat in London Fields, the one she had bought once she had moved out of the shared flat in Putney, and walked purposefully down towards Columbia Road. She is Mrs Dalloway, she thought, in her tailored jeans and her floaty top, buying flowers for her party. What a lark! What a plunge!

During the party, Delphine couldn't stop herself looking critically at the flower arrangements. When she had heard the cost of getting the flowers done by the venue, she had insisted on doing them herself. How hard could it be, she thought? She had wanted them to look like they'd been gathered casually from a garden or a meadow and care-lessly tossed into water, but instead there was something disconcertingly contrived about the generous bunches of sunflowers and roses and cow parsley and the big structural alliums. Jinan came over to her with a glass of Prosecco, and squeezed her waist shyly. 'You look gorgeous,' he said.

'That necklace is amazing,' and with the glassy-eyed courage achieved by having already drunk too much, kissed her carefully on the mouth.

'Hey, lovebirds,' said Veronica, stalking in wearing killer heels and a sleeveless pinstriped dress. 'Try not to flaunt being so happy, it's bad taste at your own engagement party,' she scolded, kissing them on both cheeks. Jinan smiled self-effacingly, slightly flushed and shiny with the heat and drinks, but was tapped on the shoulder by his best man, Dan, and pulled away to tackle a line of flaming sambucas at the bar.

'Hey, Ronnie,' said Delphine, 'I love the dress. Was it hard building the time machine to go back to the eighties to get it?'

'Not hard at all, Dee – the eighties are still alive and well in my wardrobe, thank you very much. I hate all the deconstructed crap that's out at the moment. I love your dress, too, by the way. It'll be great when they finish making it . . .'

'Oh, shut up, it's not that deconstructed,' said Delphine good-humouredly.

'But it is that short,' said Veronica, picking up a glass of Prosecco from a passing waiter. 'I do like the necklace, though. I wish I had some nice, bold bits of jewellery like that.'

'Oh, cheers,' said Delphine, looking down despondently at the stiff gold circlet with a chunky pendant of black crystals. 'You're like the tenth person who's mentioned the necklace. It's the first thing people have been saying to me tonight, after "Hello" and "Congratulations".'

'It's a compliment, Dee, I wasn't being sarky,' said Veronica.

Delphine sighed. 'I liked it before, but if everyone's so suspiciously complimentary about the damn thing, there has to be something wrong with it. It's like having a cold sore – everyone can't help but stare, and then feel they have to say something nice to cover up why they were staring.' She couldn't explain how she felt; it was as though she had made some sort of horrendous *faux pas*, and everyone was too polite to tell her. With the flowers, the necklace, the deconstructed dress even. She had wanted to be *soignée* and stunning this evening; she found it hard to admit to herself why she was so disappointed with her appearance, as that would involve admitting that she had wanted Zaki to see her, and perhaps think that she had become beautiful. But he hadn't even turned up.

Hours later, Delphine was taking a break from the dance floor, and had gone out on the deck to get some air. She kicked off her shoes and leaned over the railing to watch the lights sparkling along the slow-flowing river, which looked as black and thick as treacle in the moonlight. 'I like the lacy stuff in the vases,' said a voice behind her. 'It looks just like the weeds that grow along the motorway.'

'It is,' said Delphine, turning around to face Zaki. 'It's called cow parsley.'

'Wow,' he whistled in appreciation. 'Genuine weeds. They must have been really expensive.' There was a pause, and he joined her at the railing. 'You're looking well, Della—' he said.

'And yes, I know, it's a great necklace,' she interrupted, annoyed at him for finally rolling up when she was tipsy and sweaty and tousled and sore-footed.

'I hadn't noticed it, but I can say it's great if you like,' he said, looking at her profile, with her neat nose and curved lips. Delphine said nothing, slightly mollified, and gave a half smile. 'Well, this is awkward, isn't it?' said Zaki, after a while.

'I suppose it is,' said Delphine. 'I wasn't sure if you were coming.'

'I told Jinan I would,' said Zaki. 'I take it that your parents aren't here?'

'No, they're just coming next month, for the wedding.'

'Ah yes, next month,' repeated Zaki. 'A bit quick, isn't it, for you? You're not marrying in haste, are you?'

'What's that meant to mean?' bridled Delphine.

'Honestly, Della. No need to take such offence,' said Zaki calmly. 'I'm just asking if you've knocked up my son – he's been looking a bit chubby recently.'

'Zaki, just say if you don't approve. No one's asked for your blessing, so it wouldn't bother either of us in the slightest,' said Delphine.

'Why wouldn't I approve?' said Zaki in surprise. 'My son's going to marry the most beautiful woman on the boat. Of course I approve.' He kissed her chastely on the cheek, and smiled. Delphine felt all the tension dissolve out of her as it was replaced with another feeling; a melting spread of warmth, like a blush starting on the inside.

'Thanks, Zaki,' she said, 'for not making this too weird.'

'Not at all, Della,' he replied. 'Us cradle-snatchers must stick together.' He nodded towards the deck entrance, where a thin blonde with very short cropped hair was waving to him. 'That's Lisa, my date; she was just checking her coat. I'll see you later.' Delphine tried not to watch as he walked up to Lisa, put his arm around her, and nodded to Delphine from the door. Delphine nodded back with a cheerful, embarrassed smile; Lisa looked younger than her, even.

Back on the dance floor, Delphine danced slowly to 'Wonderful Tonight' with Jinan, and he whispered in her ear, with aching sincerity, 'I love you, I love you so much.' He said it with wonder, and buried his face heavily between her neck and shoulder; he said it like a prayer. But like a prayer, it was as though the act of saying it was what made it real, what would make it come true. Like magic. When the music changed to something more energetic, she gratefully slid away from him and sat at a table on the edge of the floor. She watched him bounce away enthusiastically with Veronica, then noticed Zaki hovering by her table. 'This is your anthem, you should dance to it,' she told him. He looked at her bemusedly, and she explained, 'The band's called Cornershop.' He didn't sit next to her, but remained standing by her side. 'I don't really get the lyrics,' she added.

'No, me neither. I never do. The worst song for me is "Whiter Shade of Pale"; no one knows what that one's about. Not even the blokes who wrote it,' he replied. 'Well, at least Jinan's having fun,' he said. 'He dances just like my dad.'

Delphine laughed disloyally, then realized what she was doing and stopped. 'I don't know what you mean,' she said stiffly.

'Oh yes you do – Big Fish, Little Fish, Cardboard Box,' said Zaki, demonstrating the gestures with his arms in swift time to the music. 'He's danced like that since he was an adolescent. Which wasn't that long ago, as you might remember.'

'I'm sure Dada Khalil doesn't dance like that,' objected Delphine, who had never met her fiancé's grandfather.

'You're right; he does more of the Cleaning Windows, Pushing Pineapples dance. Same family of moves really,' said Zaki dryly. 'Ah, here she is,' he said, as Lisa came back and pulled him onto the dance floor with her. It was only then that Delphine realized that she had been waiting for Zaki to ask her to dance; she waved to a waiter, and deciding that the moment had come to get irredeemably drunk, relieved him of a glass and a full bottle.

Delphine struggled to get through the rest of her engagement night. She remembered making an inebriated vow with Veronica over a couple of tequila slammers never to wear heels again, as it only led to the indignity of dancing barefoot on the soiled dance floor. She remembered throwing up, and as Jinan was being taken to a club by his best man and his friends, in lieu of a real stag night which he had decided against, she remembered Zaki being enlisted into getting her a cab. As she had drunkenly lost her footing and collapsed at the cab door, he had climbed in with her to make sure she made it to her flat, and she had curled up against him like a small animal and shut her eyes. She might have told Zaki drowsily, 'I'm not marrying him, you know. I can't. It wouldn't be fair. I don't love him like he loves me.' She may even have caught sight of herself, bleary-eyed and raw-faced in the cab window and said with a laugh, 'I bet you don't think I'm the most beautiful woman on the boat now.'

'Maybe just the most beautiful woman in the cab,' Zaki said in reply, pulling his coat over her, letting her fall asleep on his chest, watching her hands tighten into fists and then relax and open out like flowers. He was so drunk himself that everything was a beautiful blur. He had to carry her out of the cab and through her front door, bumping her legs and his head in the narrow hallway decorated with curly hazel sticks, and when he reached her living room, they both fell on the sofa shrieking with laughter. Delphine really, truly didn't remember anything else.

In the morning, Delphine heard the sound of the radio from the kitchen, and pulling on a dressing-gown, went in to find Zaki, who looked louche and unshaven in last night's suit, making himself a coffee. 'Oh,' she said with undisguised annoyance, as though she hadn't expected him to be there.

'I had to help you in last night,' he explained. 'You were paralytic. Not that I was much better.'

Delphine smiled weakly, to make it seem as though she didn't quite remember. Her hangover was appalling, the sound of the perky radio presenter was like a malevolent elf driving small, sharp nails along her hairline. 'What about . . . Lisa, was it?'

'I've just called her. She's OK; she went clubbing with Veronica and Jinan and the boys. Sounds like they had fun. More her scene than my stuffy old club, I guess.'

Delphine nodded, and pouring herself a large glass of water, shuffled over to the kitchen table. As she sat down, she felt a dull, inexplicable ache in her middle, between her hips, and felt forced to ask with a touch too much urgency, 'I hope the sofa was OK for you? You slept on the sofa, right?'

Zaki nodded, feeling a bit hurt, but trying to look amused instead. 'Well, that's where I woke up.'

'Oh,' said Delphine again, this time with undisguised relief.

'Do you remember anything about last night?' Zaki asked curiously. As Delphine smiled hopelessly and shook her head, he persisted, 'About not marrying Jinan. You said you weren't going to marry Jinan. You said you didn't love him enough.'

'I don't think I said that,' said Delphine. 'Anyway, don't worry. I do love him. I don't know why I would have said something like that. I guess drink just makes me miserable and maudlin.'

'That's funny, I find it makes me impossibly witty and irresistible to the opposite sex,' said Zaki lightly.

'Good for you,' replied Delphine. She paused, and said pointedly, 'Thanks for seeing me home.'

Zaki didn't need a further hint. He pushed the cup of coffee wordlessly over towards Delphine and got up to go. She realized belatedly that he had made the coffee for her, rather than for himself. Remembering her manners, she dragged herself to the door to see him out. 'See you at he wedding, I guess,' he said, and went to kiss her on the cheek. But somehow she got confused about which way to turn her head and brushed him accidentally on the lips, and he briefly, for the tiniest moment, kissed her back. The pressure from his lips was light but unmistakable, and they both pulled back in embarrassment. 'Sorry, force of habit,' he said. 'Kissing pretty girls in doorways, I mean,' he added, and walked down the communal hallway and out of the heavy Victorian door.

Delphine looked up the stairs to see one of her neighbours coming down and eyeing her with frank curiosity. 'What?' she demanded, then turned back into her flat and banged the door crossly. She sat on the sofa, which didn't really look like it had been slept on; worryingly, it looked more like it had been struggled on. She felt that dull, not unpleasant ache, and thought to herself, I'd remember, wouldn't I? If anything happened, how could I not remember? She threw herself back on the cushions and buried her face in them; there was nothing to remember, she told herself, and even if there was, there was still nothing to remember. In a few weeks she would be getting married to a sweet young man who loved her; she didn't need complications, and she certainly didn't need awkward memories; she had a whole new future waiting for her. A familiar song came on the radio, it was that record by Cornershop again. Delphine snapped off the radio, and didn't drink again until the day of her wedding, when she had a single glass of champagne; her new abstinence turned out to be well timed, as Lucky was born so soon after the wedding that most people assumed that she and Jinan were married in haste after all.

PART TWO

Players

The Other Side of the Water

IT's REMARKABLY EASY to disappear. And it doesn't
have to be dramatic or tragic or anything like that. It
doesn't have to be a car crash on a street, there doesn't have
to be a thunderbolt or a flood. All it takes is the slightest of
decisions; the decision to walk out of the front door, and to
stand on the street corner under the lamppost. And then
another decision; to choose which street to stroll down, and
then simply keep going. Another step and another step.
Baby steps, some people might say; baby steps to get to
your final destination. One brick at a time, as the village
workmen used to sing as they brought up a building with
mud blocks baked by the sun. Salami tactics, a politician
would suggest; one little slice to taste, to test the decision
out, and then another little slice. You're not committed to
anything, not yet, so it's not so very scary. The front door
is still open, and you can walk back in as easily as you
walked out. The cash register is still on the counter, and full
of the day's takings; the radio is still on and announcing the
results of the day's races, and the kettle will have boiled by
now, so if you do go back, at least you can have a cup of

tea. You didn't write a letter, you didn't do anything so banal as put your affairs in order; there's nothing to give you away, there's nothing to say you left in the first place. The only proof you have that you left is that you're sitting here, in your shirtsleeves and a light jacket, on a bench by the river, rather than sitting back there behind the counter.

Oh well. The river. Perhaps it's not as easy as all that. You walk in a straight line, and you find you're at the river, and you can't go any further. And you start to feel guilty, because you know that they will feel guilty. Portia will think that it might be something to do with her, the presumptuous little madam – as though she were that important, as though her moralizing little threat might have driven you to such dire lengths. The idea is laughable, but you don't really want the shadow of your disappearance hanging over her, the poor thing has enough pent-up anger boiling up in her already. Della will think it's something to do with her; of course she will. And Jinan will know that it's something to do with him. And through all their unexpressed culpability, they will remain together, perhaps happily, and at least Jinan will have what he wanted, which is that everything stays the same. And what about Lucky? He won't have a clue, and he won't believe it. I can count on him not to believe it; he'll think I'm on a round-the-world cruise or something. So I don't need to feel guilty about Lucky, at least.

It's pretty at sunset, the river. And it's even prettier now it's turned to night. People have walked by me in a blur; joggers, dog-walkers, businessmen, lovers, students. People have joined me on the bench, and then left again. It's as though I have been the only still point in the spinning world. There's something beautiful about it, romantic even. A lone seated figure on a summer's night. And now the clouds are gathering, and it's becoming a dark and stormy night, more romantic still. Of course I'm not stuck here; I haven't given up or given in. I'm just waiting for the perfect moment, then I'll take my next step. My next mud brick. My next salami slice. I've waited thirty years, so I don't mind waiting a little longer.

The funny thing is that it's not all to do with them. With Della or Jinan, with the tangled-up mess that Portia is so sorry I've got myself into. It's quite a lot to do with Lucky, too. I realized, when Jinan said so simply that he wanted everything to stay the same, that I wanted the opposite. I wanted everything to be different. Everything. I didn't want to be a shopkeeper in the dodgy end of Hammersmith, having an affair with my son's perhaps-soon-to-be ex-wife. I didn't want to put on that same stupid play day after day for everyone, where I perform as the maverick old man who dispenses inappropriate advice along with corny jokes, or the ageing bachelor who shags other people's wives. I wanted a life of my own, one that I had actually chosen, not one that was arranged for me; my father couldn't arrange my marriage, but he made damn sure he arranged everything else. And I was too lazy or scared to get out of it. And I thought of Lucky, who looks like he will finally get everything he ever wanted and become a famous footballer; achieving his dream so early in life. And look at me, who has achieved nothing; I don't even have a dream any more. It's a real tragedy, to reach this late stage in life and realize that you've not only not achieved your dream, but you can't even remember what that dream was. And I was the one with 'Dreamer' marked on my wristband when I was a baby in the Dhaka hospital, wasn't I? If I don't have my own dream, perhaps I should borrow one – what was that old saying? Something about how each man should plant a tree, have a son and build a house; I'd say that's a dream of sorts. Well, I threw a mango seed into the ground once near the Bangshi river, that same mango seed that little Padma had been sucking on when I proposed to Nadya; perhaps that grew. But the son and the house; well, I looked after them as best I could, but really, they were someone else's, not mine. The son never really liked me. And I never really liked the house.

So, people have different ways of taking control. Della slept with me, and her husband loved her even more for it. Jinan faked a mild heart condition. Portia made an empty threat. Lucky got good at playing in a position he hated. It comes to something when you realize that you're never going to be happy doing what you've always done, playing the role you've always been made to play, and that you're in everyone else's way as well. People have different ways of taking control, and this is mine. I'm crossing the water now, I'm on the bridge. The wires are sparkling above me, and the rain falls in a steamy drizzle; it's surprisingly warm. Perhaps it's me that's warm, as I'm finally doing something for myself. I blamed too much on fate in the past. Well, sod fate; this is my decision, finally, and no one can take it away from me. It's another baby step over the railing, and I'm standing comfortably on the edge, looking down. The river looks glossy and clean from here; not as clean and clear as the Bangshi river where Nadya washed her clothes, but clean enough to wash the tarnish off a stupid old man. Clean enough to wash away the scent of whisky and regret, and the theatrical cobwebs of the show that has been playing over and over again for the last thirty years; my own personal *Mousetrap*. No one else is on the bridge; no one has seen me. The moment is perfect, and the slow river below breaks in places, as though fish were jumping through. I'm watching the breaks and splashes – not to delay the moment, just to make it last. There was a street magician in Montmartre who worked in that little square with the fountain; he used to take pennies from people for wishes, and when he threw them into the fountain, the pennies would twist in the water and turn into goldfish, which would wriggle away like sparks of light. Nadya thought it was wonderful, magical even, that everyone's wishes had come to life, and were swimming off to make their dreams come true. Otherwise, the pennies would have just sunk to the bottom, taking the wishes with them. So this is my wish, if you like. This is my penny. And this is my baby step off the edge of the bridge. It's easy.

Roopa Farooki

KENSINGTON AND CHELSEA POST
ROYAL BOROUGH BOY TO PLAY FOR ENGLAND U18

Local boy, Luhith Khalil, 16, recently signed to the famous youth academy of West Ham Football Club, has been selected for the England Under 18. Luhith, known to all as 'Lucky', was born and brought up in the Royal Borough and lives here with his proud parents, Jinan and Delphine. He first came to attention playing for the Royal Borough Junior FC. He says on his selection, 'It's an honour to be picked, and I'll do my best to make everyone proud of me.'

HAMMERSMITH POST
LOCAL SHOPKEEPER DISAPPEARANCE BAFFLES POLICE

Police are investigating the mysterious disappearance of Zakaria Khalil, a Hammersmith legend who has run his corner shop for over thirty years. Khalil appears to have disappeared during the afternoon of 5 September, leaving his shop open, and taking no clothes or possessions. Mr Khalil was much loved by local bookies, and suggestions that he may have chosen to leave due to gambling debts have proved unfounded. He is the father of prominent lawyer Jinan Khalil, and the grandfather of rising soccer star, Lucky Khalil, and police are actively investigating the possibility that he may have been kidnapped, although no ransom request has yet been received. In a press conference which he attended with his parents, Lucky Khalil appealed to anyone with information about his grandfather's whereabouts to come forward. The West Ham player said, 'We just want him to come home. We miss him.'

RADIO 5 LIVE: WEST HAM V CHELSEA

'And what a save from young Khalil! He's been a real joy to watch this season, and thoroughly deserves his place on the starting line-up. Youngest keeper they've ever played, I should think.'

'And there's a familiar face, in his trademark grey suit. No coincidence that the England manager is watching this match, is it, Dave?'

'None at all, Khalil's making his case to the Man in Grey for an England place at next year's World Cup, and actions speak louder than words. And the pressure's back on as Chelsea regain possession . . .'

'Cox right foots it to Schwarz, Schwarz crosses it smartly over to Carlos, who's in the box and – oh! That's a questionable tackle from Marquez, and Carlos is down. Marquez is protesting, but it won't do him any good, it's a yellow card for him, and it's a penalty.'

'Khalil won't be thanking his team-mate for that one. They were on track for a clean sheet for this game, but Khalil's looking calm. Remarkable maturity for a lad of his years; still only seventeen. Schwarz, the German international, is coming forward to take it. Talented player, Schwarz, brings a wealth of experience to Chelsea, and a real threat to England's chances next year.'

'It's on target . . . [shouting] but Khalil's done it! My word! Well, practice makes perfect; that's just another amazing save. The home supporters are deafening: 'Can Khalil do it? Yes he can!' Khalil's enjoying this moment, and well might he. He's English and he's ours!'

Roopa Farooki

OBSERVER SPORT MONTHLY
HEAD TO HEAD WITH LUCKY KHALIL

Luhith 'Lucky' Khalil is the first team goalkeeper for West Ham, and is in hot contention for an England place at the World Cup in Italy next year. But the media-shy eighteen-year-old still lives at home, and dates his childhood sweetheart. He stands out among the other talented England hopefuls by making the right sort of headlines.

OSM: Lucky, you're on record for saying that you always dreamed of being a footballer, and incredibly, you were already playing at a semi-professional level at the age of sixteen. Could you tell us which footballers you most admired when you were growing up?

LK: Well, when I was a kid, it was Beckham, Lampard and Zidane.

OSM: That's interesting – all midfield players?

LK: Yeah, I played midfield until I was fourteen. But I wasn't that good; I mean, I was good, but not as good as I thought I was; I wasn't good enough to make it professionally in midfield. I just didn't have the legs for it, I didn't have enough pace or stamina. You need to have the will to run in midfield. My coach at Royal Borough put me in goal, and I've never looked back.

OSM: And what, to your mind, is the best goal ever scored?

Corner Shop

LK: One of my favourites was Michael Owen against Argentina when he was just eighteen, the France '98 World Cup. I was only little at the time, but I saw it on TV when I was older. Awesome.

OSM: On the subject of wunderkind teenage strikers, what do you say to people about the supposed rivalry between yourself and Felix Conway?

LK: [Laughs] Oh, that's just rubbish. I've been playing Conway since he was twelve and I was thirteen. He's a fantastic player, and he's done some good things since he signed for Manchester City. We've played together in the England Under 18, and he's always come through for us. A bit hot-headed, but he's young. Younger than me, I mean.

OSM: Some are saying that there's only room for one teenage star in the England squad. If it was a choice, who would you pick?

LK: It's not a choice, is it? You don't choose between a goalie and a striker. Anyone can tell you that.

OSM: Still, you're both untested on the big international stage, and the Man in Grey has to minimize his risk. If the selectors could only take one uncapped player to the World Cup, who would it be?

LK: The best for the job that needs to be done. It would be great if it was me.

Not Drowning but Waving

WELL, I NEVER SAID that I couldn't swim.
Common mistake, thinking that fifty-something shopkeepers who jump off bridges can't swim. Why would I jump off a bridge if I couldn't swim? I've had enough of my old life, not of life altogether. Life is too precious to waste – losing Nadya taught me that. I've wasted enough of my life so far; to waste the rest of it would be criminal. So I enjoyed the fall, I enjoyed the violent smack of the entry and the plunge, and then the pull back towards the surface. I'm a strong swimmer – I was brought up in Bangladesh, after all – but the current was surprisingly powerful, so I went a long way before I got out. All the way to Southwark beach, can you believe? It's not really a beach, but I call it that, because when the river is low you can see a sandy edge along the river bed, with bits of old bicycles and the odd shopping trolley. Quite an achievement, as there's not a supermarket for miles around there; I'd say the closest one must be the pink shopping centre at Elephant and Castle. Who says that the delinquent youths of today aren't motivated? I climbed up the steps at the

bank, and looked across the river. There was an enormous boat moored on the other side, somewhere near Temple. A party boat, maybe, although it was already too late for parties; the sun was even starting to come up.

I walked across to Waterloo, and the sunrise was every bit as pretty as the sunset had been. 'Waterloo Sunrise', now there's a song that should have been written. The view across the river is one of my favourite views in town; it's the one I wanted to remember, and I'm glad that it's the last thing I saw of London, as I doubt I'll go back. The early morning commuters started to appear, and many looked at me curiously – my hair was dry by then, but the rest of me was still wet. I went into the station, and withdrew some cash from the mortgage account that Dada Khalil holds on the corner shop. The old crook thinks I can't count – the mortgage was for twenty-five years, so I'd paid it off some time ago, but he still insisted that I continue with my payments. Well, it wasn't too hard to break into the account and manage it on the internet, and then it wasn't too hard to get the card reissued and the PIN number reset. At the time, I did it just to annoy him, so that when he demanded the next payment, I could show him the statement and say triumphantly, 'A-ha! – Embezzle your own son, will you?' What did he think I'd do if I didn't have debts any more? Did he think I'd run away? Well, he was right. Maybe he knows me better than I give him credit for. Not that he ever credited me with anything. Credit? Hah! That's a dirty word to my Baba – he has the soul of a shopkeeper. The beauty of the mortgage account was that no one would think to check it once I'd gone. It's not in my name. And I didn't take too much, just a couple of grand to see me through. I don't need anyone else's money; I don't even need to take back my own. I'm free now, I'll make my own way.

It's easier, these days, getting away. I mean, it's easier to leave than it was to arrive. When Jinan and I came from Paris, we had to get a train to Calais. Then get a bus to the boat. Then get the boat to Dover. Then get on the train to Victoria. It took all night, and he didn't sleep. He sat up in the plastic seats of the cafe area on the boat, his eyes getting wider and wider as he saw some Americans ordering snacks from the dead-eyed waiter running the cafe. So I bought him hot chocolates until I ran out of cash. A blonde mother with a fluffy version of the Farrah Fawcett haircut had two children sleeping peacefully beside her; she looked at me suspiciously – someone barely out of their teens in charge of a three-year-old? She made it clear that she thought I wasn't taking proper care of Jinan, buying him all those hot chocolates and letting him stay up all night. She patted her children under their blankets, as though protecting them from people like me. I couldn't understand why the sight of her contentedly sleeping children made me feel so helpless and sad. When Jinan started crying, because he was wet, because he was tired, because his hot chocolate had run out, because his mother had got run over by a taxi and had left him with an idiot stranger who didn't know how to care for him alone, I couldn't cope. I walked over with Jinan to the Farrah Fawcett haircut and asked if she would watch him for a moment, while I got some water for his nappy change. He was so stunned at being unceremoniously abandoned with a stranger that he forgot to make any sound for his tears as he saw me walking swiftly away. I went to the toilets, took a leak and washed my face, then leaned my head heavily against the smoky mirror. When I got back to the Farrah Fawcett haircut, Jinan was wrapped up in one of her blankets and almost asleep. I was so grateful, I didn't know what to say, and she smiled at me as though she had misjudged me, as though I was just another kid to wrap up in a blanket and take care of. She was a real parent, like Nadya, whereas I was a pretend parent, a player-parent. A stand-in forced onto the stage and not doing the best job; just saying the lines, and following the stage directions mindlessly. If someone had told me to Exit Stage Left Pursued by a Bear, I would have done it without question.

'He wasn't wet,' she whispered, 'he was just tired.' She nodded towards her own children, as though explaining their presence in the disreputable half-life and half-light of the night crossing. 'This was the only boat we could get at late notice. We were visiting my mother; she's not well.'

'I'm sorry,' I said, intending to show sympathy, and realized that she had misunderstood me when she repeated, 'I said she's not well,' as one might to a slow child. She looked at me as though awaiting my own explanation for being there, and for a moment it was tempting to pour out all the troubles of the last weeks, of Nadya's mouth forming an 'O' of surprise as a cab rudely took her life, of her final flight over the street, of everything changing forever. But instead I just said, mirroring her own words for the comfort of familiarity, for the hope of approval, 'We were visiting my father.' I paused, and added, 'And now we're going home,' as though saying the words might make it come true, like a prayer, like magic.

Like I said, it's easier to leave than to arrive. I just needed to buy a ticket, go through a gate and get on a train all the way to Paris. My damp passport raised a few eyebrows; it was the one I'd lost last year and hadn't got round to replacing. It was in my jacket when I walked out of the door. Well, that was a sign. I'm not quite as free-spirited and spontaneous as you think; the passport, the bank account – it all smacks, somehow, of planning. It wasn't planned, really; although in another way, it's been planned for the last thirty years. Ever since a matronly woman's contented children made me feel helpless and sad; ever since I realized that I was a fraud. It's time to stop playing roles that are wrong for me, time to avoid those slings and arrows of outrageous fortune and seek a fortune of my own, my way. I'm a different kind of player now; I'll bet on the horses and the spinning red and black, I'll play money for chess in a ramshackle studio apartment. I'll eat foie gras out of tins for supper, and have coffee and whisky and brioche for breakfast. But I won't stay in Paris, and I won't visit Nadya's grave. This isn't about endings, it's about beginnings.

It's time to start again, clean and soft and smooth as a newborn baby wimpled in muslin. It's time to send my pennies out into the water, and watch them wriggle and leap with a golden flash as they come to life and swim away. Like a prayer. Like magic. Exit stage left, but with no bear to follow me, and no baggage.

The View from the Bottom of a Bottle

DELPHINE HAS THE impression that she is standing quite still, and everything else in the world is moving animatedly about her. It is as though she is a prop on a stage set – something inconsequential, like a hatstand; something with an existence that is acknowledged by the players, but only in the sense that they try to avoid bumping into it. Since Zaki left at the end of their summer together, she is taking up very little space in the world; much less than before. Her interaction with it is pared down to the bare minimum; the handing over of payment in a shop, the receipt of change. Because of her guilt, she now takes a righteous pleasure in this state of affairs; she is almost satisfied with it. Why only the other day, she thinks, someone stood on my foot on the tube and I apologized for them, just to save them the trouble. And perhaps it was my fault, anyway; I shouldn't have left my clumsy foot in their path. Silly old me; even the little space I take up in the world is too much.

Her monstrous guilt is weighing on her, and she is succumbing to depression in such tiny slides, in such a gentle, slipping-down way, that she barely notices it. It helps that she has started to drink again – the generous, mind-twisting quantities of her youth. She is a French-woman, after all; who is she to fight her genetic heritage? The drink suffuses her with an anaesthetic calmness, and in the same gentle, slipping-down way, she sinks into the bottom of the bottle, where she nestles like a preserved embryo, a wizened, vinegar-shrivelled homunculus. A creature once full of life and potential, holding out such hope, such promise, now offering nothing but the satisfaction of morbid scientific curiosity with her eventual vivisection. Cut it open carefully, it might fall apart. Look at the dried-up little heart, still beating! Look at the blood in the veins – still red! Look at all the organs still packed into their leathery container; it's amazing that this odd animal still seems to work. The alcohol has replaced her blood, and she is now preserved for posterity by her guilt. She feels envious of other people with their common or garden guilt, who feel uncomfortable about the size of their behinds, or about watching daytime TV, or neglecting their parents or children, or being rude to people who work in restaurants. Such guileless guilt, such comfortable culpability. How well they must all sleep at night. Whereas she has broken up a family without even having gone to the trouble or personal inconvenience of leaving it herself; she has slept with her father-in-law, and after a few short months has driven him away with her clinging, selfish attention. She has lost her husband's father, and her son's grandfather; it is possible, although unlikely, that she has even driven him to his death. It is possible, although unlikely, that he is her son's father, rather than grandfather, and that none of them –

her son, her husband, her lover – has guessed this. Her crime is of epic proportions, biblical even. She wonders if her Grande-Tante Christiane back in Les Landes is still praying for her; she belatedly hopes that God speaks French.

Her languor and self-pity, senseless to those unaware of the true circumstances, which is everyone, tend to elicit irritation rather than sympathy. Instead of moping in a drunken heap, she should be busying herself making enquiries, continuing a dialogue with the appropriate authorities. Her girlfriends have not yet lost patience with her, as she has been avoiding them. This has not alerted their suspicions, as they have their own concerns. Katie is pregnant and furious about it, having only just regained her figure from her last pregnancy and finally put her little girl in full-time nursery. 'He said not to worry about the condoms,' she fumed to Delphine on the phone several months after Zaki's disappearance. 'He said it was technically impossible on the last day of my period. Technically impossible! Technically impossible is crossing a rabbit with a chihuahua. What he meant is technically *improbable*. Can you believe I'm up the duff because my idiot arty-farty husband doesn't know how to use a bloody dictionary?' So Katie is busy sipping mineral water at home, suffering from the all-day morning sickness that tends to dog the first few months of her pregnancies, and peeing on the hour.

Veronica, meanwhile, has started to plan her wedding to the dullest man in advertising. She is torn between looking sexy and confident in a clinging, skimpy dress, and having a hip party full of carefully selected witty and successful people, or looking demure in a Vera Wang meringue in a church filled with peonies and lilies, with every inconsequential, frumpy relative and their bratty children summoned to admire her. She updates Delphine on her progress with long, chatty emails, and cheerfully interprets the lack of response as a sign of continuing disapproval regarding her groom and personal motivation for the marriage.

And what of the people who live in her home, who see her every day? It seems that her son has been too upset himself about his grandfather's disappearance to notice the state she is in; his exams are over, as is his summer break, so she arranges a driver to take him to training every morning, and he does not appear again until after dinner, when he takes something out of the fridge and goes to his room to play on his hi-tech gaming gizmos. He does not account for her grief, and she supposes that he thinks she does not deserve it. His grandfather was nothing to her; he was not her hero or her ally or even her close friend, he was just a relative by marriage. So it turns out that the one person who does notice her grief, her despair even, is the one who is furiously pretending not to, as he feels he must. And so her husband behaves as though everything is all right, and that nothing of much consequence has happened at all; he shows remarkably little concern for his father's unaccountable absence, as though it is just a small prank that Zaki has played on them. As though Delphine's grey, faded-out state might be no more than the result of a minor cold. He uses schoolboy phrases to euphemize her wearying depression, to dismiss it with watered-down acknowledge-ment: 'Still a bit off-colour, darling?'; 'Still a bit down in the dumps?' It is true that even he lost some of his chirpy ruddiness when the report came of a man jumping into the river in the early hours on the day of Zaki's exit stage left, but the description was vague, and the body was never found, nor was any sign of its existence. Not so much as a stray shoe. Not enough to prove that it wasn't or was Zaki. Not enough proof for either hope or closure.

Bizarrely, in her clearer moments, when wafting vaguely around her Knightsbridge flat like a confused ghost, Delphine has some admiration for Zaki. For the decisiveness of his action; for leaving his shop open and all his possessions behind. She had said that it was hard to leave, and he had proved her wrong; not content with telling her, he had shown her. She had been a coward by comparison, letting months and months go by, making excuse after excuse. For some days after his sudden disappearance she had believed that Zaki would get in touch with her, and send for her to join him, wherever he was. In a romantic stone cottage in the Cotswolds, in the beach hut in Cornwall where they had spent that weekend; or more likely, anywhere where he might find a casino and racetrack in close proximity. She didn't pack a bag, but she looked around the apartment and tried to think what she would take with her. Lovingly chosen soft furnishings, amusing ethnic knick-knacks from expensive foreign holidays, enormous lacquered photo albums; she couldn't decide if it was all worth taking, or if nothing was. It embarrassed her how much she adored her possessions; they were just things, but they tied her down. She couldn't leave them as freely as

Zaki had left his; she couldn't leave her husband and son as freely as Zaki had left all of them. She was worried that if the call did come, she would be shown to be wanting. That she would not have the courage to leave; that she would not have the courage to have the awkward honest conversation with Jinan and Lucky. But it didn't matter, as the call never came.

Jinan, dealing with her bereavement by ignoring it as much as he possibly can, continues with their relationship as though nothing has changed. He is unusually patient and tender with her, even when she is so disinterested as to be rude. He optimistically interprets her lethargy as agreement, and her caustic remarks as interest. He seems happy to leave her nursing her coffee in the morning and return to her nursing her wine glass in the evening. He continues to make love to her frequently and with enthusiasm, beginning when she is either half awake or half asleep, and seems to be delighted by her slightest response. Only one thing has changed, and this is unconscious on his part; he no longer touches her during the waking day, not even to kiss her hair or touch her shoulder; she is grateful for this, as she does not know that she would be able to avoid flinching. Perhaps, deep down, he knows this, and perhaps that is why he does not touch her; her flinching would give it all away, and might lead to the conversation or argument that puts everything out in the open, and changes everything forever. So during the day, he is happy to share her space but not really interact with her; they are like toddlers too young to understand how to play together, so instead they play their own games side by side. Nothing must change, Jinan thinks, and he repeats what he has been told many times by all the kind people in authority in the months following his father's departure: Life Must Go On.

Must life go on? questions Delphine. It certainly does, she can't deny that, because they are all still here apart from Zaki. But she is not so sure that it must. Her dream selves, her double selves, living the separate lives for her in Les Landes, in Paris, in London, are no longer so sure that their lives must go on; and the dream self who was in the cab with a handsome stranger when her life began, is now wondering what to do with the rest of her life, which must go on, or rather, simply does.

One morning she finally gets up, and instead of drearily mooching to the kitchen with her head hung, she complains about the state of the flat – the cleaner has clearly been slacking off. She complains about the way that her husband has made the coffee, the grounds sprinkled untidily over the floor from when he opened the new packet. She complains about the greasy spatula on the counter from his breakfast, and about the damp, dirty weather. She is petty, annoying, and full of taut energy, like a stretched rubber band waiting to twang back into shape. She looks at herself reflected in the kitchen window, and sees her loose plaits, her pinched, blank face with hollow eyes, smudged with dark circles that her Touche Éclat has not smoothed away in weeks, her thin shoulders hunched in her cream dressing-gown. She looks hideous, like an awkward ghoul. She pours herself some coffee and continues to mutter bitterly in Jinan's direction. 'I bet you look at me every day and think how lucky you are . . .' she says sarcastically. After all her talk about leaving, it seems to her quite likely that Jinan would want to leave her instead; why would her well-scrubbed husband, so nicely groomed and polished, want to hang around to share his space with a skinny, inebriated harridan?

Jinan, who has been listening to this unusual and energetic morning rant with surprise, mingled with unexpected relief, replies quickly before she can continue, 'I do feel lucky when I look at you. Looking at you is easy. It's listening to you that's normally the challenging bit.' Delphine looks at him in shock, and stops her tirade instantly; she almost smiles, although the expression is awkward as she has got out of the habit. She stretches out her hand across the table towards Jinan, and he doesn't hesitate in covering it with his own fleshy palm.

I'm sorry, Zaki, she thinks over the days and weeks and months that follow, as she squeezes herself back out of the neck of the bottle, and replaces the alcohol in her veins with blood. I'm sorry, she thinks when she is making love to her husband, when she is organizing her exquisite house, when she is preparing a gourmet dinner for her family, when she is selecting cheese from the new food emporium on the corner, when she is successfully managing her gifted son into the highest ranks of national football, when she is buying a hat for her friend's wedding. I'm sorry if I used you, just as you suspected; I'm sorry I wasn't strong enough to leave or to let you go.

A Matter of Natural Selection

LUCKY IS SITTING on the step outside the shuttered
corner shop more than a year and a half after Zaki's
departure. The season is over, and the news on the selection
has come out. He suddenly feels conscious that he is being
watched, and looks around warily for men in cars with
zoom lenses. He stands up as a few kids come over; local
kids – he's seen them before in the shop, buying chocolates
and trying to steal beers from under Zaki's indifferent nose.
Zaki always dealt with the miscreants effortlessly; he'd
look up from the *Racing Post* or his crossword, take payment for the chocolates, and say in a bored voice, 'I can't
charge you for the four beers you've got shoved in your
jackets, as I can't sell alcohol to minors, so I'm adding
them to one of your dads' tabs. Whose old man is going to
foot the bill this time? Mikey, shall we take yours?' Without a word, the beers would be replaced, and the boys
would skulk out, abashed. 'Cheers, lads,' Zaki would say
as they left.

'All right, Lucky,' one of the lads says, in a prematurely
deep voice. He is about fourteen, and the rawness of his

spotty face and tender-looking Adam's apple makes Lucky feel impossibly old and worldly-wise; he is eighteen with a steady girlfriend and job – a grown-up already, just a different version of his dad. It was like he'd forgotten to be a teenager in-between being a child and an adult.

'All right, lads,' Lucky replies. There is a pause as they hang around on the corner. Lucky doesn't feel threatened by them; he towers over them. It occurs to him that a stranger walking by would assume that he was their leader.

'Still no news of Zaki, then?' says one of the other lads, a slight, mixed-race boy. Lucky remembers this lad's name, as he was the one who could turn a lit cigarette round in his mouth without burning himself, a good trick which meant that he never got caught smoking in the school cloakrooms like the others did. Peter, his name was; Peter-Peter-Fire-Eater.

'Nope,' Lucky says shortly, not being rude or polite. Niceties over, the lads look at each other, and Peter clears his throat and asks his question, revealing the real purpose for the gang shuffling over to the street corner once they had spotted him.

'Can we all have your autograph, please, mate?' says Peter, holding out one of those short biros that come free with things, and some clean slips of paper.

'Sure,' says Lucky, and taking the biro, signs the proffered bits of paper. 'What do you do with them?' he asks. 'You've all already got my autograph. And none of you are West Ham fans.'

Peter tucks away his autograph neatly in his jacket pocket, careful not to fold it. 'We're collecting them to sell on eBay. We'll wait until after the Worl . . .' he pauses with embarrassment, nudged by one of the others, and hastily rethinks what he was about to say, ' . . . after the summer, I mean. We might get more for them then, once the next season kicks off.' He smiles briefly, showing a glittering flash of train-track braces. 'Cheers, mate,' Peter says to Lucky, and he and the other lads mooch off, kicking cans down the street.

Lucky is stunned by this evidence of cunning and industry. It is somehow gratifying that his signature is helping to keep Zaki's kids in beer and cigarettes; it was like he was signing a cheque, rather than just his name on bits of neatly torn A4. They were trying to be cool, but at least two of them were wearing England shirts. He'd noticed how they had been at pains not to mention the World Cup, as though sparing his feelings. 'Don't mention the war,' he mutters. 'Don't mention the World Cup. I did once but I think I got away with it.' He decides to go inside, and hopping over the back garden wall, lets himself in.

It is slightly freaky inside the corner shop, as nothing has changed since his grandad disappeared all those months before. It's like an abandoned shrine to Zaki. The *Racing Post* and pen on the counter are still there, although Zaki's coffee cup is gone. His dad had washed and dried it, and put it back in the cupboard. The place isn't dusty, which is a bit spooky, as though someone was still living there and taking care of it. Chocolates and tins and packets are still on the shelves, and now well past their expiry date. The only obvious sign of vacancy is that the cold drinks cabinet is switched off, so the beers and bottles sit in tepid darkness. Lucky looks back towards the counter, and for a moment, quite clearly, sees Zaki sitting there, smiling in a shirt open at the collar with his paper in hand, looking ready to dispense another dollop of inappropriate advice. Bugger, thinks Lucky, I knew I shouldn't have taken that stuff with Portia. He had gone to a party with her, a party with other models and minor celebrities, in a club in London. Lucky rarely smoked or drank, but that night he had drunk a lot, to numb the disappointment over the team selection, and because it wasn't like he had a reason to be fit over the summer. Portia had dragged him to the VIP toilets, where some friends of hers were sniffing cocaine, chopping it efficiently into lines with credit cards. 'Do people still do that?' he asked, with faux innocence concealing his disapproval. 'Isn't that a bit eighties?' He had smoked some hash with Portia, and she had persuaded him to try something stronger. 'You can't condemn it until you've tried it,' she said winningly; deviously. 'It's no different from all those Catholic types who boycott movies about Christ that they haven't seen.' Lucky, normally so cautious and risk averse, so mindful of random drugs tests during the season, had taken it. He felt stupid later; why didn't he have the resources to defend himself against Portia? Even he, in the cold light of day, could see how daft her argument was. He felt even more stupid now, as several days later he was having a waking hallucination.

'What's up, Lucky?' asks Dream-Zaki, putting down his paper and stepping up to the counter. Lucky looks at him in surprise, a walking, talking hallucination – what the hell was that stuff she'd given him?

'Nothing,' he replies, feeling foolish. 'Nothing except that I'm talking to a bloody ghost, and I've gone bloody raving mental.'

'Ghost? Do you really think I'm dead?' asks Dream-Zaki with interest.

'No, of course I don't,' mutters Lucky, before adding disloyally, 'you've just buggered off and dumped us; you're probably shacked up with some bird in the Caribbean and haven't thought twice about us.'

Dream-Zaki shrugs with infuriating calm. 'Well, I had my reasons, you know. I don't expect you to understand.' He adds with a twinkle, 'If it makes you feel better, you know I wouldn't have gone to the Caribbean. Too hot, sticky and sandy; nothing to do but trail up and down a beach. Would have bored me to tears, you know I'm not the outdoor type.'

'I might go there with Portia for a week or so,' comments Lucky carelessly. 'I've never been. And it's not like I've got plans for the summer.'

'Oh, that's what this is about, is it?' says Dream-Zaki sharply. 'I take it that the selection for the World Cup squad's been announced? And you've come here to mope about it.'

'I don't know what I was expecting,' says Lucky. 'I would have been the youngest goalie ever taken. But everyone was making such a big deal about it, it was getting so hyped up in the press, I guess I just started to believe it.' He pauses and adds bitterly, 'Do you remember that little oik, Conway? The one who used to call me Frog–Wog in the junior leagues. Comes to my knee. Well, he's been selected. Fucking Wonderkid, they're calling him.' Lucky stares at his hands in disappointment.

'Oh, fuck him, Lucky. It doesn't matter,' Dream-Zaki says. 'Your time will come; you know your time will come.

You're not going to be like the rest of them, a something-nothing. You're something special, and you're going to do well, my son. You've dreamed it, remember?'

Lucky looks up sharply. 'How do you know about my dream?'

'Well, duh,' says Dream-Zaki. 'How do you think?'

Lucky peers through the gloom. Duh? His grandad would never say 'Duh', it wasn't in his vocabulary. He opens his mouth to challenge the man behind the counter, to expose him as a fraud, but Dream-Zaki is gone. 'Oi!' Lucky calls out, but there is nothing but his own voice echoing through the empty shop, the paper and the pen still on the counter. Nothing but his own reflection in the glass of the picture frame hung behind the counter, his face flickering over the photograph of young Zaki, of Lucky's teenage grandmother Nadya, and a cross-looking infant Jinan.

Lucky hears a shuffling at the back door, then Portia calls out, 'Lucky, are you there, babe?' He wishes Portia wouldn't call him babe, it is one of her new affectations; he knows it is meant affectionately, but to him it feels as though Portia is emphasizing her seniority in their relationship.

'How did you know I was here?' he asks, as she comes into the shop from the back.

'I guessed,' she shrugs. 'You weren't at home, and your driver said he dropped you off near Hammersmith tube.' She looks around. 'God, this is weird, isn't it? It's like he just strolled out this morning. He didn't take a thing, did he?'

Lucky shakes his head. He gets up to go upstairs. 'I might make myself a cup of tea; I've got a funny head after all that crap from the other night.' Portia looks like she's about to say something, then stops, and follows him upstairs into the kitchen. 'What?' he asks, annoyed by the sign that she is editing her thoughts. Everyone was being so patronizingly sensitive towards him since the selection, even Portia.

Portia smiles weakly. 'I was going to ask why you were here. But then I realized that I already knew why, so I didn't bother.'

'And why am I here?' Lucky asks crossly.

'Because you're upset about the selection, and you miss Zaki, and this place is Zaki. It even has his scent,' she says gently. 'I miss him too, you know. Sometimes I even feel guilty.'

'Why would you feel guilty?' asks Lucky, picking up the kettle. It was still full, so he emptied out the old water and filled it again, before putting it on to boil.

'I think I might have been a better friend to him, that's all,' she says quietly. She wishes she could say more, as she has felt horrendous guilt about Zaki ever since he disappeared. Did he really think that she was going to tell? She can't quite believe that she can have been responsible, but the fact of the matter was that he had left just a few days afterwards, with nothing apart from the clothes he was wearing. She watches Lucky slump down at the kitchen table, bereft, and her heart goes out to him. 'I know no one can replace Zaki for you, babe. But I'll always be here for you, I promise.'

Lucky reaches out and pulls her heavily towards him, holding her tightly and nuzzling her neck. He feels unutterably grateful, and unutterably sad; abandoned. It was one thing to have someone die on you, like his grandmother had done; quite another to have someone just walk away. Portia sits stiffly, and starts to pull herself back from him. For some reason, her reluctance makes him want to hold her tighter.

'I've just got to go to the loo, babe,' says Portia. She has remembered something; she owes Zaki something. If he has forgotten to hide his secret, then she must do it for him. She goes to the bathroom and looks for Delphine's face-cream, the Crème de la Mer. It wasn't there on the shelf. She breathes a sigh of relief, realizing that he must have put it away. But it occurs to her that at some point, they will need to go through the house and pack up everything, if it is ever rented or sold, if Zaki never returns. And the face-cream would still be here, like a bomb buried and forgotten in the ground and waiting to go off, a beating heart banging under the floorboards, a corpse of lost love dripping in a cavity wall. She looks thoroughly in the medicine cabinet, in the washing basket and finally in the airing cupboard. And there it was, the smooth, white jar of deliciously scented cream. She puts it in her handbag and goes back out to Lucky.

'What were you doing in there?' he asks petulantly.

'Nothing,' she says airily, sitting back down on his lap with a seductive little wriggle, putting her arms around his neck. 'Just thinking. You know I'm the classy type; I think on the bog.'

'Thinking what,' asks Lucky, feeling that familiar fear and almost painful throbbing he experienced whenever Portia got in this mood.

'Thinking that I might have a way to cheer you up,' she says, and begins to undo his buttons. Lucky holds his breath and submits meekly. He is still not very sure whether he likes sex or not; he finds the build-up of tension almost unbearable, and isn't certain whether the release is pleasurable or just a vast relief. His skin tingles so much that Portia's touch almost burns, and his nipples become so painfully sensitive that even brushing them against Portia's perfectly perky breasts causes a quick intake of breath. She, not unreasonably, interprets his reactions as those of extreme enjoyment. And he is still so shy of their bodies, he keeps his underwear on until the last possible moment and prefers Portia in her bra and knickers than naked, although he would never admit this to anyone. A bra and knickers is familiar, like a bikini on the beach, whereas there is something feral about her nudity, something scary. But he cannot deny the satisfaction he feels afterwards, the extraordinary tenderness of holding Portia in his arms, and kissing her gently, before she rolls away from him to go to the bathroom or light another rank fag. He supposes that this must be love, and it more than justifies the slightly undignified tussle it takes to get there. 'You know what they say about people with big hands,' Portia says huskily, her hand sliding inside his jeans.

'Yeah, big gloves,' replies Lucky, gasping as her cool palm cradles his tackle. Suddenly Portia's mobile starts going off, with one of those irritating custom ringtones that she changed almost every week. 'You'd better get that,' he says, trying to sound disappointed. 'It might be your agency.'

Portia sighs, and dislodges her hand from Lucky's jeans to get her phone from her handbag, careful that Lucky can't see the jar of face-cream nestling among the contents. She has been waiting for a callback for a Burberry shoot, and looks at the display. ID withheld, so it wasn't her agency. She flicks it open. 'Hello?' she says. 'Oh, hi Dee. Yes, he's right here. Yeah, I know, it's a pain, that. I keep telling him to keep it charged up. Either that or keep a spare battery. That's what I do. I'll pass you over . . .' She adds unnecessarily to Lucky, 'It's your mum,' as she gives him the handset.

'Yeah,' says Lucky unceremoniously for Portia's sake, as though he was irritated at being disturbed. 'Yeah, well, I said I wasn't bothered and I meant it. Portia and I were thinking of going away this summer anyway, somewhere like the Caribbean.' Portia raises her eyebrows; this is the first she's heard of it, but she shrugs her shoulders at Lucky, as though to say, 'Why not?' 'What do you mean I don't understand? What, like, are you serious? Are you fucking kidding me? Excuse my language, Mum, but are you fucking kidding me? Yeah, I'm coming home right now. No, you don't have to start packing for me, I said I'm coming back now. See you in a bit. Yeah, bye.' Lucky shuts Portia's phone and hands it back to her silently. Tears have started welling in his eyes, and they begin to drip down his cheeks. He holds Portia at arm's length, staring at her smooth, perfect face, pushing back the fashionably elfin hair, just slightly longer than the cropped hair she'd had when they first met.

'Lucky, what's happened?' asks Portia, aware that she was saying something naive and stupid; aware that she was part of something much bigger that hadn't yet been revealed to her. Lucky pulls her into his arms and kisses her tenderly and passionately. The way he used to when they were younger, when kissing was all they did; just lots of wonderful, uncomplicated, full, warm, damp kisses. He kisses her until they are both pink-cheeked and breathless, and finally he whispers to her, his voice breaking into a sob, 'I've been selected. Crichton's been injured, and they're taking me.'

As they walk out of the back door, and he locks up, he gives a brief salute towards the corner shop counter. He realizes that he is shaking; he has had a dream, and now the dream is approaching him, testing him. What if he is tested and found wanting? What if he is a something-nothing after all? Holding on to Portia for dear life, Lucky is consumed by the overwhelming urge to run, but he is suddenly unsure whether he is running away from his dream, or running towards it.

The Chess Hustler of Deauville

I BARELY TOUCHED PARIS. I arrived on one train, switched stations on the metro, and left on another. I went to Deauville on nothing more than a whim. I had read somewhere once that Churchill spent a whole winter there, drinking, playing cards and betting on the gee-gees; it seemed as good a place as any to go. It had two racetracks and a grand casino; it met my modest needs admirably. Part of me wondered if I ought to go a bit further; it didn't seem very far to escape to, the north coast of France. But if I went further south, the weather would improve, and after thirty years in England the thought of hot weather filled me with sticky dismay.

I bought a shoulder-bag and a change of clothes to put in it, and then I checked into a hotel in town – the soulless, anonymous type where all the rooms are identical moulded cubes, where the reception is never manned, and guests come in through the locked doors with a key code. I walked along the beach, looking out at the sea as though it was a vast landscape painting, something that wasn't quite real. The beauty of the grey day, the sky and sea of steel, was overwhelming; for once in my life I was absolutely certain of having done the right thing. I had loved my family enough to set them free from me, I had loved Jinan enough to leave him with the woman he cherished beyond and despite everything, and I had cared enough about Delphine to let her go. Now I was finally free myself, as I'd never been free before. The rest of my life loomed ahead of me like the sand and the sea, each minute a grain of dust and a drop of spray. I felt that I might live forever, as long as the beach spread out before me and the sea churned. I felt sorry for Oscar Wilde, scratching out his last days in Paris, begging from well-to-do acquaintances, lying in the gutter, looking at the stars; Paris sucked away your life and industry and made you its own. This place was different; this place nourished you instead. He should have stayed here, I thought, here he would have been King.

I studied the form before I started betting in earnest. A few flutters, but mainly for educational purposes. I started keeping a book, to beat the bookmakers, just as I had in London. In the meantime, I played cards in the casino, and chess for money. I broke even on the cards, and did more than break even on the chess. I had moved hotels to a family-run place a bit further out of town, as the cubicle had depressed me, and I played with the proprietor and the guests. 'Zaki, I wish I had your luck,' said Yves, the thin, anxious owner who wore wire glasses and always dressed in Parisian black and grey. 'How do you always win big, and lose small? It's unnatural!' The hotel was Yves' retirement project, and he was not enjoying it as much as he'd hoped. He was an avid chess enthusiast, and was hopelessly addicted to playing even though he rarely won, asking for another game when even I thought it was time to stop. I started losing every third game to him out of pity, and found that this had the curious effect of encouraging him to keep coming back for more; once he started beating me every third game, he began to believe that he could beat me in the other games, and then perhaps win some of his money back. He didn't realize that the house odds were stacked against him, and once I had won a month's free accommodation, I decided to stop playing him altogether. I did this the kindest way I could; I beat him ten games in a row, until he decided that it was time to stop – I let him make the decision himself. 'You're an old crook, Zaki,' he said to me mournfully, but without bitterness.

'You know what?' I replied, 'Maybe I am.' How exciting – in just a short time in France I'd become a hustler, and was earning my keep doing what I enjoyed best. Well, almost what I enjoyed best. It was time to try my luck on the nags.

There was something middle-aged about Deauville, and particularly so about the racetrack I frequented. London is a young person's town; even the older people go about trying to look young, with hair dye and collagen and botox, as though there wasn't a stage between youth and wizened, wrinkled old age. There was something refreshing about the nakedness of the middle-aged in Deauville; there was no shame in it here, you could see older couples walking around hand in hand, snogging, laughing and drinking just like normal people. And bizarrely, it made me feel quite youthful; I wasn't an old man in a young man's world any more, I was just me. One of the crowd. Not bad old, mad old, Chacha Zaki. Just bad and mad. I liked the sound of that. I felt quite dangerous. The lack of pretty young girls was also refreshing; among all the middle-aged ladies, there was no temptation, no reminders of the lovely young things I'd spent my life escorting up until now. I found myself staring at one particular middle-aged woman in the stands; she was the sort to draw attention as she was a bit loud and a bit hippy, in both senses of both words. Her generous hips were adorned in a loose ethnic dress with over-the-top embroidery around the neck and hem, and her short, dishevelled hair was dyed a violent shade of red, with lips painted to match. A ruddy tan spread across a face that had chosen plumpness over wrinkles, and she had a raucous, thigh-slapping laugh. She was possibly in her early to mid-fifties; she definitely wasn't a girl, and she certainly wasn't a lady. But there was something appealing about her; she seemed so carefree, or was it just free? She possessed something I envied. Just before I turned to go back to place my bets, she looked back over her shoulder, and saw me staring. She smiled almost mischievously, as though she had caught me doing something wrong – the complicit, ready smile of a woman who got stared at quite a lot, not always for flattering reasons, but who didn't let it concern her. I nodded at her and moved away. I wasn't lucky on the horses that day, but I didn't lose too much either. My book wasn't ready yet; I needed a bit more time for the law of averages to help me out.

Some days later, I was back on the track, drinking a short, bitter coffee and marking up my book. A shadow fell across me, and I smelt and heard her before I saw her. She wore a generous dousing of scent – something like lily of the valley mixed with patchouli – and loud, jingling bangles. This time she was wearing loose, flowing trousers, and in deference to the cooling autumnal weather, a leopard-print cardigan. Another case of tachycardia, I thought with a smile. The woman was the sort to make you smile; she looked almost comic, with her appalling dress sense and her dyed hair and exuberant sense of well-being. You got the feeling that if she got on a crowded bus, passengers who might otherwise have groaned would smile indulgently at her in her silly, optimistic get-up, and make room for her. You had to make room for her: she took up a lot of space in the world. 'Hello,' said the woman cheerfully, in French, 'You can help me win a bet.'

'*Avec plaisir, Madame*,' I said.

'My friend over there has bet me that you're a writer, as you're always scribbling in your little book. Me, I said you weren't. I said you were a professional gambler. You're not interested enough in things to be a writer.'

'I hadn't realized I was being so closely observed,' I remarked. 'And here I was trying to blend into the background.'

The woman snorted gracelessly with laughter. 'Yes, as was I. What failures we are! So, tell me, did I win my bet?'

'Congratulations, *Madame*, yes, you have. My apologies

to your friend, but I'm not one for writing things, I even struggle to fill in a cheque,' I joked feebly. It had been a long time since I had lived in France, and I wasn't quite confident enough in my French to come up with a decent joke. Besides which, something about the woman's boisterousness made me feel a little washed out, a bit pale and insipid.

The woman cackled as though I had cracked a decent joke after all. 'Yes,' she agreed, 'I suffer a similar dyslexia when it comes to writing cheques, specifically those that pay my bills. Thank God I have sympathetic creditors.'

'So tell me, *Madame*, how did you guess what I did?' I asked, feeling braver after her generous reaction.

'I saw your book, and I knew exactly what it was. I keep a book too, although more for fun than gain.' She looked back and saw her friend gesturing to her, raising a small glass of cloudy liquid. 'Ah, my pastis has arrived. Will you join us for an *apéro*?'

I looked around at the quiet bar; if I refused, it was unlikely that they would leave me in peace. The loud woman's voice would be blaring out like a horn whether I was sitting with them or not. So I accepted gracefully, repeating, '*Avec plaisir, Madame*.'

'Oh, stop calling me that. I'm not your teacher,' she said, with the only hint of irritation that I had seen from her so far. 'Call me Coco, everyone does.'

'Like Coco Chanel?' I asked, citing one of Deauville's famous former residents.

'Like Coco Chanel,' she agreed. 'Although considerably less fragrant.' She laughed raucously again, although she must have made this joke many times before. But I laughed too, because somehow she made the old, tired joke sound fresh and funny. She gave new life to old, tired-out things, I realized. That was her gift.

'Oh, of course I know Coco, everyone does,' said Yves over the chessboard. We were not playing for money this time, but he had promised me some quite superb foie gras if I won, so I was sufficiently motivated. I had sampled his wife's foie gras recipe once before; her trick was to marinade it in Armagnac, and the result was like little mouthfuls of meltingly oozing heaven. 'She is Gérard's daughter, he runs the *bar-tabac* in his village. She worked in Deauville and married an administrator in the Centre des Impôts. And she caused a great scandal when she ran off with a younger man.' Yves deliberated with his bishop, and finally committed to the move. He leaned over the board, whispering, 'A black man! With dreadlocks! It didn't last, anyway. She came back some years ago, when Gérard had his heart attack.'

'Where did she run away to?' I asked with interest, responding quickly with the move I had already planned while Yves had been prevaricating. After all, I had some experience in running away, I'd done it twice before.

'How do I know? Do I look like a travel agent?' Yves said testily. He made his next move rather hastily, distracted by wondering where exactly Coco had gone during her long absence. '*Merde*,' he muttered. 'It'll annoy me until I remember where she went.'

Yves' wife, Michelle, a short, slim woman with the effortless elegance that some older Frenchwomen seem to possess, walked in and put her hand on her husband's shoulder. Unlike Yves, she was local, and so knew everything about everyone. 'She went with him to Réunion, first of all, and then to America,' she said. 'She was always a bit funny, Coco, a bit, how do you say, a bit *spéciale*.' She pronounced '*spéciale*' in that French way which was far from complimentary, but with a light shrug, as though disowning what she was saying. She looked shrewdly at the board, then patting her husband affectionately on the top of his bald patch, said, 'I'll go and start the foie gras.' She had already prepared and sliced it – I had seen it in the kitchen under a glass cover – so it only needed to be seared in a hot pan for barely a minute on each side, and served with the pears roasting in the oven.

'Wait, Michou. Not yet,' objected Yves, while I made my move with a forced cough that should have been apologetic, but came out seeming rather smug.

'Checkmate,' I said.

Yves looked towards his wife with a new respect. 'Perhaps she should be the one playing you, eh, Zaki? I might make some of my money back.'

I next bumped into Coco at the racetrack, where she found me ripping up my betting slips methodically and binning them. 'Unlucky?' she asked sympathetically. 'You shouldn't do this to make money; it takes all the fun out of it.'

'Not unlucky,' I said, kissing Coco politely on both cheeks, 'just ignorant. I don't know enough about the horses yet. Or the punters, for that matter. '

'You know, I've kept a book for some time now,' said Coco. 'I might be persuaded to lend it to you.' She had that mischievous smile again, this time as though she was going to do something terribly wrong. 'For example, taking me to lunch might be sufficient persuasion.'

I grinned and rose to the occasion. 'I think I might stretch to lunch. Are you free today?'

'Oh, I'm always free,' said Coco, in a way that wasn't the least bit self-deprecating. 'But I'm warning you, I eat like a horse.' I took her plump arm, which was surprisingly soft, and dimpled around the elbow.

'Good, you know how much I like horses,' I said gallantly, and was almost blown away by her laugh, an infectious cackle that had me laughing too.

Friendly Fire in the Locker Room

Lucky has finished packing, and is sitting snugly with Portia in the Hour Glass, the tiny neighbourhood pub near his parents' flat. He is joining the squad for training tomorrow, and after buying Portia her Diet Coke and himself a mineral water, he asks her offhandedly, 'So, when are you going to come out? They've got a place booked for the players' girlfriends, and wives, of course.'

'Oh, babe, I'm not sure I will,' replies Portia, equally carelessly. 'I've got work, you know. I might still get that callback for the Burberry job.' Lucky looks at her in shock; he had just assumed that she would come out with him. She sips her Diet Coke delicately through the straw with an insouciant air, and he decides that she is just teasing, and relaxes.

'Of course you're coming out,' he says. 'You can always fly back if you've got a shoot. You've got no reason not to come out.'

'Yes I have,' mutters Portia rebelliously. 'This is a big thing, the World Cup. Forget all the media coverage you've had so far, that's nothing compared to what this is going to be. If I come out to mince around a load of posh boutiques, swinging my handbag with the bottle blondes and B-list pop starlet wives, everyone's going to think I'm just . . . totty.' She spits the last word out in disgust.

'Totty? Why would anyone think you're totty? You're nothing like totty,' says Lucky in genuine surprise.

'So now I'm not sexy enough to be totty?' asks Portia, bridling. 'Just because I don't pour myself into skin-tight dresses and flash my tit-tape on all occasions. I'll have you know that I could be bloody totty if I wanted to be.'

'Oh, *totty*,' breathes Lucky with new comprehension. 'Sorry, Portia, I thought you meant Toti, the Italian player.'

Portia looks disbelieving, but then stabs Lucky in the soft part of his belly with her index finger, so he groans and doubles up comically. 'Idiot,' she says affectionately. 'You really want me to come?'

'I really do,' he says. 'I'll need protecting from all those bottle blondes and B-list starlets – you can beat them off for me with that vicious finger, and your big, heavy, clever books . . .'

'OK, I'll come,' says Portia at last. 'You're right. I can catch up on my reading while the other girls are hitting the shops. And I can test out my new killer eyewear at the same time.' She pulls out a pair of designer reading spectacles, made with non-prescription lenses, and tries them on, looking critically at her reflection in her powder compact. It was a new look she was trying out; she didn't like the possibility of being mistaken for a bimbo whenever the paparazzi snapped a shot of her. 'What do you think, babe?' she asks Lucky. 'Do these make me look clever and articulate?' Lucky is suddenly unsure what 'articulate' means; he had thought it was something to do with lorries, but is pretty sure that isn't what Portia is talking about. Yet again, a word's double meaning was holding up a mirror to his stupidity. It seems to him that he has got stupider and stupider since he left school. He hides his awkwardness by taking the safest course of action – that of agreeing with Portia.

'Yes,' he says, so simply that it can only sound sincere. It doesn't seem quite enough, but Portia appears satisfied.

Lucky gets to the locker room early, and the first person who joins him is Felix Conway; the only kid on the squad younger than him. 'All right, Conway,' he says affably, trying to show that he is bearing the stubby little oik no ill will for the name-calling and occasional punching that have dogged their previous encounters. Conway was the player that he knew best on the squad, as there weren't any other West Ham players, and they had had a successful run together in the England Under-18 squad. Of course, it helped that they played on opposite sides of the pitch.

'All right, Frog–Wog,' replies Conway, but in a cheerful tone, whistling as he changes into his practice kit.

'Mate, could you stop that?' says Lucky in exasperation. It's not like Conway would dare say, 'All right, Nigger,' or 'All right, Yid,' to any black or Jewish members of the team.

'Sorry; annoying, isn't it?' agrees Conway, who promptly stops whistling. Lucky is now unsure whether he has been understood, but decides to let it go with a sigh.

He wasn't going to fall into the trap of going on about it; if Conway thought he was sensitive about the name-calling, he'd never hear the end of it. It was what made Conway such a good tactical player; if he saw a weakness, he shamelessly attacked it, whether it was forcing a hot-tempered player to commit a foul, or aggressively tackling someone's knee or ankle when they'd just come back from injury. In some ways he was a bit of dirty player, but he always managed to get a result, and so he was not only forgiven, but rewarded; he'd played first-team football most of the season.

'So,' says Conway, after a pause, 'did they find the voodoo doll in your luggage, then?'

'Sorry, mate, don't get you,' says Lucky shortly. He has decided that the best way to treat Conway is like any other rough kid on the street: not to be rude or polite, and to say as little as possible.

'The voodoo doll of poor Crichton. You must have been sticking pins in him all year to get his place on the squad. A bit funny that he breaks his ankle like that, after the season and all. You'd think someone arranged it for you. Bad break for him, lucky break for you.' Conway stops, then laughs out loud, as he realizes the inadvertent clever-ness of what he has said. 'Did you hear that, mate? Lucky break for you!' He guffaws cheerfully at his own joke, before continuing, with an eye on the door, 'Not that it was a dead cert that you'd have got his place; they'd probably have preferred Huxley if he'd been fit. My mum talked to the secretary at the FA, the not very discreet one who drinks too much at parties. She said that they were just stuck with you to make up the numbers at short notice;

they needed three goalkeepers on the squad, and at least you've had some action this season. "Frightful ponced-up little Wog, that boy, but what choice did we have?" That's what she said.' He gives a complicit shrug, and leans back on the bench.

'Yeah, I've always found drunk secretaries to be the most reliable source of information,' says Lucky, trying not to show how much he is fuming.

'Well, I wouldn't worry about it too much, mate. There's no pressure on you. You're like, the fifth choice goalkeeper; it'll be a cold day in hell before the Man in Grey puts you on the field. You're just along for the ride.'

'Whatever,' mutters Lucky, angry because he knows it's true. The chances of him playing are practically nil; the other two keepers will have to be sent off or injured before he gets a look in. And the chances of him scoring a goal, well, that's just stupid. Whereas the smug little bugger in front of him is England's main goal-scorer, and their best bet for the golden boot.

'Aw, don't look so down, Frog–Wog,' says Conway in a mock semblance of affection. 'It's about the team, remember? And you can help out in training; we all need a dummy in goal for penalty practice, although most of us would want to be up against a proper keeper, so maybe we won't be using you. Perhaps you could help bring out the snacks instead . . .'

'Yeah, I can see your mind's been on snacks recently,' snaps Lucky. It hadn't escaped anyone's notice that Conway, from being a wiry thirteen-year-old, was becoming a somewhat chunky-calved seventeen-year-old, and was now better described as stocky rather than slim. His team hadn't complained, as it hadn't affected his speed and had given him a much better advantage when it came to charging down a line of defenders. Lucky suspects that subtlety is lost on Conway, so just to make sure that the insult has been understood, he adds pointedly, 'I mean, gained a bit of weight, haven't we?'

'That's just because every time I shag your bird, she gives me a biscuit,' retorts Conway without skipping a beat. 'But it's the French Fancies I get after giving your mum one that do the real damage . . .' Lucky leaps for Conway and floors him, holding him down with his arm locked behind him.

'Take that back, you little shit,' he hisses, but then the door to the locker room opens, and their captain walks in and pulls him off.

'Lads, if you want to get intimate, we've got hotel rooms to tussle in,' he says mildly. 'I won't tell the Man in Grey about it this time, but if I catch you doing that again, Lucky, you'll be on the next plane home.'

'Cheers, mate,' says Conway with wide-eyed fawning innocence. 'I don't know what came over him – he just, like, attacked me.'

'Christ, you are so full of shit,' mutters Lucky in disbelief. 'He fucking started it.'

'Yeah, I'm sure he did. I'm sure he invaded Poland,' says the Captain. Conway doesn't get the joke, but Lucky does, and bites his lip to stop laughing. The Captain sees this, and looks a bit more indulgently at the two of them. 'I know we're a long way from home, lads. I know there's going to be a lot of pressure. But you have to remember, there's no excuses for cracking; this is big, this is the World

Cup. It doesn't get better than this, and it doesn't get any worse. Remember, you two are on the same team from now on.' The boys nod, and have the grace to look abashed, then Lucky holds out his hand apologetically to Conway, who takes it. The Captain feels terribly old and weary; this is his second World Cup, he is just twenty-seven years old, and he can't remember ever feeling free and irresponsible enough to start a fight in the changing room. Sponsored to the hilt, he isn't even free enough to choose his own brand of cola drink when out in a bar. He envies the kids their impetuousness, their youth.

When he speaks to the Man in Grey, the Captain mentions that the history between Conway and Khalil might be something more than just media-puff after all. 'I don't want anything putting off Conway,' says the Man in Grey, in his soft Scottish accent that makes him sound so sternly authoritative and trustworthy at the same time. He gave good press conferences the way other people gave good dinner parties – everyone left satisfied, impressed by the demonstration of his talents, and believing that they had had a wonderful time. 'We've got to protect him; he's our star striker, no question of that.' He chuckles. 'Besides, like I told Doris back at the FA, I wouldn't have picked the Khalil kid if I'd had a choice. Frightful, ponced-up little Wog.' The Captain nods uncomfortably, realizing that Lucky Khalil is the one who might need protecting during the tournament, and that the job has fallen to him.

A Wedding of No Importance

I T'S ODD AT HOME without Lucky, thinks Delphine.
She's following his progress every day on the news
channels and internet, and she's calling him occasionally,
careful that it is not so often as to be annoying, but not so
little as to be disinterested. Of course he's been away
before, but this trip feels different; she feels that he won't
come back from this trip, at least not as the boy he was.
He'll come back grown-up, having taken on the expectations and yearning of a whole country – what boy couldn't
be changed by that? He would either be crushed by the
pressure, or stand up stronger and taller than ever before.
Sometimes Portia answers his phone for him, sounding
crisp and efficient, and perhaps even a little . . . proprietor-
ial. Delphine realizes that this is the start of a bloodless
coup; she is being gently ousted by Portia – the writing was
on the training-ground wall the first time he forgot to give
his mum the usual peck goodbye, when he saw Portia
standing there, waiting for him. He might move out when
he comes back, she realizes with a shock; he'll move in with
Portia. They both earned decent incomes, far more than

she'd earned when she first started in marketing; there was nothing to keep him at home apart from her cooking. She bites her lip, and starts painting her toenails with a suddenly intense concentration.

'Hello, darling,' calls Jinan, as he walks in the front door. He finds her sitting at the dressing-table, her feet propped up on a stool as she varnishes her toenails, the late evening sun streaking in the window and catching the ends of her hair, turning them almost gold. He kisses her hesitantly on the top of her head, so as not to disturb her, so as not to spoil the tableau with his chubby, sweaty self, and sits heavily on the bed, removing his tie. When he thinks of Delphine, she is always at the dressing-table; it's where he would have her painted, if he was the sort of man to give time to such things. 'Delphine at the Dressing-Table', like Bonnard's wife in the bath. He watches with admiration the gentle, precise strokes of the brush, which leave her toes shining like little scarlet jewels. Sometimes he thought that Delphine was a frustrated artist herself, forced to use her body as her most readily available palette. Pencils, kohl, coloured creams and pots of fine silver and gold dust, all blended together by her as she re-created herself each day. However, because Delphine always looked consistently wonderful to him, he frequently struggled to see the results of all her labour. It was as though he possessed a funny kind of sympathetic blindness that made it impossible to see her flaws, or even acknowledge them; a little like people with that illness that makes them unable to recognize faces. Jinan would peer at Delphine's face in the same myopic way before an evening out, in order to check that she was already made up and ready to leave. Once, a long time ago, he had got it wrong; they were due to meet friends for dinner, and he had got back from golf a bit late. He had dashed into the house, and on seeing Delphine all in black with her hair pulled back stylishly, showing her smooth and gleaming forehead, had assumed that she was ready to go. He had been trotting back out the door when Delphine had yelped in insulted outrage, 'Do you really think I'm going out like this?' How could he explain that as she always looked the same to him, there was little she could do to make herself lovelier, and that it wasn't intended to offend, no, not at all? On that occasion, it turned out that Delphine had not only not yet done her make-up, she hadn't even dressed. She had just got back from yoga class a little late herself, and was still wearing her loose yoga trousers and a T-shirt; her hair had been scraped back, not pulled back stylishly, but he hadn't seen any of that. He had just seen her.

'Christ, it's hot out there. It's a relief to get indoors. And to get that tie off. It's like a noose in this weather,' he says amiably.

'I don't know why you wait until you get home before you take your tie off; you could take it off when you walk out of the office,' Delphine replies distractedly. She is thinking about Lucky and Portia moving in together; hopefully they'd stay somewhere close by. Portia wouldn't want to go anywhere near to Lucky's team's ground, it wasn't trendy enough for her. But then, maybe Knightsbridge wasn't trendy enough either. She might want to go somewhere like Chelsea, or Notting Hill. Or maybe somewhere even further, somewhere miles up the Northern Line, like Camden or Hampstead. Somewhere Delphine would never

have an excuse for visiting. She'd never see him. Oh
God . . .

'I've got to keep up appearances; you never know who
you might bump into in the car park, or waiting at the
lights. Can't be seen without a tie; it's an act of weakness.
And I've got that promotion coming up, remember? The
one that'll put me in charge of long-range planning; no
more nuts and bolts work on M&A, if that happens.' Jinan
says this happily; the promotion, which carries a place on
the executive committee, is practically a dead certainty, and
the well-known fact that his son was on the national
football squad was not endangering his chances one little
bit. Jinan liked being recognized in his work; it was one of
the things he measured his self-worth by – prowess at work,
beautiful wife, successful son. He could just as well be
called Lucky, he thinks with satisfaction, without the
slightest tell-tale niggle from recent memory bothering him.
As though he had never had a phantom heart murmur,
never played his father at chess and won. Everything was
unchanged, beautifully and wonderfully unchanged; it had
taken Delphine a little bit of time to adjust to this state of
affairs, but he had been patient, and had been rewarded.

Delphine smiles weakly. 'Mmm, long-range planning.
Nice gig that; no one will ever be able to tell if what you
do is any good, as it's all too far in the future. You can
spend all day surfing and playing pinball on your laptop.'

Jinan laughs, a bit uncomfortably. He wishes Delphine
would take his work a bit more seriously – he was more
than Very Important now, he was One of the Most Important, but she didn't seem to appreciate the difference. 'The
house is looking fantastic,' he says, changing the subject.

'Kasia's really pulled her socks up since you had that chat with her.'

'Mm-hmm,' assents Delphine vaguely. 'I'm not sure it was my motivational speech that did it. I think it was when I rearranged the furniture, and showed her all the dust-balls underneath that were big enough to start growing their own ecosystems.' She has finished her nails, and sprays them with some expensive mist that promises to set them more quickly. 'Anyway, she didn't get slack maliciously. She was just a bit distracted; she's finally applying for teacher training, you see.'

It seems to Delphine that everyone but her is aspiring to something better: Jinan to his promotion, Kasia to her new career, Ronnie to her new life as a wife, and Lucky and Portia to their trendy new home; this last has swiftly moved from conjecture to certain, unavoidable fact in her head. She herself aspires to nothing any more; she tried, she sank, she bobbed back up to the surface, and now she is just treading water. She doesn't want anything, and she wants for nothing; it's not so unpleasant. What was it someone had said to her once? That there are only two tragedies: the first was not getting what you want, the other was getting it instead. Far better to forget about aspiring, and avoid tragedy altogether. 'Well, that's done,' she says, looking with satisfaction at her toes and fingernails, and then feeling faintly silly for how pleased she is with them, as though a decent nail job was really something significant enough to take pride in. 'Much better to do it tonight – there's never enough time in the morning, is there?'

Jinan stretches out on the bed, then bounces up with a tigger-like enthusiasm. 'You know, I'm really looking forward to Veronica's wedding tomorrow. It's been ages since I went to the wedding of someone I actually liked.'

'You clearly haven't met the groom,' Delphine says darkly. Poor Ronnie, with her boring, twice-divorced, elderly, unprepossessing, overly possessive future husband; the media man of her dreams. There are only two tragedies, thinks Delphine. It sounds like something Zaki would say. She must have heard it from Zaki.

Katie notices first. She whispers it urgently to Delphine after Veronica has sailed down the aisle, her smooth dark back and gleaming shoulders rising magnificently from a frothy wedding dress that has much more cachet than a Vera Wang meringue, as it has reputedly been hand stitched by a famously reclusive and exclusive dressmaker somewhere unpronounceable in deepest Wales. Veronica is trailed by her adorable nieces, looking like chocolate cherubs wrapped in frilly silk, scattering pink and yellow rose petals that match their sorbet-coloured gowns and the sparkling beads in their corn-rows. 'Dee, how long has it been since you've seen Ronnie?' she asks.

'At least a month; not since the hen do, actually. She's been so frantic. And I've been busy negotiating Lucky's endorsements, since he got the call-up for the squad.'

'Me neither, I've barely been getting out at all, not with this bloody bowling ball banging against my pelvic bone every time I take a step,' Kate replies, gesturing towards her impossibly pregnant belly. The baby was already over-due. 'And that scrap of a dress she wore at the hen do left nothing to the imagination, did it? I mean, she wasn't even wearing a bra—'

'What's your point?' interrupts Delphine, sighing sadly as Veronica has reached the altar and her disappointing husband-to-be has taken premature possession of her, holding her hand firmly as though he is afraid that she might think better of it and dash back out the way she came, trailed by the chocolate-sorbet cherubs and their empty flower baskets. Go, Ronnie, go, she urges silently, although without much hope.

'Well, just look at her tits! They're enormous – they were nothing like that a month ago!' says Katie in a stage whisper, over the organ music. Jinan is glaring at them disapprovingly; he has heard the words 'tits' and is trying to look stern. As a non-Christian, he tends to be very stiff and reverent in churches because he has spent so little time in them.

'My God, you're right. They're fabulous!' mutters Delphine in an uncertain mix of outrage, admiration and envy, glancing down at her own diminutive bosom. Another thing about her that was 'Really minimal, darling'. 'Shit! You don't think she's had them done, do you? Some creepy sort of wedding present for him?'

'God, Dee, you're such an innocent,' giggles Katie, before grimacing and holding on to her tummy. 'Ouch, fucking ouch. He doesn't like it when I laugh, I think he's just head-butted my cervix.' She pats the bump soothingly for a minute and murmurs to Dee as the organ music stops, 'Does she look like a woman who's just been through nipple-slicing surgery? I reckon she's got herself knocked up; it always hits the tits first.'

'Oh God,' says Delphine sadly, 'I guess she really has to

marry him now,' for all the world as though they weren't already sitting in a flower-filled gothic church, clutching custom-made orders of service wrapped in silk ribbons and listening to choristers warbling the first hymn in exaggerated harmonies, with her own husband's untrained tenor booming out enthusiastically. It seems that none of these things are as real or important as the fact of Veronica's increased bosom; nothing else matters. Katie stifles a laugh at Delphine's exaggerated hangdog manner, and groans and clutches her tummy once more.

During the champagne reception outside the church, Veronica races up to them and screams with delight. 'Babes! Have you forgiven me? I'm so sorry I couldn't have you as my bridesmaids! It's just that if I had, I'd never have heard the end of it from my mum, asking why I didn't pick my sisters. So much easier just to have the flower girls.'

'And much more photogenic,' agrees Katie. 'Your nieces are so cute, they're like something from a Mothercare catalogue. We'd have looked like bloody Jack Sprat and his wife, walking up the aisle behind you. Well, Dee would have been walking. I'd have been rolled along by someone with a stick.'

'You look beautiful,' says Delphine sincerely, and rather solemnly. She hugs Veronica close to her, and nods irreverently down towards her bosom. 'So tell us, what's that all about?'

'Christ, is it that obvious?' squeals Veronica. 'I thought everyone would just think I suddenly had great boobs!'

'They might have done if you'd covered them up a bit more in the past, Ms-I've-got-a-push-up-bra-and-I'm-gonna-use it,' says Katie dryly. 'So how many weeks are you gone?'

'About six, I think. I didn't have a clue about it at the hen do – I'm glad I didn't drink too much that night. Hubby over there is so excited, you'd think it was his first, not his third.' She adds in hushed excitement, half whispering so the rest of the guests can't hear, 'Can you believe it, girls? I'm going to be a mum!'

'I'm so pleased for you, honey,' says Delphine. 'It's the best thing ever. I know it's what you've always wanted.' She finally has a reason to congratulate Veronica sincerely that day, and she can finally understand her decision; Delphine now realizes that the groom was just a means to an end, a way to get what Veronica had always dreamed of. Like the flower-filled church and the custom-made programmes, in fact like the whole elaborate wedding, he really didn't matter at all.

Delphine couldn't help reflecting during the reception, the speeches and the cutting of the spectacular mountain of a cake from Patisserie Valerie, that Veronica and Katie's lives were beginning again, and hers had almost ended. They had had wonderful careers, and now they were starting up and increasing their families, whereas Delphine's life was practically over – or worse than that, was staying exactly the same. It was as though she was frozen in time; once Lucky left, which might be in a matter of months, or even weeks, she would no longer be a mother. She would be a nothing. Not even a corporate slut. It's funny, and sad, she thinks, that all she ever wanted to be, once she had achieved such early success in her job, was a *maman*, and that now it was done, she had nothing left to look forward to. I'm too young for my life to be over, she thinks disconsolately, and I'm too old not to have really lived.

Looking around the room, at guests who had brought small children, breastfeeding, cuddling, talking away quite normally while they held wriggling babies on their laps, Delphine remembered what it was like to be a new mother. She had been worried that she wouldn't be very good at it; that all her expertise lay in marketing and organization, not in caring and nurturing. It was something that required skill, of that much she was certain. That was why she'd been so stern with clumsy, well-meaning Jinan; he'd never been very good with his hands, and she just didn't trust him not to drop Lucky, not to bang the baby's head against the door-frame when walking into another room, or to fasten the nappy firmly enough for it not to fall open. She hadn't trusted him at all. 'Support the head,' she had squealed fearfully whenever he held Lucky. 'Support it *properly*!' Yet funnily enough, when Jinan wasn't around, when there wasn't someone looking on as she performed the role of Supermum, she herself had felt strangely uncomfortable, and rather awkward. Like an actor backstage at an empty theatre, waiting for the show to begin, but without a script for support or an audience for approval. She would sit and look at Lucky, and think, 'Well, what do I do now?' She would say her lines. 'Good boy! Maman loves you so much,' and perform the set pieces at the set times: nappy change, bath time, feed. But she felt she was, somehow, doing something wrong. As though she might be saying the wrong lines in the show, but no one was correcting her. She was relieved when Jinan came back in the evening and she could scold him for his own awkwardness, and demonstrate once more what a good and accomplished mother she was. During the day, the only relief she had was Zaki. The black hole of her engagement night had been forgotten by unspoken consent, and he turned up regularly with grandfatherly gifts for Lucky, making up silly rhymes and games for him, and singing little songs. It might only have been her imagination, but sometimes she thought she saw him looking at Lucky rather more pensively than he needed to; was he wondering what she sometimes wondered too? It was possible, but very, very unlikely. Wouldn't one of them have remembered?

She had been so occupied with Lucky, so in love with him, really, that she couldn't imagine herself having another child. And so, when she finally went off the pill when he was settled at school, it hadn't been too much of a disappointment when they didn't. But all these years afterwards, she was asking herself, why weren't we able to have another child? Why didn't we? And how did we manage to have Lucky?

She wondered whether that was what Zaki had begun to think. It was one thing to steal your boy's wife, quite another to steal his son as well. The one thing you do for your child is try and protect him from the things that can hurt him, keep him safe; so what do you do if the thing that can hurt him, if the thing that is threatening his safety, is you? You must remove the threat, and so you leave – you really have no other choice. Couldn't that have been why Zaki had run away? It seemed so simple to her now, so obvious. He had been all posturing bravado and disdain when it had come to Jinan, but part of her had always suspected his secret, that he loved Jinan every bit as much as she loved Lucky. That he was much fonder of Jinan than he had been prepared to admit.

Delphine is aware that she is being looked at, and realizes that Jinan has broken off his conversation with Tony, Katie's husband, and is waiting patiently for her attention. 'I've heard the good news about Ronnie,' he says. 'It'll be nice to have another little baby around to spoil, won't it?'

'Yes, it will,' Delphine says, wishing she felt as cheerful as she sounded. 'Babies are great,' she adds with a grin to Tony, but even though her voice is steady and there is no wistful catch in her throat, she feels hollow when she says this. Jinan looks at her again, and sees something in her smiling face that no one else can see, something frozen in her features that is almost piteous. It pulls at his gut in as deep a way as Lucky's first infant bawling did – an intensely physical reaction that makes him want to reach for her and hold her. So he does, almost without thinking, and Delphine sits meekly and accepts his unsolicited hug, amazed that he has tacitly understood her need for comfort, and humbled by the unselfishness of his response.

The Guilty Comforts of Ugly Furniture

COCO LIVED IN A small flat in town, almost as small as the studio flat I had lived in with Nadya in Paris. She had had some training with an antiques dealer in her youth, and her place was filled with eclectic finds from the local markets: dark, beautifully carved old tables mingled with ostentatious art deco, ethnic statuettes and sequinned bedspreads. She had the most hideous armchair imaginable, covered in tattered chintz, that was the most comfortable thing I had ever sat in; I sank into it, and felt that I'd never be able to get up. 'I couldn't stay in antiques,' Coco explained to me over stewed espressos so thick that the surface tension kept the sugar lumps on top, until we eased them down with our teaspoons. 'I liked going to the markets, or to people's homes; I liked discovering new stock, but I hated selling it. I hated having to sit in a shop all day. I have an inbred hatred of shops; it's the result of my cretinous upbringing in the *bar-tabac*. My father was amazed that I didn't want to take the place over from him; he thought it would be my greatest dream to manage his cruddy little shop. I told him when I left that he had the soul of a shopkeeper, and you know what . . .' She paused, and I filled in the end of her sentence for her.

'. . . he took it as a compliment,' I said with confidence. 'Yes, my father was the same – he was a shopkeeper, and he made me one too. I wanted my son to be something different, something creative. He didn't become a shop-keeper at least, but he became a lawyer. Almost as bad.'

Coco nodded sympathetically. 'My daughter became an administrator, like her father. The very dullest thing she could have chosen. It was my fault, because her father was the very dullest thing I could have chosen. I think, in fact I know, I married him just to escape the bloody shop. When it was clear that my *apprentissage* in antiques was not too successful, my father said, 'Don't worry, Coco. You can come home. You can work in the shop.' I had no job, and nowhere else to go, so I accepted Didier's proposal. I didn't know him very well; I wasn't even particularly fond of him. It's like when you're hitchhiking in the rain: you take the first car that stops.'

'How long were you with him?' I asked, putting down my espresso cup and melting back with guilty pleasure into the soft blowsiness of the hideous armchair.

'Sixteen years,' she shrugged, with a hint of embarrass-ment. 'I got pregnant almost straight away with Claudette, and I wasn't brave or clever enough to leave earlier. Then I met Fabien, and I got brave, although I was still not very clever; he was eight years younger than me, and very roman-tic, but I should have known that we had no future.' She gave a very Gallic shrug and pouted, an eloquent little gesture that she often made use of. 'But when you are in love, you don't think of these things,' she said with cheerful resignation, stretching up her arms and putting them behind her head. 'Claudette, she was furious with me. She stayed with her father and took her Bac exams, and refused to speak to me for months. I would call, and she would hang up. She sent back my letters unopened. She didn't really forgive me until Fabien and I separated, but even now she doesn't approve of me. I think that I embarrass her.'

'So you came back when you separated?' I asked, noticing again how soft and dimpled her arms were; the undersides were quite pale in contrast with her lurid purple smock, and I had an absurd urge to touch them, to stroke them as you might stroke a cat's satin underbelly.

'No, I didn't come running back when Fabien left. I stayed in the States; I was working as a croupier in Atlantic City, and I liked it there. But I had to come back when Papa had his heart attack. He didn't ask me to come back, but I did. He needed my help; he wouldn't let anyone else run the stupid shop while he was ill, and my poor *maman* had her hands full looking after him and Mémé – that's my grandmother,' she explained unnecessarily, as most grandmothers of that generation were known as 'Mémé'. 'And of course Claudette was too busy pushing her paper around in her unimportant job to help.'

'So you ran the shop for him?' I asked in surprise. 'I thought you hated the place?'

'Just until he was better. What else could I do?' she said, with the same shrug and pout. I realized that I was growing rather fond of Coco; it was like she was another part of me, with the same disappointments and dreams of escape, with our fathers with the shopkeeper souls, and our disapproving offspring. I wondered if I were to look in a mirror, perhaps the ornate, scrolled one that hung heavily on Coco's wall above her fireplace niche, I would see myself as I saw Coco: someone past their best and a bit ridiculous in appearance, but who, despite everything, hadn't yet given up on life, on love, on their dreams. I wondered if this was how other people saw me. Coco was watching me questioningly, and asked with a smile, 'So, you think I was stupid to come back, no? You think I was stupid and weak to come back and take over the shop I hated. I did it for my father; he is a kind man, a gentle man. A gentleman, even.' Her lips pronounced '*gentilhomme*' distinctly, and rather ruefully, as though his kindness had been her undoing, and she would have done better if he had been a cantankerous old sod like so many other old men, my own Baba included. It hadn't occurred to me that a good father could be the undoing of a renegade child; it was normally the other way around.

'I would never describe you as stupid or weak,' I said sincerely to Coco, before overplaying my hand. 'If I had to describe you, I think I might say you were clever and brave.' I was aware that I was being rather too charming, rather too smarmy in directly contradicting her earlier words, but I couldn't stop myself. I was hypnotized by the paleness of her soft, full arms. I was astounded to find myself thinking what it would be like to be held by them; perhaps it would be almost as comfortable as the ancient, ugly chair, which was enveloping every inch of me so miraculously.

'You are flattering me,' she said with disapproval, 'or worse, you are teasing me. You should meet my father, he is also a difficult one to resist. Not because he is charming, like you, but because he is . . . himself.'

'I'd like to meet your father,' I said unthinkingly, without fully realizing the implications of what I'd said. Coco was as surprised as I was, but her open, merry face displayed nothing but pleasure, and she flushed rosily, so that her cheeks matched her cherry-painted lips. After waiting a moment, possibly to check that I wasn't going to backtrack on what I had just said, she finally spoke: 'I think he would like to meet you, too. I'll arrange it; perhaps we can go over for lunch on Sunday.'

I thanked Coco for the coffee and made to leave, giving her the usual polite kisses on both cheeks. But this time, at the door, after the kisses, she put her arms around me and with irrepressible enthusiasm, pulled me to her in a bear hug. Her arms were every bit as soft and cushiony and comfortable as they had promised to be. 'Until Sunday,' she said, letting me go and smoothing down her awful purple smock over her baggy, silky trousers. Her lips were too bright, and managed to clash with both her smock and her hair, but her eyes were bright too. She was loud, in both senses of the word, and she was hippy, in both senses of the word; she was not a girl, and certainly not a lady, and she had appalling taste in clothes and quirky taste in furniture. No wonder it had taken me so long to notice that she was, actually, rather pretty.

The Making of a Model

THE WEEK AFTER his mother's best friend married a media mogul, Lucky is reading the papers. It is the night before the third group stage match, and he has been told firmly that he must be in bed by 10.30 p.m. But even though he knows there is absolutely no possibility of him playing the next day, he is too excited to sleep. He is not breaking any rules, as strictly speaking, he is in bed. And his light is turned off, so if anyone came to check, there would be no sign that he was still awake. But he is awake, and he is hiding under the hotel duvet reading the tabloids with a torch, like a kid trying to hide porn from his mum.

The papers are predictable; there are inches and inches about Conway, who has been even more insufferable since scoring a hat trick in the first group game against Australia. At least there is a less than flattering cartoon of him, looking unfairly chubby and bearing the legend 'The Fatboy Felix Strikes Back'. He rips it out to show Portia; she probably wouldn't get the *Star Wars* reference, so it might be one of the few times he got to explain something to her rather than the other way round. There is quite a bit of speculation about the fitness of their second striker, who has had an injury-prone season and didn't manage to play a full ninety minutes in the friendly, and some heart-warming articles about the twins recently born to one of the midfield players. Lucky's name is mentioned only once, in an article about the wives and girlfriends – the Wags, as some wag from a Sunday paper still insists on calling them. There are a few photos of Portia looking both stunning and intelligent; her non-prescription glasses have been as effective as she had hoped and have caused quite a stir, and he is mentioned in passing as her 'childhood sweetheart'. Lucky doesn't like the phrase, which is often bandied about in reference to them; it implies that their relationship is already over, and that she's now in the market for an adult sweetheart.

In the next set of papers, there are even more photos of Portia. She seems to have become the darling of the press pack, possibly because she is one of the youngest of the team girlfriends. As one of the few non-blondes, she is certainly the most recognizable in a crowd, and those glasses, again, make her unmissable. The more Lucky thinks about it, the more he realizes that she is really quite special among the other girls, most of whom look almost identical at a distance, with long highlighted hair, enormous sunglasses and sporting similar combinations of skinny jeans and strappy tops recently purchased from the Milan boutiques. Of course, Portia was already a successful model, and she knew how to self-promote and get herself seen and photographed in much the same way that an actress would know how to deliver a snappy line; but Portia was also skilled enough to maintain a teasingly reluctant air at the same time. The Lady Di act, someone had called it; the doe-eyed skipping away from the cameras while at the same time ensuring that her hair was perfect and that they got the best angle and lighting. It might have been calculated, but it was so much more appealing than the wannabe attention-grabbing antics of the other girls, who spent most of their nights getting wasted in the bars out of boredom, then calling their boyfriends tearfully in the early hours, forgetting that the lads were on England duty and playing for their country the next day. The Captain's wife was notoriously neurotic, so much so that there were rumours that the Man in Grey was thinking about banishing her back to Blighty.

Lucky had listened to the lads complain in the dressing-room about the raucous behaviour of their girlfriends. He had tried to look sympathetic, he had made the right sounds, and he had even tried to feel smug about his own perfect Portia, who went for a polite few drinks, then returned to her main job of manipulating the media while she sat in well-lit public areas with a book and her clever glasses. But the truth was Lucky hadn't felt sympathetic; he'd felt a little jealous. Why didn't Portia ever call him in drunken desperation, to say slurringly that she really, really loved him, that she really, really missed him? Because he missed her; not the Portia that was in the papers, the cunning self-image she had fashioned, who wore clothes that were deemed elegant when they were long, and frivolous when they were short, but who was never, ever labelled slutty. He missed the Portia she had been before; the previous Portia, who had rucked up her school skirt to climb over a wall and help him practise his goalkeeping, who had chewed the end of a biro while she concentrated on a sudoku puzzle at the corner shop counter, who had righteously charged him for a Coke that he had thoughtlessly shoplifted. Portia the brave, the smart, the just; the keeper of small confidences and unhappy inner thoughts; his dark, brooding angel. This is the Portia he looks for when he calls to the Portia who has taken her place; he knows that she is still in there somewhere, and that everything else that surrounds her is just pretty, shiny wrapping.

The Delightful Consequences of Playing with Cards

JANUARY WAS A QUIET, grey month in Deauville; with the goodwill and bustle of Christmas over, the town could no longer pretend to be anything other than what it was: a beach resort out of season. I took a break from the nags and the tables, and found myself spending much of my time with Coco, turning up unannounced at her funny little flat when I was in town.

I had first called in out of politeness; I found myself walking by her place just after New Year, and it occurred to me that she might have seen me, and that it would be rude not to stop and say hello. Especially after I had spent Christmas with her family. Her father, a kind old gentleman who obsessively polished the bottles in his beloved *bar-tabac* on Sunday afternoons, had asked me over for Christmas when I visited for lunch. He and his wife were quite insistent when they realized I had no family locally, and after a pastis *apéritif*, two good bottles of red and rosé during the soup course, main course, salad course, cheese course and pudding, and a large whisky as the *digestif*, I found that I was too well fed and merry to argue. Besides,

I wouldn't have admitted it to them, but I had been desperate to avoid the hotel as much as possible during the festivities. I'd nursed hopes that Yves and Michelle would disappear off to one of their grown-up children in Paris, and leave me king of the manor, but instead their grown-up children and hordes of rug-rats had all descended some days before the *réveillon* on Christmas Eve, and were not leaving until New Year. I couldn't bear all that childish good will; I knew where I was with Coco and her picture-postcard parents and her arthritic Mémé. In fact, Christmas had been quite a jolly affair, just a slightly more lavish Sunday lunch, and had provided the added entertainment value of disapproving Claudette turning up briefly to sniff at her mother's hairdo and outfit. She had bought Coco a sober grey trouser suit, which Coco, to her credit, accepted with a ready smile, as though any gift from her daughter brought her pleasure. Her smile only faded when Claudette tactlessly insisted that Coco wear the suit during the dinner party she was planning with her in-laws; Coco was right, Claudette was embarrassed by her.

So there I was, knocking on Coco's door, and she was so cheerful and welcoming, I felt slightly ashamed that I'd had to think twice about it. So I found myself knocking again, and again; she wasn't always in, as she occasionally helped out some local artisans with their accounts and paperwork. It was the way she earned her pocket money; that and occasional rental income from the holiday villa in Réunion which she had bought with Fabien and now owned outright. It tickled me a bit that I was finally the one laying siege to someone, just as others had carelessly dropped in on me when I was the fixture in the corner shop. With Coco's energy, common sense, warmth and candour, the listless afternoons seemed to pass quickly, even though we often did nothing more than drink endless coffees and talk.

Coco surprised me one afternoon when she offered to do a reading for me; she went to an elaborately carved wooden box that was sitting unassumingly on the shelf, pulled out a package wrapped in black silk, and unwound it to reveal a deck of tarot cards. 'I didn't know you read cards,' I said suspiciously. It was the black silk that threw me; it hinted of ceremony, it had the taint of . . . belief, and although Coco was quite hippy in lots of ways, she had always struck me as quite a practical woman, not the sort to get involved in faddy things.

'Ah, but these are truly special cards,' she said, amused by my discomfort.

'Because a cursed gypsy gave them to you?' I hazarded sarcastically.

'Yes, of course. And also because it's the same deck they used on *Live and Let Die*. You know, the Bond movie. Where he replaced every card with the Lovers, so the girl would sleep with him.'

I chuckled a bit rudely. 'You've not done that, have you?'

Coco tutted at me sternly, and her censure seemed all at odds with her flaming hair and coin-belted skirt, like a schoolgirl trying to ape the headmistress. 'You are not at all funny, Zaki.'

'Your family thinks I'm funny – they laughed at all of my jokes,' I replied, cheerfully unabashed.

'They are polite,' sniffed Coco dismissively, and she started to lay out the cards. 'A girlfriend in Atlantic City gave me these, and showed me how to do a reading. It's easy – this represents what you were, this is what you are, and this is what you will be.'

'There's really no point doing this,' I said, stretching back on my favourite ugly chair. 'I already know who I was, and who I am, and I don't care about who I will be; I don't believe in fate. Not any more.'

'I don't believe in fate either,' said Coco approvingly, 'but I do believe in chance.' She gestured towards the cards. 'This is just for fun. The most interesting thing is how people react to what you say.'

I leaned forward and swept all the cards back together, shuffling them like a normal deck. 'OK, if you believe in chance, I'll take a chance on a card,' and I picked one off the top and put it flat on the table. 'Ouch,' I said, looking at it. It was an unpleasant-looking card – a medieval-style keep had been struck by lightning and was collapsing in flames. 'I don't think I want to know what that means.'

Coco looked it up in her little book that had been hidden in the box with the cards. That reassured me somewhat, that she didn't know what the cards meant by heart; it seemed that her interest really was just for fun. 'The Tower: it means that something terrible and tragic has happened, or will happen; the lightning punishes the guilty ones who have exploited and abused others. Not so nice,' she said matter-of-factly.

'Your turn,' I said, proffering the deck. She took the top

card, looked at it, blushed, and put it back face down. 'Show me,' I insisted, amused by her embarrassment. 'What, is it The Lovers or something?'

'No, you conceited man,' she muttered, and reluctantly turned it face up for me.

'Oh,' I said, looking at the scythe-wielding, skeletal figure of the Death card. 'Not so nice, either.'

'It's not so bad; I know what this card means, it's the one that everyone knows. It just means that everything will change,' she said, shrugging her shoulders.

'If it's not so bad, why are you disappointed?' I asked. I saw a slight flush begin to heat her cheeks again, and suddenly had a feeling that I could guess the answer myself.

'Because I don't want everything to change,' she said, looking straight at me. One of the things I liked about Coco was that she kept no secrets; she was as transparent as cellophane. Her blush deepened across her round, apple cheeks, practically reaching her ears and matching the short, bright hair tucked behind them. I suddenly felt a little reckless, and reaching over to her, I pulled her onto my lap in that sinfully comfortable chair and kissed her chastely on her snub nose.

'How about changing just a few things, instead?' I suggested.

'You are presumptuous,' she declared with unconvincing tartness. She struggled to get out of the chair, but it fitted snugly around her hips and held us both in. 'And you are certainly not as handsome as you think.'

'But despite that you like me,' I said, finally letting her escape from the chair. She blushed again, and started picking up the cards that had fallen off the table. 'You must know by now, I like you too, Coco,' I said, astonishing myself with my sincerity. I must have startled her too, as she looked at me with tears welling in her big brown eyes, and flung her arms around me, kissing me with her cherry-red lips. I could see us reflected in that mirror of hers, the ornate one which hung low above the little fireplace niche, looking like the most mismatched pair you could imagine: me tall to her small, me thin to her thick, me faded to her flamboyant. I could have been thinking, 'Oh my God, I've barely been in Deauville for more than a few months and I've lumbered myself with an elderly girlfriend as round and gaudy as a Christmas bauble, and her family to boot.' I could have been thinking, 'Just break off the kiss, leave, and look embarrassed and apologetic, and she'll be too good-natured to hold a grudge.' I could have been thinking, 'Perhaps it's time to try another town with a better casino; perhaps it's time to blow all my funds and head to Las Vegas.'

But instead I was thinking how dull and inanimate I looked next to her radiant roundness; instead I was thinking how wonderfully her soft body with her enormous, matronly bosom filled the circle of my arms; instead I was thinking how warm and happy I was, suffused with a rosy glow that started somewhere in my stomach and travelled outwards, as though I was the one that was blushing. I was thinking how the hole in my dry little heart, which had been withering ever since Nadya flew over the street, was finally closing up. With Delphine, all the overwhelming passion and the tenderness that I had undeniably felt had always been tempered with caution; with the knowledge that she would leave me that first long summer, and with the guilt that we both tried to ignore the second summer, when we were older, but not really much wiser. But now I didn't feel that same treacherous, awkward passion; I just felt safe, as though in Coco's warm and generous embrace, I had finally come home.

The End of the Season

IT WAS COCO'S IDEA to go to Las Vegas. She mentioned it one morning while we were eating croissants in her ludicrous four-poster bed, getting flaky crumbs over the sheets that stuck to our skin in the slightly damp apartment. The Deauville summer season had come and gone, and despite the valiant efforts of Coco's little electric fire nestled in the fireplace nook, the damp that had disappeared with the sun returned persistently in the autumn. 'God, I miss the heat,' she said, warming up the coffee on her stove, then pouring it out and bringing it over to the bedside table. She shrugged off the dressing-gown that she had worn for warmth rather than modesty, and slipped naked back into bed. Dipping the remaining tatters of her croissant into the coffee, she tucked them carefully into her mouth, trying to avoid coffee drips on her splendidly round breasts. Coco was the sort of woman who looked much better naked than with her clothes on; her generous ivory curves were gentler and almost classical in proportion when they weren't straining against fabric. Although her face was ruddy from too much sun, the rest of her skin was pale and delicately veined and as soft as a baby's, spreading like silk in a tempting, voluptuous expanse across her belly and thighs. Once I'd seen Coco without her clothes, it was all I could do whenever I saw her not to get her out of those terrible rags and tumble her into bed. 'The only thing I didn't like about Atlantic City was the cold winters. That's why I wanted to go to Las Vegas to work – a girlfriend and I talked about renting a place there and getting jobs in one of the casinos, but we never did.'

'I went once,' I said casually, putting my arm around her, under her breasts where I could feel their comforting weight on my forearm. 'I went with my girlfriend for a week, and did all the big casinos. We both got really drunk one night and Ayesha suggested that we get married, just for fun; we ended up in some drive-in chapel, and while we were queuing I started sobering up and wondered desperately how I was going to get out of it.'

'How did you get out of it?' asked Coco with interest.

'I remembered that she was already married,' I said with a shrug. Coco looked at me in disbelief, then exploded in laughter, snorting with such unladylike enthusiasm that I joined in.

'You are terrible, just terrible,' she said, finally calming down. 'I wish I had gone there. I thought I had lots of time to do things in America, but then I had to come back so suddenly.' She looked into her coffee, and pouted unconsciously. 'You may think that this sounds foolish, but I still think that I am young. I think that I am too young for my life to be over, I still want to do the things that I couldn't before. I still want to go to Las Vegas.'

'Well, you should,' I said, nestling comfortably against

her. 'What's keeping you? Your father is back in good health, your daughter certainly won't miss you, and the artisans can manage without you doing the paperwork.'

'You stupid man,' exclaimed Coco. 'You! You are what's keeping me. If I go, I have no idea if you'll still be here when I get back. You might have gone back to London, or to Bangladesh, or the other side of the world for all I know. And I am enjoying being with you. You are the first man I have met who has not judged me for my smoking, drinking, gambling and eating, and what's more you are wonderful in bed.'

'Stop it, I'm blushing,' I said, realizing that she was the first woman who had not judged me either for the smoking, drinking and gambling. Perhaps what they said was right; common interests were the key to happy relationships; or at least, common vices.

'Unless . . .' Coco started to say thoughtfully. 'No, you'll think I'm stupid.'

'Unless what?' I said, putting aside my rapidly cooling coffee.

Coco said nothing for a moment, and then suggested hopefully, 'Unless you come with me. We could leave this bloody damp place and enjoy the desert. And you could gamble all night. You'll know better, but I heard that it's always like daylight in those casinos, and at three in the morning they pump oxygen in to keep everyone awake.'

'Sounds like heaven,' I said derisively, pulling her over to me and covering myself with her damp, delicious flesh.

She squealed with delight. 'You mean it? You mean yes?' In fact, I hadn't meant to agree, but she looked so excited that I didn't have the heart to tell her; I kept forgetting that Coco was appalling at registering sarcasm, she was so nice and cheerfully brash that she rarely used it herself. Besides, there was nothing so bad about going to Las Vegas, the pumped-in oxygen notwithstanding; if I was going to be serious about this running away business, after almost a year out of England, it was about time that I went a little further.

Coco, despite her fluffy exterior, was quite determined when she got an idea in her head, and she booked the tickets for as soon as she could manage. Once she had decided to leave Deauville, it was like every spare minute or hour she had to spend in the town was utter torture. She took hurried leave of her friends, and ignored the gossip that dogged her – that silly, infatuated Coco was running away again with yet another disreputable coloured man. The worst thing for her was saying goodbye to Claudette, who seemed determined to avoid the interview by refusing her mother's calls; eventually, the night before we were due to leave, Coco went to her house and waited for her to come back from work. Claudette wouldn't let her in the door, and Coco returned to the flat in tears. 'I used to think that I just embarrassed her because I dyed my hair and didn't wear sensible grey outfits with tan tights. Now I think that she just hates me.'

'She doesn't hate you,' I said comfortingly, not sure if I was lying or not. 'She just doesn't understand you. My son was the same, but we worked things out.'

'The son whom you never see, who doesn't know if you

are alive or dead?' asked Coco for clarification, without any hint of irony.

'Yes, that's how we worked it out. He's happy now, and so am I,' I said cheerfully. 'I should have left years ago.'

'I did leave years ago,' said Coco disconsolately, 'and I'm not sure it helped. She said that she just wants an ordinary *maman*, but I don't know what that means. Does she want me to live alone with a cat in my flat, knit booties for future grandchildren, and wait for her to visit once a month?'

'Probably. But she's a big girl now, and she should have learned that the world doesn't revolve around her. She should love her mother for who she is, not who she wants her to be. I mean, you don't judge her for her bloody boring mundane administrative little existence.'

'How can I?' shrugged Coco. 'It's probably my fault, anyway – I abandoned her with Didier . . .' she trailed off and started packing her bag, an ethnic embroidered rucksack that was even smaller than my minimal holdall. Coco clearly travelled very light, and after throwing in a pair of sandals and a few tops and trousers, she then managed to fit all her toiletries in an outside pocket – just a toothbrush, a bar of Marseille soap, a tube of moisturizer, two lipsticks and a powder compact. She had already put most of her personal possessions in the cellar that belonged to the apartment, so that the place could be easily sublet in our absence. I found myself thinking of Della for the first time in months, of the bijou suitcase that she had packed for our weekend in Cornwall which was easily twice as big as Coco's bag, and stuffed to the seams with pots and potions and cosmetics and coordinating outfits and no less than four pairs of shoes. 'I have to carry my life with me,' she had said by way of rueful apology when I met her on the platform at the train station, and humped the suitcase into the main racks as it was too big to go overhead. Coco's bag, by contrast, still had plenty of space when she had finished packing. She looked at me quickly, then as though slightly embarrassed by what she was doing, took the grey trouser suit that Claudette had given her for Christmas and rolling it up, placed it carefully on top of the other clothes where it wouldn't get crushed. 'What?' she asked defensively, raising her chin at me while she closed her bag. 'I might need it, for job interviews or something.'

'Nothing, nothing at all,' I said, not admitting how touched I was by the fact that Coco had taken almost nothing at all, just so she could fit in the last thing her daughter had given her, a gift that wasn't even given with love. Claudette was a spiteful little cow, yet her mother still loved her, and somehow that love redeemed them both. Not for the first time I felt slightly ashamed of myself. I wondered if I really deserved Coco; she was so much bigger than me, and not just in dress size.

Chips from Someone Else's Plate

As the team celebrates reaching the last sixteen of the World Cup, only Lucky is miserable. He feels that he is the laughing stock of the crowd and country, the only member of the squad not to have played. Even when they had Togo on the ropes at three–nil, the Man in Grey still hadn't taken the chance to put him on – instead, he had put on the second choice goalkeeper, and the only two remaining substitutes who hadn't yet had a match. There hadn't been any room for Lucky, and now that they have reached the knockout stages of the tournament, the stakes are higher, and it is even less likely that he'll get picked. In fact, it is practically impossible.

The rest of the team are in fantastic spirits in the dressing-room. As he turns his back on them to get changed, he can hear Conway mouthing off to one of the defenders: 'Two days off, man! I'm going to go off and get shagged senseless.' The defender replies in a low, secretive voice, and Conway, much less discreet, gives a surprisingly filthy laugh. 'Yeah, she's the fittest by far, I'll bet she's a demon in the sack – those prissy, neurotic ones always are.

If she was my bird I'd give her a damn good seeing-to, never mind the curfew. And then I'd turn her over and do her again.' Lucky freezes, and turns around slowly. If Conway was talking about Portia, he'd fucking murder him. But surely even he wouldn't be so callous as to talk about Lucky's girlfriend so obviously within his earshot. He gives Conway a dark look, and carries on changing, but then he sees Conway give him a cursory glance as he says, 'And the poor tart's gagging for it. I've heard from Tiffany that he kisses her Mondays and hugs her on Thursdays.' Lucky feels the heat rise to his face in the already hot dressing-room; he hasn't slept with Portia since they've come out; he's been too tense and nervous, and their time together outside training is so short that they've barely had time to catch up. And to be honest, a reassuring kiss and cuddle from her has been all he's wanted. But why would Portia tell anyone that, least of all Tiffany, the most gossipy of all the footballers' girlfriends? Conway looks straight at Lucky as he smirks and says quietly, but distinctly enough for Lucky to hear, 'I'd say that the bloke's lost his balls since we've been out here.' Then he calls out towards Lucky, 'Oi, Frog–Wog, why are you looking like a wet weekend? We won, or didn't you notice down there at the bottom of the barrel?'

Lucky leaps across the dressing-room and drags Conway off the bench and to the ground; he's shaking him like a rat when he is pulled off by the rest of the team. 'You dirty-minded little shit,' he spits. 'You take that back!'

The Captain appears, already showered and with a towel around his neck, looking disconcertingly like the deodorant ad he has recently starred in. He calmly empties his bottle of mineral water over Lucky. 'I know it's hot, Lucky, but there's no reason to get hot-tempered. This is a good day. We won. So what the hell's wrong with you?'

Conway pulled himself up heavily from the floor. 'The big selfish moron is feeling shirty because he's not good enough to play, that's all.'

'You're priceless,' says Lucky in disbelief. 'He was talking about wanting to shag my girlfriend, I heard him.'

'Oh, for Christ's sake,' says the defender who'd been sitting with Conway, 'he wasn't talking about Portia, Lucky, he was talking about . . .' but he is stopped by Conway, who kicks him urgently.

'No point lying for me, Jack,' says Conway to the defender, and he holds his hands up sheepishly towards the Captain. 'So he heard me; I was just saying his bird was shaggable. That's not a crime – every tabloid hack back home says the same thing, and I don't see him giving them a kicking.'

'Yeah, well, keep your opinions to yourself in the future, Felix,' says the Captain shortly to Conway. 'If you had the good luck to have a girlfriend or a sister, you might have learned by now that young women aren't just objects to be drooled over on page three.' He turns to Lucky and says harshly, 'I'm warning you, Lucky, if you can't keep cool off the pitch, the Man in Grey is never going to trust you on the pitch. Sticks and stones, remember? If the opposition know that they can get to you that easily, you're worse than useless.' The Captain can see how miserable Lucky is looking, and feels himself soften. Lucky was just a kid really, a kid who loved his girlfriend more than his dressing-room reputation; there are worse ways to be. He adds kindly, 'And whether you believe it or not at the moment, there might be a time when we'll need you. If that time comes, you'd better be there for us.'

'Of course I will,' mutters Lucky, feeling ashamed. As the Captain leaves, he stalks over to Conway and says, 'This isn't over, you lecherous little dwarf.'

'Oh, for Christ's sake, Lucky,' repeats Jack, the defender, rolling his eyes with exasperation. 'Chill out; we weren't talking about your precious Portia. We were talking about the Captain's wife.'

Conway is shaking his head with relief at the narrow escape of almost being caught lusting over the boss's girl, and grins wickedly at Lucky. 'Hey, but tell Portia that if she really isn't getting her meat and two veg at home, she can always eat out with me – any time.' He doesn't give Lucky a second glance as he and Jack walk away. Lucky is left standing in the hubbub of the dressing-room, with no other player bothering to catch his eye, feeling even more foolish and alone than he thought possible.

'You made a mistake,' says Portia, 'that's all.' They are snacking on room service in Portia's hotel room, while the rest of the team are having a celebratory dinner. Lucky couldn't stand the thought of attending, and had asked Portia to pretend to be poorly so he could excuse himself and look after her like the caring boyfriend he really was. Portia is having a single glass of champagne and a poached salmon salad; she doesn't fall on the bread rolls like Lucky does, and appears the very picture of controlled moderation. Lucky had taken a long time to choose from the vast menu card. He makes it a point to order things when he's out that he wouldn't get at home, and after studying all the posh dishes on the menu, he'd decided that his mum probably made them better. He eventually went for a cheeseburger with chilli and curly fries, something his mother wouldn't make in a month of Sundays. When it arrived, he had been amazed at the capable ease with which Portia had charmingly greeted the waiter, and handed over a tip. Lucky knew that tipping was the done thing to do, but he never had a clue how much to give, so he tended to hide in the bathroom to avoid having to give anything at all. 'In fact, it's nice to know that you care enough to defend my honour,' Portia adds.

Lucky shrugs. 'Do you want a chip?' he offers generously, slurping down his Coke.

Portia shakes her head. 'No thanks. If I wanted a chip, I'd have ordered some. I wouldn't steal yours.' She sips her champagne delicately. 'And besides, it's just ridiculous to think of little Felix Conway lusting after me. I mean, he comes to about here on me,' she says, indicating her chest.

'That's probably just where the dirty little bugger would want to be,' says Lucky sourly. He asks grumpily, 'Why don't you want a chip? You like chips. And most girls love nicking chips from other people's plates. I wouldn't mind, there's more here than I want anyway.'

'For God's sake, Lucky, I don't want a bloody chip,' says Portia, beginning to sound a little bit irritated.

'Well, I don't want any more, so they'll just be wasted,' says Lucky petulantly, pushing the plate away, his cheeseburger only half demolished. He looks like a toddler about to have a tantrum. Portia sighs, and finishes her poached salmon with three neat movements of her fork: slice, spear and swallow. She takes her glass of champagne and goes to the balcony to smoke. Lucky waits a few minutes, fiddling with his cutlery, wishing he wasn't such a hormonal prat. He eventually finishes his burger and goes out to join her, putting his arms around her and burying his head in the side of her neck. 'I'm sorry I'm such a loser. I don't know why you put up with me,' he says sadly.

Portia puts her arms over his comfortingly. 'Because you're special, Lucky. That's why I put up with you. And you're not a loser.'

'That's not what everyone else is saying,' says Lucky. 'They were talking on Radio 5 Live today – they said that the only way I'd get a game at this World Cup would be if we lost in the semifinal and had to do the third-place play-off. They said that I might get put on in the last minute of injury time, just for a laugh, and to scupper the bookies.'

'Sticks and stones, Lucky,' says Portia, just like the Captain. 'It's all just puff to fill the air time. You're out here, and they're not. How many kids can only dream of being in the squad?' She looks out to the distance, and sees a flash from the hotel grounds. 'Long lens, let's go back inside,' she says, pulling him back with her.

Lucky sits in the armchair and starts to pick at the bowl of rejected chips. 'I know it was my dream, but now I'm here it's just not enough. If I could just play, I could show them. And if I played badly, at least then I could understand people ripping the piss out of me. But I'm not even doing anything, I'm just like the Lucky mascot on the bench;

there may as well be a stuffed toy there as me. I'm just so, so . . .' He struggles to find the right word, grunts with the effort, and glumly grabs a fistful of chips which he stuffs into his mouth.

'Frustrated,' says Portia. 'Of course you are. It's frustrating because you're not in control, you can't change your position, and you can't change the circumstances. But a wise person said that whatever you are, you can still make a choice. The decisions you make are still yours. You can choose to rise above this, because you will play one day. It might not be here in Italy, but you will play. I know you will, and you know I never lie to you.'

Lucky feels unbelievably touched. 'Thanks, Portia,' he says gratefully. He thinks about what she said, and realizes that her comforting, sage tone sounded familiar – disconcertingly familiar, in fact. Then, with what for him is a flash of genius, he realizes why. 'Portia, that wise man who said that you can still make a choice, whatever you are? That wouldn't be the wizard off Harry Potter, would it? Didn't he say it to Harry Potter in that movie we saw last week on DVD?'

Portia flushes, as she thinks that Lucky might be right. She honestly hadn't remembered that herself, so the chances of him placing the quote should have been infinitesimal. 'Might have been – so what if Gandalf said it to Harry, it's still true, isn't it?'

Lucky shakes his head; he isn't going to be outdone when it comes to knowledge of fantasy teen fiction. It's his only strength. 'Not Gandalf, that's *Lord of the Rings*. You mean Dumbledore,' he said.

'Potayto, Potahto,' says Portia dismissively, as though she was the one who had said something clever rather than Lucky.

Potayto, Potahto. It's another one of her new phrases. Portia is giving him a knowing look, the type of look she gives him when she is about to explain something to him, or correct him. To avoid her saying anything more about Gandalf or Dumbledore, he deliberately misunderstands her. 'Potatoes? No ta, I've still got my chips.' He adds cheekily, 'You can have one if you like, I know you love chips . . .'

Portia wisely ignores him, and lying back on the bed, starts leafing through the menu for puddings. 'You know, it's true what Tiffany has been saying about the Captain and his wife. Is it still gossip if it's true? Anyway, they haven't had sex since they've been out here. He's too wound up – he really believes he's going to bring the World Cup back for England; he's saving everything for the pitch. Like the top cyclists on the Tour de France – they abstain too.'

'Does it work?' asks Lucky with interest.

Portia looks at him sharply. 'Don't get any ideas. Every other girl has had their bloke pouncing on them the moment the game is over, and the only thing you want to pounce on is a Coke and a cheeseburger. I might start thinking that you don't fancy me.'

'Oh, but I do,' protests Lucky furiously, remembering the comment that Conway had made about a kiss on Mondays and a hug on Thursdays. He'd have to do better with Portia. He bounces onto the bed next to her, taking the menu and dropping it on the bedside table. He kisses her, a long rapturous damp kiss that he wishes wouldn't end, and with some regret, that he thinks he hides quite well, he starts to unbutton her thin blouse. 'Just as long as you hold me afterwards,' he says, not sure if he is really joking.

Viva Las Vegas

'Y OU HAVE ROSE-COLOURED glasses about Deauville. You think that we're all picturesque, or worse, quaint,' said Coco, over the buffet breakfast in the hotel. On arrival, we had decided to check into a decent place for a week or so, before our strained finances caught up with us. I was hoping that I would beat the house at cards, and Coco was more pragmatically looking at a paper which had listings for rooms to let, and job vacancies.

'I don't think that you're quaint,' I argued mildly. 'Perhaps, maybe, the tiniest bit . . . *mignons*, that's all.' I had started this conversation by complaining about Las Vegas, comparing the crass, greedy environment unflatteringly with genteel Deauville, and Coco had bizarrely decided to take offence.

'Not *mignons*, not cute. Quaint,' repeated Coco firmly, draining her coffee cup and putting it down with a weighty clunk. She waved to the friendly waitress. 'More coffee, please,' she said in thickly accented English, which had the slightest whisper of a lisp. I had forgotten how charming Frenchwomen sounded when they spoke English, even ones with normally strident voices like Coco. She looked at me disapprovingly and continued, 'It's not so flattering to be considered quaint, you know. Some people might even consider it patronizing.'

'Well, it's better to be quaint than vulgar,' I said brusquely, and saw Coco blink and draw back, suddenly looking a little hurt. 'Oh, don't be silly, of course I don't mean you,' I said impatiently. 'I meant Las Vegas is vulgar. And of course Deauville is picturesque and quaint, and your father's village goes off the scale. If you didn't want to be quaint, you should all stop being so postcard pretty in your little stone houses with your *potagers* and painted shutters, and try living between a rowdy estate and a massive flyover instead.'

'Ah, your 'ammersmith 'ome,' said Coco in English, deliberately dropping her Hs as she knew it made me laugh. 'So that was not so picturesque?'

'Not really. Some bits of Hammersmith are considered quite nice, but not where I lived. And it wasn't nearly sparkly enough even to be vulgar, no matter how many shiny lager cans and silver chewing-gum wrappers littered the street,' I admitted. 'If it's any consolation to you, I don't think that everything about Deauville is picturesque. For example, I don't find your charming daughter pictur-esque in the slightest.' Coco gave me a little smile and a sigh, a gesture that was halfway between affection and exas-peration. She shook her head ruefully, and went back to looking at her listings.

I don't know why I was so down about Las Vegas; it was only our first week there, and I had made a little money on blackjack, which I had so far managed to avoid losing on roulette. I also remembered how much I had enjoyed it when I had come with Ayesha, despite the disastrous visit to the wedding chapel. But something about it now just made me feel sad and nostalgic for Deauville, for the seaside and the funny little streets, and the friendly *bar-tabacs* lovingly tended by people like Coco's dad. Perhaps it was the combination of sparkle, and the grubbiness between the wall and the carpets in the big gaming rooms. Perhaps it was too much pumped-in oxygen. Perhaps it was simply the girls; the showgirls, the cigarette girls, the wait-resses, and even the hookers outside. They were all so beautiful and manicured, with teased hair and clothes on the playful side of slutty; they should have all been home-coming queens in their home towns, and yet here they were, hawking their goods in an artificial desert complex where most people stayed for no more than a week.

'Or perhaps you are simply getting old?' said Coco disconcertingly, as though she had been reading my mind. 'You like Deauville because it is comfortable, and familiar. And Vegas is neither – it's uncomfortable, it's strange, it's vulgar, but at least it's fun. And that's why we came, isn't it? For the fun of it?'

Coco, as always, had a point. 'Wait until after break-fast, and I'll show you who's getting old,' I threatened, just to make her giggle. The waitress finally came over with the coffee, and as she poured it, I tried not to look at the too-young face with too much make-up, and the bitten nails underneath the fake French manicure. Perhaps not everyone wanted to be a homecoming queen in a hick town anyway.

Some weeks later, Coco had drawn a blank in getting a job, but was enthusiastically planning a trip to Cancun with the last of our money, as she had always wanted to go to Mexico. 'Fabien and I once went to San Diego to stay with a relative of his, and we took the tram to the border, to Tijuana. But it wasn't the same. And that was a horrible town, full of American daytrippers like us, just there to buy cheap pharmaceuticals.'

'What happened with you and Fabien?' I asked with interest; in my experience, most women loved telling you about their past partners, and it surprised me slightly that Coco only ever mentioned her ex-husband and Fabien in passing.

Coco did her little shrug and pout combination. 'Perhaps it was doomed from the start. I was like you, I found him picturesque. He had beautiful skin, like ebony, and the most amazing hair that he kept in dreadlocks. He was originally from Réunion, but he worked in Paris as a sous-chef. And then he came to Deauville.' She gave a little smile. 'I liked him because he was a dreamer. He was younger than me, so perhaps he could still afford his dreams. I had been married for sixteen years to a man who was so dull that he was practically grey, and all I wanted to do was escape. That's what he promised. That's what we did.'

'So what went wrong?' I asked, feeling a little bit jealous

of Coco's younger man with the ebony skin. I knew what it was like to fall in love with someone for their pure beauty; I had seen Nadya on a river-bank, her arms had gleamed like polished stones in water, and that had been enough.

'He fell out of love with me,' said Coco simply. 'I think it was when I changed the colour of my hair. When he met me, my hair was purple, so purple it was almost blue. But one day, when I was walking down the street in Atlantic City, I saw myself in a shop window. And I felt ridiculous, a forty-something woman walking around like that. So I went to the hairdresser and got it dyed red instead. He hated it; old-lady red, he called it. He said it was like I'd given up on being myself.'

'Oh,' I said, not sure how to react. 'Did you dye it back?'

Coco shook her head. 'You know, at the time, it didn't even occur to me. Maybe that was my way of showing that I'd fallen out of love with him, too.'

The phone in the room started to ring and Coco answered it automatically in French: 'Allo,' she said, then crying out 'Maman!' gleefully, she started rabbiting away about her Cancun plans. Something stopped her short and she started listening, and tears rolled down her face. I listened to the conversation in helpless silence, standing next to her, my hand on the back of her neck. She finished the call, then looked up at me from the seat by the phone. 'You heard all that?'

'Yes,' I said. 'Does it look bad?'

'Worse than last time,' Coco said. 'I have to go back, he needs me.' She started crying quietly, while I kneeled beside her and held her; then she said, 'Will you come back with me?'

'Of course I will,' I replied. 'You didn't need to ask.' I went to get some tissues, and started drying her eyes. 'Don't cry. He's a tough old bird, your dad.'

'I'm not crying for him,' said Coco in a strangled voice, 'I'm a selfish *chienne*, because I'm crying for myself. I'm crying because I have to go back, and it will be exactly the same as it always was. I'm crying because I'll have to look after the shitty *bar-tabac* for Papa, and I'll never get away from it.'

'It doesn't need to be exactly the same,' I said. 'We can make something different, before we go back, if you like.'

'What do you mean?' sniffed Coco, looking at me suspiciously.

'I mean that I've always preferred married women. I'd quite fancy going back to Deauville with one – a bit of a souvenir, if you like, of Las Vegas. I hear that you can find them by the drive-in chapel. It's on the way to the airport,' I said, walking casually around the room to pick up my meagre possessions, and putting them back in the holdall. I turned back and saw Coco had stopped crying, and her eyes were as big as saucers as she smiled at me in wonder.

'I had no idea that you were such a romantic,' she said.

'Well, I just got to thinking,' I said, 'you said a while ago back in Deauville that you felt too young for your life to be over. I thought about that, and decided that I was too old not to have lived. So it's time to start living. With you. If you'll have me – even though I'm presumptuous and not nearly as handsome as I think.'

'Oh, Zaki,' said Coco, getting up and putting her arms

around me, 'of course I will.' She added in an uncharacteristically soft voice, her face buried in my shoulder, 'You
didn't need to ask.'

We couldn't get a flight until the next day, so we made it
to the chapel that evening, and it was during the actual
ceremony that I made a surprising discovery. 'Colette? I
didn't know that your name was Colette,' I said with a
frown.

'Of course it is – you think my parents christened me
Coco?' replied Coco in her thickly accented English.

'Why didn't you tell me?' I asked, a bit annoyed.

'I didn't hide it – it's right there in my passport if you
ever wanted to look. You're just not curious about things –
that's why I knew you weren't a writer that day we met,'
she said, before adding reasonably, 'Besides, why didn't
you tell me that your name was Zakaria?' The minister was
sniggering openly at us, Coco in her hippy trousers clutching a cheap bouquet that we had picked up on the way in,
me in my jeans and a rumpled shirt. 'What's so funny?' she
asked him tersely.

'Oh, heck, nothing,' he said, laughing even more openly.
'I mean, we get a barrel-load of folks through here who
don't know each other's surnames, but nothing like this.
You sure you all don't need some more time, to . . . hmm
. . . get on first-name terms?' He was practically in stitches
at the cleverness of his little joke.

'Oh, shut up and say your lines,' I muttered.

'Sure thing,' said the minister amiably, getting over his

fit. 'I'd hate to screw up one of the . . . hmm . . .' he paused once more for dramatic effect, and even had the cheek to wink at us, '. . . happiest days of your lives.'

Afterwards we sat in a Mexican restaurant and ordered all the delicacies that Coco would no longer have the chance to try in Cancun: chicken in black chocolate *mole* sauce, fajitas and tacos, deep-fried ice-cream, and lethally strong margaritas. 'You know what?' she said, her cheeks red and shiny with the chilli and the tequila and the heat of the restaurant. 'I think that obnoxious man was right. I think it was.'

I knew exactly what she meant. 'One of the happiest days of our—'

'Yes,' she interrupted, 'exactly.' And she held my hand across the table, with a beaming smile on her face so bright that it practically lit the room.

The Messy Miracle of Birth

DELPHINE IS GETTING READY to visit Katie and the new baby at home. Katie cares rather more for Wimbledon than the World Cup, and as it is Wimbledon women's final day, Delphine has bought her a bottle of pink champagne and made a classic Eton mess with strawberries, cream and meringue, so that Katie can get into the spirit of the thing while having baby Lily clamped onto her at home. It is a baking hot day, and the tube will probably be unbearable, but Delphine unselfishly decides not to take the car, as Katie will probably want her to drink a glass or two of champagne with her; Katie loves champagne, but unlike Delphine is incapable of drinking alone.

Katie finally popped two days after Ronnie's wedding, insisting that it was the result of all the dancing and gorging on chilli-laden guacamole dips during the evening festivities. She had told Delphine that exercise and chilli were meant to work wonders in getting recalcitrant babies to make an appearance. 'Sex is the best thing, of course, gets all the hormones racing, but bloody Tony is refusing to come near me.' Delphine had nodded sympathetically, loading up her own plate with nachos and chilli guacamole, privately thinking that it needed a bit more lime juice, while Katie had continued forlornly, 'I suppose I shouldn't blame him, I completely went off sex for the first few months, and now I'm so enormous it's barely feasible. Having sex with a space hopper really isn't that appealing . . . But I just don't have the motivation to do it on my own.' Delphine had almost sputtered out her inadequately limed guacamole with laughter.

Delphine had only seen Katie once since the birth, which had been an unexpectedly difficult one that had taken over twenty hours and eventually required ventouse vacuum extraction to drag the baby out. She had gone to see her in hospital the day afterwards; the baby girl looked surprisingly chubby and finished, with none of the usual funny imperfections or blotchinesss of newborns, apart from the patch on her head where the suction cap had been attached. She supposed it was because the baby was practically two weeks old already, having been born so late. Katie, on the other hand, was far from her usual rosy and dimpled self; her glorious hair had been freshly washed and spilled like sunshine over her shoulders, but it only served to make the rest of her seem pale and washed out. 'I'm too old for this,' she moaned to Delphine, waving away proffered chocolates and flowers distractedly. 'Lily's a hungry little monster and wants feeding every two hours; I'm just not fit enough, I've got no bloody business breeding at almost forty.'

'Don't tell Ronnie that,' chided Delphine. 'Besides, you're looking great. I can't believe you just had a baby.'

'Aww,' said Katie, 'it's so sweet of you to lie, but I look like something the cat dragged in. The worst thing was that bloody suction cap; the doctor thought I had an epidural in place – he hadn't realized that the midwives had allowed it to wear off so I could push Lily out more effectively, and he just shoved the bloody thing up. It was utter agony, like giving birth in reverse. And then my contractions stopped for ages, so they all sat around for ten minutes tapping their fingers while I drained the gas tank dry, with the baby and the suction cap stuck halfway up where the sun doesn't shine, until I finally had another contraction so they could yank her out.' Katie paused, with half a smile. 'She was gorgeous, though – completely perfect and without a mark on her, like she'd already been washed. She only got a bit grubby when bloody clumsy Tony cut the cord and managed to spray blood all over her. Still, it was utter agony,' she repeated. 'I'm getting Tony neutered at the first opportunity.'

That had been two weeks ago, and poor Katie had been run ragged by doting grandparents and family visitors while baby Lily remained as demanding, Tony remained uselessly underfoot, and her little daughter Tasha got bewildered and jealous.

Delphine finally arrives at Katie's Balham home, feeling sweaty and crumpled in her cropped trousers and light sleeveless shirt, but gratified that the champagne has at least remained cold in her chiller bag.

'Perfect timing,' says Katie, opening the door before Delphine can ring the bell and wake the baby. 'I've just got Lily to sleep, and she should hopefully be down for a couple of hours. Hoorah! Two baby-free hours!'

Delphine picks her way through the hallway, trying not to notice how Katie's home looks like a bomb hit it. 'Where are Tony and Tasha?' she asks, looking for somewhere to sit in the living room. She scoops up a hotchpotch of papers, children's crayons and colouring books, fairy princess stickers, NHS leaflets and wrinkled muslins from the sofa, and puts them carefully in a pile at her feet. 'Tony's taken Attila the Toddler out to the park. I asked him to; they were both driving me crazy,' answers Katie from the kitchen. 'Tony's been a complete pain, he's constantly whingeing about the mess, but does absolutely nothing about it apart from pick things up and put them in piles everywhere.' Delphine tuts disapprovingly, glancing with surreptitious guilt at the pile that she has just made herself. 'And Tasha is being impossible. I mean, she was impossible already, but she absolutely loathes Lily, and you just can't persuade a hysterical infant not to hate her baby sister.'

'I guess it's understandable,' says Delphine sympathetically. 'Tasha had this nice, ordered little life, and suddenly there's this noisy, demanding creature that's stolen her mummy and turned everything upside down.' She looks around at the mess, and feels a bit uncomfortable sitting while Katie is doing things in the next room. 'Sweetie, do you want a hand with that? Why don't you sit down while

I make us some tea? I'll even run a hoover around for you if you like, and do a quick tidy while you put your feet up.'

'You angel!' exclaims Katie, coming into the living room, brandishing the champagne and dish of dessert that she has finally unpacked from Delphine's gift bag. 'And it's already chilled! God, I can't think of anything nicer to have on a summer's day! Sod tea, let's have some of this! And sod the housework! I'd rather have a gossip and watch the tennis, than watch you do the hoovering. It's Tony's job anyway.' She carefully pops the cork, and pours the champagne into a couple of flutes. 'Besides,' she says confidentially, 'there's really no point in tidying up; believe me, I've tried, and it just looks exactly the same the next day. It's as though tidying up just encourages Tony and Tasha to mess up the place; this way, they just add a bit more mess to the mess that's already there.'

'Quentin Crisp said something like that,' says Delphine, helping Katie dollop out the strawberry and meringue mixture into bowls. 'He said that he stopped dusting, as he discovered that the dust didn't get any worse after a few years.'

'Didn't he also say that sex was no substitute for masturbation?' replies Katie. 'After six months of abstinence, I'm beginning to wonder if he had a point. Cheers,' she says.

'Cheers sweetheart, congratulations on gorgeous little Lily,' says Delphine, and just as they clink glasses and are about to take a sip, a heart-rending screech is heard from upstairs; a long, shrill note that arches across the house and descends into guttural whimpering.

'Oh, for God's sake,' says Katie bitterly, but she doesn't

move, and bravely forces herself to stay for five minutes on the sofa, clutching her champagne anxiously but not sipping it, waiting to see if Lily will manage to settle herself. 'If I go straight away, it just encourages her to stay awake. And then I have to pat her and walk the floor with her for another twenty minutes,' she explains wearily to Delphine. They sit there under siege from the tiny body upstairs, from the insistent wailing, which increases in frequency and volume to a choked, screaming sobbing that sounds almost painful, and Katie, possibly feeling like the worst mother on earth, eventually puts down her glass and all but runs upstairs.

More than twenty minutes later, she returns, looking harried, and downs half of her glass of champagne in one go. She sits in front of the tennis and starts wolfing down her meringue, too, as though she is trying to finish it before Lily starts up again. 'Mmm, this is so delish, Dee,' she says. 'Did you see Ronnie's email from Borneo? She's staying in this fantastic hotel, on the beach and next to the rainforest. I'm so jealous of her, it feels like I'll never get to fly long-haul again. Not with two puking kids; three if you count Tony.'

'Yeah, I'm a bit jealous too,' says Delphine. 'The photos looked fantastic. I should do more travelling, really.'

'Well, there's nothing stopping you,' says Katie, looking at Delphine, who didn't seem even slightly sweaty or crumpled to her. She looked slim, chic, perfectly groomed and manicured – everything that Katie currently was not. 'I really envy you – you and Jinan can go and do whatever you want, this part of your life is over.' She waves a hand over the cluttered room, the organic nappies and scattered toys, the damp, laundered nursing bras draped over the cold radiator. 'You're free.'

Delphine returns Katie's glance with a slight smile, and a rueful shake of her head. 'You don't get it, do you, Katie? I'm the one who envies you.'

Katie looks astonished. 'What on earth for?' she asks, thinking of the rubbish-tip house, the toddler who is taking tantrums to a professional level, and the adorable but greedy baby that is draining her in every physical and mental way possible.

'Because this part of my life is over,' says Delphine simply. She resists the urge to whine to Katie, who has enough to contend with at the moment; she resists the urge to confess, and say that she doesn't feel free, she feels trapped. She feels that she is too young for her life to be over.

On the tube home, Delphine gives up on the Simone de Beauvoir autobiography that she has started reading and picks up an abandoned newspaper instead. She skips through the news about the Middle East and stops at the problem page; this is the type of page where the readers get a preview of the problem, and can contribute their own opinions alongside that of the professional columnist. There is something seductive about the simplicity of putting down a matter of vast emotional depth in a few bald lines, and hoping that this will be enough to convey the pain, confusion and turmoil of the suddenly tender heart writing it; tender because they are exposing themselves in the most stark, brutal way, to an audience who neither knows them, or cares to know more. They are reduced to just a smattering of printed lines, a pair of initials and a home town.

I have started seeing a much younger man, whom I adore, but I worry that we have no future. My children profess not to judge, but they do not support the relationship, and make it clear that my partner is not welcome at family events. When we go out in public, I can see that other women find him attractive, and he has been mistaken for my son on more than one occasion. Am I making a fool of myself?

JD, Manchester

I do not love my husband any more. He is an artist, but has been 'resting' for several years, although he helps with the care of our child while I work. I have felt increasingly dissatisfied with our relationship, and am beginning to feel that he is sponging off me. He is still attractive, but I am no longer attracted to him, and even find that he bores me. Although he recognizes that we have problems, he has no desire to separate or divorce, possibly because he is too comfortable to move out, and does not wish to start working again. I think that he is a good father, but I am not sure that this is enough to make our relationship work. I am not too old to start again, and I think that I deserve better.

KS, south London

Delphine bites her lip thoughtfully, and scans the other letters on the page. So many problems, with different contexts and permutations and prejudices, but all with the same basic question. Should I stay or should I go? The first few lines from KS in London made her stop short, as it could have been written by Katie, who was clearly enjoying life with Tony even less now that she had to stay at home and spend all day watching him litter up the house.

Delphine looks at the replies to the first letter from JD, which are predictable but not particularly satisfying, from one reader's pithy, 'I say you go, girlfriend! Your kids are jealous and will get over it,' to the columnist's long rant about how relationships with nothing in common but sex are doomed, as are relationships which aren't supported by the wider family, and especially relationships when the woman is older than the man, as men don't have the nurturing qualities of women and so are only happy to be with older women as long as they retain their looks, but not when they start to get incontinent and forgetful. Delphine raises her eyebrows – how did the columnist manage to interpret that it was a relationship based on sex from that sedate little letter? Perhaps she had rather more information on JD than the newspaper could be bothered to print. She started to think about a letter of her own; it would be tempting, somehow, to get it off her chest. A message in a bottle, sent out to whoever might pick it up, and feel moved to answer.

I am unreasonably unhappy with my husband of over eighteen years, who is better than me in almost every way, and who I do not deserve. He is six years younger than me and seems to love me. He says it frequently, and we have an enjoyable sex life. He is unaware that I had a recent affair with one of his close relations, and that I was planning to leave him. I was too cowardly to leave, and so my lover left me first. My husband is unaware that I do not feel passionately for him, and possibly never did. He is unaware that I resented giving up my career to run his home perfectly, and to raise our son, as I led him to believe that getting out of the rat race is all I ever wanted; at the time, this was true. He is unaware that I feel trapped in our beautiful home. I do not think I love my husband; in many ways I find him petty and irritating, although on occasion his kindness is so sincere that I could cry. Sometimes I feel like running away, like my lover; not to be with him, as I do not know where he is, but to be like him. To be free. As it is, I live the same clockwork life, managing our household and some of our son's business affairs, and filling my time with meaningless chores and superficially enjoyable leisure activities. I feel that I am too young to have stopped living; I feel that I am too old not to have properly lived. Would it be better for everyone concerned if I left? Someone please tell me, simply and without explanation, judgement or caveats, should I stay or should I go?

DK, central London

As Delphine tries to order her jumbled thoughts in her head, she feels suddenly very foolish. What did she expect anyone to say? Consider his happiness, not your own, you selfish, faithless, deceitful woman. Think of someone else for a change. You are right, DK from central London, you don't deserve him. She looks around her, at the blank, nodding faces on the tube, and feels accused, as though she is sitting within an arm's length of her own jury. The tube pulls into Waterloo, and feeling stifled, she jumps off. She keeps walking until she comes out into the street, and finally breathes properly, even though the outside air is just marginally cooler and less muggy than that of the underground. She decides she might as well distract herself at Tate Modern, but just a few minutes strolling in the heat makes her feel dizzy again, and she is now unsure if her shortness of breath and the funny feeling in her head is really caused by her guilty musings, or just by too much champagne on a hot day. The beating of the sun on her bare head feels almost violent, and she has scarcely walked down The Cut before she decides it might be best to abandon the Tate and to continue her journey home instead. She reaches Southwark tube, and looks regretfully down towards Blackfriars Bridge; it would surely be cooler along the river, but she doubts if she would be able to make it there. Besides, the river always makes her think of Zaki, which is something she wants to avoid; it is unlikely, wherever he is, that he is thinking of her. If anything, he would be thinking about the bet he might have on the World Cup final tomorrow. He'd want to bet on Argentina, the favourites, but with his grandson in the England squad, he'd have to put some kind of side bet on them as well, wouldn't he? Or perhaps he was more interested in the Wimbledon men's final, which was happening the same day. That was more of a sure thing – everyone thought that the defending champion was going to walk it. I'm rambling, she thinks, and steps out of the sun, and under the canopy of Southwark tube station, teetering dangerously at the top of the stairs; the heat and the dizziness in her head suddenly feel like nothing compared to a stunningly painful cramp in her lower stomach that goes all the way to her groin. She cries out, collapses, and everything goes mercifully blank.

Delphine is dimly aware of being lifted into something that looks rather undignified, more like a pram than stretcher, and taken out of the station into an ambulance. She thinks she tries to say something to the paramedics, but they don't answer, so perhaps she didn't say anything, or else they didn't hear. She wonders if she might be dying, as she suddenly feels astonishingly lucid inside, but blurred and slow on the outside, as though she is swimming underwater. She can see the irony – there she was agonizing about running away, but it may turn out that she doesn't have any choice in the matter anyway. The cramps start again, more painful than before, and she thinks that she is given some sort of anaesthetic, as she either passes out or drifts off, she's not certain which.

'Delphine,' says Jinan, 'Delphine, can you hear me, darling? You're going to be fine. Do you know what happened? Do you remember anything?'

Delphine shakes her head; she is in a hospital room, with a TV monitor fixed high on the wall like in a cheap hotel. The sheets are stiff and very white. Jinan is wearing the clothes he wore that morning when he went off for golf. Everything seems very normal. 'What was it?' she asks. She feels totally numb below her waist, and she can't even twiddle her toes.

Jinan hesitates, and just says it quickly, like pulling a plaster, hoping that the faster it is said the less painful it will be. 'You had a miscarriage. Quite a late one – you were about thirteen weeks. A spontaneous miscarriage, they called it; the womb just contracted and pushed the baby out. They don't know why it happened; sometimes it just does, if the baby or placenta isn't healthy enough. You lost a lot of blood, that was why you fainted. You were bleeding so much, even afterwards, that they had to put you under to check that . . . everything had come out, the afterbirth and everything.'

'Oh,' says Delphine. It seems hopelessly inadequate, but it was such unexpected news that she didn't know what else to say. Why would she get pregnant now, if she hadn't for years? It made no sense. 'Are you sure?' she asks, and then wishes she hadn't. She feels like an idiot.

'Yes,' says Jinan simply. She becomes aware that he is holding her hand, as he squeezes it with a featherlight pressure. 'Didn't you know? About the baby?'

Delphine shakes her head. 'I'm not sure I believe it. I wish I had known.' She thinks that she should feel sad, but she finds it hard to feel sad about the loss of something that she never knew she had. The poor baby, living just thirteen lonely weeks, not even noticed by its own *maman*, not caressed, or sung to, or loved. 'The poor baby,' she says out loud.

Jinan doesn't quite meet her eyes. 'That baby almost killed you. I didn't know you wanted another baby. I didn't realize that you'd gone off the pill.'

'But I've not been on the pill,' says Delphine. 'Not since Lucky was six years old.' They sit together in silence, realizing how little they know each other. All these years, Jinan had thought that she was using birth control; all these years, she had thought that they might have been infertile together after all, and had even questioned Lucky's paternity. It just turns out that they had simply been . . . unlucky. It was almost laughable.

'Did you see the baby?' she asks.

Again, Jinan doesn't meet her eyes. 'I didn't want to. It had hurt you and made you ill, I was too angry to look at it.' He feels ashamed admitting this, and taking a deep breath, manages to say, 'It was a boy, another boy. I think you'll be able to see it, if you want. If you'd like to say goodbye.'

'Are you all right?' questions Delphine, looking at him with concern. He seems less well than her; the dark polo shirt disguises it, but he is sweating profusely, and he looks unnaturally pale for him. Not so much pale, in fact, as grey. He is shaking with the effort of speaking calmly.

Jinan nods his head violently, trying to master himself, but finally explodes: 'I thought you were going to die,' he wails, burying his face against her dead legs and almost howling with the relief at letting the words out. He starts to sob, 'I rushed to the hospital, and I saw you there covered in blood, and I thought you were going to die. And

I didn't care about the baby, I just wanted the bloody thing out of you so you wouldn't be hurt.' Wiping his tears on her hospital sheets, he carries on, 'I was thinking about those old dramas, when the doctor asks if you should save the wife or the child, and I was just thinking, save my wife, save my wife, save my wife . . .' Delphine, shocked by the outburst, doesn't know what to do, and just puts her hand tentatively on the back of his head, stroking his hair. Jinan raises his head, trying to smear away the insistent trickle of tears that he simply can't stop, that seems to inflate his whole face into a puffy, indistinct mess.

'You know, Delphine, I lied to you once. When you'd just had Lucky, you asked me who I'd save out of a burning building – you or the baby. And I told you the baby, because that's what I thought you wanted to hear. And you nodded, and said, good; you said you'd rather I saved the baby. But I lied. I wouldn't have saved the baby; even if I'd known that you would have hated me forever for it. I would have saved you first. I wouldn't have been able to help myself.' Delphine feels her throat go dry, and her eyes well up at the same time. She thinks she ought to say some-thing, but she just can't think of the right words. She tries all the same.

'You know, I don't deserve you—' she begins to say haltingly, but is interrupted by Jinan, who says, 'I know I don't deserve you,' as though he hadn't heard what she had said, or had heard but misunderstood it. 'I know I don't deserve you, but I love you. I'll always love you. I know I don't have very much to offer you – I'm not funny, or unconventional or brave, and I can be small-minded and petty and annoying, and I wasn't even strong enough to look at our unborn child. But I do love you. I can at least offer you that. I know it's not enough . . .' he trails off.

'It's enough,' says Delphine, her hand still stroking the back of his head. 'It's more than enough.'

The nurse comes bustling in, and as her pulse is taken, Delphine asks if she'll be allowed home that evening. 'Oh no, dear,' says the nurse. 'You've lost a lot of blood. You'll be overnight at least. Maybe even tomorrow night, depending on what the doctor thinks.'

'Does that thing work?' Delphine asks, pointing towards the TV. 'If I'm still here, I'd like to be able to watch the final tomorrow. The football final, I mean.'

'I should think so,' says the nurse, marking up Delphine's chart. 'You need to buy a card from downstairs for it. It's a pay-as-you-go. I'll go and tell the doctor that you've come out of the anaesthetic.' She strides off efficiently, and Delphine turns towards Jinan, who is still red-eyed and is looking at her open-mouthed with surprise.

'Well, we don't want to miss it, do we? He might still play. Will you come back and watch it with me?'

'Of course,' says Jinan, with a slight sob in his throat that he tries to suppress.

'And let's not tell him that I've been ill. I don't want to worry him, at least not tonight,' says Delphine. She squeezes Jinan's hand, and as he crouches unhappily by her bed she feels a rush of tenderness for him that surprises her with its force. She doesn't say anything more to him, as she knows that it is better that she doesn't. She will get well, and then she will go home, where she will be cared for, and will care for in her turn. She thinks she finally knows how to be happy now, and she mentally shreds the letter she had written, and consigns it to the darkest, deepest recesses of memory; she will be happy, as she will give back what she most needs to the man who has continued to love her despite everything; she will expiate her wrongdoing, she will deserve his love and become a better, happier person, as she will finally give back what she has received.

Polished Bottles in the Village Bar-Tabac

Coco's father was still unwell, and likely to be stuck in hospital for some time, but he still looked delighted to see his errant, red-haired, middle-aged daughter and her equally elderly beau. '*Félicitations!*' he beamed, and insisted that he and his wife would throw us a proper reception party as soon as he got out.

'I really don't think so,' I muttered to Coco as we left, but her mother stopped me with a disapproving 'Tch!' that reminded me disconcertingly of my father.

'Now is not the time to be selfish, Zaki,' she said, with that thin-lipped look that some women do so well and to such impressive effect. 'You are family now. This will give him something to look forward to. He needs a reason to get better.' Coco said nothing, but looked at me with wide-open, appealing eyes. I knew better than most that when you're floundering in the deep and dirty water, sometimes you need a reason to float. So I copied Coco's little mannerism, I shrugged and pouted, and both she and her mother nodded with approval, as they took this as a Gallic shorthand for grudging assent.

The reception was one thing, the *bar-tabac* was quite another. 'With two of you it will be so much easier,' Gérard had said, like a fragile saint in his hospital gown, his veined and pale as parchment feet poking out from underneath and looking heartbreakingly vulnerable. 'My Coco was just overwhelmed with it before, the poor little flea.' He chucked his daughter on the soft flesh under her chin, and held her like she was a delicate thing, instead of the strong, wide-hipped woman that she was.

'No, absolutely not!' I stormed to Coco in her little apartment that evening. 'There's no bloody way that I'm running the village shop. I'll jump in the river first. In fact I did jump in the bloody river! I didn't run away from one shop just to end up in another.'

Coco just looked at me miserably. 'I know. I hate the bloody place too. I ran away as well, remember. But what can we do? Maman can't run it, and Mémé certainly can't. And we can't afford to pay someone to do it. We're family, we're the only ones who can look after it. I'm sorry, Zaki, but when you married me, you married them too.'

'I'm the one that's sorry, Coco,' I said meanly, still not calmed down, 'but I didn't see that little bombshell in the small print of the wedding contract, and I certainly didn't marry you to become an indentured slave.'

'No, well, why did you marry me, then?' she asked, getting cross herself.

'For the fun of it!' I said. 'Remember?'

'Ah, that's good. Because this is nothing if not fun,' replied Coco. 'I'm having so much fun, I think I'll go and find a cafe to sit in, and spread all this fun around.' She walked off, and waited at the door for a moment for me to stop her; when I didn't, she just left.

It was two in the morning before she returned, and I was sitting in the armchair, half dozing by the electric fire, waiting for her. 'I was beginning to worry,' I said.

Coco took off her coat and her long fringed scarf. 'I didn't think you'd still be here,' she admitted. 'I was avoiding coming home because I didn't want to walk back into an empty apartment. I think I was just getting used to having someone there for me, someone to worry about me. I didn't like to think that it was over so soon.'

I pulled her into my arms; she was freezing from the night air, and her hair was damp from the rain. 'I didn't mean to shout,' I apologized. 'I know it's not your fault that your father's ill. If anything, it's his fault for being such a bloody nice man that no one wants to let him down.'

'You were right to shout,' said Coco, pulling herself away and beginning to undress in front of the electric heater. 'I talk all the big talk about dreams, about living the life I want, and instead I always end up back here, minding the shop. It's like I have travelled nowhere since I was nine years old.' She looked at me and said, 'I have been thinking, Zaki. It's not fair of me to ask you to take on the shop with me. I'll handle it myself. And if you want to leave, I won't stop you. It was wonderful, what we did in Las Vegas. It was romantic and impulsive, and I will never forget it, but I know that you have your dreams too, and watching someone mind a shop probably isn't one of them.' Coco wrapped herself in a dressing-gown, and went into the bathroom.

I stayed in the ugly, comfortable chair, and looked into the bars of the heater. Coco had humbled me yet again. I had thought that I was better than her when we first met, simply because I had considered myself better looking – or at least better dressed. But inside, I was gnarled, withered and ugly. I had none of Coco's generosity of spirit, her strength for self-sacrifice. She was a big woman, and she made me feel very small indeed. I had managed to get quite old without remembering the lessons that my loved ones had taught me – that of unconditional love. Nadya had it, Jinan had it, and Coco had it. She was willing to let me go for my happiness. But I had lost Nadya, I had left Jinan, and now I had been released from any obligation towards Coco – the woman who had made me feel alive, who accepted me and even loved me just as I was, without conditions or judgement. A woman capable of all sorts of weaknesses, but who never, ever deceived. Did she really think that I would walk away from her, just because I might have to put in a few hours in a village shop while her invalid father recovered? That would make me, quite possibly, the stupidest man I knew.

Coco came back into the room, her face scrubbed and shiny with face-cream. 'So,' she said.

'So,' I repeated, 'I have been thinking.'

'Yes,' she said, trying to look impassive, but her lip and chin quivered slightly.

'I have decided not to take you up on your generous offer to abandon you. I regret to inform you that you will not be getting rid of me so easily. And it is with great reluctance that I will take up the challenge of showing you how to run a bloody shop.'

Coco's lip quivered even more. 'Oh, Zaki,' she started to say, but instead of waiting for her to fling her arms around me, I went to her first, and put my arms around her, kissing her softly. Then, with some difficulty, I carried her, giggling, to her oversized, overstuffed bed, where she bounced when I joined her.

'It won't be so bad, Zaki,' she said, cuddling against me. 'It might even be fun.'

'I seriously doubt that, Coco, but fortunately I have a bit of a crush on you, so I don't mind how bad it is,' I replied.

Some months later, I was sitting in the *bar-tabac*, pouring myself a whisky at midday on the dot, looking at the racing papers. The occasional person from the village came in, as did the odd tourist for postcards and canned drinks. Coco and I were planning to go to the track later that day, so we'd put a sign up announcing an *exceptionnel* closure. I had recently subscribed to the English papers, just so I could follow what Lucky was up to without having to dabble on the internet, and saw he'd been selected for the World Cup squad, as a late replacement. There was a photo of Portia next to him, looking delightful as always, wearing a strange pair of glasses that she surely didn't need. Well done, Lucky, I thought. At least one of us was living his dream. That's what I had thought I would do when I arrived in Deauville, but here I was just over a year and a half later, in the bosom of another family, running another shop, which I was shutting just as cavalierly to head off to the races or the casino with someone's wife. The only difference was that this time the wife was mine, and tended to still be in my bed the next morning rather than disappearing in the night. And it was a nice difference, no doubt about that. It wasn't a bad life; it's just that it was pretty much the same as the one I'd left behind. With nicer scenery. Perhaps Coco was right, perhaps I did think this was all picturesque. Maybe if she'd been a cockney running the dry-cleaner's up the road from me in Hammersmith, I might not have fallen for her in the same way at all.

I started thinking about Oscar Wilde again recently – down and out in Paris, lying in the gutter, staring at the stars, and I thought of what he'd said about there only being two tragedies: never achieving your dreams, or achieving them all. I was thinking of Lucky, achieving his dream so young; it was an unexpected tragedy to get what you want so early in life – where did that leave him to go? And here I was, at the other end of the scale. When I was a young man, I had a dream, but I was so far from it for so long that I had practically forgotten what it was. It was Coco who helped me remember. My dream was simple: it was to live with my soul mate by my side, free from all the petty practicalities of life. Well, I had a good run at it, and almost made it in the end, but if it only half worked out, that's just the way things go sometimes. Call it fate, or accident, or chance – call it a flaming tower in a tarot deck or a bloody tragedy if you want – but whether you believe it or not, sometimes you can't fight the house odds. And sitting in the cool shade of the shop, guarding Gérard's proudly polished bottles, with the early summer sunshine glinting on the trees outside, with the crickets chirping and the bees buzzing, and the prospect of a bloody good race this afternoon, with Coco's thigh-slapping laugh as an accompaniment, I wasn't feeling all that bad about it.

So maybe that little tag on my wrist at birth said 'Shopkeeper' after all.

Time to Go to Work

LUCKY IS SITTING on the sidelines, watching the game so closely that it's as though it is all being played in his head; he is experiencing every pass and kick and throw-in as though his own muscles had twitched and contracted to make them happen. There had been doubters, there had been disappointment, but here they are, in the final for the first time since they had won in 1966. They had not been a fancied team, they had been criticized at home for lacklustre performances, for rarely scoring in open play, for falling too readily, for never winning by more than a single scrappy goal, but they had advanced, and they had gone through. If anything, the criticism has galvanized the team more than wide-eyed support could have. 'Just let us do our jobs,' the Captain had said to a hostile press conference before the quarter-finals, and they had gone to work and proved them wrong. Perhaps they had benefited from a suspect decision against Spain in the semis; perhaps they had been lucky; but that didn't matter any more, as they are here.

Lucky no longer cares that he won't play; Portia was

right, he will play again. It's not his fault that he wasn't called up, and at least he didn't lose his dignity in any memorable way, not like Conway, sitting next to him and kicking the ground furiously, barred from the final. He catches Lucky's eye and turns on him furiously: 'What are you staring at? Do you fucking want some or not?' like any England lager lout dancing shirtless in a bar, spoiling for a fight and eyeing rival fans hungrily. Lucky says nothing and turns away, and Conway spits on the ground at his feet. 'You make me sick, you do. You call yourself English, but you don't give a shit that we're not out there. You're just a fucking Frog–Wog traitor.'

In fact, Lucky feels astonishingly grown-up for accepting his situation; so grown-up that he doesn't bat an eyelid when Portia suggests that they move in together in the autumn. He would have said before that they were too young; that neither of them knew how to cook, or how an iron worked. Of course, he had wanted to get married when they were sixteen, but that was a romantic notion; living together was somewhat more practical. But they weren't really all that young – plenty of students younger than them moved out to strange cities to study; his own grandfather had run off to Paris with his teenage wife when he was eighteen. Of course they could move in together; he had come to Italy a boy, and was leaving it . . . a slightly wiser boy, toughened by the unflattering glare of media exposure, so that he was finally strong enough to ignore it.

Conway isn't playing as he picked up two yellow cards in the semi against Spain for quite unnecessary offences. After his opening games, he hadn't been as successful in scoring as everyone had hoped, and most of the key goals had come from midfield players during set pieces; the free kicks, corners and throw-ins. The Man in Grey had accordingly marginalized Conway and built up the midfield, to Conway's despair and frustration. 'It's a different game if we're two goals ahead,' he had said to Conway, 'then we'll give you all the service you need, we can afford to. Until then, we're playing deep.' But they had never gone two goals ahead, and Conway's frustration on the field had grown until he had fouled a Spanish defender quite outrageously; a misjudged tackle just a few minutes later was enough to send him off, and have him miss the final. Conway had cried his way off the field, and Lucky was reminded of the game they had played when he was fourteen and Conway was thirteen, and how Conway was still a little kid after all, under all the bravado. Conway had gone sobbing into the dressing-room, and hadn't emerged even with the win at the final whistle.

Lucky is so immersed in the game that he doesn't see how close they are getting to the final whistle now. They are one goal ahead, from a free kick scored by the Captain in the opening minutes of the second half, and now there are just nine minutes to full time. Eight minutes . . . seven minutes. He can see the England supporters in the crowd, staring at the clock, wishing the time away, willing it to go faster. They would all lose the next six minutes of their lives, if they could. Two cigarettes, thinks Lucky, would do it for them; one cigarette takes three minutes off your life. He is sure that Portia is chain-smoking for England in the wives' and girlfriends' box. Then the inevitable happens; the Argentinians break through the tired England defence, and the striker is facing an open goal, with just the keeper before him, caught way off his line. The England goal-keeper leaps in instinctive desperation, but goes for the striker rather than the ball; a deliberate foul, stopping a goal-scoring opportunity. He is shown a red card and sent off, and a penalty is given, and converted. The striker drops to his knees and kisses the ground. The Argentine support-ers are in tears of joy, the England supporters are just in tears; the teams come off grimly a few minutes later. Extra time.

The England players are valiant, and with just ten men manage to keep the Argentines at bay for most of extra time. Everyone is thinking about penalties now; the Eng-land team has avoided having to go to penalties in the tournament so far, managing to win by one precious goal each time since reaching the last sixteen. The Argentinians are playing defensively but with an almost confident swag-ger; they're just waiting for the shoot-out now. They had won their semifinal on penalties – not one of them had missed – and they all know England's poor record at penalty shoot-outs. A few minutes before the end of extra time, there is a dangerous scuffle near the England goal. A goal kick is won, and the England team's second-choice goalkeeper clears the ball, but then slips on part of the churned-up pitch, and falls awkwardly, with a look of undiluted agony. Everyone is remembering his former injury-prone season, and he is stretchered off. The physio is shaking his head. 'Cruciate ligament,' he says to the Man in Grey and his assistant, 'very possibly. If it is, he won't be playing again for months.' And suddenly Lucky isn't playing the game in his head any more, as all eyes are on him. And the Man in Grey isn't calling out to the players on the field, but is walking towards him, and taking him by the arm.

The Man in Grey has no time for players who have already left the pitch; he doesn't give the slightest glance to the injured keeper coming off, he is looking at Lucky intently, holding him around the shoulders and telling him, 'It's time, Lucky. You're on.'

'But sir, we might go to penalties,' Lucky stammers idiotically. He had wanted to debut in this World Cup, but how could he go on for the last five minutes, and lose the World Cup for England? How could he lose the last remaining shreds of his dignity?

The Man in Grey has no time for doubt; he has never supported Lucky before, but he knows he must support him now, and make him believe that he deserves this chance. Lucky is suddenly the most important player in the world to him. 'I didn't bring you here for fun, Lucky. I brought you here because you're one of the best goalkeepers in England, and because we've got a job to do. You've had an easy ride up until now, and I know you haven't been happy about it. But now it's finally time to get off your backside, and off the bench. I need you, the team needs you, your country needs you. It's time to do your job, Lucky. It's time to go to work. And remember, if you couldn't do it, you wouldn't be going out on that field.' Lucky nods, and races out to the cheers and despairing groans of the crowd. Some of the rowdier England fans start to chant, 'I'd rather be a Paki, I'd rather be a Paki, I'd rather be a Paki than a Kraut,' and Lucky is unsure if this is intended to show their support or derision.

The assistant glances over at the Man in Grey, and aware of cameras, holds his clipboard high enough to cover his mouth, pretending to be deeply occupied with the list of penalty takers that he had already scribbled down. 'Very inspiring, Greg. Do you think he can do it?'

The Man in Grey shrugs and looks at his shoes, showing the cameras nothing but the top of his own neatly cut, wiry brown hair. 'I'll be bloody amazed if he saves a goal. But no one's expecting him to save a goal; I wouldn't expect the best keeper in the world to save a goal in this situation. I'm expecting our other lads not to miss.'

Lucky stands in the goal in the dying minutes of extra time, the heat of the day finally fading away. The play is nowhere near him, it is all on the other side of the pitch. He doesn't get a foot or hand to the ball. He stands on his line, in readiness, with nothing but his hands for defence. He is the centre of the spinning world, and when the whistle goes, and the players prepare for penalties, he finds it difficult to leave the goal, the place that he has been chosen to defend, to join his team-mates. He finds it difficult to look back and see the net looking so exposed as he is backslapped and encouraged by the lads on the field, and he finds that he does not really take in their backslapping or their encouragement, as he feels that he is now, really and truly, on his own.

Living on a Fault-Line

LUCKY IS GOING OUT to buy flowers for his mum in hospital on a glorious July day. His girlfriend is fussing in their sleek apartment on what used to be called the wrong side of the river, and is telling him not to dare be late coming back. She is throwing him a party, to mark the twenty-fifth anniversary of the game that made his name, that made him notorious, that made him the headline filler of newspapers for months, and not necessarily in a good way. 'I really don't want a party,' he had said, and she had pouted and given him a kiss in the way you might give a little boy a sweet to stop him being sulky.

'Everyone says they don't want a party. What they mean is that they really do,' she had said with dismissive indulgence, and had carried on with her plans. She was much younger than Lucky, some sixteen years younger, and had the confidence of youth, which Lucky finds appealing and appalling in equal measure. Whenever Lucky was cross with her about something, and was trying to get her attention during her interminable phone calls, she would tell her girlfriends down the line, within Lucky's earshot,

'Ooh, I have to go. My man needs me again, he's SO demanding,' and Lucky didn't know whether to be pleased or offended.

Suzanna has lived with Lucky for almost two years, but doesn't really know how he feels about the game; she was a just dimpled darling of a toddler when the game was played, dressed in England colours on the match day, and asleep in her cot through most of it. She felt none of the ecstasy and agony, the passion and the penalties; for her, the game is the stuff of legend, or myth. It isn't something that involved real people or real pain, and she doesn't really identify her laid-back, sleekly groomed pundit boyfriend with the raw youth who was thrown out in front of the firing line. She just knows that it was one of the biggest games in England's recent history – they haven't reached the final since – and that Lucky played a part in it. As far as she's concerned, that deserves a party.

'I'll tell Mum that you sent your love,' says Lucky a bit reproachfully as he leaves, reminding Suzanna that she hasn't. His mum has just had a painful operation, a hysterectomy, and Suzanna has been so wrapped up with the party arrangements that she hasn't even asked after her.

'Yes, do,' says Suzanna guilelessly, as with her youth came a certain selfishness, a complete lack of remorse or doubt relating to any of her words or deeds. 'Make sure you buy her some nice flowers from us, and tell her we're all thinking of her.' Then she repeats, 'But don't you dare be late. That guy from the BBC is coming over, he's going to do a bit of filming. He wants to ask you about the game.'

'Yeah, course he does,' says Lucky. 'See you,' and he

pecks her on the cheek and strolls out of the apartment, taking the stairs rather than the lift. The thought of being interviewed about the game doesn't dismay him any more; he's done it so many times over the years that he doesn't even have to think – he always gets the same predictable questions, and just trots out the same tired phrases in response. It was practically all he was ever asked about, as it was the only interesting thing that had ever happened to him in his life, apart from when he and Portia had that messy divorce; that had earned him a fair few headlines, too.

He walks across the bridge and buys some roses and delphiniums from a stall, where the fresh-faced girl arranges them beautifully, and wraps them up efficiently and elegantly in brown paper with pale raffia string. She looks at Lucky curiously, as though she recognizes him but can't quite place him. He smiles, and when he pays, gives her a tip for the careful work. He tips people now, as over the years he has finally worked out when it is appropriate, and how much to give; I've grown up, he thinks a bit smugly, a bit sadly. These days, Suzanna looks in admiration as he confidently tips, just as he once looked at Portia.

He starts to walk up towards the Kings Road, but it's quite a way to the Chelsea and Westminster Hospital on foot, so mindful of time, he hails a cab and speeds there in a matter of minutes. He finds his mother in a private room, shamelessly watching soap operas. She is still in pain, but thrilled to see him. 'Another unexpected visitor! You didn't have to come today, Lucky, I know you've got that party.'

'I'm not that bothered about the party,' he says, and

sees an empty cappuccino cup on her little side table. 'Who else is here? It's not Dad, is it? I thought he'd still be at work.'

'He is, darling,' says Delphine, and doesn't quite meet his eye. 'Oh, there she is – she just popped out to the ladies. The visitors' loos are miles away; you're not allowed to use the patients' loos, for some reason.'

Portia walks into the room and is visibly shocked to see Lucky, but recovers almost instantly, like water smoothing itself back to a calm pool after the disturbance of an unexpected pebble. She walks around the bed and kisses Lucky on the cheek. 'Well, hello there. Don't I remember you from a courtroom battle in a galaxy far, far away?'

'Hello, Portia,' Lucky says dully. She is looking very well indeed; he expects to feel bland and grey next to Suzanna, who is bursting with youth and vitality, but he feels disappointed to still feel so bland and grey next to Portia, who is older than him, after all.

Portia considers him for a moment too long, then leans over towards Delphine. 'Well, it was lovely to see you, but I mustn't monopolize you any more. You're looking marvellous, as always. I can't believe you've just had a major operation.'

Delphine smiles beatifically, a serene, older lady smile that she has recently perfected now that she is too old to be sexy. 'Portia, it's so sweet of you to lie, but I look like something the cat dragged in,' and they both laugh, as though it's a private joke between girls. Lucky guesses that she must have said something similar when Portia first arrived.

Portia kisses her goodbye. 'I'll be off. Harrison will be

coming to pick me up shortly, so I'll grab another guilty cappuccino and fag before he finds me.' She nods politely at Lucky. 'Well, goodbye,' and then she is gone.

Lucky sits and chats with his mother, but is obviously distracted. It was unnatural that Portia looked so well, even though she had been a model and it was her job to be good at presenting herself. It annoys him that she has been visiting his mother when his own girlfriend can't even be bothered to send good wishes without prompting. He didn't even realize that Portia was back in the country; she lived in the States these days. After a few minutes, Delphine says, 'Oh, for God's sake, Lucky. Go downstairs and talk to her. She's flying back out again tonight, and you can come back and see me any time. And besides, I'm watching my soap.' Lucky hesitates, just enough for Delphine to know that she should insist. 'Go! Go!' she says, flicking him away with her hands for emphasis, 'Or I'll miss Tim saving Melanie from the kidnappers.'

'I don't know why you bother watching the soaps,' says Lucky, kissing her hurriedly goodbye on the cheek. 'You always know what's going to happen in them anyway.' He skips downstairs and finds Portia sitting outside the nearest cafe where she is allowed to smoke, the one opposite the hospital entrance.

Portia doesn't look too surprised to see him. 'Tim and Melanie, right?' she says. 'I've been in the country for a week, and I know exactly what's happening in all the major soaps. Pathetic, isn't it?'

'Do you mind if I join you?' he asks politely.

Portia shrugs her shoulders and nods with a half smile. 'Why not? It'll be a novelty to speak without a lawyer each as a chaperone.' Lucky orders a coffee and sits down with her. He doesn't ask how the kids are, as he already knows: Taylor is travelling the world and rediscovering his Asian roots in Dhaka, currently staying in Dada Khalil's old house, although the old man himself died many years previously at an astonishingly ripe age, ironically from diabetes – the disease of too-much-sweetness that his first wife had died from in relative youth. And Jasmine has just finished her first-year exams at Columbia University in New York, and is on holiday with friends in the Hamptons. She'd be coming to London to visit him next month.

'So, how's Harrison?' he asks. He has never met Harrison; in the photos that he has seen, he looks like one of those smarmy American lawyers that you see on TV, with suspiciously good teeth.

'Fine; how's Suzanna?' Portia replies without skipping a beat.

'Fine,' shrugs Lucky.

'You know, I've got whisky older than her,' she says with a wry smile.

'I think I've got whisky older than you, even,' replies Lucky.

'Well, that's the niceties over with,' laughs Portia, with relief. 'And how are you, Lucky? Really. It's not an easy day for you, is it?'

'Oh, every day's easy,' says Lucky, touched that she has remembered. Not that she has remembered the day itself, as it was somewhat unavoidable – it was all over the papers and the TV. But touched that she has remembered how it made him feel. 'I really can't complain.' His coffee arrives, and he sips it thoughtfully.

Portia frowns as she looks at his coffee. 'When did you start taking it black?'

'Since Suzanna made it her mission to look after my waistline,' says Lucky ruefully. 'I've decided to find it charming rather than annoying; I'm taking it as a sign that she cares.'

Portia looks at him approvingly. 'That's very philosoph-ical of you, Lucky. A sign of growth, as they say in LA.'

'What's it like over there?' asks Lucky with interest. 'It's clearly agreeing with you, you look fantastic.'

Portia accepts the compliment with a contented, cat-like smile. 'It's great, if you don't mind living on a bloody fault-line. And no one smokes, and no one drinks, and everyone has dinner way too early. It's all very healthy. Well, apart from the poison that we all inject into our faces.' She indicates her smooth forehead and the area around her mouth with a delicate gesture. 'The trick is to start doing it when the lines have barely appeared. Then no one can expose you with those unflattering before and after photos.'

Lucky laughs. 'It's so good to see you,' he says unthink-ingly, then realizes what he has said and feels a little bereft. Portia the brave, the smart, the just, the keeper of small confidences and dark secrets, the mother of his children, who now lives an ocean away.

It was all his fault – despair and disappointment had made him a monster; not straight away, but slowly it had eaten away at him, until he felt that he was merely tolerated by club and country. He had never lived it down.

Portia sees the cloud cross his face and recognizes it immediately, even though she has not seen him at such close quarters for years. 'Would you have changed anything, if you could have? I never asked you before, it seemed so silly, and obvious. But would you have?' asks Portia suddenly, leaning across the table towards him. She is close enough to kiss.

Lucky closes his eyes and shakes his head, not to say no, but just to clear his mind. He had thought about this for years, during his darkest times when he had curled up in the bottom of a bottle, or in someone's unwelcoming bed. He had been the defender of the goal; that was his remit, that was his job. He was the one who was chosen to prevent the goal from being, yet the goal had happened. He had let it happen. Once it had left that kicking foot, neither he nor anyone else in the world had been able to prevent it – they had all watched, powerless, hypnotized. They all knew that it was going in. It was fate. It was myth. It was legend.

The tragedy wasn't that Lucky hadn't saved the goal for England. The tragedy was that he had scored the goal. He had taken the last penalty that had won the World Cup for England. He had become a god, he had become notorious. He would never do anything in his career so amazing again, and he would never be forgiven for once having been so good. He had been tolerated by club and country while he behaved outrageously and then became a mediocrity, remembered for what he had once been. His life had been over when he was eighteen. But what would he have done, if he could have gone back to that scared eighteen-year-old on the field, who was about to achieve all his dreams? Would he have told him, would he have whispered in his ear, 'Miss it. I dare you to miss. I'm begging you to miss. And when you miss, I will say congratulations. Congratulations, because now you can have a career. Congratulations, because the rest of your life is still ahead of you'?

'I don't know,' admits Lucky. 'I still don't know, after all these years, even after everything that happened. It wasn't my choice, I guess. I wouldn't have been brave or clever enough to make the goal or miss it; it was just . . . dumb luck. Something I've specialized in, I guess.'

'No regrets, then,' says Portia, a little disappointed. She had hoped for something more than this; something less nonchalant, less tolerant. Something angry, from the heart.

'Of course I have regrets,' says Lucky, looking straight at her. He drops his gaze down into the depths of his coffee, as she remembers he once used to look into his whisky glass. 'I regret that I never found out what happened to Zaki; I only heard from him again that one time, after the game. I regret that I never appreciated those days we spent hanging about at the corner shop, kissing when no one could see us. Those were the best days of my life, when I still had a life and a future to come, and I never even knew it. Most of all, I regret that I never appreciated what we had until it was too late.'

'It wasn't all your fault, Lucky,' says Portia. 'I'm not proud of the way I was either. I became a real media-hungry bitch, back then. I wasn't cut out to be a celebrity – I thought too much of myself.'

'Maybe you just thought too much,' says Lucky. 'You always were the clever one.' He sighs, then repeats, 'So, like I said, I really can't complain. I've got a nice flat, a nice girl who's throwing me a party because she thinks I'll like it, I still get work commentating, and I've got two healthy kids. What more should a middle-aged man want?'

'Peace of mind?' suggests Portia.

A tiny sputter of laughter escapes Lucky involuntarily. 'Now that would just be greedy,' he says.

Portia lights another cigarette. 'You know, I went into therapy for a bit. Not over you, just generally for stuff. It's what you do in LA if you don't want to bore your friends. And the shrink told me that the way you reacted was understandable, as it's hard to get what you always wanted, harder than not getting it. We're trained to accept disappointment in a way that we're not trained to accept success. She said that there were just two tragedies: one was getting what you always wanted, and the other was not. I found out later that she was just quoting some pithy little witticism from Oscar Wilde, but I still thought it was interesting. Like Orson Welles; he could never make another movie to match *Citizen Kane*, and it was the first film he ever did. But at least he tried. Some people might have given up altogether. And you tried too, Lucky. You should be proud of that. Not just of the goal that you scored when you were eighteen, but of what happened afterwards – that you tried, and that you were brave enough to try.'

Lucky has been listening intently, and the gentle, caring words are too much for him. Portia has no reason to be so kind to him, and he can feel himself welling up. He wants to say, 'I miss you. I miss us,' but realizes that it is useless; he is sure now, anyway, that she already knows.

Portia's phone beeps, and she stands up. 'Harrison's arrived. I'd better go.' She leans over, and kisses Lucky gently and firmly on the lips. 'Take care of yourself,' she says, and walks away without looking back.

Lucky returns home in time for the party. Suzanna is delighted, as all the guests have arrived promptly and in good spirits, the décor looks superb, and the expensive caterers have excelled themselves. Felix Conway has even turned up, fat and in his forties, with his curvy blonde wife of the last ten years. Lucky does his bit for the man from the BBC, and holds court among his friends and colleagues, playing his role with aplomb. An England hero. Fêted for what he did years ago, when he was someone else entirely. It is a convincing performance, but it is just a performance, more or less. Surrounded by good will and good wishes, Lucky has the sense of someone who has walked onto a stage, and who must say his lines, who must do what is expected of him. Someone who doesn't have control of his own fate, and who doesn't even have enough power to exit stage left. He suddenly understands, finally, why Zaki ran away.

The Stuff of Myth and Legend

THE WHISTLE BLOWS for the first penalty, and the
Argentine player takes it, and slips on a piece of
churned-up pitch, just as England's second-choice keeper
did. The ball flies high over Lucky's net, and the England
fans cheer, while the Argentine manager furiously shouts at
the referee for the shot to be retaken, but it isn't given. The
Captain takes the next penalty for England, but kicks it at
a good height for the goalkeeper, who manages to block it;
there are screams of rage that the advantage has been given
away so easily. Nerves have got the better of everyone, but
now as the Argentinians recover, so do the English. They
remain level on penalties right into sudden death, until the
final Argentinian comes forward and Lucky miraculously
saves the shot. He doesn't so much save it as have it collide
with him, but he keeps it from going in. The young
Argentine player who took it, also in his first World Cup,
is in tears and inconsolable. If England make their next
penalty, they will go one ahead and win the tournament.

And Lucky, their last man on the field, is the one who
has to take the shot. He walks to the spot as though he's

walked there a thousand times before, puts the ball down, and stares at the goal – his old friend to defend, whom he must now defeat. He was the gamekeeper, now he is the poacher; a keeper turned striker. He looks into the eyes of the goalkeeper opposite, and thinks, 'I know you. I know which way you'll leap. I know, because you're me.'

Delphine and Jinan are sitting on her hospital bed, tightly holding hands, looking at the tiny screen with pale concern. 'My poor, poor Lucky,' Delphine thinks; she has never seen him look so brave and so alone.

He runs and strikes, his lucky left foot connecting, the ball shooting like a bullet towards the goal, and then there is nothing but the moment. Sweeter than the dread pregnancy of anticipation, more potent than the complacency of has-been memory. Later there might be press conferences and parades and celebrations, later there might be documentaries and disappointment as he ages and fails, later there might be his older, greyer self jealously guarding his place in the commentary box. Later he might reflect that this is the only deed for which he will be remembered, and even as he was written into the history books, all else that he once was or could ever be was already being erased from memory. Later he might drink himself into an angry, antisocial stupor with the inexplicable tragedy of potential that was fulfilled too early, leaving him with nowhere else to go.

But now there is only the perfect stillness as he stands spread-eagled at the centre of the spinning world.

There is only the moment, and him.

Zaki is watching in the *bar-tabac* with a dozen other expats squeezed in, and punches his fist in the air as the deafening cheers threaten to raise the roof. Lucky is his hero; he has succeeded where Zaki has failed, he has achieved his dream. Zaki had promised himself he would leave his family in peace, but he will get one final message to Lucky – he must – and he will say simply this: You're something special, Lucky. And you have done well, my son.

He will not tell Lucky that there are only two tragedies; he hopes Lucky will never have to find out.

Acknowledgements

I owe a particular debt of gratitude to my husband, Phil Richards, for this book; he looked after our infant son while I was writing and gave me unlimited snacks, support and sympathy. He also cast a detailed eye over my final manuscript, proving to me at long last that there really was a practical application for his football fixation and addiction to Radio 5 Live.

My father, Nasir Ahmed Farooki, a charming, unconventional and unrepentant gambler who made his home in many places, passed away in 2002 in a hotel in Deauville. Although he died long before the writing of this book, my memories of him (coloured by both fondness and frustration) inspired some of the themes of *Corner Shop*. I hope that he'd have enjoyed reading it.

My mother, Niluffer Farooki, was always at the end of the phone if I needed a break from the splendid isolation of writing, and her proud and spirited advocacy of my work was a source of great strength to me.

And finally, I'd like to thank my thoughtful and diligent editor, Julie Crisp, and the whole team at Macmillan for all the hard work and enthusiasm they put into this book; and my agent, Ayesha Karim at Aitken Alexander Associates, for her unflappable calm and encouragement.